I0761683

BONE ASH

Tow Ubukata

New York

BONE & ASH

Tow Ubukata

Translation by Kevin Gifford
Original cover design by Koichi Sakano (welle design)

Yen On
150 West 30th Street, 6th Floor
New York, NY 10001

Visit us at yenpress.com • facebook.com/yenpress • twitter.com/yenpress
yenpress.tumblr.com • instagram.com/yenpress

First Yen On Edition: November 2025
Edited by Yen On Editorial: Anna Powers
Designed by Yen Press Design: Wendy Chan

Library of Congress Control Number: 2025029931

ISBNs: 979-8-8554-1308-3 (hardcover)
979-8-8554-1309-0 (ebook)

10 9 8 7 6 5 4 3 2 1

HJM

Printed in South Korea

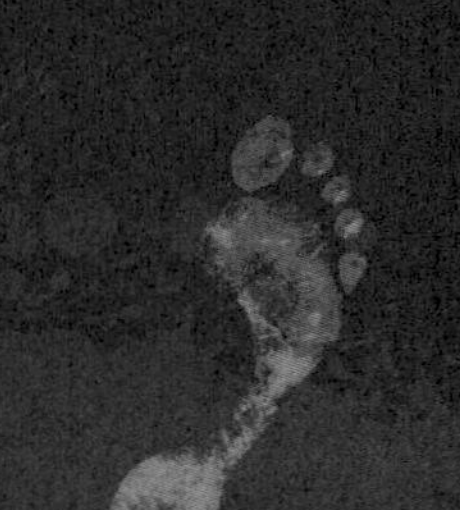

BONE & ASH

Contents

Photos: Adobe Stock, Shutterstock

Chapter 1 Release—2015

1

—What an odd staircase.

Mitsuhiro Matsunaga stopped after going down a fair distance, overcome with regret.

The stairway went deep underground. Each flight was ten or eleven steps high, and it just went on and on. Every time he thought he was almost at the end, there'd be another landing, and then the next flight of stairs would appear.

It was perfectly normal for construction sites like these to have lots of exposed concrete around, but there were no lights at all, which was strange. Mitsuhiro adjusted the headlamp on his helmet with a gloved hand, hoping to make it shine downward as much as possible. That was the only source of light he had. Having to constantly stare at his feet as he descended was starting to make his neck stiff.

—How much longer do these stairs go on?

As he rubbed the back of his neck to loosen it up, Mitsuhiro realized that he had an intense urge to turn back. The more he went down, the more irritated he was about having to climb all the way back up later. The claustrophobia of being this deep underground began to slowly spread out across his mind. He was anxious that he might be trapped in this total darkness forever. But most of all:

—Why is it so dry in here?

The basement should have been damp, but this stale air was almost painful for his eyes and throat. It was getting on his nerves, and he wanted to return to the surface as soon as possible to get some fresh air. At the very least…

—This stench, like burning bones…

There was no logic to it, but the air made him feel uncomfortable. He wanted to be out of it, even if for just one minute.

But that wasn't possible, so Mitsuhiro instead took his phone from his jacket pocket and checked the time. It was a bit past seven thirty in the morning. He had one more hour to complete his investigation and report back to the office.

"*I want speed to be your priority here*," his boss, Yasushi Takenaka, had told him on the phone just before six. With Takenaka and the rest of Mitsuhiro's team working on this emergency, there was no time to entertain fantasies about heading back up and coming down again later.

—Let's just get this over with.

Mitsuhiro forced himself to continue down the stairs, feeling like he was jumping into the bottom of a dark hole.

"We have to wrap this up before it gets any more difficult for us."

When Takenaka called him, Mitsuhiro was already wide awake and out of the shower. He was already aware of the problem, even without an early-morning call from his boss. He quickly got ready in his dim bedroom, grabbed his bag, and opened the door.

"See you later," murmured his wife, Miyoko, without moving her head from the pillow. "Tough day ahead, huh?" She waved at him, her other hand resting on her large belly. She was in her seventh month now, so she could hardly even stand up quickly, much less bend over. Even putting on her socks was a struggle.

Mitsuhiro returned and lightly grasped Miyoko's hand, placing it by the pillow. She sighed peacefully through her nostrils.

He left her there and went out into the hallway, then checked into the room nearby. Their daughter, Sae, had kicked the blanket off the bed, so he put it back on her, stroking her head. She sighed as well, just like her mother had, which made him smile a bit.

Now that she had started first grade, there was no need for him to drop her off and pick her up at kindergarten any longer, and that was a big relief for a working couple. They still had to prepare for the new baby, but Mitsuhiro was sure he and Miyoko would make it work. After everything they'd learned from their first, he had much more confidence about that.

Leaving Sae's room, he went up to the entryway, picking up a pair of nonslip shoes from the shelf and putting them on. These were meant for navigating construction sites; if he wore regular shoes, it'd be all but asking for an accident.

In another moment, he was out of the door and in the elevator. Mitsuhiro had purchased a corner condo on the fourth floor; he'd take the stairs for exercise when he had the time, but he didn't feel like it right now.

Once he got out and walked through the auto-locking front door, he was taken aback by the sound of heavy rain and the surprisingly chilly air.

It had been hot and sweaty since June began, so it caught him wholly by surprise. Out of consideration for Miyoko, he hadn't opened the curtains in the bedroom this morning...but still, the fact he didn't notice the rain at all showed just how much modern construction shielded him from the outside. No wonder there were laws about providing ventilation; otherwise, oxygen might not be able to get in.

Letting out a sigh, Mitsuhiro ran off, holding his bag above his head. The station was just across the street, so he only had to go about five hundred feet from his building to reach his subway entrance.

—*Good thing we decided to live near the station.*

It was on the pricier side, but it couldn't be much more convenient for commuting. Miyoko was into stuff like feng shui, things that went completely over Mitsuhiro's head, but she was the first to agree to this location.

—*She called it a "power spot," didn't she?*

Mitsuhiro brushed the raindrops off his suit as he rode the escalator down.

That was some kind of trend lately, he heard, but he didn't know what kind of "spot" it was supposed to be. Probably it was Miyoko's way of showing gratitude for all the convenient urban benefits their condo provided.

The sound of the rain was no longer audible as he reached the underground floor, and the dampness of the wind blowing in had also disappeared. He bought a sandwich and some tea from the kiosk, put them in his bag, and hurriedly passed through the gate for the Den-en-toshi commuter line into Tokyo.

The train he boarded was sparsely occupied, and the air conditioner was blowing hard enough to give him a chill on his skin. Mitsuhiro found a seat as far away from the vents as possible, took out his company phone, and got himself caught up on the incident.

Twenty-two hours had passed since it broke out. The crisis-management team at IR tried to document any incident that took place within twelve hours, so this was a performance nobody was proud of.

IR, or Investor Relations, was essentially a PR department aimed at investors, which made its job fundamentally different from dealing with mass media. The IR group had to communicate the current status and future outlook of a company's board, finances, and performance in order to present a transparent view of the firm, improve its brand value, and attract investor interest. They could hold press conferences as well, of course, but their main objective was to minimize the risk of unexpected changes in the stock price.

Mitsuhiro was a member of the IR team for the financial planning bureau at Shimaoka Corporation, the main hub of Shimaoka Group, which was currently betting its corporate future on the redevelopment project taking place at Shibuya Station. The group consisted of over forty companies encompassing five main businesses: railroads, real estate, resorts, lifestyle services (chiefly department stores), and construction.

This redevelopment project was launched in the early twenty-first century, bringing all of these core businesses to the table together. It was being closely watched by every type of investor, so IR's role was to function as a kind of central crisis-management center for them all.

Not long after Mitsuhiro had joined the firm, his boss, Takenaka, had told him about the phrase "earthquake-proofing fraud" and how it had haunted him between 2005 and 2006. The MLIT—the Japanese government's Ministry of Land, Infrastructure, Transport, and Tourism—had publicly disclosed twenty-one hotels, condominiums, and other properties that had fabricated the seismic resistance of their buildings, triggering a massive public outcry. The companies took a major hit to their reputation, and the police set up a task force to arrest all those responsible.

"A lot of the arrests were actually for other crimes, but there was so much rage across the country, they had to do *something*."

Takenaka had spoken in hushed tones, like he was still fearing all that anger...but fortunately, the Shimaoka Group wasn't badly hurt by that scandal. The directors at the time, though, were almost morbidly fearful of any potential blowback, so they decided to boost the on-site verification and crisis-management teams over in IR around that time.

Now, in 2015, after several reorganizations, IR's crisis-management group was being headed by Takenaka, who had a great deal of PR experience. He had a gift for calmly reading two or three moves ahead and giving just the right instructions, and Mitsuhiro and his coworkers never found themselves scrambling to make a decision or releasing incorrect information that harmed more than helped.

The most dangerous situation in crisis management is when you're obligated to make an announcement while something is keeping you from all the pertinent information. If you don't know what happened, why it happened, and how you'll prevent a recurrence, all you can do is say a bunch of hollow, made-up nonsense. Sometimes, the C-suite would order you to report total falsehoods, and you'd be at your wits' end trying to figure out how to toe the line and say something comforting that still managed to be true.

"There's nothing you'll regret more than doing IR work for a company that normalizes coverups," Mitsuhiro's colleagues from other firms would tell him. "You make one misstep with the media, they blow you away with a big exposé, and now your own family's calling you a liar."

So far, at least, Mitsuhiro had never dealt with that sort of situation, a testament to both Takenaka's talents and the relative sanity of the managers above him.

After arriving at Shibuya Station, Mitsuhiro went out not at the Sakuragaoka side, where Shimaoka's corporate headquarters was located, but through the east exit, where the construction site was.

The whole area was an intricate maze of temporary walled-off paths. The layout would change month to month, and despite his knowledge of the construction schedule, even Mitsuhiro often got lost. It must have been even more of a hassle for the general public. The team managing the company's media presence in the local community was trying to spin it as "a sight you'll only get to see for now," but the feedback had been less than positive. Once construction was over in a few years, it'd be incredibly easy to go in any direction you wanted around here, but until then, everyone had to familiarize themselves with this ever-changing labyrinth.

The "Labyrinth," speaking of, was one nickname for the Shimaoka East Department Store that once covered this whole area. That building was known for being something of a jungle as well, but now it was demolished, the culvert underneath exposed, and construction was underway on a new forty-seven-story high-rise, tentatively called the East Wing.

Mitsuhiro headed for the East Wing's foundation site, typed in the code for the number lock on the door of one soundproof construction wall, and went inside. Before him was a giant square hole in the ground, and near it was the cover from one of the culverts redirecting the Shibuya River. Part of the East Department Store used to stand here.

In normal times, there'd only be a shallow puddle of water at the bottom of the culvert, but now the river was audibly rushing by. This culvert had been left in place in order to address potential flooding; water usually went through the main sewer line directly under Meiji-dori Avenue, one of the main thoroughfares in the district, but when the flow from districts like Sendagaya and Udagawacho increased, water started going through the Shibuya River culvert, located underground right in front of the rail station.

—Good thing I'm not investigating some kind of waterproofing mistake.

Mitsuhiro imagined himself soaking wet and peering into a sewage-choked culvert. That was horrifying enough, but what if he slipped? He'd make one of those "Top Ten Worst Ways to Die" news articles, and that wouldn't be too funny for him, would it?

He climbed the prefab stairs to the construction site's prefab office, recalling Takenaka's stern reminder to his team: "You need to keep in mind three things during an investigation: safety first, safety second, and safety third."

Upon opening the door upstairs, he saw two men wearing "Shimaoka Construction" work outfits and armbands. One was talking on a desk phone about the weather forecast and when they could reopen construction. The other man, an older one, stood up and walked over to Mitsuhiro.

"Um, are you the guy the head office called about earlier?"

"Yes, I'm Matsunaga from the IR department. I've been ordered by my boss to investigate here."

"Right, I heard about you. With this rain, though, most of the crew's not at work..."

"That's good for me, actually. I'm not too sure how long this survey will take, after all."

"Do you need someone to guide you? I can probably leave here around eight, once more people show up."

The man scratched his forehead with a thick finger. He and his colleague were stuck here at the office for now. They were probably handling the night shift. This huge rainstorm right when they were about to clock out was pretty bad luck for them.

"I'll be fine on my own," Mitsuhiro casually replied. "I've been here plenty of times, and I have all the drawings. I won't be going anywhere outside the safety fencing anyway."

The man frowned. He probably didn't even want to imagine an amateur like Mitsuhiro wandering around a place like this. Mitsuhiro, too, wasn't exactly thrilled to be following these orders.

"I'm just going to look at the East Wing's underground, so I don't think there'll be any danger. Can I borrow a helmet and armband? Oh, and some work gloves if you can."

The man looked relieved to hear it. Weather conditions wouldn't be a problem underground, and the piles supporting the main structure had been very carefully inspected and verified before being driven in. Unless he took a tumble in the dark, it'd be perfectly safe.

"You can use the stuff on the shelf over there. The checkout sheet's hanging on that shelf, too."

"Thank you very much. I'll just borrow this, then…"

Mitsuhiro grabbed a clipboard and ballpoint pen hanging by a string from one of the columns of the plastic shelf, writing his name, the date, and time in the "equipment used" rows. He put on a helmet with a headlamp, an armband, and a pair of gloves before lightly bowing to the man and leaving the prefab office.

Staying under all the temporary structures to avoid the rain, he proceeded over to the East Wing foundation. The blueprint files were on the tablet he was carrying in his bag, but he didn't need to look at them. He had read through them all while preparing an investor-targeted construction progress report, and as he'd told the man in that prefab office, he had been here multiple times.

So he climbed over a line of waterproofing sandbags to enter the underground level of the worksite. All the machines and heavy equipment were silent, letting him clearly hear the sound of the rain hitting the steel plates overhead. During normal construction, the sheer noise would make conversation nearly impossible, but now everything was quiet. The rain made everything seem dark, and while there was a large portable lighting array on the far side, it was all shut off for now. The lights were there to keep the heavy equipment from creating large shadows that workers could walk into, rendering them invisible to operators. Such situations had actually resulted in the majority of injuries and deaths involving heavy construction machinery until new procedures were initiated a little while back.

—It'd be nice if they could put some more lights on...

But he knew this was impossible. Turning on the temporary lighting would require powering up the generator—in other words, the whole site would need to be put into full operation just for Mitsuhiro's sake. They'd also need people checking on the generator to make sure it was operating properly. When nobody was around (save for the two in the prefab office), it wasn't a reasonable thing to ask for.

Wrapping the strap of his bag across his body to free his hands, Mitsuhiro turned on the headlamp, using the light to proceed underneath the speckled steel-plate-and-concrete ceiling. Soon he saw the stairs to the second basement floor, a temporary structure made of metal plates and pipes bolted together without any decoration.

Here he removed his tablet from his bag, pulling his right glove off with his teeth as he activated it. As he listed up the necessary files, he marveled at just how useful a tool this was. It was five years ago, in the year 2010, that the iPad had first appeared on the market; it had spread so quickly that now it was one of the greatest tools the company provided him. Before, they'd need to spend time and money taking pictures with instant cameras; now they could take hundreds of photos without any extra cost, view the images on the spot, and even create documentation with them. It was so much easier.

Now Mitsuhiro was looking at this tablet, studying the worrisome images on it.

Seven photos were lined up together on the screen, forming a continuous image. Each one was from a different article posted on social media—well, *article* wasn't the right term these days. This was stuff posted on an application called Twitter, and although each post was only 140 characters, you could attach images and video to "tweets."

Twitter use had exploded in Japan beginning in 2008, especially among younger people, and it swiftly became a tool for corporate advertising and government PR. As widespread as it was, of course, not all of its users put it to good use. Maybe there's just something about the internet that brings out a malicious streak in people. Mitsuhiro always thought so, and what he was seeing now was nothing but a whole mess of malicious content.

East Wing basement. A rash of construction errors

East Wing basement. Just being there makes you sick

East Wing basement. Sore throats; something absolutely harmful coming out

East Wing basement. The wall after the fire—just seeing it gives me a headache

East Wing basement. Another fire here—I can hardly breathe, I want to quit

East Wing basement. All workers hospitalized

East Wing basement. Human bones are coming out from that hole, but nobody's saying anything

The person posting all this went by the handle "Mole Unit-01." It was a pretty silly name. His bio only said that he did civil engineering work, and the rest of Mitsuhiro's team was scrambling to identify him.

This guy's first tweets were sent around last fall, and they mostly consisted of trivial stuff like "Lunch now." Recently, though, he'd switched gears and begun posting a series of defamatory tweets about the worksite. Each one began with the phrase "East Wing basement," and each one had a different image from the site attached to it, likely taken with a phone. None of the photos showed any obvious negligence or mismanagement, but the text went on about construction errors, harmful materials, fires, hospitalizations…and now human bones.

It could no longer be overlooked. Accidents and fires caused by hazardous materials were the kind of news that easily spooked investors. Even the top management would stay up at night over it, and Mitsuhiro and his boss, Takenaka, were no exception. It would be foolish not to be concerned.

So the first objective of Mitsuhiro's investigation was to confirm that the tweeted images were, in fact, from this site. If they were, he then had to confirm the current situation. These images might've been faked, after all, so a quick and careful investigation was needed at once.

Putting the first image in full-screen mode, Mitsuhiro put the glove back on his right hand and went down into the darkness of the second floor, looking for the location this photo matched.

2

He was soon able to match five of the seven images with reality. They were all from the East Wing construction site, so it was impossible to claim that the images were wholly unrelated to the tweets...but it was also almost certain that none of the claims from those posts were true. Mitsuhiro still felt uncomfortable about it—perhaps even a little angry now—and that was likely why he was getting thirsty.

Before he tried to track down the remaining two images, he sat down on a pile of construction materials and started on the breakfast he had brought along. Eating here in the dark underground with nothing but his headlamp to guide him ensured the experience was completely unappetizing. He couldn't have purchased that sandwich too long ago, but it was weirdly dried up. He washed it down with some tea as he looked at the five images he'd taken with his tablet.

The first "construction error" one, he realized, was referring to the piles—the steel and concrete driven into the ground to support the structure of the building. It turned out the ground layer supporting the building ran deeper than expected, so the piles didn't reach fully into them. However, after checking the progress report he had saved on his tablet, Mitsuhiro found that crews had already completed work to embed the tips of the piles more than a meter into the supporting ground.

—Some "construction error."

He wanted to shout at whoever had sent this tweet. All it took was a little extra low-risk construction work to address it. Still, the malice behind this tweet was far more serious than he had first imagined. After all, it was these piles that were causing the most concern for his boss and the management at large.

The whole thing started with the Park City condo complex project that started in 2005. It was completed in two years, and then in 2014, seven years later, some of the handrails in the corridors of one building began separating from the walls. The following year—in other words, February of this year—the main contractor examined the frame of the building and found that while it was generally sound, the western block had sunk by two centimeters across all the floors.

They conducted a drilling survey to determine the cause, and it confirmed that some of the piles below the building didn't reach down to the ground layer meant to support them. Out of the fifty-two piles put in place, eight either didn't reach the supporting layer at all or failed to be rooted at least one meter in. One pile also had an incomplete cement footing. These should have been the underground pillars supporting the building; instead, they were just floating around freely in the earth.

To make matters worse, subsequent investigation revealed that the ammeter data used to confirm the reach into the supporting ground layers had been doctored. There were four apartment buildings in total and a total of 473 piles supporting them, but the data for a staggering 70 of them had been tampered with.

Japan's Ministry of Land, Infrastructure, Transport, and Tourism took this very seriously, ordering an investigation to search for any other falsified data. They found a total of 360 cases, over 10 percent of the 3,000 or so projects they surveyed, and the repercussions quickly spread nationwide. The problem wasn't just with the ready-made concrete-pile industry—even large firms were found to have faked their data, leading to further distrust. The number of investigations was likely going to reach 20,000 nationwide by the end of the year, and now everyone was associating pile construction with at least some degree of data fudging.

All the piles in this Shibuya redevelopment project were being closely monitored, the data being double- and triple-checked to ensure nobody was making up any numbers. It was causing the schedule to gradually slip, and the burden of the work was building up like a set of body blows.

In essence, these tweets could be the work of someone with ties to the industry who was pinpointing this project in particular in order to shift the blame. It was IR's job to quickly confirm that these accusations had no basis in reality and prepare materials to counter the tweets.

Mitsuhiro had repeatedly compared the images of the five sites he had already checked on with the pictures from the tweets.

Just being there makes you sick

The image from that tweet was taken in one corner of the worksite on the second basement floor, but there was nothing wrong to be seen anywhere.

Something absolutely harmful coming out

This was a picture of a wall from the same second-floor site. The toxic-gas detection system was functioning normally; the only thing Mitsuhiro could find was the slight smell of sewage. That could be due to the diversion work on the underground culvert, or it might be from the large water tank being built underneath the station's east exit to drain water during heavy rain events.

The wall after the fire

Another fire here

These were taken from the foundation space adjacent to the water tank. One site report stated that some of the lighting cables shorted out due to the extreme dryness, leading to a small fire. The smell of burning metal in this underground space couldn't have been pleasant, but as far as Mitsuhiro could tell, there were no longer any signs a fire had taken place.

This, too, felt like a pointed attack, and not like the one aimed at the piles. It targeted the site's lack of manpower—not just a seller's market for workers, but a tremendously serious shortage. The birthrate was declining, the population was aging, and the younger generation that should have been inheriting the skills of their blue-collar elders were avoiding the construction industry entirely. Unless they welcomed in a large number of foreign workers, large-scale construction like this would become all but impossible in much of the country.

That problem was compounded by the sudden demand for construction following the earthquake and tsunami in 2011, several major redevelopment projects launching at the same time, and then the 2020 Tokyo Olympics, first announced in 2013. All this reconstruction, redevelopment, and revitalized tourism were good things, but the Olympics demand in particular had only exacerbated the worker shortage.

This was supposed to be a year of recovery for Japan's construction industry. A lot of the major construction contractors had seen a downward trend in their financials, but they were all doing much better now, and by June, every firm was seeing significant profit increases over the previous year. Construction investment, also on the decline, was showing signs of its own recovery. Fears of a labor shortage could easily bring about another downturn; without enough workers, projects across Japan would grind to a halt. Costs would exceed profits everywhere, and the industry as a whole would fall off precipitously.

Amid all of this, the Shibuya Station redevelopment was now something that the Shimaoka Group, its related firms, and the local landowners couldn't back out of.

The underlying cause of this was in the gradual aging of this station's travelers and commuters, along with a new direct line making it possible to get between Yokohama and Ikebukuro Stations in less than an hour.

The impact was clearly seen in the sales of the department store connected to the Shibuya Station building, its shelves lined with products aimed at the local elderly population. Families who used to be frequent visitors quickly dropped out of sight. The nature of the customer base had taken a turn for the worse as well, with people bringing a Mardi Gras–type atmosphere to the streets of Shibuya for things like Halloween and live showings of World Cup games. The police did their best, but there'd been broken shutters and signs, along with trash-lined streets. The "fashion capital" image of Shibuya was taking a serious hit, and the neighborhood as a whole was losing its appeal.

At this rate, people thought, Shibuya would become nothing but a stopping point on the way to somewhere else. It was seen as a crisis, and it brought people with often conflicting interests together to create a redevelopment project on a scale and time frame like nothing seen before. The rise in job openings this presented would normally be welcome, but the reality was that chronic worker shortages were now the norm at all construction sites. Staff weren't willing to put up with poor working conditions and low wages—and even if a site was free of problems, bad rumors like these were still enough to keep people from applying.

—Is someone in the industry trying to sabotage this site?

That greatly expanded the suspect list—rival firms, subcontractors with a grudge, even factional strife within their own group. In a case like this, you could be caught off guard at any moment.

—I can't make the call by myself.

Mitsuhiro tried to keep himself from getting all gloomy about it. He'd find the two remaining locations, ask Takenaka to make a decision, and the real work would come after that. He put the sandwich wrapper in a plastic bag, rolled it up, and tossed it into the bag he had slung over his shoulder.

—It sure is dry, though.

He sipped his bottle of tea. It was probably the least refreshing breakfast he'd ever had the misfortune to endure. He thought about putting the bottle back in his bag, but he was thirsty, so he took another sip, and then another. Now there was only a third of the bottle left.

—Funny that I'm so parched on such a rainy day.

He hadn't thought to borrow a dust mask since there wasn't any work going on. Now, as he emptied the bottle, he realized he should've at least brought along a regular anti-flu mask or the like.

—Better finish this up before I turn into a dried husk.

Stowing the empty bottle in his bag, he put his gloves back on and stood up, tablet in hand. He went down to the third basement floor with the two remaining images on his tablet as he looked around.

All workers hospitalized

This tweet had an image of a narrow passageway with bare concrete walls.

Human bones are coming out from that hole

This picture showed a square hole dug into the soil surface, a concrete wall in the background.

These were both distinctive enough that Mitsuhiro figured he'd recognize them immediately, but it was not to be. Nothing he saw seemed to match the photos, so he left the East Wing for the time being, looking around the area that'd serve as an open plaza under the station's east exit in the future. He saw no success there, either. If the "East Wing basement" reference was to be believed, the poster wasn't talking about the zone underneath the major crossing in front of the station. But he was running out of areas to search. Puzzled, he walked around the temporary structures—and as he passed by the underground water tank, something strange appeared in the light of his headlamp.

鎭

A character written in dark gray paint or something. It was larger than Mitsuhiro's height, running from the floor to the ceiling.

—What's that for?

He looked at it from a distance, since if he got too close, the character would start to disappear in the light from his headlamp. It was a kanji character, but one not seen in day-to-day Japanese life—he had no idea how to read it or what it could mean. But as his light shone on it, he realized from the movement of the shadows that there was a space between the wall and the temporary structure to the left of the character. He looked at this structure; it was lined with some kind of material, as if to soundproof it. He couldn't see what was behind it.

The space was large enough for two people to fit side by side, and on the floor of it was a large square hole. Mitsuhiro thought it'd match one of the remaining images, but this wasn't a dirt surface, and it wasn't just any hole. It was a stairway—not a temporary one made of metal plates and pipes. These were bare concrete stairs.

Mitsuhiro raised an eyebrow. He had no idea why they'd go through the trouble of hiding these stairs with that temporary structure. It was like some kind of facade to hide a service entrance in a commercial building. The staircase's position was strange as well. If you listened carefully, you could hear the faint sound of water overhead. The air here was dry, but above the ceiling, there was an onrush of rainwater going through. But aside from that:

—What're they gonna build deeper than the culvert?

He hadn't heard anything about building a new water reservoir. He checked the blueprints on his tablet. They showed a blank space, no diagram indicating the presence of stairs. Maybe someone overlooked something, or maybe this was here before the project began. If these stairs were built around when the Shibuya River was first diverted, that'd make them at least fifty years old. Maybe they'd fill it with earth and concrete later, just to make sure no workers fell into it.

Mitsuhiro crouched down, peeking in. Exactly ten steps greeted him, with a landing below that made a right turn. If he wanted to look any farther, he'd have to go down, and since he had already looked everywhere else, down it was. He tried to sigh and coughed a little instead. His throat was burning. The coughing stopped after he swallowed a few times, but he couldn't help but feel thirsty again. He really wanted to finish this up and get something to drink, or else he'd be craving water before long.

Hoping this would be the final step of his investigation, Mitsuhiro descended the stairs, his boots clattering against the steps. He knew the air would grow colder and more humid down below. That was how basements worked. In no time at all, he'd be seeing puddles, and the air would get all musty on him.

But he was wrong. As soon as he walked along the landing, went down the second set of stairs, and reached the next landing, he began to blink. His eyes were irritated—now *they* were dry, too, not just his throat. The air brushing against his cheeks stung so fiercely that he wondered if a fire had been burning here just a few minutes ago. In a construction site that used concrete, dryness was your worst enemy. Cement hardened after it was mixed with water; unlike with clay, absorbing the water was what made it harden. If it dried out before it was fully hardened, it could lead to cracking and collapse. It was vital to "cure" the concrete, maintaining the right temperature and humidity for it to set correctly. Given that fact, this dryness was awful. Or, really, simply abnormal.

—What kind of equipment could've made this place so dry?

It smelled weird, too. Not the usual sewage smell—it was sharper on the nose, drier, like something had been heated up really high in an oven. Mitsuhiro thought he had smelled it somewhere before, but he couldn't remember where. Instead, his brain gave him the image of his father, who had died when Mitsuhiro was in his twenties. In his mind, his father was wearing a business suit, which was out of the norm for him. The last time Mitsuhiro saw him wearing one was when he was saying his final goodbyes to him, in the coffin.

—Why am I thinking about that?

Mitsuhiro wiped his sweaty brow and went down another flight, to another landing. Your dead father is the last thing you want to think about alone in a dark basement. As he descended, he was struck by a sudden chill—a sign of panic, perhaps.

Maybe this was the cause of his excessive thirst and the weird connections he was making in his mind. Height and confined spaces were the two major phobias a construction site could easily trigger. If you couldn't control your instinctive fear, you could wind up causing a major accident for yourself.

That reminded him of something his late father had taught him. He'd owned a construction company. Mitsuhiro had known him to be a tough man, mentally and physically, but dependable and a born charmer—until that impression of his father changed. Out of nowhere, he had begun to get sick a lot. He had grown taciturn and difficult to deal with, and his eyes always looked dark somehow. Now that he was dead, Mitsuhiro was no longer sure which one was the "real" version of his father.

—Again. I'm thinking all these unnecessary thoughts.

He took a few slow, deep breaths to calm himself down. His father had told him that it'd help him relax. But no. That didn't matter.

This truly was a deep staircase. He had passed by several landings now, but they didn't lead out to any floors at all. And how could the air be *this* dry?

—What's at the bottom of this thing? A blast furnace?

As he looked around at the next landing, trying to find the cause of this dryness, he suddenly saw something strange.

Footprints. Coming from downstairs. They were so clearly there on the floor, it made him raise an eyebrow. Why would anyone leave footprints like this?

He bent down and looked at the floor. There was a light dusting of something on it, like soft snow. He ran the index finger of his gloved right hand across it; it left a streak, just like actual snow. But it was a white dust, kind of like fine ash. The ashes of something burned at an incredibly high temperature.

This must have been the cause of the odor. If he blew on this ash, it'd fly up and get inhaled. Praying that it wasn't asbestos of any kind, Mitsuhiro rose up and rubbed the fingers of his gloves against the wall to remove any residue. Perhaps this was the dust buildup from cutting through concrete. Now he especially regretted not wearing a dust mask as he held the tablet to his chest, took a handkerchief from his jacket pocket with his left hand, and held it to his mouth as he began descending again.

Soon, there were no more stairs leading down. He had finally reached the bottom…and a narrow passageway was ahead.

The thought of having to venture even further through this unpleasant air was incredibly uncomfortable to Mitsuhiro. He wriggled his tongue around, trying to summon more saliva in his mouth as he continued down the passage.

—There it is.

Suddenly, he stopped and brought up one of the tweeted images on his tablet.

All workers hospitalized

The words jumped out at him, giving him goose bumps. Pushing away the thought that staying in such an unnatural atmosphere really would make him sick, he compared the image with what he saw. There was no mistaking it. The sender of that tweet definitely took the photo right here.

Mitsuhiro did the same thing—after taking off his right glove and putting it in his pocket, he used the tablet to take a photo of his own. Then he walked ahead, right hand still holding the tablet while his left kept the handkerchief over his mouth. Positionally speaking, he had to be directly underneath the East Wing by now, having crossed under the culvert. This was the deepest part of what the tweet called the "East Wing basement," a place so deep that no one involved in the construction project would bother entering. If anyone was coming here often, there'd be footprints all over the place.

Now a door was suddenly visible at the end of the passage. It had a lock on it, the type seen at many construction sites: a metal door with a PIN-based lock on it. You had to know the right numbers, or you couldn't open it.

This would mark the end of the investigation…if the door had been closed. But despite the imposing lock, it wasn't. There was a dark space about four inches wide between the door and its frame.

—What's this lock even for?

Mitsuhiro felt a surprisingly intense sort of anger, one he couldn't immediately suppress. Maybe it was a sign of panic manifesting in another form.

When you try to push down your fear, anger wells up until you can no longer control it.

Mitsuhiro took a deep breath under his handkerchief and slowly exhaled. He managed to suppress both his anger and his fear, scowling at the ever-rising dryness and odor, and pushed the door open with his foot. He had to, because his hands were full—although, really, he didn't want to touch the door with his hand. It was a completely illogical thought, but he was afraid he might burn himself.

The door made a creaking sound as it swung open. He entered, sincerely hoping there was a damp space on the other side, and shone his headlamp into the darkness.

It was a surprisingly large space. He had his light on, but without any prior knowledge of his structure, he had no idea what he was looking at. He could make out concrete walls and a vaulted ceiling, but he couldn't tell how high that ceiling went, and he was stepping on bare earth right now. That white lime-like substance he saw on the stairs was spread over the soil as well, creating clouds of dust as he slowly advanced. Despite how much the space around him had changed, the air was still the same. In fact, it started to seem drier and drier, like he was in a walk-in oven or a sauna where someone forgot to add any humidity.

Suddenly, the face of his dead father flashed across his mind again. A gaunt face. His father in the coffin, dressed in his suit, sleeping in his final resting place.

Takenaka had once asked Mitsuhiro if his father taught him how to read blueprints. Yes, he said—then he was surprised at how proud saying that made him feel. He thought the stress of running a subcontracting firm had caused his father to have a physical and mental breakdown. The face of his mother, exhausted after caring for her husband so long, flickered into view. He had sworn many times that his own wife would never have to experience that.

—This is so crazy. Why do I keep on recalling my dead father?

His heart pulsed. Maybe he was dehydrated. That was right up there with heat stroke as a factor in construction-site accidents.

Then, in the light, there it was.

A hole in the back of the space. A vertical shaft several yards square.

—That's it! It has to be it! The last image! I finally found it!

Mitsuhiro shouted with joy in his heart. If the air didn't feel so weird around him, he might have actually whooped out loud. Instead he held his breath, removed the handkerchief from his mouth, and quickly took several pictures with his tablet, not bothering to compare them to the tweeted photo. With each flash, a table by the wall beyond the hole appeared and then disappeared back into the dark. There seemed to be something on it, but he couldn't tell what it was.

Human bones are coming out from that hole

He suddenly recalled the words, and they made his hair stand on end. He almost dropped the tablet, and as he tried to clutch it to his chest, he took in a deep breath of that dry air. It immediately set his throat on fire, making him cough and put the handkerchief over his mouth again. From now on, he resolved, he'd always wear a dust mask on these investigations. Better to keep one in his bag at all times, really.

The coughing had subsided, but Mitsuhiro was still having trouble breathing. It was time to get out of here before panic really did set in. With that in mind, he turned around, looking for the door. There was none. That doorway should have been right behind him, but now there was just a concrete wall.

He hurriedly turned his headlamp left and right to illuminate the wall. There was no way in or out. He extended the light range a few more yards, but he could only see the wall.

—The door disappeared.

Feeling rushing waves of agitation, he tried desperately to calm himself down.

Hang on. It couldn't have just disappeared. The darkness made him lose his sense of direction. He thought he made a beeline for the hole, but he was actually walking in a broad arc, and now he was looking at the wrong wall.

—Footprints. Right, I left footprints. Just follow them back.

But when he shone his light on the ground, he couldn't see any. Nothing but the pure white reflected back at him. No, the footprints had been erased by a new layer of white. That white ash, the remnants of something burned at high temperature. It was crazy. Mitsuhiro's heart was pounding, his temples throbbing. *Calm down. There has to be a way out. There must be.* He repeated it in his head as he made a clockwise circle around the hole, taking care not to fall in.

He began to feel like a kid lost at a stamp rally—the kind of event train companies ran all the time, where you took the train to different stations and got your paper stamped at each one. The thought made him shudder.

What if this was the purpose of those seven tweeted images? What if it was all done in order to lure someone into this space deep underground?

—Stop being stupid. Why would anyone do that?

But his mind was already on to the next thing. He recalled a series of graffiti messages he saw in a bathroom stall once. You'd look at the door in front of you, sitting on the toilet, and you'd see "Look right" on it. You'd look right, and you'd see "Look up," and so on. You'd follow this trail, and it'd always end the same way:

Dumbass

That was what he'd been doing the whole time. He was being made into a fool. He had been lured into this dark cavern in the middle of the city, and now he was trapped inside. *God dammit. Calm down. There's no way the exit just disappeared. Maybe the door closed on its own, and it just looks like the wall. There's a way out. If you get trapped, the boss or someone on the team will come looking for you. So calm down. Calm down. Calm down...*

Panic was about to overtake him, but he urged himself to move along the wall. He was bound to find the exit that way. It was a perfectly rational thought, but he was so impatient and uneasy that he rushed at the wall anyway. Maybe his body thought he could break through it or something.

With a thud, he felt a heavy impact on his shoulder. His helmet hit the wall hard and bounced back.

Every movement was panicked now. That was the state he was in. He was suddenly very aware of the smell, and all of a sudden, he was reminded of an MRI machine, that narrow space where they examine your brain. The first one he got was also the first time in his life he had ever felt claustrophobic. He'd nearly panicked, like he was being placed in a coffin. Like his dead father.

There, in front of his father in the coffin, someone had said to him:

"This is the last farewell to the deceased. You will not be able to see his face any longer. Please approach him and say your final goodbyes now."

The final goodbyes. Why the final?

—Because it was a cremation.

Mitsuhiro rubbed his shoulder against the wall, staggering as he walked. He was shocked by the answer that suddenly came to him. He *had* smelled this before. It was the smell that had wafted faintly through the air after the coffin containing his father's body, suit and all, was pushed into the oven and the lid was closed. The smell of someone turning into bones, then ashes.

Human bones are coming out

The palpitations were intense now. He could hear nothing but his own heartbeat. No, it was intensifying the silence around him, making his ears ring painfully.

Just being there makes you sick

He felt like at least one of the blood vessels in his brain was about to pop. He might've been able to calm down if he at least had something to drink. Then again, he likely would have just drunk down everything he had. That was the kind of thirst this was. These ashes, the remnants of the fire, were completely robbing him of all moisture.

I can hardly breathe

He found himself biting his hand with the handkerchief. He was dissolving into full-blown terror. But just as he was about to scream in overwhelming fear, something slammed into his thigh. It was a table, attached to the wall. The thing that had appeared in the flash from those photos. Now there were white fluttering objects on it. They were *shimenawa* and *shide*—the heavy ropes and zigzag-shaped paper streamers seen decorating Shinto shrines.

They were also used at construction sites, usually for groundbreaking "earth-appeasement" ceremonies and the like.

Looking closer at the table, he could see trays of these *shide*, and the *washi* paper used to make them. There was something shiny on one of them. A small piece of metal—a key of some kind. Likely the key to the door he had just gone through.

As he tried to go around the table, he noticed a large stepladder lying on the ground in front of it. Moving away from it, he looked at the table from the front.

Now, he finally realized, it was a shrine—a small wooden shrine against the wall, a little higher than Mitsuhiro's head. It wasn't some ancient Shinto altar; it appeared to be brand new. The *shimenawa*, that sacred rope of straw, was tacked right up to the wall between the altar and the table. Behind it, on the wall in dark gray paint, was that character:

鎭

No, he intuitively realized, it wasn't paint. It was ash. It had been written with the ashes after something had been burned up.

Mitsuhiro consciously relaxed his jaw, taking the handkerchief and hand out of his mouth. He took a natural deep breath. The stench in the air moved away, and cool, misty air flowed into his body.

For the first time since he had started down the stairs, he could breathe properly. Immediately his pulse slowed down. Sweat began to ooze from his skin, like he was ejecting steam from every pore.

Mitsuhiro, grateful for the clean air, began to wonder if this was a small underground enshrinement. He had heard that places like these were often built inside large buildings in Japan. They were also called "ritual halls" or "sanctuaries," and only a few people were allowed to enter them.

Part of him wanted to thank this shrine for the fact he could now swallow the saliva in his mouth without difficulty, but that seemed a little unscientific. There had to be a structural reason why the air was only humid right here. He felt considerably calmer as he thought this over. It wasn't like this altar was the sole reason why he could breathe properly again. Of course not.

Then he looked at the table. With his left hand, still in a glove, he rubbed the surface. Nothing was accumulated on it. The white lime-like dust on the stairs and the dirt was absent on the table. Someone must have been frequently wiping it off—or something else was keeping it from piling up. The idea that the altar could keep itself divinely free of dust was too preposterous to consider. Surely it served as a kind of landmark. It must have been placed at this special point where the air was cleaner for some reason. That was the rational way of thinking.

He now found himself completely at ease—and on top of that, something curious now appeared in the light. It was a thick black wire hanging down from far overhead toward the right side of the table—a cable. At the bottom end of it was a simple switch, capable of being turned on or off.

—Is there power going to this?

Mitsuhiro walked up to it in disbelief and turned it on.

With a flash, orange light poured in from all directions. It was as if the sun had set, and all the streetlights had come on at once.

Thanks to this light, he could see that this space was almost a perfect square, about twenty yards wide on each side. That large square hole was in the center of the space, and the altar was on his side of it. The door he had lost sight of was on the other side of the hole, right in front of the altar, and it was still open. It was such a simple setup, he wondered how he got so lost in it.

The lights weren't on the ceiling but hung from the four corners of the room. The reason was obvious: The ceiling was just too high. It was so deep and vaulted, he couldn't even see it with the headlamp alone.

—What's this stepladder for?

It was a little too big to be needed for replacing those lights. It was almost as large as a regular ladder, in fact.

—Is it for getting in and out of that square hole?

Mitsuhiro walked up to the hole, but he was suddenly distracted. For the first time, he noticed something on the left side of the wall facing him—some kind of heavy machinery. The center of each wall remained dark, the light from the four corners not quite reaching, and this pure-white machine shimmered in the middle of it, stunning him.

—A pile driver?

It resembled an excavator, but instead of an arm at the end, there was a pump and a large hammer. This equipment was meant for forming cement-milk piles in the ground, using the so-called pure-pile method. The three-point prop and pump were folded up for now, but when fully assembled, the machine was over thirty feet tall. There were some concrete piles lying beside it as well, ready to be driven down.

How in the world did they get this down here? You couldn't carry it down the stairs, so Mitsuhiro assumed they used a crane to lower it. Then they put a ceiling over this space and just sealed it all up, driver and all. Or did this space lead all the way to the surface? No way. There was no giant hole this size in the middle of Tokyo.

None of this made any sense. All the pile-driving work had already been completed. Piles were one of the most sensitive current topics in the construction industry, and if there was any change to their implementation schedule, Mitsuhiro would have known about it, especially if there was additional work to be done.

And why would equipment painted this blinding white color be used underground? There weren't any regulations on the color of heavy machinery like this, but it was common practice to employ bright, conspicuous colors like yellow to prevent accidents. White machinery would stand out in cases like daylight mountain excavation, but using this underground seemed completely unreasonable. If anything, it'd make the equipment blend in with the walls in lit areas. Mitsuhiro hadn't even noticed it in the dark until now, in fact.

But as he looked at this enigmatic piece of equipment, he heard a metallic jingling from the hole. Then a voice, almost like a groan.

"Is… Is somebody there?"

Mitsuhiro wanted to shout out loudly, but the thirst and surprise stifled his voice.

—The door had been open.

He should have considered the possibility that someone else might be in here. Maybe someone had fallen in the hole trying to flip the light switch by the altar. So he looked into the hole to call out again to whoever was in there—but then his voice left him.

The bottom of the hole was a flat, bare dirt surface, and it was littered with trash. There were plastic bottles, along with what appeared to be food wrappers. Surrounded by this trash was someone leaning against the wall, legs sprawled out.

He was either asleep or unconscious, not moving an inch. He appeared to be a man, considering the bushy beard. His gray hair was long and shaggy, and his thick coat and pants looked worn and dirty.

—Is a homeless guy living here?

That was Mitsuhiro's first impression, but that was impossible. The people who slept in parks and under railway overpasses around here had been cleared out for this redevelopment, yes, but it would be impossible to sneak past all these security guards and workers to set up shop in a construction site this size.

Having no idea how he got in or why he was here, Mitsuhiro then noticed something strange on the man's left leg. Around the ankle of his sneaker, which was so dirty that Mitsuhiro couldn't tell what color it originally was, he could see a metal ring that reflected the light from his headlamp. A thick chain, silver in color, extended from it, leading to some unseen place below.

Fearfully, Mitsuhiro got down on his knees, put his gloved left hand over the edge of the hole, and peered down. There was a cone-shaped concrete block there, like a giant bollard of some sort. It was too big and heavy for one person to carry around. The chain was tied crosswise to this block. It was likely secured with a lock or something.

—He's not living here by choice.

Now Mitsuhiro understood what he was seeing. He didn't think he could explain it well at all, but he could at least see what kind of situation this man was in.

A person was chained up at the bottom of a large hole dug into a deep underground space.

3

"Are you okay?!"

Mitsuhiro couldn't help but shout to the man at the bottom of the hole.

The man with the shaggy gray hair leaned his back against the wall and twitched his chained leg, flexing and straightening his knee a bit. It was a reflex movement, like a sleeping person trying to shake off the discomfort in their chained ankle. The resulting jingle of the metal links made Mitsuhiro flinch. The eerie sound, echoing across a room an unknowable number of floors below the ground, sent chills down his spine. His headlamp and the four orange lights in the corners were now working in tandem to fend off the darkness, but the abnormally dry air was still making his skin tingle, and the discomfort and irritation were now accompanied by an undeniable fear.

This smell, especially. It wasn't a musty basement smell or the stench of sewage, but rather the lingering scent of a raging fire. Mitsuhiro had associated it with things like ovens left on by mistake or incinerators that had just burned a load of trash, but now he couldn't help but think of a different scene. The relaxed expression on the face of his father, lying there in his formal suit as if he had been freed from something. The distinctive smell of a crematorium hanging in the air.

Human bones are coming out from that hole

He wasn't sure if he'd soon fall into another panic—but just then, the chain jingled again. Mitsuhiro wanted to beg him to please stop doing that, but of course the man wasn't doing it on purpose.

"Can you hear me? What happened?"

But the man was either asleep or didn't want to be in the light, because he twisted his head and kept his face down.

Why was he in this hole deep underground? The first idea that came to mind was that he was a victim of an attack by his fellow construction workers. That sort of thing used to happen a lot, he had heard. The rough types you saw in this business would get into arguments over gambling debts or who loaned money to whom, or fought over who'd get work and who wouldn't. Sometimes, they just liked bullying the weak. Occasionally it would get way out of hand—literally hanging people up in the air or leaving them in unventilated containers in the dead of summer. All sorts of things.

That was back when there were more workers than jobs, and people had to fight for whatever they could get. With the chronic worker shortage now, that sort of behavior would quickly scare away whatever applicants they could find.

In fact, maybe this was the man who sent out that series of tweets? Had this guy's coworkers found him disparaging their worksite, and they decided to take matters into their own hands? That made more sense…except the man in that hole didn't strike him as the type to be very social-media savvy.

"Um… Can you hear me? Are you awake?"

Mitsuhiro called out to him a few times but stopped as he became aware—and afraid—of two things. One was that the echoing made his voice sound just as eerie as the chains. The other was that he feared the edge of the hole might collapse if he leaned over it too much, sending him down with it.

He stepped away from the hole, covering his mouth and nose with the handkerchief again. Unconsciously, he was heading toward the small shrine… and from there, he remembered that there was a safer way to reach out. That large stepladder in front of the table.

Taking the handkerchief off his face, he put it in his pants pocket, not doubting for a moment that the air was perfectly fine around the shrine. He put his tablet in his bag, placed the bag on the table, and then took out the right work glove he had jammed in his jacket pocket. After putting it on, he looked at the stepladder in thought. There was a good chance this would reach the bottom of the hole. There'd be no reason to leave it here otherwise.

That, and he was weirdly convinced about one other fact. The air in that hole had to be incredibly dry. If the altar was seemingly "generating" clean air, that hole must be the source of the not-so-clean air.

Clink.

The sound of the chain made him jump again, as grateful as he was for the interruption to his idle thoughts. There was no time to waste. He had already gone through a lot of trouble tracking down these images, and now he had run into this emergency. He needed to do what he had to and get back to HQ.

But he also knew deep down why he was taking his time. He didn't want to leave that shrine. He wanted to cling to that table and pray that the hole in front of him would just disappear. The fear of going down into it was almost primal.

Of course, as part of the crisis-management team, he couldn't just run away without even trying to figure out what was going on. If he did, he'd be kicked off the team and lose the job he had spent so much time hunting down. A job he chose because he didn't want to wind up like his father.

—You're letting your mind wander again.

Get moving. Get this over with fast, go back to the office, and regale your team with your little heroic tale. Add in a joke or two.

As he gave himself this order, he was about to lift up the stepladder when his eyes were drawn to something on the table. One of the trays, covered with Japanese paper and the *shide* streamers, had a key on it. He had thought it went to the door on the wall, but then a flash of an idea suggested otherwise. If it was placed right by the stepladder, he might as well take it with him. It seemed like a rational idea—proof, he felt, that he had regained his composure.

So Mitsuhiro took the key and slipped it into the breast pocket of his jacket. Then, with a quick "Okay" to himself, he picked up the stepladder and approached the edge of the hole. As long as he held on to this, he was sure, he'd be able to manage even if he fell in somehow. It was such a reassuring thought, he almost wanted to hug this thing.

Instead of opening it up into an A shape, he kept it closed as he placed it by the hole. Slowly, he lowered it down, letting it slide along his hands, careful not to accidentally let it land on the man below. He adjusted the angle of the stepladder so that the base would be close to the wall. Soon, he could feel the ladder's rubber feet touching the bottom of the hole. The top of it was just below the lip, but that was good enough. As he had expected, it was long enough to let someone climb up from the bottom of the hole to where he was standing.

Brushing away the white dust that slowly rose up from the bottom of the hole with one hand, Mitsuhiro bravely turned his body and put one foot on the stepladder. He pushed hard, embedding the ladder into the ground a little, and checked to make sure it wouldn't tip over with his weight before putting his other foot on it. He went down a few steps, grabbing the sides with both hands. Careful not to pinch his fingers or hands between the closed sides of the ladder, he made his way down until he was standing at the bottom.

This ground was softer than expected, reminding him more of sand than soil. The hole felt almost conical in shape, as though an enormous antlion would be waiting for him at the center of it…which was silly, of course. That concrete block would've sunk into the sand long ago, to say nothing of the man chained to it. The thought was terrifying, but he quickly put a stop to it.

He pressed on, flashing his headlamp side to side as he kicked aside the trash in his way, and finally reached the man leaning against the wall. Mitsuhiro peered at his face. The man, exposed in the light, had thrown his head back, blocking it with both hands.

"What the hell, man?" came a high-pitched voice. "Stop shinin' that in my face. I'm just sleepin' in here."

The tone was completely normal. He seemed so at ease it was almost anticlimactic. He certainly wasn't desperately calling out for help or struggling for his life after being brutally assaulted.

"Sorry."

Mitsuhiro changed the angle of his headlamp so it shone over the man's head. For some reason, it occurred to him that he should be recording this.

He thought about going back to get his tablet, but instead he removed his right glove and took his company phone out from his jacket pocket. Turning on camera mode, he pointed at the man.

"Excuse me one second," he said, and then he took a picture of the man quizzically looking up at him, hands lowered. He then took some shots of the ring on the man's left leg, the chain, and the concrete block.

"What're you taking pictures of?" the man asked. He sounded a bit agitated at being treated as a curiosity.

"Oh, I'm sorry. This is part of my job."

Mitsuhiro didn't really think it was. Attempting to parse this bizarre situation was more his boss Takenaka's job. *This* was more a self-protective impulse, motivated by not wanting to be blamed for any problems that might arise later. But this suddenly drove the man into activity, startling Mitsuhiro.

"Job? I can still work, y'know."

"Um… Huh?"

"As long as I can eat, I can work. I can work…"

The sad desperation in the man's high-pitched voice was more than irritating. It was frightening. He claimed to be able to work, but how could he, chained up like this? It was almost like punishing him for *not* being able to work. It was cruel.

"All right, all right. Calm down, please. What are you doing in a place like this? Did someone bring you down here?"

"Ahh, I dunno anymore."

"…You don't know?"

"I dunno why, but I have to be here, don't I? Ugh! What a pain in the ass. I just wanna go to sleep!"

The man sadly flailed his legs around, making more noise with his chain. The sound was still hard to put up with. His voice, and the jingling, echoed inside the hole, stirring up Mitsuhiro's emotions from every possible angle—as pathetic as it was irritating and impossibly creepy. The man's rotten body odor wafted through the air. Mitsuhiro almost wanted to spit and yell at him to shut up.

"Please calm down. I'm going to take this off now. Come outside with me and tell me what happened."

He was more quieting down his own mind as he said it, putting his phone in his pocket and examining the lock on the ring. The man stopped ranting for a moment, suspiciously eyeing Mitsuhiro, who was adjusting the angle of his headlamp to illuminate the keyhole. He said he'd take it off, but if the key he brought along wasn't a match, there was little he could do. He'd have to return to ground level and call for backup or borrow some kind of saw to cut the chain with.

Praying that he was right, he inserted the key into the chain lock. He wanted to get out of there as soon as possible…and he hoped he would never have to come back.

The key fit perfectly. He twisted it. With a click, the lock came off the man's leg. He took a deep breath, his relieved body suddenly slick with sweat.

"Ohh? You got it off?"

The man flashed a contented smile.

"Yeah. Let's get out of here."

"We're leaving?"

"Yes. C'mon, let's go. Here."

Mitsuhiro couldn't hide his frustration. He was getting angry with this man who couldn't explain why he was here, and he didn't want to waste any more time. This newfound forcefulness pushed the man to shrug, stand up, and stagger toward the stepladder. Putting on his work gloves, Mitsuhiro watched as the man opened up the ladder, secured it so its sides were flush with the wall, and easily climbed up. After all that doddering, Mitsuhiro had feared they'd be down here for a while, so this was a great relief as he grabbed the ladder himself.

Immediately, he was struck by the image of something raising itself up behind him and giving chase. It was a tremendously powerful premonition, and Mitsuhiro almost screamed. He was so terrified, having no idea what was chasing him, that he couldn't even look back to see. If he did, he thought, there'd be no turning back.

—*Calm down. There's nothing behind you. Just a big empty space.*

But the image of being left alone in this vast dark ocean appeared in his mind. A cold, sharp fear pierced his entire body from behind. Overwhelmed by the sensation, Mitsuhiro gritted his teeth and climbed up the stepladder. He couldn't afford to slip—otherwise, he'd be swallowed into the bottom of the hole, never to emerge. He was breathing hard as he ascended.

The man had now climbed all the way out, disappearing over the edge of the hole. Mitsuhiro soon followed him, crawling out on hands and knees atop the dusty ground. He continued crawling all the way over to the altar, then stood up, clinging to the table and panting with fear.

He was back in the safe zone. He thought so, anyway, but it was far from safe. He felt like he was merely clinging to a tiny inner tube in the pitch-black sea, desperately trying to keep his face above the surface.

The man was standing there, looking dazed.

"Let's get out of here," Mitsuhiro barked, the dry air irritating his throat. The man gave this an apologetic nod. Considering his previous situation, he really deserved some sympathy. Right now, Mitsuhiro should have been winning this man over, convincing him not to tell the outside world about what happened at this site. Minimizing the potential damage to his company was supposed to be his job here, but right now, it sure didn't seem that way.

Mitsuhiro didn't know if some idiot construction worker did this or not, but all the trouble this would undoubtedly cause filled him with frustration. Or maybe it was fear.

Clutching his bag in his hand, he made for the only door in the room. He had left the stepladder down in the hole, the key in the chain lock, and the lights on as well, but he didn't care. He wasn't about to switch them off and take that long walk back in the dark.

—If anyone has a problem with that, tell it to the idiot who didn't put a light switch by the door!

Feeling a little ill, he kept the handkerchief by his mouth as he climbed the stairs. Occasionally, he'd look back to make sure the man was following him. At first, he did so silently. But as they both made their way to the surface without a word, the man suddenly shouted out.

"Fire!"

Mitsuhiro turned his gaze upward. He had only been looking at the dusty staircase in front of him, oblivious to the smoke and strange smell that had begun to drift down. He hadn't even noticed that unnerving, burning smell in the dry air.

—Fire? Where could there be a fire? The generator isn't even running.

Another fire

He almost took out his tablet, attempting to figure out where the fire might be coming from, but naturally, that wasn't the smartest move right now. The most pressing issue was the smoke. It was blowing downward at them; they had to move right now. There was no way he could stand there checking blueprints while they were being bombarded with potentially toxic smoke in this cramped stairwell.

"Let's get out of here now!"

Mitsuhiro saw the man shrink back and decided to give him his handkerchief.

"Put this over your nose and mouth."

The man eagerly accepted it. That handkerchief, Mitsuhiro suddenly recalled, was a Father's Day gift from his wife and daughter. But it was too late to worry about such pleasantries, especially now that the man already had it.

Mitsuhiro was deeply frustrated, but he covered his own mouth with a gloved hand and climbed the stairs, holding his breath as best he could. That irresistible fear stalking him from behind wasn't there any longer. Now the fear was overhead.

And as he endured the pain of climbing these stairs while breathing as little as possible...

I can hardly breathe

...he bit down again, this time around the base of the thumb. He tried his best not to fall, his eyes alternating between the smoke reflecting the light of his headlamp and the dust billowing off the stairs. His knees and thighs were in agony. His lungs were burning hot, and his heart was beating so fast, he thought he might have gotten sick. Something about restricting his breathing as much as possible while doing all this aggressive physical exercise almost made him laugh—or maybe he really *was* giggling as he scrambled up the stairs.

He was ready to break, but he still struggled and put one leg in front of the other. Then he thought he really would break, but still he persevered. This time, when he really *did* think he was at the end, that he had absolutely nothing left, he finally reached the open floor above.

鎮

The character on the wall appeared in the light from the headlamp, but in no time at all, Mitsuhiro was surrounded by smoke, unable to see anything. He tried to make sure the man was all right, but he couldn't. Instead, he bumped into a nearby wall. Following the wall with his shoulder, he used his memory of the floor plan to try to reach the stairs to the surface. His head was pounding, and he feared he was about to pass out or pop a blood vessel and die right here. His hand was in terrible pain, but he wouldn't stop biting on it.

Suddenly, a figure appeared and pulled his other hand forward.

"This way! This way!"

It was the older guy from the prefab office. He had his helmet on, along with goggles and a dust mask. His guidance allowed Mitsuhiro to reach the stairs without another moment of hesitation, his legs shaking with fatigue by the time they reached the surface. The sound of rain was audible again. He felt a cool breeze blowing in, as the realization that he was finally safe again washed over him.

He kneeled on that dark, damp floor, put his bag down, and dropped on all fours, too desperate for air to thank his coworker yet. His eyes, nose, and throat ached; his head throbbed; and it felt like someone had stomped on his chest. He wished he could be strapped to a stretcher or wheelchair or something and taken to the hospital right now.

"I'll bring some water. Stay here."

The worker, apparently sensing Mitsuhiro's difficulty breathing, turned his headlamp off, removing his goggles and mask as he jogged over to the office. He was back in around two minutes, an unopened plastic bottle of water in his hand. Mitsuhiro took it in a great hurry, opened it, and gulped it down with audible greed. He wanted to breathe, but he didn't want to take the bottle away from his mouth either, so he huffed as much as he could through his burning nostrils, downing the entire bottle nearly all at once.

Remembering the pain in his hand, he looked at the damage. The base of the thumb on his work glove was partially chewed off, blood seeping out from inside. The bright glare from his headlamp on it remind him to turn it off, and he did so shakily. He blinked his aching eyes, rejoicing at how doing it didn't leave him in total darkness anymore. The area was dimly lit, full of ugly-looking concrete and prefab structures, and the smell of sewage seeped out from the culvert...but it was still far safer and more comfortable than the bottom of that underground pit. This was where people actually belonged.

"I came here as fast as I could when the alarm went off," the coworker said, waiting for Mitsuhiro's breathing to settle down. "Do you know where the fire started?"

"Not sure," Mitsuhiro managed to squeeze out of his sore throat, still on his knees.

Before the older man could ask any more questions, his younger companion emerged from the unadorned steel stairway. He was in his own helmet, goggles, and dust mask, a fire extinguisher in his hand. Mitsuhiro hadn't noticed him before, but he had come down with the older worker.

"Is there any fire to put out?" the older worker asked.

The younger one nodded. "On Floor B2. Some of the materials and plastic sheeting we had piled up in there were on fire."

The older man stared at him. "Floor B2? Really?"

"Yes, sir," the younger man replied, removing his mask. "I don't know what the cause was, but I didn't see any potential arsonists or anything."

Mitsuhiro could feel himself growing pale. "Arson...?" he said. The workers hadn't said that it was, but their attitude suggested that it was highly possible. That, and they seemed to be watching Mitsuhiro pretty carefully. Another beat, and he realized that he was their prime suspect so far.

"I… I have no idea what happened. I tried to leave the basement, and the smoke was already all over the stairs."

The two men remained silent, so Mitsuhiro pushed through the pain in his nose and throat to keep talking.

"All I was doing was taking photos. I didn't do anything that'd start a fire. I didn't touch any switchboards or generators. I don't have anything to start a fire with. The guy in the basement was with me, too."

That last sentence startled the two workers. Mitsuhiro was so relieved to survive this ordeal that he'd forgotten to mention the man at the bottom of that hole. The young worker had come up from below with no apparent health issues, so Mitsuhiro assumed that man was safe as well.

"There was someone in the basement?" the older one asked in shock.

"Yes… I don't know why, but he was stuck in this sort of ritual altar down below. I think I got separated from him because of the smoke. Did you see him around where I was?"

The young worker turned toward his older associate, looking worried.

"Does he mean the room at the very bottom we can't go into?"

The older one didn't answer the question, instead turning toward the stairs.

"Let's go look for him. It might be an arson, so…"

He beckoned the younger staffer to join him. They both went down the stairs.

Mitsuhiro found a place to sit down. The little water droplets in the air felt pleasant to him. It felt like whatever had been eating him up from inside was now leaving his body.

—I hope I get my handkerchief back.

That was his first thought. It made him reconsider what order he should be tackling all the questions in his mind. He was still fairly certain that someone had locked him in that room, at least for a while. He also wanted to see how all of this might be connected with the tweets.

After the fire

The fire had started when Mitsuhiro released that man. Almost as though it was trying to drive him back down into the depths.

Another fire here

His temples began to pulsate. He felt a tingling sensation in his neck. Was there some kind of toxic gas rising up from the bottom of that pit? Had it started the fire?

No… There was no scientific basis for that. It was too out of this world to mention in his report. He was inclined to believe it, having experienced that bizarrely dry air for himself, but it was just too farfetched. If any sort of gas caused the fire, after all, the basement with that pit would've been the first to be engulfed in flames.

They needed to presume arson here. Maybe the arsonist was angry that the man he had chained up down there was released. Mitsuhiro stood up, fearing the criminal might jump out and attack him, but the workers returned just then.

"Did you find the man?" he asked.

They both stared back in silence. From their expressions, Mitsuhiro realized that he now had some new problems. He thought about going back down there in an attempt to solve them. He had a terrible feeling now that he was about to be blamed for something he didn't do.

Without knowing how or why, the man at the bottom of that pit had disappeared without a trace, taking one of Mitsuhiro's belongings with him.

4

"Those are all the images of the hole you have?"

"Yes," Mitsuhiro hoarsely replied, and his boss, Takenaka, gave him a concerned look.

"Okay. When the Chief comes around, you can just give him a verbal report. Go to the hospital and get yourself checked out."

"I'm feeling a lot better now..."

Mitsuhiro rubbed his throat. As soon as he'd left the construction site, he had gone to a nearby convenience store to pick up a few things—eyedrops, lozenges for his throat, bandages, and so on. The first aid seemed good enough for the time being.

He'd also purchased a folding umbrella, along with some wet wipes. He had used up all his wipes in the toilet over at the main office, cleaning that dust off his clothes and shoes. He also remembered to buy two bottles of spring water, along with a mask. If they'd had goggles as well, it would've been perfect, but they didn't sell those.

"If you suddenly fall ill on us, it'll just be more work and trouble for the team, you know."

"I do."

Mitsuhiro obediently agreed. If a member of the crisis-management team collapsed on the street after inhaling toxic substances at a worksite, it would be a burden on everyone. It would be shameful to cause that kind of nuisance for his team.

"Now, just to be sure, you didn't actually see any human remains around this hole?"

"No, nothing. I asked the on-site workers as well, and they said they never heard anything like it."

There was that smell, though, a voice in his head whispered. The smell of people burned down to the bone, and beyond.

—But was that really it?

In the familiar surroundings of his main office, everything that had happened to Mitsuhiro down below seemed like a dream, detached from reality. He had shared the images he took with his boss, and they looked over them on the tablet together...but it was just a bunch of scenes from a construction site, an uninteresting collection of images on their tablets. No reason at all for such terror.

"No remains, and no harmful gases, either..."

Takenaka crossed out "human bones are coming out," "something absolutely harmful coming out," and "just being there makes you sick" with a red pen on his printout. It contained a list of the tweets in question. "A rash of construction errors" and "all workers hospitalized" were already crossed off.

"We can discount the 'all workers hospitalized' one, too?"

"I couldn't find any evidence to back that statement up," Takenaka grumbled, putting his red pen down. "That just leaves the fire."

Mitsuhiro couldn't help feeling like he was being accused of something. After getting caught in that fire, and then suspected of accidentally causing it, he was getting angry.

On his tablet, Takenaka brought up an image of the materials that burned in the fire. Mitsuhiro had asked the workers to come back with him and get that photo as well. He made sure to borrow a pair of goggles and dust mask from them, too.

"We're waiting on the fire department's investigation," said Mitsuhiro, "but if it turns out to be arson, I think the disadvantages outweigh the advantages for us, don't you agree?"

"Well, if it wasn't caused by an error on-site, that works for us."

"Yes, but if word gets out to the public, it still won't be good. We won't be able to deny the possibility that this arsonist is still accessing the site without getting caught. Having firefighters and police officers around is going to delay our work. We'll be questioned about our management. It'll lead to more security costs, and we might run into worker shortages if people leave. It all means this Twitter user's attack succeeded, and that could mean more attacks in the future. All minuses in terms of investor sentiment."

"But if the fire department determines that it's arson, it becomes the police's job after that, right? Better than the media getting ahold of it and putting their own spin on it."

"Yes, of course. We need to avoid holding a press conference where our executives have to apologize over something that's not actually a big deal. If all we have right now is an ongoing investigation, the firm's gonna be reluctant to announce anything publicly. We might wind up having conflicting information later on if we do. First, we have to thoroughly investigate; then we report the findings and implement measures on-site to prevent a recurrence."

A knock on the door made Takenaka stop talking.

"Hello. It's Sugawara."

A large man in work clothes came into the meeting room. The employee ID hanging from his neck read "Kento Sugawara—Chief." His breast pocket contained a pair of large glasses and four pens, all different colors.

This was the site manager for the East Wing, as well as the man who oversaw all aspects of the Shibuya redevelopment project, including how they negotiated with the local residents. That meant he was the de facto director of the entire project.

Mitsuhiro and Takenaka stood up and bowed. "Sorry to make you come all the way out here," Takenaka said as he walked up to him.

Sugawara stopped him with a friendly smile and a wave of his hand as he went around to the other side of the conference table. "I was just in a meeting at the head office. I heard there was an incident on-site, so I came to see what was up."

He pulled up one of the chairs and sat down opposite the two men. Takenaka and Mitsuhiro also sat down, the former handing over a tablet showing a group of thumbnail images.

"These photos were taken by Matsunaga here as part of his investigation into some tweets posted by someone who appears to be working for us."

Sugawara looked at Mitsuhiro for a moment, nodding. Mitsuhiro bowed slightly back at him. He thought for sure that Sugawara would take out those glasses from his breast pocket and put them on, but he didn't. Instead he blinked a few times, running a less-than-sure finger along the screen as he scrolled up and down.

"Is this the Shinto shrine they built for the groundbreaking ceremony? Huh. Where was it?"

"In the basement, sir, about as deep down as it gets." Mitsuhiro opened up the blueprints on his tablet, pointing to the area with the stairs. "There was a stairwell here…"

"Ahh, the ritual hall. I didn't think anyone could go in there. How did you get in?"

"The door was open. Judging from the tweeted images, someone was going in and out of it."

"The door? Usually they put a steel plate over the entrance to the stairs. Some of these things were built over eighty years ago, after all. We have a specialized contractor maintaining the area and everything."

Takenaka leaned forward.

"A specialized contractor…?"

"Tamai Construction, one of our subcontractors. They're the ones who built this shrine as well. They mostly manage ritual halls like these, unlike ordinary construction companies. I'm sure they've helped us out with other sites, too, but I don't know exactly what sort of work they did here."

"You don't know what they did either, Chief Sugawara?"

"It was all under the auspices of the previous chairman…or maybe the one before that. They're still taking on work that existed back before I even joined the firm."

"Do you at least have an idea of what sort of work they do?"

"More or less. This is essentially a Shinto ritual, so it's more about the 'proper' thing rather than anything technological. We don't really have much say in it at all. We don't have the plans here, anyway. I think only our president and chairman even attend these ceremonies, and they're only held when a building's completed or demolished, so we're talking once every few decades. Honestly, I'd have forgotten all about it if I didn't see it right here."

"And the budget for this comes from our construction costs?"

"Yes, it's filed under 'groundbreaking ceremony,' 'ritual-related costs,' 'facility construction costs for ritual hall,' and so on."

Mitsuhiro took a notebook out of his bag and wrote the pertinent key words down.

Sugawara looked at his watch, apparently wanting to get to the point. "This isn't all you wanted to talk about, is it?"

"No," said Takenaka, pulling the tablet away from Sugawara's side. He put two images on the screen before giving it back, both taken by Mitsuhiro. One showed the man chained at the bottom of the pit, and the other showed the aftermath of the fire.

As Sugawara looked at them, his expression grew more and more serious. He wasn't angry or sullen about it; it was more like he was trying to stand firm when faced with a truly extraordinary situation. Seeing these photos didn't make him exclaim in surprise at all. Instead, he remained silent, waiting for an explanation from Takenaka and Mitsuhiro. After all, this was the man who was pushing forward this redevelopment project on a scale like nothing before it.

Mitsuhiro suddenly recalled a time when he had wished to become like that himself. For a moment, the image of his father, back when he was cheerful and healthy, superimposed itself over Sugawara. Now wasn't a good time to be thinking about the deceased, of course, so Mitsuhiro didn't mention it out loud.

Instead, he briefly recounted what he experienced at the scene once Takenaka prompted him. Sugawara only occasionally interjected a few words here and there, listening quietly without asking any extraneous questions. When Mitsuhiro finished his story, Sugawara finally spoke, slowly and thoughtfully.

"First, we need to contact Tamai Construction and confirm whether they opened up the entryway to the stairs. I'll bring this up with both them and the chairman."

"We'd like to ask some questions, too," Takenaka immediately replied. "Would that be a problem?"

"I don't think so, but I don't know if you'll receive answers either. When it comes to constructing these sites, it's ultimately the chairman who gets the final say."

"All right. Thank you."

"Next, about this man—is there any possibility, do you think, that he's doing this of his own free will?"

Mitsuhiro and Takenaka looked at each other, surprised at Sugawara's suggestion. Sugawara, on the other hand, seemed to find this quite reasonable.

"There are no signs of a struggle," he continued. "We're not the police, so we can't be sure, but this area is filled with unhoused people refusing to move out. We're working with the local government right now to try to improve the situation, but it takes time. In the past, we've seen activists handcuff themselves to fences or railway poles to protest their eviction. Sometimes residents will pay the homeless to protest on their behalf, either to drive up the price of land or drive it back down. I wouldn't make statements like this in public, but you know what I mean. There might be someone in the local support groups who knows this person, too."

Takenaka glanced at Mitsuhiro, who wrote "unhoused" and "support groups" in his notebook. Suddenly this investigation seemed much wider in scope than before. He began to wonder whether he could complete it in the short time he had.

"Do you think this person chained up in there was homeless?" Takenaka asked.

Sugawara inclined his head a bit. "I don't know, but at first glance, it does appear to be that way. We'll also need to investigate how he got in there, and where he disappeared to. I'm sure he'll show up on our security cameras, so I'll obtain a copy of the relevant footage. I also know that some subcontractors have been bringing their own people on-site lately, citing our staff shortages. We'll reexamine the identities of these more informal workers as well."

"All right."

Takenaka nodded deeply. His attitude showed how grateful he was that on-site people like Sugawara were taking the initiative to carry out such troublesome work.

"Finally, this fire," Sugawara matter-of-factly continued. "I'm sure this was arson. There's no way a fire could've just started by itself here."

Mitsuhiro and Takenaka were both taken aback by his firmness on this point.

"This is the job of the fire department and the police, so I'll consult with Legal and my higher-ups. We'll make the necessary arrangements to ensure this doesn't delay our schedule. We'll also boost security and check everyone who enters and exits the site, and we'll also go back over the informal workers I mentioned earlier as soon as possible. On-site workers are very sensitive to this sort of crime, so I think they'll gladly step up to tell us if they see anyone suspicious."

Mitsuhiro hurriedly took notes as the completely unfazed Sugawara smoothly described the preventative measures to be taken.

"Do you have any plans to make an announcement?" Sugawara asked.

"Hmm…" Takenaka paused. "At the moment, there's not much we can announce… I'll ask my managers, and Legal as well."

"I think the higher-ups might be reluctant to," said Sugawara as he got up from his chair. "I'll let you know when I learn any more details. If you find out anything, too, please let me know."

Takenaka and Mitsuhiro also stood, politely thanking him as he left the room. Then Takenaka sat down at the table, bringing up his tablet's thumbnail list.

"These images should suffice as the results of our emergency investigation. Thanks a lot for your help. From what the Chief just said, you'll have a lot more to deal with, though."

"Yeah. I'll try to learn about Tamai Construction and the homeless-support groups. If we can find out who the man in the basement was, I think that'll give us a clearer picture of the whole situation."

"Right. For now, gather the relevant accounting paperwork and make the appointments you need. How are you feeling?"

"Much better now."

Takenaka seemed unconvinced by Mitsuhiro's raspy voice and gave him a serious look.

"You really need to get checked out at the hospital today, all right? You're lucky to have a boss in *this* industry who'll tell you to take time off, so don't squander it. You'll have a lot more work before long at this rate anyway."

Mitsuhiro took him up on the offer. However, he only made the appointment with the local general hospital after having lunch with his team and sharing all the latest data with them. He wanted to leave earlier, but he missed his chance after everyone wanted to hear about Mitsuhiro's novel experience. Before hitting the hospital, he also had to find Tamai Construction–related items from past accounting data, gather info on facilities and nonprofit groups that help the unhoused in Tokyo, and make appointments with people at both places.

The internet and search sites made information gathering far easier than before, but he still left his office with a bundle of printouts in his bag, unsure what would be relevant in this unfamiliar territory that lay in his future. He wanted to say hello to Takenaka and his friends, but the whole team was out on errands, so he was the only one left at the office.

He looked over these printouts while enduring the long wait at the hospital, even though he thought he had made an appointment. He began by looking at the budget data, and what he saw stunned him.

Ten million yen had been allocated in the East Wing construction site for "Shinto ritual decor"—an outrageous amount of money for a small shrine and some woven ropes. The overall cost for the ritual hall was twenty million yen—could it really cost *that* much for someplace so bare-bones, with four naked light bulbs on each corner? Even though all this work was supposedly done decades ago? Plus, they were planning to pay the same amount of money for additional pile-driving work for the site. Why in the world were they doing that? He had no idea.

He wondered if the East Wing was a special case, but no—expenses for "groundbreaking ceremonies" and "ritual-related" items were always sky-high in Tokyo, making Mitsuhiro wonder if it was some kind of tax write-off for companies. Or maybe it was a way of laundering money that'd be embarrassing if its real purpose got out? He felt uneasy bringing these kinds of damning documents out of the office, like he was holding a wad of cash.

Opting to go over them in detail at home, he put them all away in his bag and kept it on his lap. He wanted to go home and talk to Miyoko ASAP, telling her about everything that happened and getting her opinion on this accounting data. She was on maternity leave at the moment, but she worked in Accounting at Shimaoka, so she'd be able to judge how sensible (or not) these expenses were.

A short time later, he finally underwent his exam. His throat was swollen, he was told, but otherwise there was nothing wrong. To be doubly sure, they took a CT brain scan, an X-ray of his lungs, and an EKG reading—basically a full physical, a bit earlier than usual.

The whole ordeal took twice as long as Mitsuhiro expected, and by the time he'd received his medication and headed home, it was already well into the evening, the continued rain making it seem particularly dark.

He returned to Shibuya Station, proceeding through the crowded premises. In three more years, there'd be convenient pathways everywhere, greatly smoothing the flow of people, but for now everyone went around in what felt like a state of constant panic.

Before heading down below, he called Miyoko's mobile phone. "I'll be home soon," he told his daughter, Sae.

"I'm gonna make you *okonomiyaki*!" she cheered, making him smile and hope he made it back without a moment's further delay.

As he hurried down the stairs, passed through the turnstile, and stepped onto the platform, he felt a sudden sense of discomfort. His neck was stiff, and his heart began to race.

The hole was there—right nearby, that accursed hole.

He felt beads of sweat forming on his brow, unable to take his eyes off the deep darkness within that round hole of the subway tunnel.

—*Stop it. You're starting to develop a phobia.*

Mitsuhiro rested against the platform wall, wiping his forehead with his bandaged right hand and taking a deep breath.

—*Did Dad get scared like this, too?*

A question he asked as a child came back to him.

"What do you do if you get scared when you're working up high or in the dark?"

"I count upward," his dad had told him, *"and take slow, deep breaths. In my case, once I'm a little calmer, I recite the names of my family members in my mind. Then I'm all better."*

"You don't pray to God or anything?"

"Well, for me, your name and Mom's do the trick. Like a protective talisman God gave me."

That was what his father would say back in his brighter, more cheerful days.

Miyoko. Sae. Miyoko. Sae. Mitsuhiro chanted the names of his wife and daughter in his mind. They hadn't decided on a name for the next child coming up, but of course it existed in his mind, too. It did, in fact, have a very welcome effect. He had to skip one train, but by the time the next one arrived, he was ready to lean away from the wall and walked up to catch it.

Once he was inside the car, he grabbed a pole by the door and braced himself against it, feeling like he was about to walk into darkness. But once the train went into motion, his heart didn't speed up at all. Instead, he could feel the train moving at breakneck speed, carrying him farther and farther away from that damned thing. The cut on his right hand ached as he gripped the pole. He relaxed his hand a bit, breathing a deep sigh of relief.

5

"Okay, here you go! Please enjoy and let me know if you need anything!"

Sae recited the latest phrase she had learned—they had gone to a *ryokan* in Hakone before she began elementary school—lifted a can of sparkling water with both hands, and poured it into Mitsuhiro's glass.

"Ah, thank you, Sae."

He raised the glass, pretending to drink from it. He was already on his fourth glass of sparkling water, and his stomach was full of the giant *okonomiyaki* that Miyoko helped Sae cook—although the little girl had sworn she did it all, since Mom's belly was so big. Some parts of it were burnt, some not cooked through enough, but there was no doubting it was delicious. He had to be very patient as Sae drew a smiley face with the sauce on his warm pancake, made "stars" with the mayonnaise, sprinkled wiggly bonito flakes on them, and called them "Hattifatteners," after the wispy Moomin characters…but after the three of them had finished two and a half full *okonomiyaki* pancakes, he was on the verge of becoming uncomfortably full.

"Here you go!"

Miyoko put a stop to Sae's merciless second helpings.

"Sae, Daddy's already full."

"Nuh-uh! Here you go!"

"His belly's going to be bigger than mine," Miyoko said. Sae blinked a couple of times, then put down the can of water, twisting herself on her chair to try to look at Mitsuhiro's stomach. He had already showered and put on a T-shirt and sweatpants, and now he was trying to slouch as much as possible.

"See? Look how full I am!"

He patted his stomach through his shirt. It made Sae laugh and get off her chair.

"Sae, sit down!"

Ignoring Miyoko's order, Sae jumped up on Mitsuhiro's lap, legs thrown ahead of her, patting his stomach as well—or, really, poking at it with her little hands.

"That hurts, Sae—"

Mitsuhiro couldn't take any more and let out a loud belch. Sae stopped at once and looked up at him, as if to make sure she correctly parsed what just happened.

"Daddy, no!" Miyoko laughed.

Mitsuhiro covered his mouth with his hand and looked up, his eyes wide and apologetic.

Sae started laughing again, imitating her mother. "Daddy, no!"

Mitsuhiro followed suit, laughing as he picked up Sae and put her back on her chair. "Here, sit back down."

Ding-dong.

Since he was up already, Mitsuhiro went over to the intercom on the wall. The monitor was on, indicating that someone at the building's front door had tapped his apartment number on the keypad to call him. But nobody was on the video feed. Mitsuhiro picked up the receiver, just in case.

"Hello?"

No response. He waited, choosing not to press the unlock button for the lobby entrance, but no one appeared on the screen. A little ding-dong ditch? Well, even if the caretaker's office was unmanned after eight PM, it seemed unlikely that some kid would try that with a surveillance-camera-equipped condo building.

Mitsuhiro shrugged and put the receiver back. The monitor automatically turned off.

"Someone visiting?" Sae asked.

"No, I think it was a wrong number. Or maybe the machine's acting up."

"It rang with nobody there? Some kid, do you think?"

Miyoko's face was clouded a bit. When something goes wrong with a piece of security equipment like an intercom, it can make any city dweller feel a tad uneasy.

"Maybe I just couldn't see him. The entrance door didn't open up, so nobody went inside."

"Someone invisible?" Sae blithely asked. Her choice of phrasing unnerved Miyoko even more. Something about the word *invisible* seemed eerie to Mitsuhiro as well, regardless of whether anything would personally happen to him or not.

"No, I don't think so," Mitsuhiro said, brushing her off. "I just don't think there was anyone there." He took Miyoko's hand, smiling at her, and Miyoko smiled back.

Ding-dong.

Miyoko's hand tightened around his. Sae quickly stood up on the chair, turning to face the monitor on the intercom.

"Nobody there!" she shouted, enjoying every moment of this. It was starting to unnerve Mitsuhiro.

"Sit down, Sae," Miyoko said, her hips rising off her own chair. Her voice was full of anxiety-driven irritation.

"Stay there, Mom," added Mitsuhiro, looking at the monitor again. Once again, no one seemed to be at the entrance. The automatic door was visible in the left side of the screen, but it wasn't moving. He wondered if someone might be hiding in some corner of the camera view, but no one was.

He picked up the receiver and said "Hello?" His voice was louder than before.

"There's really no one there?" Miyoko asked, finally standing up.

"No one there!" Sae said in Mitsuhiro's place, standing up in her chair and only adding to Miyoko's irritation.

"I *said* sit down!"

Sae's eyes widened in surprise. Mitsuhiro put the receiver back on the phone and patted his daughter on the head, trying to assuage his wife.

"It's fine. I think it's just some mechanical issue."

Some unknown tension was making it feel like his heart was being bound up tight inside his body. But he didn't want to act selfish here, telling them to be quiet or raising his voice. The thought of his father after he had changed so much rose up from somewhere in his mind.

Ding-dong.

Before Mitsuhiro's eyes, the monitor activated again, revealing the fully deserted entrance. There was something coarse and almost antiseptic about the view, the intertwining shadows like otherworldly stains.

Miyoko came to Mitsuhiro's side, squeezing his hand. Her anxiety must have finally spread to Sae, because she was now out of her chair and clinging to the legs of both her parents at the same time.

Mitsuhiro tried to pick up the receiver, but Miyoko tugged on his hand and kept him from it. That annoyed him a bit, but he knew that was just his anxiety flaring up. Having them both cling to him like this caused an instinctive sort of discomfort; not being able to move freely made it harder for him to protect them. But unlike how his father usually reacted, he didn't push them to the side. Instead, he reached out with his free hand and lightly patted Miyoko's arm, then Sae's back, trying to calm them both down.

They were silent as could be. It no longer felt like a friendly dinner. Mitsuhiro thought about letting the receiver hang off the wall but then recalled that doing so would shut off the intercom entirely. Instead, he waited for the monitor to turn itself off.

"I'll go check out downstairs."

"What?" said Miyoko, in what could be construed as either a question or an implicit no. *Why would you bother doing that?* was likely what she wanted to say.

"Maybe someone down there who doesn't know how to use the keypad is pressing the wrong number."

"But there was no one on the screen."

"Well, maybe they were just off-screen. If it's someone suspicious, I'll call the police, okay? That's what they're for."

"Yes, but—"

"You gonna call the police?" Sae interrupted her hesitant mother, convinced it was the right idea.

"Not yet. For now, I—"

Ding-dong.

The monitor flicked on again, revealing an empty space. The intervals were clearly getting shorter, and the repetitive ringing was now almost physically painful. He had never paid much attention to the noise before, but now he was getting angry at how invasive and disruptive it was to his family's peace. If there was no way to stop it like this, he wanted to turn the whole thing off or tear it off the wall. That, of course, would only make life more difficult for him, so he had to find another solution.

"I'll be right back. I'll be fine, okay?"

Mitsuhiro held Miyoko's hand, squeezing it a little, as he urged her to let go. Understanding that she had no choice, Miyoko stopped clinging to his hand and pulled Sae toward her.

"Take your phone with you."

"Of course. I'll call you from downstairs."

"Can you stay on the line on the way down?"

"It'll get cut off when I'm in the elevator. I'll call you down there."

Mitsuhiro tried to assuage her, even though keeping the line busy would make it harder to call the authorities. He picked up his key from the living room shelf, put it in his pants pocket, and unplugged his partially charged phone. Miyoko grabbed her phone from the same shelf, and she and Sae followed him to the front door.

He opted for the same shoes he wore when he left home this morning. Something firm and nonslip. If someone bad *was* down there, it'd be better to wear something that gave him more agility.

"I'll be right back, all right? Lock the door, just in case."

Mitsuhiro made an effort to sound cheerful as he walked out the front door. Miyoko and Sae kept looking at him through the open doorway. He smiled, waved, and gestured at them to close the door before turning down the hallway toward the elevator lobby. They both anxiously waved back—and then the door closed. He heard the faint sound of the lock clicking shut.

He called the elevator and got in. His face was expressionless, his teeth clenched and eyes narrowed. He stared, unblinking, as the doors opened again.

Confirming that no one was getting in, he strode out of the elevator. The moment Miyoko and Sae were gone, he realized, he was beginning to have quite aggressive thoughts—anger that his wife and daughter were being frightened like this. At this rate, he was liable to start yelling at whoever he saw on the other side of the entrance door.

But no one was there.

He looked at the regular glass door on the other side of the automatic-locking door, then farther on to the street outside. It was still raining lightly, but he couldn't see anyone going in or coming out.

As he stood there, keeping his distance from the automatic door so it wouldn't open, his phone rang.

"Hello?"

"Hey, is anyone there?"

"No. Nobody."

"Even though the doorbell keeps ringing?"

"Huh? You're still getting that?"

"Yeah. But nobody's ringing it? Why is it ringing?"

Miyoko sounded angry. Mitsuhiro realized her emotions were spreading to him, and he gritted his teeth to keep his anger from escaping him, breathing slowly through his nose.

"I'm sure the wiring's messed up or something. I'll go look, so wait there."

He walked toward the automatic door he had been careful not to open, trying to reassure her. Taking the phone away from his ear, he braced himself in case someone rushed in the moment the door opened. But no one did.

Mitsuhiro moved sideways toward the control panel on the entrance side, keeping the normal glass door leading outside in his sight, and looked at the display.

401

For whatever reason, the screen on the control panel was showing the number of his apartment. Did someone type that in, and now some bug was making it stay on there? Or was the machine broken? As he tried to figure it out, the doorbell rang. It wasn't very loud, since this was just the control panel at the entrance, but it sounded like the machine was making noise on its own. Just as he thought, it was some kind of malfunction.

"Hey, are you okay?"

Miyoko's voice came through the control panel's speaker. She was answering the intercom.

Mitsuhiro smiled at the camera, cheerfully waving his hand. "It's totally fine. There's nobody here. It's just the machine acting up. I'll turn it off now."

He said it loud enough for Sae as well, since she was probably listening in. Still, Mitsuhiro kept an eye on that glass door while he jabbed the delete button on the control panel. The *1* disappeared. A second press and the *0* was gone, and finally the *4* was deleted as well.

"Did the sound stop?" he said into his phone.

"It's not ringing now, no..."

"I'll keep an eye on this for a bit."

"Are you sure? Be careful."

"I'm fine."

Mitsuhiro kept talking to Miyoko and Sae as he watched the control panel. He could sense that Miyoko was calming down. The control panel remained quiet, no longer having a mind of its own.

"I'm going back up. I'll open the door from here, okay?"

He'd need to ring the intercom to have Miyoko open it for him, but he didn't want to make her nervous again. So, phone still to his ear, he took the key fob out of his pocket and pressed the button on it to open the automatic door. Everything had a remote control on it these days. Starting an engine or opening a door with a button was a novelty at first, but now it was becoming completely ordinary.

Just to be safe, he kept a close eye on the entrance, but no one showed up, and no other building residents were around either. The rain must have been keeping pedestrians away.

Going into the entrance, Mitsuhiro watched the automatic door close behind him. *I think that did it.*

Finally, he could feel a natural smile rising his face again.

"I think I fixed it," he told Miyoko.

"Oh, great."

She sounded relieved as well. He could hear Sae cheering about it, too.

"I'll be right back up, okay?"

Feeling like the job was done, Mitsuhiro ended the call and got on the elevator. Then he suddenly felt something odd on his right index finger. He raised his hand, looking at it.

There was some kind of faint substance stuck to it. White dust, or maybe a powder of some sort. As he rubbed it off his finger, he thought he caught a whiff of something. The same odor he had smelled deep underground, in that parched, desiccated air.

Oh, no way.

The elevator doors clanged open, startling him. He remembered that dark hole, then froze in fear, realizing he was right in the middle of an elevator shaft. The doors began to close. He hurriedly pushed them open with his hands and rushed out into the hallway. He felt like he was starting to develop a fear of the dark. It was just one panic attack, but it seemed to have left a deep impression on him.

It's okay. Breathe and count. Repeat the names of family members in your head. Miyoko. Sae. Miyoko. Sae. And the baby that's about to be born. It's okay now.

Mitsuhiro let out a deep sigh and headed toward his apartment. The door to his place wasn't remote-controlled, of course. He inserted the key, unlocked it, grabbed the door handle, pushed it down, and pulled it open.

He could feel the air move. The air that had been clinging to his body flowed smoothly through the open door. *It must be the difference in air pressure*, he thought as he went in and locked the door behind him. It was raining out, and barometric difference made the outside air flow into the room.

But the air he felt now didn't seem particularly dry. Something different from the outside air, amid the drizzle, seemed to have followed him from the elevator. Or maybe it had been lingering around the entrance all along. Calling him. Trying to get into this room. He hadn't noticed it, and now he had inadvertently brought it with him, maybe, without even realizing it was following him.

Where on earth could it have come from?

That hole. Crawling through the subway tunnel.

Just as his heart began to accelerate again, Sae ran down the hallway and embraced him.

"You're back!"

Miyoko appeared behind her. "You can't run around like that so late. It's noisy," she scolded, but Sae wasn't paying attention.

It all helped Mitsuhiro regain his senses, pushing the thought just now into the back of his mind. He took off his shoes and picked up his daughter. She clung to his neck.

"Thanks," he told them, smiling as he walked up to Miyoko. His heart wasn't settling down quite yet, but it didn't seem to be getting worse, either.

He was optimistic that, by the time he returned to the dining room and sat down, he'd be able to shake off this sudden panic—and from there, he'd find a way to permanently be rid of it.

But while he was still in the hallway, Sae pointed behind Mitsuhiro and yelled out.

"Ahhh! Daddy, your feet are dirty!"

Miyoko turned around, and Mitsuhiro did the same. Sae twisted around so she could still see while in her father's arms.

Right inside the entrance, there was a single footprint. A large right footprint, as if someone had stepped into a tray of white powder and then come inside.

Miyoko silently looked down at Mitsuhiro's feet. She stared at his short summer socks, frowning as though she didn't like him wearing socks—even though *she* was the one who kept complaining about him being barefoot around the house. He sweated too much, she said, and the smell would stick to the slippers and the floor without socks.

No, the problem wasn't the socks. Noticing the anxiety returning to Miyoko's face, Mitsuhiro hurriedly apologized.

"Ah, I'm sorry. Some dust from the construction site must've stuck to them."

He put Sae down, took off his socks, then went to the front door, knelt down, and used one sock as a rag to wipe up the footprint.

"Wait. Don't put that in the laundry basket."

Miyoko went to the kitchen and brought back a small plastic bag from her last trip to the convenience store. She opened it up, and Mitsuhiro dropped the socks inside.

"Did you take off your shoes at work?"

"Of course not. I think it just worked its way inside."

"It's not asbestos or something, is it?"

"None of that, no. It's fine. Probably just dust from cutting concrete."

But as Miyoko carefully tied the bag shut, she suddenly turned toward the front door again.

"That *was* your footprint, wasn't it?"

Miyoko's face was stiff, as if she was frightened by her own question. Mitsuhiro understood what she meant. A strange thought was now hovering in the air between them. They both knew how ridiculous that thought was. They tried to laugh about it, but they couldn't. Instead, they just stood there awkwardly.

An invisible visitor.

No, that was ridiculous. Clearly a crazy idea. They had to move on from this, or else he'd pass on his strange new phobia to the rest of his family.

"Well, if you're worried, let's just throw them out. I'll wash my shoes tomorrow. Lemme get my feet clean for now."

Mitsuhiro took the bag from Miyoko's hands, went to the kitchen, and threw it into the trash. Then he went into the bathroom and washed his hands and feet. He almost stopped himself, reasoning that he had taken a shower right after getting home, but he didn't want to keep his mind focused on why that familiar dust was on his hands and feet.

It was inside of him now.

He hoped the scent of soap would somehow eliminate that smell.

An invisible visitor.

Mitsuhiro forced himself not to say those words aloud, pushing them deep into his mind. He wiped his hands and feet with a bath towel, forced himself to smile, and returned to the dining room, where his family was waiting.

Chapter 2 Tamai

1

"So," Miyoko said, "this includes not just the construction costs but also the maintenance costs afterward, right?"

She kept the red pen in her hand as she followed the printed numbers with her eyes, drawing a line on the paper. Mitsuhiro leaned over to take a peek, so Miyoko turned the sheet toward him. There was a red underline highlighting the part indicating that the contract was valid until June 30, 2045.

"You're right. I didn't notice."

"Me neither. The format for these ritual halls is a lot different from a normal purchase order, so I didn't know what it meant at first."

"What's the difference?"

"It's just, like, really old-fashioned. All this stuff is written in old-timey characters."

Miyoko pointed with the tip of her pen. Mitsuhiro looked at where she indicated. A lot of the expressions were written in old-style Chinese characters, which had fallen out of common usage some decades ago. They were easy to misread.

"Wow. So if this ends in 2045, we're paying for it for thirty years? How common is that?"

"Well, thirty years is the general rule for land-lease contracts. But this isn't like buying the rights to use the underground space beneath some land, like for a subway tunnel."

"So does that mean the land belongs to Tamai Construction?"

"There'd be something about a land-use fee in here if did. This contract's only talking about maintenance and management—you know, like arranging for security or planting trees on the sidewalk. I don't really know what a 'ritual hall' looks like at all, but..."

"Well, it was just a barren basement. Dirt floor, concrete walls, and a little shrine sitting by itself."

Miyoko furrowed her brows. The scene in her head must've been a creepy one.

"Those really exist?"

"I was pretty surprised, too."

After all, the room also had a large square hole with a person chained up inside. He didn't mention that part, though. No need to make Miyoko feel *that* kind of uneasy.

Thanks to Sae going to bed early, he and Miyoko had some quiet time to talk now. He didn't intend to bring up work, but when he mentioned there were some papers he wanted her to look at, she'd volunteered to check them out immediately. "After all these household chores," she'd joked, "I'm starving for work-work."

And Mitsuhiro knew she meant it. She had been constantly rebelling against her parents, who took it as a given that she'd leave her job once she began having children. They had griped at Mitsuhiro more than once over how long he planned to keep their daughter working and whether his job didn't pay enough to keep them afloat.

Having Miyoko be a full-time housewife *would* help in some ways, but it'd certainly affect their financial leeway—and most of all, he couldn't make her quit when she was still eager to build her career. It varied by the department or group, but Shimaoka, where she and Mitsuhiro worked, wasn't the type to discriminate against women aiming for career advancement. The Japanese government was kind enough to recently start promoting female participation in the workforce, another consequence of the nation's current labor shortage. His in-laws were easily swayed by authority that way, so when Mitsuhiro told them that even politicians were saying the times were a-changing… Well, they didn't necessarily agree, but they stopped arguing about it at the dinner table, at least.

So Mitsuhiro showed her the documents, figuring it'd help take her mind off things, but he didn't mention the guy at the bottom of the hole. No need to scare her and make her feel ill or whatever. She was more serene now, but when her morning sickness started to really kick in, it seemed like the entire world was beating her up. Even the slightest stimulus, the tiniest unpleasant topic, would lead to intense physical discomfort or negative emotions. They had stopped watching TV together long ago, and that was because of how much it upset Miyoko at one point. For a time, she'd feel nauseous whenever food appeared on the screen, and news about tragic crimes or accidents would overwhelm her with sorrow. Miyoko had privately confided to her husband that even Sae's favorite cartoon show, *Anpanman*, featuring a cast of anthropomorphized versions of popular foods, was too much for her.

He could tell she wouldn't want to hear about dark basements and shrines right now, so he changed the subject.

"So, yeah, apparently this was built for the groundbreaking ceremony. We paid ten million yen for it."

"Right, a lump sum that covers thirty years. Counting the construction, that'd be three or four hundred thousand or so a year? That's not a huge amount compared with all the construction taking place around it, but I'd need to see if there were any additional costs incurred in this contract—"

Miyoko let out a wide yawn. Sleepiness was another symptom of her pregnancy, and he had seen her fall asleep out of nowhere several times before, complaining that she just couldn't keep her eyes open. Still, at this time of night, her drowsiness was perfectly reasonable.

"Sorry to keep you up so late. Maybe you should go to bed."

"Yeah, I will. What about you?"

"I want to finish this first."

Miyoko nodded and stared at the papers, but her eyes were a little distant. "You think my work will still be there when I go back to the office?"

"Of course it will. You know how much the department relied on you."

"I sure hope so."

Miyoko sighed, but she didn't seem deeply worried about it. The concern that she'd be forced to quit after giving birth had been a lot more present back when she had Sae. In the few years since then, it had become far less likely for women in Japan to leave the workforce the moment they started a family.

Miyoko glanced at the sparkling water in his glass. "You really want a drink, don't you?" she said. "Just a little is fine, you know."

To be honest, she was exactly right. Maybe it was that unnerving doorbell thing during dinner. But Mitsuhiro shook his head.

"I never really liked drinking at home. I had to see my dad abuse it all the time."

"Well, maybe if you drank with him, he would've been happy to join you."

"Maybe."

Mitsuhiro chuckled, but in his mind, he could see his father silently pouring the contents of a convenience-store single-serving cup of sake into his mouth. His gaze would always be fixed on nothing in particular, like he was staring intently at some dark specter within himself. Every time Mitsuhiro saw his father like that, he wondered not so much why he had become that way but instead when that dark thing had begun to take root inside of him.

"I just don't wanna wreck my liver like Dad did. I want to see old age."

The topic was veering toward chronic illness and death, perhaps inevitably. But fortunately, it didn't seem to upset Miyoko.

"Well, sure. That's what I want, too. Isn't that right?"

Miyoko smiled and rubbed her large belly. She wasn't speaking to Mitsuhiro but to the unborn child within her. Mitsuhiro smiled back and reached out to give her stomach a pat of his own.

"I'm going to bed," Miyoko said, the words almost swallowed by a yawn.

"Sure. Good night."

After seeing Miyoko off to the bedroom, Mitsuhiro sipped his water and picked up the papers he'd brought home. It was true—the more he flipped through them, the older they seemed to get. He kept diving into the stack, wondering how far back they went, and toward the end, he came across copies of a few memos. The first one was very brief, stating that on the occasion of the "business opening" in "the fortieth year of the Meiji era," "Tamai-sha" would perform the "water-god ceremony" for "ten thousand yen," as per the "agreement." The payment was to be made by a company called "Tamagawa-sha," which sounded a lot like "Tamai-sha" but was apparently different. It was confusing.

The fortieth year of the Meiji era? What year was that?

He took his smartphone out to look it up. It turned out to be the year 1907, and further investigation showed that 10,000 yen back then was equivalent to approximately 10,180,000 yen today.

What was opened, exactly? It was none other than Shibuya Station itself—to be exact, the Tamagawa Electric Railway.

Delving further in, Mitsuhiro found several other copies of similar memoranda, all exchanged with either "Tamai-sha" or "Tamai Construction Company." One was dated approximately thirty years later, in 1938. The Tokyo–Yokohama Electric Railway had acquired Tamagawa Electric Railway and was constructing the Tamaden Building, slated to open with the brand-new Tokyo Express Railway stop that went through Shibuya Station. At that time, in addition to an "earth-appeasement ceremony," another "water-god ceremony" was held—and the costs, reflecting inflation, amounted to fifty thousand yen. That would also be around ten million yen in modern terms.

Sixteen years later, in 1954, the Tamaden Building was renovated and converted into an event hall. Tamai-sha, now officially known as Tamai Construction Company, prepared an invoice for something called the "removal ceremony." The payment was made by Shimaoka's headquarters at the time, and the cost was listed as "one million yen," reflecting rampant postwar inflation. In modern terms, that would be approximately twelve million yen. (This hall later became the west wing of a larger department store. It was slated for demolition at the moment, concurrent with the construction of the East Wing.)

Ten years later, in 1964, a fee for an "additional removal ceremony" was paid to Tamai Construction Company. This was in connection with the construction of the Tokyu Toyoko Line's ground-level Shibuya Station building, known for its roof that resembled rows of barrels, which was carried out in preparation for the Tokyo Olympics that year. The expenses amounted to "2,500,000 yen," which again was around ten million yen today. That was directly proportional to inflation at the time, which suggested that the payment was based on some unknown adjustable factor, such as land prices.

Thirteen years after that, in 1977, another "removal-ceremony fee" of "four million yen" was paid. That was the year the New Tamagawa Line, later renamed the Tama Monorail, opened in Shibuya Station. From that year onward, it became possible to travel all the way to the core of Tokyo without having to leave Shibuya Station for a transfer. This, however, introduced inconvenient underground transfers, which Mitsuhiro knew about reading the history of Shimaoka development in the region. The complex layout of the ticket gates, along with the stairs you had to go up and down, marked the beginning of Shibuya Station turning into a kind of urban maze for visitors.

Nineteen years later, in 1996, ten million yen was paid to Tamai Construction for an "earth-appeasement ceremony" and "water-god ceremony." This was the year of the JR Saikyo Line's expansion, which required extra construction on Shibuya Station's south side. The "ceremonies" were likely part of this new construction, which introduced a new south exit to the station.

That was the last of the memoranda. Mitsuhiro thought he could find more if he combed the company archives, but for now, he had enough to understand how Tamai was connected to Shimaoka...or Shibuya at large, to be more exact.

Basically, for over a century now, Tamai Construction had been responsible for the religious ceremonies associated with the development of Shibuya Station. Regardless of the nature of the rituals, however, the term *water god* threw Mitsuhiro for a loop. After all, he had just been nearly overwhelmed by the parched, dry air underground. If there was any water deity around there, it must have left long ago. Or perhaps it was still residing in that little altar underground, and that was why the air around it was so pure.

—No, no, that's ridiculous.

Mitsuhiro pushed the thought out of his mind, gathered the documents, and bundled them together. He put them in his bag, forgot about work, and sat alone, sipping some water to relax.

Why did he feel so strangely at ease when he was alone like this, after his family had gone to bed? He felt peaceful, accomplished, as if he had finished everything he had set out to do. Indeed, he thought, if he was feeling this way, maybe having a drink wouldn't be so bad.

Then he heard the sound of running water behind him, from the kitchen faucet. He didn't need to turn around to imagine Miyoko filling a glass with water, but he'd already sensed something was off.

Due to the effects of her pregnancy, Miyoko couldn't drink tap water at the moment. There were several boxes of mineral water for her in the small storage room next to the front door. She used it for drinking, cooking, even rinsing out after brushing her teeth. Thanks to that, Mitsuhiro had also started to lose his tap-water habit, but Sae hadn't. She didn't quite have the wrist strength to open those large mineral water bottles on her own, so she found it easier to stand on her little step stool and pour tap water into a cup.

Mitsuhiro stood up and peered into the kitchen. Then he froze. Sure enough, Sae was standing on the step stool, greedily drinking water. But instead of pouring it into a cup, she had stuck her small head into the sink and was drinking right from the faucet.

This was not normal thirst. Her behavior was almost animal-like, as if she'd go crazy unless she drank as much as possible right now, and it made him rear back.

"What's wrong, Sae? Are you thirsty?"

He called out to her, but Sae didn't even turn around as she relentlessly gulped down the water. He could see that her hair was not only touching the sink, but some of the ends were even going into the drain.

"Sae, stop that," he sternly said. "I'll get you some water in a cup."

This was a shock. Not her actions themselves, but the fact that he felt something eerie in the actions of his own precious daughter.

But Sae didn't respond. Mitsuhiro reached out and jerked the faucet shut, then grabbed her small shoulders and tried to pull her out of the sink.

At that moment, it struck again.

Ding-dong.

The sound of the intercom doorbell sent more shocks down his spine, like he was being electrocuted. *That thing must really be broken*, he told himself, slowly backing away and looking at the monitor on the wall. It showed an empty front entrance.

Miyoko came out of the bedroom, her voice trembling with fear.

"Again?"

"Yeah," Mitsuhiro hoarsely replied. He wanted to calm Miyoko down, but before he could, his body froze in anxiety. He couldn't take his eyes off the empty front entrance. Was anything moving? Could he see a shadow somewhere on the screen?

"Sae?" Miyoko said, startled by something else. The next thing they knew, the faucet was running again. Sae was still loudly, greedily drinking down the water.

"What's wrong?" Miyoko pleaded, her voice almost tearful. She grabbed Sae's shoulder in a panic, pulling her away from the sink. And as Mitsuhiro's gaze shifted between the monitor and the two of them, the monitor turned off.

"Sae. Hey, Sae. Are you okay? Can you hear my voice?"

Miyoko kept talking, but Sae only turned her dazed face toward the flowing water.

Mitsuhiro hurried to the sink and slammed his palm against the faucet to turn it off. The water's sound was unbearably grating, unlike anything he had ever experienced before. The same went for Miyoko's continued pleas and Sae's silence.

Mitsuhiro took a deep breath and spoke as calmly as he could.

"You're drinking too much water, Sae."

Suddenly, he remembered this one time when Sae had guzzled down the contents of an entire water bottle during a picnic. As he recalled, she wasn't thirsty so much as seeking her parents' attention. Mitsuhiro and Miyoko had told her to knock it off, but still, it was just an amusing family moment.

This was completely different. Looking directly at Sae's drenched, vacant face, Mitsuhiro felt a pang of something akin to grief. Drops of water were falling from her hair, wetting the collar and shoulders of her pajamas.

"Really, what's wrong, Sae? Come on, Sae..."

Miyoko took a washcloth hanging on the shelf and wiped Sae's forehead and hair. All of her actions were full of an urgent desire to get her daughter back to normal.

Sae reached for the faucet. Did she *still* want more? Mitsuhiro, eyes wide open, grabbed her hand to stop her.

"No. Don't drink so much."

"I'm hot," Sae said. Sweat was beading on her forehead.

Miyoko put her hand on it. "I think she has a fever."

Mitsuhiro could feel the heat on Sae's hand, too...but there was something extremely strange about it. The wet patches on Sae's pajamas were disappearing. The droplets of water had stopped falling from her hair. Miyoko seemed to notice as well, gently scooping it up with her hands. The hair cascaded smoothly down from her hands. It was dry. Sae's pajamas were completely dry as well.

"I'm hot," she said again.

"You have a fever. I'll put a cooling patch on you."

Miyoko quickly took her hands off Sae's hair and looked toward the medicine cabinet.

"It's the visitor's fault," Sae muttered.

"Huh?" Mitsuhiro asked, still holding her hand.

"I'm hot because of the invisible visitor."

Miyoko startled and turned to look at Sae.

Ding-dong.

* * *

Mitsuhiro inhaled sharply as Miyoko clung to him.

"Why's it ringing again?" she said. "Didn't you fix it? It's been ringing nonstop!"

Mitsuhiro wanted to say the same thing, but he silently let go of Sae's hand and tapped Miyoko's shoulder, urging her to step back. He nodded slightly, trying to reassure them, and stepped back to where he could see the intercom monitor.

The building entrance was empty, but now the image was unusually cloudy. Maybe the camera was breaking down as well now. It looked like something white was sticking to the lens. White powdery stuff…

"I'm hot!" Sae screamed.

Mitsuhiro looked toward her…just as an intense light struck his eyes. Sae's pajamas, around the shoulders and abdomen, were bursting into flames with a popping sound.

Miyoko let out a shrill scream and tried to beat the fire away, but it wouldn't go out. In a flash, it spread across Sae's writhing body, then to her hair.

"Sae!"

Mitsuhiro let out a horrified scream, overcome by unimaginable terror as his daughter was consumed by flames. He grabbed Sae's burning body, thrust her back into the sink he had been trying to pull her away from a moment ago, and turned the faucet on full blast. Miyoko also grabbed a plastic bottle from the refrigerator, unscrewed the cap with trembling hands, and poured it over Sae, who was screaming in agony.

Desperately trying to extinguish the flames, Mitsuhiro was overcome by regret. Maybe the fire in the basement wasn't arson after all. Maybe it was caused by that substance filling the air down there. Maybe that should have occurred to him sooner.

The two of them kept pouring water on her, desperately trying to remove her burning pajamas. But the flames only grew more intense, devouring her body with dreadful hunger.

The horrific smell of burning hair and skin choked Mitsuhiro and Miyoko, stinging their eyes until tears were streaming down their faces. All three were screaming at the top of their lungs. The two parents didn't care about the scorching pain on their own skin as they tried to put out the flames, but it was no use.

Before their eyes, their daughter was no longer herself. Her flesh and internal organs had swelled in the fire and heat; her skin cracked with a crunching sound, and blood began to spurt out, leaving only the sickening smell of charred bodily fluids.

2

When Mitsuhiro opened his eyes, there was no more nightmarish glow from the fire burning his daughter, only the dark ceiling of his bedroom. His hands should have been melting away with that unbearable heat, but they weren't.

Instead, his entire body trembled violently, his teeth chattering loudly and making a worrisome clamor. He was drenched in terrified sweat. When he tried to wipe his forehead, his palm was already soaking wet.

—That was the most terrifying dream I've ever had.

Overcome by a sense of exhaustion, he closed his eyes, then opened them again, too afraid to fall asleep.

Slowly he got up, being careful not to wake Miyoko next to him, and left the bedroom. He turned on the light and stared at the sink. Sae's step stool was propped against the wall. There were, of course, no signs that any fire had taken place. The memory of Sae shoving her head into the sink crossed his mind, but by now, his fear had subsided considerably.

He took a cup from the shelf, turned on the faucet, filled it with water, and drank. He was a lot thirstier than he had realized, and he finished it in no time.

What an unbelievable dream that was. But when did reality end, and when did the dream begin? He put the cup down, turned on the dining room light, opened the bag he had left on the chair, and flipped through the papers.

He saw the underlines that Miyoko had put on them. The copies of the old memos he had seen toward the end. He had put them all in his bag, washed his face and brushed his teeth in the bathroom, then went to the bedroom. The dream had been inserted somewhere in the middle of that memory; he was sure it wasn't real. Sae hadn't gotten up and started guzzling water. Nor did the doorbell ring again.

No, it was all just a dream.

He closed his briefcase, returned to his chair, and breathed a sigh of relief. Dream or not, he never wanted to see anything like that again. If such a thing happened to him in reality, he'd never be able to recover. He would've shattered into pieces. *Now* he felt like having a drink—but he didn't. It was past four o'clock, and there was no alcohol in their home anyway.

Mitsuhiro returned to the kitchen and had another cup of water. With the cup in his hand, he went to Sae's room and quietly opened the door to see how she was doing. Sae was sleeping with her arms and legs spread wide, blanket kicked off. He touched her small forehead just to be sure, but she didn't feel feverish.

He placed the cup on the desk next to the bed and left the room. He started to return to his bedroom, then thought better of it and filled another cup with water before taking it in with him. After placing it on the small bedside shelf, he lay down.

Miyoko let out a faint sigh and reached out with one hand toward his shoulder. Mitsuhiro gently held it, closing his eyes. He felt tremendously fatigued.

Sleep came quickly. He didn't dream again that night.

The alarm rang at seven, and by the time he woke up, his memories of the dream were already growing vague. Still half-asleep, he stared at the cup, wondering if it was him who filled it up or someone else.

He took it over to the bathroom sink, rinsing his mouth with the lukewarm water he'd poured into it overnight. Ah, right, he'd gotten the water in case he got thirsty later. Not that it mattered now. He quickly shaved, then gave the bathroom over to the now-awake Miyoko and went to the kitchen to put the cup away.

Sae appeared with the same cup in her hand. “Hey, Daddy, there was water here when I woke up.”

“Oh… I put that there. I thought you might get thirsty.”

“It’s not good. I want the cold water Mommy drinks.”

“Okay, give me a sec.”

Mitsuhiro took the cup, poured the contents into the sink, took a plastic bottle out of the refrigerator, and poured some chilled mineral water into it. Sae happily took the cup with an appreciative “Yay, cold!” and went to the dining room, giving it little sips.

By the time he was out of the bedroom and ready for work, Miyoko had breakfast going. He draped his tie around his shoulders and helped out, grateful for a morning where they could all eat together as a family. He had the shorter commute to thank for that. He was so glad they bought this condo. He had every intention of staying here for good—at least twenty or thirty years.

After breakfast, Sae put on her yellow school hat and backpack, and Miyoko said goodbye to both of them. As soon as they reached the lobby, Sae asked Mitsuhiro a sudden question.

“Did somebody come visit yesterday?”

She seemed confused, as though she wasn’t sure whether she dreamed it or not.

“It was just the intercom messing up,” her father replied, not thinking much of it. “It’s fixed now, so don’t worry.”

“Oh, okay. I thought I had a dream or something.”

“It was scary, wasn’t it? The doorbell ringing so many times?”

“Uh-uh. It was fine.”

Sae smiled. The image of her hair catching fire faintly flashed through Mitsuhiro’s mind, but he instinctively pushed it away and left the building with her.

“Careful on your way to school, Sae.”

"'Kay. Bye, Daddy!"

They smiled at each other and waved goodbye, and as Mitsuhiro was about to head for the station, Sae called after him.

"Bye, invisible guest!"

Mitsuhiro stopped crossing the street and turned around. But Sae had turned away from him, walking toward a group of children wearing hats like hers. He stood there for a moment, then shook his head and smiled, looking to both sides. An invisible guest? The morning sun was shining down on the busy street, and the memory of the words didn't make him uneasy at all.

What a strange thing to stick in her mind. Children sometimes liked to talk about things they couldn't see, after all. He just hoped she didn't scare Miyoko with that stuff.

Not giving it any further thought, Mitsuhiro went down the station stairs on his way to the ticket gate, but then he changed his mind and went to a convenience store to buy a bottle of water first. He had no deep reason for it, just that having one in his briefcase would give him peace of mind. He had a feeling that keeping a bottle of water by his bedside at night would become a habit shortly, too, but again, he didn't dwell on the thought much.

He stepped off the train at Shibuya Station and made his way through the stuffy air inside, following the ever-evolving flow of people moving this way and that. Once outside, he was greeted by a fairly steep slope. The highway here went across the neighborhoods of Akasaka, Aoyama, and Shibuya; they had the characters for *hill*, *mountain*, and *valley* in them, respectively, and that was no coincidence. East of Shibuya Station was Miyamasuzaka, and to the west was Dogenzaka, both filled with lots of ups and downs. It was clear why Shibuya became what it was—if they wanted to get trains through there, they either had to build along river paths or start digging tunnels.

After climbing one such slope, Mitsuhiro finally entered the lobby of his company building, letting the air-conditioning envelop him. It wasn't the worst commute, but it was still a decent bit of exercise.

As soon as he put his bag on his desk, his boss, Takenaka, called out for him.

"Did you see the doctor? How are you feeling?"

"Yes, I'm fine, thanks."

Takenaka nodded. He must have been relieved that Mitsuhiro's voice was back to normal.

"You're going to interview the construction company today, right?"

"Yes, I have an appointment."

Takenaka lowered his voice. "Well, be careful. We had an attempted arson, remember."

"All right, sir."

Mitsuhiro also frowned a bit.

"Let me know before you go in. I'll call you in an hour. Make sure your phone is set to ring."

This was a precautionary measure the company had in place to prevent employees from being stranded in an emergency. Construction frequently involved land transactions, so it was often unclear what sort of individuals or organizations you might be dealing with. You could make necessary preparations if you knew in advance that the other party was the yakuza or otherwise working for them, but sometimes you'd run into people who committed crimes impulsively. Takenaka had once been negotiating when he was suddenly told "no more excuses," had his phone taken, and was all but held captive for a while, so he wasn't being needlessly cautious.

"Got it. Thanks."

"What about the homeless-support groups?"

"I made appointments with the main ones in the district. I'll be going down the list."

"Good. I want to resolve this case before the shareholder meeting at the end of the month."

So did Mitsuhiro. The East Wing construction was one of the key elements of the whole Shibuya redevelopment project. Imperfections of any sort would not be tolerated, and it was the IR department's mission to keep everything well protected.

Confident and excited at being entrusted with such an important task,

Mitsuhiro wrapped up the team meeting, gathered his belongings, and left the HQ. His first destination was Akihabara. After getting off at the station, he followed the map on his phone and walked along the building-lined street near the riverbank before finding his destination. Before getting into the only elevator, he called Takenaka and informed him that he was going into Tamai Construction's office.

"Talk to you in an hour, then."

Reassured by this backup, he checked the nameplate by the door and took the elevator to the fourth floor.

Stepping out into the external corridor, he saw summer sunlight streaming in between the ceiling and the handrails. Beyond them lay the road and the river. A steel ashtray was placed near the emergency staircase, but it was recently cleaned, and a sticker reading "No Gang Activity" was affixed to the frame of the office door. At least it wasn't run by the sort of rough-and-tumble types who wouldn't bother to keep a building in good shape.

When he pressed the intercom button, a surprisingly cheerful female voice answered.

"Hello, Tamai Construction Company."

"Sorry to suddenly drop in. This is Matsunaga from Shimaoka. I called you earlier."

"Ah, yes, yes. Just a moment, please. I'll open the door."

Her voice was so bright that it caught him off guard as the door promptly opened. It wasn't locked, so she must have come over to open it for him. A smiling, elderly woman wearing a shirt and skirt in subdued colors appeared.

"Please, come in. It's not large, but..."

"Thank you."

She politely handed him her business card. "A pleasure to meet you. I'm Chiyo Tamai from the General Affairs department."

Mitsuhiro took a business card out of his breast pocket, bowed, and exchanged cards with her.

"I'm Matsunaga. Nice to meet you as well."

"Please have a seat here," Tamai said. "I'll go get the president right away."

Just beyond the door was a reception area surrounded by thin partitions. A set of sofas had been arranged around a low table in a U shape. One wall was lined with bookshelves containing a variety of legal books, references on construction-related laws, economic white papers, and case studies of construction accidents in Tokyo. On top of the shelves was a small well-worn Shinto altar, the branches of a tree with lush green leaves provided as an offering. Mitsuhiro guessed they were from a sakaki tree, an evergreen often seen at shrines, but he wasn't sure.

Instead of sitting down, Mitsuhiro remained on his feet, observing the office. On the other side of the partition was a tight array of filing cabinets and desks, and a man wearing armguards was busily sorting through documents. On the shelves next to him were models of buildings and houses, giving the impression of an architect's office. It certainly didn't look like a gang hideout, at least.

Soon, four people came from another room and entered the reception area. They were the woman who opened the door earlier; a wrinkled, elderly man in work clothes; and two men in their midthirties, also in work jumpsuits. Mitsuhiro assumed that the oldest man was the president, but one of the younger men approached him first, handed him his business card, and bowed his head.

"I'm Yoshio Tamai, president of Tamai Construction."

He was the smallest, slimmest, and youngest-looking of the group. Behind his thick glasses, his round eyes cheerfully darted around. Mitsuhiro was surprised but still bowed politely and exchanged business cards.

"I'm Matsunaga from the IR department at Shimaoka. Thank you for taking the time to meet with me today."

"Not at all. Thanks for coming all this way. This is Koji Tamai, our vice president and general manager."

President Tamai motioned to the man next to him. "Koji Tamai," the elderly man muttered as he handed Mitsuhiro his business card. He appeared to be taciturn by nature, with an expression that hardly changed. Having all these Tamais in one place was starting to get confusing, but then President Tamai introduced another young man.

"This is our other general manager, Sota Araki."

"I'm Araki. Nice to meet you."

Suddenly, a different surname. This man was tall and well built; he looked the most engineer-like out of the four. Mitsuhiro exchanged cards with Araki as well.

The president gestured for him to sit down, and Mitsuhiro did so with all four cards still in his hand. They placed their cards on the table and expressed their gratitude for taking the time to meet each other.

Just then, another older man appeared with a tray holding plastic bottles of tea and cups for everyone. The president helped pour, and everyone passed the cups around.

"Oh, it's chilled," the president said. "That's thoughtful of you."

"Hee-hee! I certainly thought so," said the server with a proud smile.

"You bought these at the convenience store earlier, didn't you?" Araki said with a grin.

"Oh, don't say that," the woman said, laughing and tapping Araki on the arm.

"It's true," said the man who brought the tea, smiling and bowing slightly to Mitsuhiro before leaving the reception area. It was a convivial sort of atmosphere, free of any sense of hierarchy, and everyone seemed to get along well with each other. Thanks to that, Mitsuhiro's pre-visit jitters had melted away...but at the same time, he couldn't completely let himself unwind.

Maybe their interactions were almost too friendly—it seemed a tad artificial, perhaps. They were all so polite to Mitsuhiro—"It's such an honor to have you visit our company," "I know this is a lot of trouble for you," "Yes, yes, we really should apologize for all the inconvenience"—but despite the familial atmosphere, it felt like they were trying to keep their distance. The unwritten rule seemed to be that guests were welcome but to be kept at arm's length as much as possible.

—Feels like I'm out in the countryside.

When you visit a chamber of commerce or the like in a rural area, you'd usually receive a warm welcome, but nothing approaching friendship. Deals like a large land purchase or lease in the area—and the big-box stores that could potentially be built on them—tended to raise hackles. Anyone who affected local business owners was no friend of theirs.

After this merry-go-round of welcoming remarks, President Yoshio Tamai slowly got down to business.

"So we received a call from Chief Sugawara about an incident at a ritual hall?"

"Yes, that's right. I understand that Tamai Construction manages the East Wing basement."

Mitsuhiro took his tablet out of his bag, opened a file he had prepared, and showed them images of the hall he'd found in the basement, along with the square hole.

"Ah, yes, yes. That is one of the duties we inherited from our predecessors."

"Is it usually blocked off like this?"

"Yes. It was dug over a hundred years ago, so I can't call it very safe."

"The stairs down were exposed and accessible when I examined them."

"The usual blockade had been removed to prepare for a certain ceremony. Right?"

Yoshio Tamai turned to Araki.

"Yes," Araki replied. "We had to set up the ritual, and with the heavy rain, we didn't expect anyone to come so early in the morning."

"But you left it wide open? What were you thinking, Sota?"

Yoshio's tone suddenly became quite frank, enough to catch Mitsuhiro's attention. The closeness between them, unique to a family-run business, was evident.

Araki frowned, as if to remind him they were in the presence of a guest, and Yoshio cleared his throat.

"Well, we apologize for the inconvenience caused by our carelessness." Araki bowed his head to Mitsuhiro, then immediately turned toward Yoshio. "But, sir, we can't just seal it up with the removal going on inside."

"If you remove the barrier, you have to notify the director. You know it's been a troublesome ritual hall for us."

President Tamai's voice grew sterner, and Araki bowed his head again. "I'm sorry," he said, not arguing this time, and the president sighed back at him.

"Normally," the president continued, "a barrier is set up to prevent people from entering the ritual hall. However, due to the recent construction work, there is a great deal more empty space in the surrounding area. As a result, the barrier that had been set up when the hall was built decades ago has completely disappeared. We've had to set up a temporary barrier ourselves, but I'm afraid that's made access far easier."

Mitsuhiro nodded at the president's words but deliberately frowned to show that he didn't like what he was hearing.

"I'm sorry. By 'barrier,' are you referring to some kind of structure?"

Tamai, Araki, and the others fell silent. All four of them looked at Mitsuhiro, as if trying to gauge his level of ignorance.

Then, as if suddenly remembering something, President Tamai said, "We're still cleaning the shrine in Sotokanda today, right?"

"Kenichi is doing it," said the elderly Koji Tamai, speaking up for the first time since greeting Mitsuhiro.

"Why don't we perform the purification ritual while we're at it? It's due next week anyway. It might be good to have someone from headquarters take a look."

The other three nodded at Yoshio, completely ignoring Mitsuhiro's question. This made him uncomfortable, along with the way they wanted to vaguely deal with "headquarters" rather than him. The implication was that Mitsuhiro Matsunaga didn't matter—they were only dealing with him because he was an errand boy from Shimaoka HQ. Now he wanted to know whether they knew the man in the East Wing basement, but he didn't like how they seemed to be dodging the topic. Considering all the other appointments he had, he couldn't help feeling anxious.

Of course, as an IR department employee, he couldn't show any personal discomfort, so he asked the president in a tone that sounded as ignorant and apologetic as possible, "Did you want to show me something?"

President Tamai smiled in approval of Mitsuhiro's attitude. "Well, most people don't know what we do at all. We have a ritual hall we're working on that's within walking distance from here. Would you like to take a look? I think it will help you understand our business more."

"If it's not too much trouble, I'd love to. Thanks."

"Oh, no trouble at all. Just follow the rules—and it's nothing complicated, either. Stay out of unauthorized areas, don't touch anything, and don't move anything."

"Certainly. Not a problem."

Mitsuhiro gave his agreement, but he was also curious. Or maybe it was the anxiety festering in his heart coming to the surface. Don't enter, don't touch, don't move anything… Didn't he violate all three of those rules in the East Wing basement?

"By the way, if I break the rules or do something I'm not supposed to, will I have to pay damages or anything?"

The group fell silent. This silence was completely different from the previous one. The small reception room was filled with tension, as if they had just been informed of some terrible on-site accident. It was deeply unsettling.

"Oh, um, I was just asking out of curiosity," he hastily added. "I didn't mean anything by it."

President Tamai let out a deep breath. The others looked at each other, as if trying to brush off a bad joke.

"Was that rude of me? I'm sorry; I don't know anything about this."

Mitsuhiro bowed his head and apologized.

Yoshio pressed his lips into a thin line before replying. "Well, that depends on what exactly happened. Sometimes it's easily settled, but other times, there's not much we can do. If we make certain bigger mistakes, we may have to rebuild the entire ritual hall to appease the spirits."

"Appease..."

Mitsuhiro thought about the character he saw on the wall of the basement. 鎭, it said. Now he realized that it was the old way of writing 鎮, which meant *appease*.

Mitsuhiro saw the character in his mind's eye, realizing it had been used to write "earth-appeasement ceremony" in the old memos he read before. For the first time, he'd realized that it was the same one written in the East Wing basement.

Yoshio Tamai nodded back at him. "By that," he said, "I mean that it becomes a matter of whether someone who breaks the traditional rules will be cursed by the spirits, and whether the spirits can be appeased or not."

3

"There are various kinds of curses," Yoshio Tamai said, taking off his glasses and wiping the sweat with his handkerchief. "None of them are things you can scientifically explain, but at the same time, you can't dismiss them as mere figments of the imagination."

Mitsuhiro had to use a fist to wipe his own sweat as he looked at the giant boulder in front of him, illuminated by the bright sunlight. "I see," he replied, pretending to be impressed.

Yoshio, Koji, and Sota Araki had taken him to the opposite side of Akihabara Station. At the foot of a nineteen-story building, one of the area's local landmarks, there was a panel titled "Site of Ishigaki Ruins," and Yoshio had encouraged Mitsuhiro to read it.

Mitsuhiro wasn't sure why he had to do that but went ahead and did so. Apparently feudal lords and samurai and the like used to have residences in this area, and parts of the stone walls from their excavated houses were reused for monuments in the square, as well as sites for urban foliage and such.

—So what?

Mitsuhiro tried not to show his annoyance, but he felt more and more like he was dealing with country folk here. Whenever he went to some local chamber of commerce to say hello, he'd invariably be taken to check out the local sights and be lectured about their history. Takenaka had once told him that this was their way of introducing him to the local history he'd be destroying when some large-scale construction project rolled through, and that he'd better not let them see a hint of boredom. If people from big firms showed respect for the local history, he said, it'd often make negotiations easier.

Still, for the life of him, Mitsuhiro couldn't see why he was going on this walking tour of Akihabara. It's not like Tamai Construction was even contracted to preserve these stone walls or whatever.

"You see this large stone?" explained Yoshio. "It's proof that the clan who lived here was wealthy enough to transport such enormous objects. The area around what's now Akihabara Electric Town was largely home to lower-ranking samurai, so stones like these are less common to see around here."

Yoshio no doubt felt this was necessary, but Mitsuhiro just responded with an interested nod and an "I see," unable to connect this to their current business. Yoshio was probably aware of Mitsuhiro's confusion to some extent, but he continued talking, as if he was duty bound.

"In Tokyo, you can see evidence of family fortunes like these everywhere. After all, most of the old city of Edo was owned by either samurai clans or religious shrines and temples. The families who lived here did everything they could to maintain their status or hopefully make it grow. They'd do things unimaginable in this day and age, even."

"Right."

"And this area, you know, has a history of fires."

"A history of fires?"

Mitsuhiro repeated the words, marveling at the leap in conversation.

"At the beginning of the Meiji era, they built Akiba Shrine here, a place to pray to the gods for fire prevention. It was originally called Chinka, or 'Extinguishing' Shrine, but when it was renamed Akiba Shrine in the Showa era, this district came to be called Akiba-ppara or Akiba-hara."

"Was it an open field, or…?"

"Much of this area was a firebreak. When the last major fire took place, they cleared the burnt-out area and kept it unbuilt to prevent future fires from spreading."

"Just a barren field? Fire must've been a real threat back then."

"Yes. It's said that Edo, now Tokyo, once had one of the highest fire rates in the world. That on top of earthquakes and wars, too. Regardless, Akihabara has a special connection with Tamai Construction, and I wanted you to know about that as well, Mr. Matsunaga."

"I see. Thank you very much for the tour."

To be honest, Mitsuhiro didn't really understand what Yoshio was talking about.

"Now, it's hot out here, so shall we go inside? The shrine should be cleaned by now. Come with us and take a look at our workplace."

"Yes, I'd love to see it."

Finally, they were able to go in. It was scorching outside, and the heavy rain from the other day now seemed like a mirage. Mitsuhiro wanted to beg them to let him inside, but he kept his mouth shut and followed Yoshio and the others to the service entrance of the nineteen-story building.

This was mostly office space, but it also contained an event hall, so there was a freight entrance as well. Yoshio and the others showed their passes to the security guard at the reception desk, cheerfully greeting him. Mitsuhiro gave his business card, signed the guest book, borrowed a pass, and joined them inside.

The air-conditioning was comfortable enough, but since this was the service entrance, there was no real decor at all. They walked down a large, plain corridor, opened one of the doors, and went down to the basement.

Opposite a door with a plastic sign reading "High Voltage," there was a door with a numeric keypad.

Mitsuhiro casually looked up at it…and gasped.

It was the same door. The door to the hole in the East Wing basement. That one had been open at the time, but this one was firmly shut. Yoshio used his body to block the door as he unlocked it, preventing Mitsuhiro from seeing the number code.

Everyone stepped through, and Yoshio closed it behind him. He seemed well used to this. If they were going in and out of the East Wing basement, had they left the door open on purpose? Mitsuhiro idly wondered to himself.

"Off we go," Yoshio said, descending the dimly lit stairs. They went down around ten steps, turned right on the landing, and repeated the process several times. The disturbing experience in the East Wing basement came back to Mitsuhiro's mind, but they reached the basement floor much sooner than expected. It was probably about a third of the depth of the East Wing.

Now they were in a place that resembled an underground parking garage. It was brightly lit by fluorescent lights, with shelves and water pipes along the walls. On the shelves were several large flashlights, buckets, rags, dustpans, and other cleaning tools, as well as bundles of sacred *shimenawa* ropes and paper streamers.

In one corner, there was a doorway without a door and a pair of shoes. Beyond the doorway was pitch-black, due to a complete lack of lighting. Because this garage-like room was so bright, it looked like a dark hole in the wall more than anything else, making Mitsuhiro feel a chill down his spine.

He couldn't afford to give in to this phobia. He took a deep breath, trying to calm himself down and stay inconspicuous. Ever since that East Wing basement descent, he had been developing a sense of fear inside dark spaces. As a member of the crisis-management team, he needed to overcome it as soon as possible. If he got scared every time he entered a construction site, he might get assigned to counseling or something—or removed from the team entirely.

"Careful, now. It's a little dark in there."

Yoshio and the other two took flashlights, illuminating the dark entrance. Mitsuhiro's eyes widened. A long passageway led into the depths, but the floor was unusual. It was a polished wooden floor, just like the hallways of traditional Japanese inns. The bright light did wonders for his fear. He seriously considered keeping a flashlight in his briefcase from now on.

"The ritual hall is up ahead. You can see the marks of purification on both sides."

Yoshio shone his flashlight on the walls to the left and right of the doorway.

鎮, or *appeasement*, was written on the right side; 祓, or *purification*, on the left—both with some kind of ash-like material.

"I saw that character in the East Wing basement over in Shibuya," said Mitsuhiro, pointing to the right side.

"Yes. It indicates that this was a ritual hall where an appeasement ceremony needed to be held. It has now been properly purified, so you must not go inside the shrine itself here or touch anything."

"Right," he replied, wondering if he should tell Yoshio what he had done.

"Oh, take off your shoes here, please."

He obeyed Yoshio's instructions without question. As he entered the passageway, he felt a pleasant chill through his socks. Seeing a proper wooden floor in this damp basement was a surprise, but it creaked only slightly under his feet, apparently still in good condition. The lacquered surface reflected the strong light of the flashlight like a mirror.

The three men bowed politely toward the back of the passageway before proceeding. Mitsuhiro followed suit.

They walked down the long corridor until they reached a dead end. Then they turned right, bowing in the direction they were facing, and Mitsuhiro did the same. The same wooden floor extended out. They walked down it for a while before reaching another dead end.

The group turned right, bowed, and proceeded. Mitsuhiro followed them, unsure what was happening here. They came to another dead end, turned right again, and bowed their heads.

"Are we going around in circles?" he couldn't help but ask. If they had turned right three times, wouldn't they end up back where they started?

Yoshio looked back over his shoulder. "This is called the '*sazae* corridor.' It's designed like the shell of a *sazae*, or sea snail, with the pathway winding around in a spiral. You walk around in circles until you finally reach the ritual hall. There are several approaches to creating these entrances and barriers, but for this one, we restored it to its original state."

"So this space was here before?"

"It used to be much shallower. When the previous building here was demolished—I think around 2006?—the previous president, who oversaw the construction and management of the original, recommended moving it farther underground. Typically, when a space needs to be purified, the only option you really have is to move it to a purer location."

"Does 'purer' mean 'deeper underground' here?"

"Yes, well, in Tokyo, there are very few places where the bone ash hasn't seeped into the soil."

"Bone ash?"

He didn't understand what the term meant, so he repeated it back.

"Yes."

Yoshio nodded as if this was common knowledge, turned right, bowed with the other two, and continued on.

Bone ash? Mitsuhiro also bowed and followed, but before he could ask what it meant, they were at the next turn and everyone bowed in silence, so he kept missing his chance. The passageway was getting shorter and shorter now.

"We're almost there," said Yoshio. He must have been counting the number of turns this whole time—and sure enough, as soon as they turned the last corner…

—An old prison cell?

The phrase popped into Mitsuhiro's mind. He had never actually seen a dungeon-style prison cell before, but he reflexively associated this with the term. Maybe he had seen it in some samurai drama once. In any case, it was a dimly lit room, about twelve feet to a side, sealed off by thick, heavily stained wooden bars. Some of the wooden bars had hinges and a lock on them, forming a low door that required bending over to pass through. From that door, a man holding a flashlight and a broom emerged. He gave a startled glance to Yoshio and the others, lit up by the flashlights.

"Whoa, what's going on? Did something happen, boss?"

"Ah, sorry, Kenichi," Yoshio said, pointing his light toward his feet. "I wanted to call you to say I was coming over, but I guess you're out of range down here."

"Oh, okay. I turned off the lights, but are you here to inspect the cleaning?"

"No, no. This is Mr. Matsunaga from the Shimaoka HQ. We wanted to give him a tour of our worksite."

"Ah, I see. My name's Kenichi Tamai. I'm an employee of Tamai Construction, and I'm also the son of—"

"He's my son," Koji interjected.

"He is?" Mitsuhiro asked, pretending to be interested. It was funny how much of a family business this was. "Oh, I'm sorry. I'm Mitsuhiro Matsunaga from the IR department at the Shimaoka HQ. Can I ask where we are?"

"This is the ritual hall I'm in charge of. Um, are we letting him in, President?"

Yoshio turned to Mitsuhiro instead of Kenichi.

"It's probably best not to step inside, no. Would you mind just looking in from the entrance?"

"Not at all."

"All right. Give us some light, Kenichi."

"Right away, President."

Kenichi crouched down and crawled back inside the door. His flashlight flickered, illuminating the area behind the bars.

For a moment, Mitsuhiro thought he spotted someone sitting in the dark room, which sent a jolt down his spine. The figure was dressed in a kimono, quite different from everyone else in their work coveralls. He hadn't sensed it at all before now, and if he didn't know better, he would have said it suddenly teleported in out of nowhere.

Kenichi took a long lighter from his pocket and lit the oil lamps hanging from the four corners of the ceiling. The soft light filled the interior of the cell, and the figure sitting in the center of the room became clearly visible.

It wasn't human at all. It was an elaborate, almost life-size wooden doll, like an oversize version of the ones sold in tourist-trap souvenir shops. No wonder he didn't notice it before now. Mitsuhiro took a deep breath, being careful not to draw attention to himself.

Once all the lamps were lit, Kenichi stood by the wall so Mitsuhiro could see inside.

"Now, Mr. Matsunaga, bend down and take a look. Be careful not to touch anything."

Mitsuhiro knelt down in front of the door, his bag in his arms, and peered beyond the wooden bars. It was a sturdy space, likely covered in concrete, and it featured wooden pillars, ceiling boards, white plaster walls, and a small shrine on the side. In the center of the tatami-mat floor sat a doll dressed in traditional clothing, and behind it was a lacquered shelf and a large, heavy wooden box.

"This doll," Yoshio said, "is said to be modeled after the original *mi-keshi* that was enshrined here."

Mitsuhiro didn't quite understand what that meant.

"The original...?"

"Yes. It was probably offered here a long time ago."

Mitsuhiro was suddenly overcome with a cold chill. *Enshrined. Offered.* Such words had a terribly disturbing connotation here. Still on his knees, he looked up at Yoshio beside him.

"Offered...as in this doll?"

Yoshio shook his head. "A person."

"What?"

"A man was enshrined here. Alive."

4

"A man...?"

Mitsuhiro muttered it in a daze. He couldn't believe it was real.

Next to him, Yoshio Tamai crouched down and peered inside through the bars. "I guess you could call it a *sokushinbutsu*, a Buddhist monk entering mummification by his own volition. Mummies are rare in Japan's humid weather, but they said that this one was very carefully preserved. This land was once samurai territory, and during the Meiji era, a water-transport company bought the land and found that beneath it. Wisely, they left it as it was. Later, during the Sino-Japanese War in the 1930s, the company became a state-owned enterprise. When they constructed their first building here, they followed precedent and didn't touch the ritual hall."

"So the body of a man had been here all that time?"

"Yes. He was said to have remained here untouched for decades. Him and that box over there. There were also remains inside of it."

"Inside? A whole body?"

"No, not the entire body. Just mummified human hands. Apparently, there were several packed tightly inside, all severed at the wrist."

Mitsuhiro shuddered again. All he had to do was open that lid, and that's what he would see. He would have fainted on the spot.

"Are they still there?"

Mitsuhiro pointed fearfully at the large box, but Yoshio shook his head.

"It now contains wooden carvings in the shape of hands. We can't just leave such things in place nowadays, of course. In 2006, when the building in front of here was demolished, the remains were all properly processed then. The previous owner consulted with the company that owned the building, the police, and the temple he was affiliated with. The remains were determined to be over two hundred years old, and no criminal activity is known to be involved. So, after cremation, the ashes were taken by the temple as unclaimed remains."

"And you've been managing this place ever since?"

"Yes. After preparing the requisite substitute image, Tamai has been keeping this site enshrined ever since. Temples and shrines can't take responsibility for things outside of their premises, so our family has been managing these halls across generations. Otherwise, a hall might place a curse upon anyone who comes here."

"A curse…"

As soon as he uttered those words, Mitsuhiro swallowed hard, feeling thirsty. Yoshio nodded as he peered at Mitsuhiro through his thick glasses, which glinted among the flashlights.

"The person enshrined here was, in so many words, a human sacrifice to bring prosperity to the family that owned this building."

"A sacrifice? Because…well, it looks like a prison cell."

"Indeed. Perhaps the person was punished for offending the head of the household. Or maybe they were an important figure, like a retired clan leader. Either way, this was an era when human life was treated with far less worth than it is now. But that doesn't mean life was worthless, either. On the contrary, it was quite valued. That's why someone like this man was deemed worthy to be offered to the gods."

"But did people really make these human sacrifices back then…?"

"Ritual halls where people were enshrined like this have been found in at least a hundred sites I know of across Tokyo, including former prisons and so on. That doesn't mean it was commonplace, though. Even among wealthy families, such extreme measures were only taken if the head of the household hoped to bring the gods down for his clan's benefit, if you will, or if the family was on the brink of ruin. Of course, there's also the possibility that this was erected following an accident of some sort."

"Accident…? Like, you mean a worksite accident?"

"That's one way to put it. People who offer their sacrifices to the gods are called *mi-keshi*, and since ancient times, this has been associated with the idea of 'disappearing' or 'erasing oneself.' That's because flying too close to the sun—in other words, becoming too close with gods, or spirits, or bone ash—invites curses upon them, and they're forced to sacrifice themselves to appease them."

Mitsuhiro frowned at the absurd logic. Then Yoshio smiled faintly, averting his gaze from him.

"Most people, with their modern sensibilities, might think 'Wow, what the hell?' But our basic belief is that such so-called absurdities are exactly what form the backbone of this world. My duty is to offer our thanks to the gods, but I don't know when I myself might be cursed by the bone ash."

Mitsuhiro stood up again, returning to Yoshio's height. Observing such a mysterious sight in an unnatural position had made his whole body stiff.

For a moment, it seemed Yoshio was about to continue speaking, but he remained silent, staring at the doll.

"What is that 'bone ash' thing?"

Yoshio seemed puzzled. The others from Tamai Construction around him also gave Mitsuhiro looks, as if to say, *You don't even know that much?*

"Let's discuss that on the way out. Kenichi, could you turn off the lights?"

"All right," Kenichi replied, using a small metal snuffer to extinguish the lamps. The darkness once again filled the interior of the cell and swallowed up the doll sitting down there, along with the eerie box full of hands.

Kenichi crawled out on all fours, closed the door, and turned the large metal lock on it.

"Let's head back up."

Mitsuhiro followed Yoshio back up the passageway they'd come from. This time, they were making left turns as he continued listening to his story.

"In olden days, wealthy families would try to summon gods, or sacrifice people and keep their spirits alive, in order to protect themselves and grow richer. Modern people are usually more individualistic, but the samurai of the past tied their whole identity to the status of their clan. They considered themselves a very literal part of their family. You may argue whether that offered much in the way of freedom, but either way, that was the conventional wisdom of the time."

Mitsuhiro, being a modern man, couldn't quite understand this, but he nodded along.

"The gods and spirits enshrined at ritual halls are there for the sake of the family that built them. They're not like the *jizo* Buddhist statues on street corners that grant individual wishes to anyone passing by. On the other hand, 'bone ash' can be seen as the accumulation of countless personal grievances. Each one may be as small as a mote of dust, but a mass of them can defile the gods and spirits, and even turn a ritual hall into a house of curses."

"Hoh..."

"Our company manages over a hundred such sites in order to prevent any sacred grounds from being defiled by bone ash. We perform daily purification rituals, and sometimes, we also perform exorcisms or appeasement rites."

"And your family's been doing this for generations?"

"That's right. I'm the fourth generation. During the last war, there was a Shinto priest who was displaced by the Tokyo air raids and lost his property to the Americans. That priest was also named Tamai. He had nowhere to go, so he was taken in by the Araki family—his younger brother's in-laws. The Arakis were carpenters, and through their connections, he began conducting earth-appeasement ceremonies and eventually started to manage ritual halls. I suppose he had a talent for these rites—purification, exorcism, appeasement—so people started calling for his services from all over."

"So the Tamais and Arakis are related to each other?"

It was a family business through and through. Mitsuhiro was impressed to see a company span four generations. A common saying around Shimaoka HQ was "With a family-run company, watch out for the third generation." Apparently, it was often that third-generation owner who destroyed the company or led it to its ruin in some way. If Tamai had made it to the fourth generation, it means they had deftly avoided the traps and pitfalls of change over the years.

"Yes, you could say that," Yoshio said, suddenly sounding a bit vague. "And so Tamai has seen it as its duty to perform purification rituals, exorcisms when curses strike, and appeasement rites when curses persist, all across Tokyo. The curses in this city are unique things—most are caused by bone ash. The bones and ashes of those who were burned to death in fires have seeped into the very soil."

"Burned to death…"

Finally, the reason it was called "bone ash" was becoming clear to him.

"Yes. As you know, Edo—and later, Tokyo—was known for fires. The city was ravaged by more than a hundred major fires over the span of 250 years, or one every two or three years. Even in modern times, you had the Great Kanto Earthquake in 1923, then the air raids over Tokyo during World War II… Now, wherever you go in Tokyo, the soil is literally saturated with the remains of those burned to ashes. The remains of thousands, or millions, accumulated over hundreds of years."

"Right in the soil… I never even considered that."

"The soil in the Kanto region where Tokyo lies is acidic enough that it dissolves bone over time. Any remains are completely obliterated. In Europe, on the other hand, remains can still exist for hundreds of years afterward. It makes it easier to perform rites on them, in a way."

"It does…?"

That was all Mitsuhiro could say. He had never thought about it before, and now that thought made him feel uneasy. Did parents who take their children to play in the nearby park ever think about how the soil contained human bones and ashes?

"Yes. The previous generation at Tamai went through a lot of trouble, actually. When Tokyo began to see more high-rises and underground development, it led to a lot more bone ash being uncovered. Your East Wing in Shibuya is one of the most prominent examples."

Suddenly, the topic had turned toward the East Wing. Mitsuhiro was relieved that they hadn't forgotten the reason for his visit.

"I have a question about that," he quickly asked. "When I was investigating the East Wing, I saw someone in what appeared to be a ritual hall in the basement…"

"Yes, that's the *mi-keshi* that we hired. Right, Sota?"

"Right. That would be Mr. Hara… Yoshikazu Hara. We were asked to bring him on as a *mi-keshi*."

"How do you write that in characters?" Mitsuhiro asked, not expecting to learn the name that readily.

"Like this— 原義一. He's worked for us since he was young as a laborer for the previous president, so we know him well."

Mitsuhiro took out his cell phone and made a note.

"Was Mr. Hara in the East Wing for some kind of ceremony?"

"That's right. When we placed the substitute image you saw earlier, the *mi-keshi* hired by our predecessor stayed there for seven days and seven nights. He slept next to the substitute image in complete darkness. That's how they stabilize the image, along with the ritual hall. But in the East Wing, the ritual hall is deep and very complex, so they had the *mi-keshi* stay there to monitor whether the bone ash was causing any curses."

"Was he chained up for this ritual?"

"No, that had nothing to do with the ritual," Yoshio casually replied.

"Mr. Hara requested it," Araki added. "He told us he was developing symptoms of Alzheimer's disease, just like his wife. He wanted to chain himself down there so he wouldn't wander off if he had another episode."

Mitsuhiro was stunned.

"You mean…it was his own decision? I thought he was forced in there—"

Yoshio Tamai waved his free hand. "Forcing him would have led to a curse. It would have brought even more resentment and grudges into the space. The East Wing is a place of great importance to us, and doing any such thing would be strictly forbidden."

"Importance? How so?"

"It's where the water god of the Shibuya River is enshrined. The river is now fully an underground channel, but it's still a sacred site for the water god, as its source lies within the Shinjuku Imperial Garden. The god was there long before the first vertical shaft of the ritual hall was dug about eighty years ago. It's an indispensable deity for purifying the valley where the ashes of the deceased flow."

They were now out of the corridor and back in the parking-garage-like space. Kenichi put the cleaning supplies back on the shelf, and as the five of them climbed the stairs, Yoshio Tamai continued his story.

"That, of course, is why there's a risk of any *mi-keshi* on the site being cursed, so we pay Mr. Hara a considerable sum for his work. Apparently, it's been very hard work, since the old eastern building was constructed on the site. They had to dig extremely deep to keep the ashes away and call the water deity back."

"Um… Well, I'm sorry. I think I misconstrued why he was there…and I'm afraid I let him out."

"Right, I heard about that from Chief Sugawara. I'm sure the sight would surprise anyone if they didn't know about us."

Yoshio's voice was gentle. It grew sterner as he turned toward Araki.

"The blame lies with the site manager for not closing the barrier properly."

Araki bowed his head silently. He didn't seem all that terribly remorseful, though; he even seemed to be silently accepting how absurd all of this was. Maybe Araki had some kind of reason for his actions, but Mitsuhiro didn't see one.

"Um, so where does this Yoshikazu Hara live?" he asked, fairly winded after climbing all those stairs.

"He's homeless," Yoshio nonchalantly replied, not out of breath at all. "He sold everything, including his house, so his wife could be put into a memory-care facility. His financial struggles were what inspired him to become a *mi-keshi*."

"…So he's living on the streets?"

"That, I don't know. We've tried introducing him to support centers and such, but given his condition…"

"I see," replied Mitsuhiro, but internally he wondered how true it was. Was it *really* his own choice to be chained up in a hole? It was far too deep for him to climb up from. Even without the chain, there was no way he was getting out.

"I'm sure," Araki said, "that he'll contact us again once he remembers what he was trying to do."

"Um," said Mitsuhiro, hesitantly but firmly, "I'd like to speak with Mr. Hara as well, if possible." As part of the crisis-management team, he couldn't allow any inconvenient truths to be covered up, lest they be exposed later by a third party and damage the company's image. Thorough, complete investigations were his duty.

"I'll have him contact you, too, Mr. Matsunaga. Is that okay with you, Sota?"

"Not a problem."

Araki bowed his head to Mitsuhiro. Something about the man made it hard for Mitsuhiro to fully trust him. Maybe because everything he'd heard so far seemed detached from reality. As they approached the surface, he was becoming more and more convinced that this was a family of shysters trying to extort money from big companies with loony stories about eternal curses and the like.

"Do you know the name of Mr. Hara's wife and the facility she's in?"

"Yes. Megumi Hara. She's at a nursing home for the elderly in Gotanda—"

Yoshio readily provided the name of the place.

"Also, there's a pastor for a church in Shibuya who runs a support group. He knows Mr. Hara well, too."

He gave the group's name.

"Oh! I was planning to visit them right after this. I thought there might be a chance that homeless people were entering the site to protest being evicted from the area."

Mitsuhiro wasn't shy about revealing this. He wanted to make it clear that he wasn't here to conduct a half-hearted investigation.

"Ah, good. Well, please say hello for me."

Yoshio, too, acted like he had nothing to hide as they reached the end of the stairs. He unlocked the door, and as everyone exited to the ground floor, he closed it firmly behind him.

Mitsuhiro appreciated being back on the surface, with no more stairs to traverse. He wanted to sit down somewhere, but the four men kept on walking over to the service entrance on the first floor of the building. Mitsuhiro returned his pass to the security guard, wrote down the date and time of his departure, and stepped out into the blazing sunlight.

"Thank you very much for your time," he said politely.

"Not at all. Oh, right—there was a fire, wasn't there?"

Yoshio brought it up without any warning at all.

"What?"

"The director told me there was a fire at the site while you were there. I'm sure it's nothing, but please take this just in case."

Yoshio rummaged in the pocket of his work outfit and handed Mitsuhiro what he found. It was a slightly large amulet, the kind you could buy at any shrine. The words "Tamai Prayer" were embroidered on it.

"Thank you very much for the thought," said Mitsuhiro—but he didn't expect that Takenaka would much appreciate such a gift. Ethically speaking, he should avoid accepting anything from someone he was questioning for an investigation. Gift giving was a habit among those hiding something that'd damage their reputation. With this, however, Yoshio was framing it more as part of his duty than a gift.

"I would suggest keeping that with you at all times for a while. It's like a vaccination. If, despite that, you or someone close to you is afflicted by a curse, burn the contents of the amulet and use the ashes to write something on your body or the wall of your home's entrance."

"Write something? What should I write?"

"Anything is fine, actually, as long as it's accompanied by a prayer. It can be a single line, even, or a dot. However, my predecessor said that character from before is the most effective thing. Do you remember the one on the right side of the entrance to the *sazae* corridor you saw today?"

Mitsuhiro nodded.

鎮

He'd taken a picture of it in the East Wing so he could check on how it looked anytime, not that he thought it'd be necessary. Yoshio must have taken a lot of pride in the fact that he was descended from the chief priest of a Shinto shrine. Mitsuhiro thought so, at least. Faith was the Tamai family's way of life, and also their business, so he thought it was best to play along with them…for now.

"I'm very grateful for everything you showed me today."

"I'll waive the purification fee for you. It's actually rather pricey."

That sounded like a joke from Yoshio, but Mitsuhiro couldn't be sure if it actually was.

After parting ways with them, Mitsuhiro headed for Akihabara Station, stuffed the amulet into his briefcase, took out his phone, and called Takenaka's number. As he sorted out what to report in his head, the memory of the amulet was already drifting out of his brain.

5

"I feel like I just journeyed to another planet."

Mitsuhiro sat down on a bench at the muggy Akihabara Station platform, put his finger to the ear that wasn't holding his phone, and tried not to be distracted by all the trains and announcements as he talked.

"Sheesh. So you went down there without any phone signal? How d'you think that makes me feel as your boss, huh?"

Mitsuhiro could see why Takenaka was rebuking him, but he hadn't completely thrown caution to the wind.

"The building had good security, though. Surveillance cameras, a guard with my business card, everything. If they held me captive, I think the guard would have notified you that I hadn't left the building."

"Sometimes the guards are in on it, you know. In my earlier days… Ah, never mind."

Takenaka trailed off. It probably occurred to him that lecturing someone who brought back solid results would just discourage him.

"Talk about stepping into the lion's den, huh? Great work on figuring out his name and who he is. I don't really get the whole 'ritual hall' and 'exorcism' side of things, but once we confirm with Mr. Hara that he volunteered for this and there's no criminal activity involved, that'll wrap up our investigation."

Like his subordinate, Takenaka believed that taking Tamai Construction's word for it wouldn't suffice here.

"I want to visit that memory-care facility before I return to Shibuya for my appointment with the homeless-support group."

"Please do. It may give us some leads for our investigation into those tweets."

"Oh…? Any new ones?"

"Yeah, there was one a few hours ago. It said 'I've finally been banished. I'm cursed. I'm cursed, and it's all thanks to the East Wing. They even took away the place I called home.'"

Mitsuhiro groaned, unable to hide his exasperation. He felt sorry for this poster's hard life, but why did he have to name-drop the East Wing again? He was just making things worse for everyone.

"It's clearly slander by this point."

"True, but we can't ignore his obsession with the East Wing site. There's also the arson, remember."

"Did they confirm it was arson?"

"That's what the fire department found, so they reported it to the police. The Chief is handling the response, securing the site, and adjusting the work schedules. We haven't linked the arson with the Twitter poster yet, but the police are investigating on the assumption that it's someone hostile toward the site."

"Is there any chance of the police leaking information to the media?"

"The director said that wouldn't happen while the suspect is still unknown, but honestly, I can't say. Not even the police can ignore an arson at the East Wing site. If they hit a dead end in the investigation, they might leak it to the media, so we need

to take separate precautions. For now, though, I want you to focus on investigating that unhoused person."

"Understood. But this isn't gonna be easy. Now it's two suspects with no fixed address?"

"If they have access to the internet, they must still have a phone. Keep an eye out for any posts mentioning their whereabouts."

"Got it. I'll return to the office once I'm done with my rounds."

He ended the call and put away his phone. He finally felt like he was back in reality, but he was unsure how to write up the report. To put it bluntly, they had chained up a person with early-onset Alzheimer's and locked him in a dark basement for some kind of woo-woo human-sacrifice ritual. It was beyond inappropriate. You could easily call it laborer abuse, but Tamai Construction would likely insist it was part of their job. It would have been much easier to handle if this was just some homeless guy chaining himself to the site to protest his eviction or something.

For now, gathering information was top priority. Pushing aside unnecessary thoughts, Mitsuhiro boarded the train. Once he sat down, his legs were able to recover from the exhausting climb up and down the stairs.

He got off at Gotanda Station and made another call, sticking a finger in his ear again. He was requesting a meeting with Megumi Hara at the care facility. As expected, the receptionist was reluctant, since Mitsuhiro wasn't a relative. However, when he explained that her husband Yoshikazu Hara had developed dementia himself and was currently missing, the receptionist softened her tone.

"I want to get everything ready so I can rush right over if Yoshikazu Hara appears at your place."

The receptionist agreed to the proposal. The facility wouldn't want Yoshikazu Hara to show up without going through the admission procedures, then hole up inside or wander around the neighborhood. However, Mitsuhiro's purpose here was only to question him; he had no intention of protecting him.

In any case, that conversation went smoothly, so he headed toward the facility while checking the map app on his phone. He avoided the scorching sun as much as possible along the way, walking in the shade and finishing the water he had in his bag. Once he did, he bought another cold drink from a nearby vending machine.

When he arrived at the facility, he showed his employee ID at the front desk and said he was the one who had called. A female caregiver came over at once and led him to the recreation room.

"I'd appreciate it if you could avoid any topics that might upset her. Try to keep the conversation strictly to where her husband might be."

There were seven or eight elderly men and women there, each watching TV, talking to visitors, or sitting at a table, slowly painting pictures. As soon as Mitsuhiro saw them, it felt like time was slowing down. As if a current that had been flowing like water was now oozing as slowly as honey.

"Megumi, this is someone who works with your husband."

The nurse called out to a petite woman in a wheelchair by the TV. Her limbs were as thin as twigs, and she looked like a balloon that had slowly deflated over the years thanks to a tiny hole.

"Is something wrong with my husband?" the woman asked, bemused.

"My name is Mitsuhiro Matsunaga, ma'am. I'm a colleague of Yoshikazu Hara… We're acquaintances. I just came to say hello."

"Ohh. I see. When will he be here?"

"Well… Did he say when he would arrive?"

"He said he'd be here soon." The woman smiled. Apparently, she had just been told that. There was no trace of anxiety or loneliness.

"Okay. Do you know where he might be now?"

"Where he might be? Did he go somewhere?"

A frightened look flashed in the woman's eyes. The caregiver immediately bent down to calm her.

"No, not that. He just wants to see your husband for work."

"Work? Ohh… Are you from Tamai, perhaps?" The woman brightened up again.

The caregiver looked at Mitsuhiro, wondering if that was the case.

"I'm from Shimaoka, which has a contract with Tamai Construction."

"Ahh, yes, yes. Well, I don't know much about my husband's job. But the people at Tamai said he's a fine worker. They said he was a whiz at applying that plaster, you see? So even after he stopped working, they would sometimes come over, you know, and ask him for help."

Her relaxed tone made Mitsuhiro feel a bit impatient, but he didn't rush her, matching her tone of voice.

"Right, yes."

"But, you know, whenever they do their work, the two of them are always bothered by that smell." The woman looked around, as if she couldn't say it too loudly, and placed her hand over her mouth, eyes twinkling. "'Smells like burning bones,' they said."

Mitsuhiro felt uneasy, like this was code for something that the woman expected him to know. The caregiver gave Mitsuhiro a suspicious glance. Apparently, Mitsuhiro had seemed frightened by her words.

The woman reached out and tapped Mitsuhiro's arm lightly. "But Tamai will give you a charm, so don't you worry."

Those words reminded him that he had one in his briefcase right now... but that wasn't what he wanted to ask about. Before he knew it, his heart was pounding. He couldn't wait to get out of there.

"Where do you think Yoshikazu might be now?" Mitsuhiro asked again.

But the smile quickly disappeared from the woman's face.

"Now, who is this?" she asked her caregiver, confused by the presence of a stranger.

"He's a colleague of your husband's."

"Well, he must be here somewhere." The woman turned her head this way and that, as if he was just around the corner. "He said he'd be here soon."

She smiled at Mitsuhiro. He smiled back, then looked at the caregiver, not sure what to say next. The caregiver nodded, stood up, and gently patted the woman on the shoulder.

"Okay, thanks a lot, Megumi. I'll see this man out now."

"Yes, yes. Ask him when he's going to be here once you see him."

"Certainly. Thank you very much."

Mitsuhiro, suddenly feeling exhausted, followed the caregiver out of the recreation room and back to reception.

"She's getting worse, I'm afraid. I doubt she'll remember that conversation for longer than a few minutes. It might be better if we're there when you visit her next time."

Realizing that he likely wouldn't get much more information, Mitsuhiro handed over his business card. Pleading wouldn't do much here.

"All right. Please let me know when Mr. Hara shows up."

Mitsuhiro entered the facility's phone number into his cell phone, thanked them, and left. After visiting Tamai Construction, he was now building another contact network related to Yoshikazu Hara. He should have been satisfied with that, but he couldn't shake the feeling that this was likely a dead end.

You can't be admitted to a facility unless you have enough savings for it. One out of those two must have been at the end of their rope. Yoshio Tamai told him that they had lost their home, along with everything else.

Sensing a pang of sympathy, he returned to the station and noticed a scruffy-looking man crouched in the corner of the building. Could that be Yoshikazu Hara? He thought about it for a moment, but the face and build were all different. Mitsuhiro had looked at the photo many times by now, and he was confident he wouldn't miss Hara if they passed each other by.

Still, he couldn't help but stare at the man for a moment. He said he'd be at the facility soon, but he was lost, with nowhere to go. That was why he had to go down into that hole in the basement. The thought made anxiety suddenly well up inside Mitsuhiro. He looked away from the man.

Why was he feeling so anxious? Somewhere in his heart, he believed that unhappy people had a magnetic pull that would draw him into their misery if he got too close. The thought may not have been grounded in reality, but it unexpectedly shook Mitsuhiro as he quickly entered the station.

Even when he returned to Shibuya Station by train, he was plagued by the thought that the man he was about to meet would see right through him. He had plenty of time before the appointment, so he entered a chain soba-noodle restaurant and had an early lunch. As he slurped down the noodles, his mood gradually calmed. He was grateful for the way his mission, and his desire to be thorough with it, was keeping his personal anxiety and agitation at bay. That was one of the benefits of belonging to such a large company.

His father was always keener on running a small business, and he had never been able to enjoy the benefits of belonging to such a solid firm. He had lost everything, including his home.

As Mitsuhiro left the soba restaurant, for some reason, those two facts flashed through his mind at once. That anxiety and fear welled up from his stomach, leaving a bitter taste in his mouth.

—Don't be stupid. My father didn't lose his house. He's not living on the streets. I'm not in danger of losing my place either.

Mitsuhiro told himself that as he crossed the intersection in front of the station in the tropical heat and walked along the sound barrier bordering the construction site. Suddenly, he smelled that dry, strange odor again.

—Is it from underground here?

He remembered Yoshikazu Hara, who had been in that dark hole.

Mi-keshi... Erasing oneself. What a nasty word. You'd only make such a request of someone no one would notice was missing. Those were the sort of people Tamai Construction was chaining up in there. Mitsuhiro suddenly trusted them a lot less now.

In any case, he had to find Yoshikazu Hara, figure out what had happened to him, and determine how much of it was Mitsuhiro's own doing. And even if he couldn't get Hara into a facility, he could at least take him to see Megumi Hara. With that in mind, he entered a café, told the staff he was waiting for one other person, and sat at a table for four where he could see the entrance.

He pulled up the organization's website on his phone and double-checked the photo of its leader. Soon, the man entered the café. He was much taller than expected from the picture, and his appearance was sleek.

Dressed in leather shoes, slacks, and a blue shirt, he exuded a soft aura from head to toe.

When Mitsuhiro stood up and bowed, the man noticed him immediately and approached.

"I'm Mitsuhiro Matsunaga from Shimaoka. Thank you very much for your time today."

"My name is Tomohito Okuyama, head of Helping Hands Mutual Aid. Nice to meet you."

"Please have a seat. Would you like something cold to drink?"

"Yes, thank you."

Okuyama called the waiter and ordered the same iced coffee Mitsuhiro had. "I was a little surprised to receive a call from the company that's redeveloping Shibuya," he calmly said. His expression was soft—transparent, even. His website said he was a pastor, but he didn't seem like a very stern one. His friendly, warm smile made even Mitsuhiro, who wasn't here for religious assistance, feel that he could trust him.

"First, thank you very much for seeing me on such short notice."

"I understand you're looking for someone?"

"Yes. I just found out his name today." Mitsuhiro took his tablet out of his bag and showed the man the image of Yoshikazu Hara's face and upper body, lying in that basement hole. "This man's name is Yoshikazu Hara. Do you recognize him?"

He kept his tone deliberately polite. Tamai Construction was also searching for Yoshikazu Hara, so he wanted to secure Okuyama's cooperation here, just so his investigation covered every possible facet.

"I have, yes. He's come to help prepare meals many times, among other things. We serve lunches at our church, so I've spoken with him several times there as well. I understand that his wife is in a memory-care facility at the moment."

"Right, yes. It seems he sold off all his assets to cover the medical costs."

Okuyama sighed deeply. Whatever he was lamenting, it was heartfelt.

The drinks were brought over right then, but he didn't touch his right away. Instead, he spoke solemnly.

"It's a rising trend, sadly. In the past few years, there's been a sharp rise in the number of people who don't want to accept public welfare, even if they're far too impoverished to make ends meet."

"Oh? Why is that?"

"Politicians and the media."

Okuyama shook his head in despair.

"You mean… Ah, yes. There're a lot of news stories about how we should restructure the welfare system."

"It's not restructuring. They're just cutting it. That, and you have these fancy politicians on TV acting like receiving welfare is something to be ashamed of. As if the poor have no right to live."

"Right. I've seen people on TV like that. But does it actually have much of an impact?"

"It's everywhere now. I've never seen things like this before. It's not at all uncommon to see efforts to kick the homeless out of certain areas…and with all due respect, your company's redevelopment project has displaced a lot of them, too."

"I'm aware, yes. We have people consulting with the administration to find a solution…"

"Right, and the administration is now actively trying to turn away those in need of assistance."

"What?"

"And even worse, our requests for space to hold food banks and provide shelter on cold winter days are being refused now. These measures were at least tolerated before, and it was seen as common sense to do so. Now they're being rejected outright—while people are starving and freezing right before our eyes. Even when we go through all the proper procedures, we're told no. We can only get people to listen when we bring a lawyer into the picture. It's becoming hard to believe this is happening in Japan.

Before we knew it, this trend has spread throughout the city—throughout the country, really."

"I had no idea."

"Well, a lot of people still don't fully grasp the severity of the situation. Right now, though, public support—which was never sufficient to begin with—is crumbling like a building in an earthquake. What's more, the fact that politicians and the media are actively working to dismantle it makes me fear that we'll all be facing desperate times before long."

"I didn't think it had become that bad."

Mitsuhiro really wanted to talk about Yoshikazu Hara at the moment, but he found himself agreeing with Okuyama. Maybe he had developed some sympathy for his position.

"Every politician's number one drive is to stay in power—that hasn't changed at all. But the fact that they've started targeting vulnerable populations to that end is deeply troubling to me. And to top it off, they're blaming the weak for their own problems. The struggling people I know are the most honest and hardworking individuals I've ever met. Yet, due to family circumstances, illness, or injury, they simply can't make it work for themselves. 'What's so wrong about looking down on people like that?' some may ask. Well, it ends up encouraging the idea that it's better for people like them to do whatever it takes—even dishonest or immoral things—to make money. It's a trend that I strongly believe is starting to take hold among our younger generations as well."

"Recently... What was it? I heard about young people who are called 'half gangsters' or something strange like that."

Okuyama nodded sadly at the vague observation. "A lot of young people don't bother joining traditional gangs or organized crime syndicates. They're a lot more unpredictable as a result. I often talk with people who help young people find jobs, and they tell me that some of these new groups are becoming more organized than even the yakuza. Ultimately, this phenomenon arises from a lack of public support and that universal need among us all to fill the void when you have no dreams or hope in life. And this is true for people of all ages and genders."

Mitsuhiro solemnly nodded, trying not to be too moved by Okuyama's sincere plea. He had never been very interested in the young drifters who strutted around Tokyo like they owned the place, committing crimes and violence. At the same time, he couldn't immediately see the connection to people who got chained up in basements for money simply because they were unable or unwilling to go on welfare.

"If Mr. Hara's wife hadn't fallen ill, would he have been able to enjoy his old age? You know, get rewarded for all his hard work?"

Sensing Mitsuhiro's intention to return to the subject, Okuyama nodded slightly and smiled. "That may be true. But I think Mr. Hara was well aware of his situation. He just refused to accept welfare. I remember him saying that there was only one duty left for people like him. He didn't discuss his work in detail with me, but..."

"What was that duty?"

Okuyama seemed depressed just saying it. "'To become a sacrifice for the sake of society and humanity.' His words."

6

Mitsuhiro was so surprised by this that he felt himself talking faster.

"Mr. Hara himself said that? That he'd become a sacrifice?"

"Yes. Does that ring a bell?"

Okuyama looked back at him suspiciously.

"No, not really..."

Mitsuhiro hesitated, wondering if he should mention Tamai Construction. But judging from Okuyama's expression, he was unaware of the weird custom the term *sacrifice* suggested. As an IR employee, Mitsuhiro couldn't possibly tell a third party about Yoshikazu Hara being chained up in the East Wing basement. Mitsuhiro couldn't even guess how much that could damage the company.

"You know, I...I just thought it was an odd turn of phrase."

"So did I. I figured he was just being sarcastic about the state of the world and everything, but…is there something I should be concerned about?"

Okuyama prodded him again. Mitsuhiro could tell he was an observant man who wouldn't miss even the slightest change in tone or expression. It was a skill he'd likely gained dealing with as many people as he did each day. He wanted to ask Okuyama what he thought about the people at Tamai Construction, but that seemed like too much of a hornet's nest.

"The other day, Yoshikazu Hara was found at one of our construction sites. I'm looking for him because I've been assigned to investigate how he got in and out."

"You mean he broke in?"

"That's part of the investigation."

"Something happened at that site, didn't it?"

Arson, Mitsuhiro's mind immediately suggested. But he couldn't say that out loud.

"Some materials were damaged. And, no, I don't think it was Mr. Hara at this point, but he was in the same area, so we need to talk to him. The problem is that, like his wife, he seems to be showing symptoms of dementia…"

"Right. Mr. Hara asked me for advice about that, but we couldn't find a facility that would accept him, and eventually he stopped showing up to my parish. I know that he has a cell phone, but we haven't been able to reach him. We contacted the police about it, but they brushed us off, pretty much."

Okuyama quietly shook his head as he spoke. He was clearly worried, but he seemed to trust that the methodical approach would work best here, rather than dwelling on matters unnecessarily. That was the kind of calm strength he exhibited.

As Mitsuhiro watched Okuyama finally take a sip of his iced coffee, he thought to himself how he could never do this man's job. Taking care of someone he had no connection with was unimaginable to him, and he could never see himself dealing with problems like these so calmly, especially if he felt the same rage as Okuyama against the injustices of society.

"Do you think Mr. Hara's condition is worsening? Could he be wandering the streets right now?"

"That's likely the case, I'm afraid. I've been checking common gathering places for the unhoused around here, along with Tokyo's main support center. I also checked his former house and the facility where his wife is staying."

"If it's not too much trouble, could you give me the addresses of those places?"

Okuyama readily provided the information.

They agreed to contact each other if Yoshikazu Hara was found, and that was the end of their business. Still, they continued to chat for a while longer. Okuyama had an impressive strength of character, and he was kind enough to offer some advice for the search, like how to approach the unhoused and what to do if things got violent.

Okuyama left first, and Mitsuhiro paid the bill and left soon after. The pleasant air-conditioning made it possible for him to comfortably walk on the asphalt without sweating for a bit, despite the boiling heat. He decided to look around the nearby parks before returning to the office, so he soon took off his jacket, slung it over his shoulder, and unbuttoned his shirt.

—It's been a hot one this year.

He recalled the TV news deeming it an "unprecedented rise" in temperatures, with heat records being destroyed worldwide.

As he climbed the hill, he passed an unusual-looking man holding an umbrella, despite the lack of rain.

"Oh, a sun umbrella?" he muttered, surprised. The idea of a man sporting one of those was bizarre to him, but given the intensity of the sun right now, maybe that was the smart thing to do. A decade or so ago, when the Ministry of the Environment announced their "Cool Biz" campaign—reducing air-conditioning usage, encouraging looser office dress codes in the summer, that sort of thing—he thought it was just a publicity stunt. But before he knew it, even at Shimaoka, they were allowed to wear short-sleeved shirts and go tieless from June to the end of September. It really did help a lot.

Mitsuhiro used to think that climate change and global warming were a bunch of nonsense, but surrounded by all this unusual heat, he was starting to think they might actually be true.

—Hope the guy didn't get heatstroke.

He imagined Yoshikazu Hara lying motionless in a corner of some street, unable to get help, and felt an odd pang of sadness.

—Sacrificing himself for the greater good.

If he took Okuyama at his word, maybe that was what Hara had done already. Something had gone missing in society, and this lack of support was just like being trapped in a pitch-black inescapable hole.

With that thought in mind, he searched a nearby park for Yoshikazu Hara but failed to find him. Okuyama had advised him not to stare or peek into the tents made of plastic sheets, so he kept his distance and only peered briefly at them. For now, that was enough.

Maybe it was the heat, or maybe they'd just decided today was a good day for it, but five or six people had come out of their tents and were sitting in the shade, chatting about something. Mitsuhiro clearly remembered Yoshikazu Hara's face, and he could say with certainty that the man wasn't there. Mitsuhiro considered approaching the group, but it was hard to tell how much time it would take to ask everyone whether they knew him. Okuyama had told him that the most important thing was to be as thorough as possible with each of them, but Mitsuhiro didn't want to go peppering everyone with questions and making them suspicious. Some of the more sensitive ones might think he was going to report them to the police or subject them to verbal or physical abuse.

For the time being, he decided to check the locations of the local homeless hangouts, turning his mind toward the people he knew existed but had never considered part of his reality. He needed to consult with his boss about how to approach them anyway, as well as talk things over with the employees responsible for their eviction. If Mitsuhiro got into a dispute with these people or their support groups, leading to more drama on Twitter or elsewhere, the whole purpose of this investigation would be cast into question.

Mitsuhiro took out his phone as he climbed up a sloping street and checked the Twitter user's posts. The user still called himself "Mole Unit-01," and his profile discussing his civil engineering job hadn't changed. A few hours ago, he had posted:

I was cursed thanks to my shitty job at the East Wing

It was just another text tweet, or more like someone talking to himself. The problem was that he was attacking the East Wing in the process.

—He could at least say where he is, or what he's doing, or something.

He put his phone away angrily.

Returning to his company building, he basked in the chilly lobby for a moment, then put on his jacket and buttoned his shirt. When he got on the elevator and went up to his floor, he was spotted by Takenaka, who was talking to someone from another department in the hallway.

"We'll talk later," he told his conversation partner, and they bowed slightly to each other before Takenaka approached Mitsuhiro and pointed to the nearby meeting space.

"Thanks for doing all that. We'll talk in there."

"Was that guy from Corporate Planning?"

"Yeah. I have to compare our financial results with our shareholder materials by the end of this week."

In these modern times, even with short-term financials like this, you had to show shareholders that the company was being well managed and its future was looking up. Major redevelopment projects requiring more than ten years to complete often appeared to be suffering losses in the short term, so companies frequently needed to be creative with the information disclosed to shareholders.

"The government's still hell-bent on favoring shareholders in their policies, as always," Takenaka said emphatically as he sat down on a chair in the meeting space. "We have to take all possible measures to protect the company."

The greater the number of investors seeking immediate profit, the more pressure there was to show those profits in the quarterly results. Even essential projects for the medium- to long-term future of the company could be rejected by them, and if that happened, the company would lose any path to forward growth. Mitsuhiro would have preferred it if his job involved collecting fun, positive information right now, but under the current circumstances, he was tasked with minimizing the impact of a scandal that could have adverse effects on their stock price.

"I'm working to resolve the current situation as quickly as possible," Mitsuhiro said, determined to get it over with.

"Right. Once the scope of this investigation narrows a bit, I'm sure we'll begin to see how we can resolve this."

However, Takenaka already seemed to be anticipating a long investigation process. A swift response was necessary, but he wasn't reckless enough to want to resolve this issue at any cost. They could quickly silence everyone involved, yes, but that would just leave more problems for the future.

"I'm sure," Mitsuhiro said with some remorse. "At this point, though, the scope's still expanding."

"Did you establish any contacts today?"

"Yes. I reached out to Tamai Construction, his wife's care facility, and the head of the mutual-aid association that he often worked with. I didn't question anyone about the Twitter poster."

"That's okay. Better to cast a wide net at first."

"Of course. But if we do, support groups and such might not be good enough. We may need to reach out to the homeless living in the area."

Takenaka seemed to have considered that point as well. He nodded, looking conflicted. "If Yoshikazu Hara and the Twitter poster remain missing, we may need to do that."

"Can we ask Twitter or something for the user's information?"

"I consulted with Legal, but they said information disclosure requests usually take a while. The way privacy protections work, even the police have trouble obtaining phone numbers."

"And if he has no fixed address, we're gonna have to just track him down ourselves..."

"I know that Chief Kento Sugawara always attends the eviction briefings. He'd know all the administrative officials involved, along with the heads of all the relevant support groups. He knows a lot about our company's internal workings, too. I'll contact him to see if he can advise us."

"Thank you."

Mitsuhiro wanted to achieve results on his own and get rewarded for his efforts, but getting these higher-ups involved was also a relief.

"So where are you going to look?" Takenaka asked.

Mitsuhiro replied that he'd search online for the locations Okuyama had given him, along with other sites and organizations involved with them, and create a master list.

"That could be dozens of places if you're not careful. It's hard if he's got no fixed address. I want you to be careful with the locations you select. We need to cast a wide net, but I'd advise against handing out cards to everyone you meet."

Such behavior, Takenaka explained, could spread the impression that there were big problems at the construction site.

Mitsuhiro saw the value in being prudent here as well, so he replied, "Yes, sir," before asking another question. "Do you think I'd get permission to borrow a company car?"

Takenaka groaned, but his voice and expression told Mitsuhiro that it'd probably be okay.

"Yeah, in this heat, pounding the pavement's way too inefficient. We're dealing with a potential Alzheimer's patient, and we'll probably have to move him around after we find him… I'll talk to Finance about this. If you can send me your report at this stage, I'll decide how much information to share. We have to be supremely cautious with this case. I know I don't need to remind you, but be very careful not to mention this to anyone in other departments."

"There's the arson, too," Mitsuhiro said softly.

Takenaka tightened his lips and nodded. "I'll consult with upper management to decide how to respond, including what we'll do if the police leak anything. Meanwhile, I want you to conduct a thorough investigation. Speed is important, but don't try to rush it before the shareholders' meeting rehearsal. We may see more incidents like this in the future, so treat this as an opportunity to polish your investigation and response skills."

Even Takenaka was keenly aware that this was an era where individuals could attack companies with nothing but a smartphone.

"Right," Mitsuhiro replied, and then he returned to his desk and quickly prepared a summary report. But he hesitated to include the words Yoshikazu Hara had reportedly said.

"Become a sacrifice for the sake of society and humanity."

Metaphor or not, it was disturbing. If whoever received this report read that quote after learning about "duties" carried out by Tamai Construction, wouldn't they get the impression that Shimaoka was ordering Tamai to perform these outdated, inhumane rituals? Certainly, if Mitsuhiro read something like this, he'd be shocked at the absurdity of it. Writing it made Mitsuhiro wonder if it would damage his own reputation.

Still, he decided that he should leave that judgment call to Takenaka, so he wrote down everything he'd experienced and sent it in an internal email. Many of the older employees still liked to be given printed copies; Takenaka, on the other hand, preferred to retain all documents as images or PDFs instead. For an office employee, it went without saying which type of boss was easier to work for.

After finishing the report, he used the map app on his tablet to create a screenshot of the area from Shibuya to Shinagawa. Between this and the cameras on his devices, it was amazing how much more efficient his work had become.

He then used some editing software to add marks to the map image. These were the locations where he might be able to find Yoshikazu Hara and the Twitter poster in the future. He also marked out the approximate route for driving around the area and sent the image to his own cell phone.

After confirming that it had been received on his phone, he checked Twitter again. There was a new post on the account.

No matter where I sleep, I smell fire. I'm completely cursed now. Please don't let me die in these flames.

* * *

The image of his daughter in his dream suddenly came back to mind, and his hair stood on end.

Feeling his heart beating wildly, he told himself to calm down. But suddenly, his throat tightened as he smelled that strange dry odor again. He looked around frantically, wondering if anyone else had noticed, but no one else seemed to notice what was in the air.

Mitsuhiro took several surreptitious deep breaths and waited silently until the fear subsided. *Now I'm having episodes*, he thought, regaining his composure. It was like accidentally hitting the funny bone on his elbow, the way the fear had overwhelmed him out of nowhere.

This time, the trigger for it was pretty clear, which only strengthened his resentment toward the poster. It was thanks to this guy's tweets that he'd ended up deep in the bowels of the East Wing in the first place. Here was a guy being paid to do a job, and just because he had some hard luck, he was attacking a project involving thousands of people. It was ridiculous.

The anger pushed his fear further aside as he closed the Twitter app. Then he noticed that he had a message from Takenaka. He'd be allowed to use a company car starting tomorrow. He appreciated that his boss always worked so fast.

Mitsuhiro sent a thankful reply and stated that he'd continue his investigation now that he'd finished his report. Then he made several appointments—with nonprofit groups, volunteer organizations, government-support centers, and Chief Sugawara—packed his belongings, and left his desk.

Outside, the afternoon sun was beating down as intensely as ever. He quickly took off his jacket, slung it over his shoulder, unbuttoned the collar of his shirt, and walked down the hill.

He checked the main homeless gathering places around Shibuya Station. He didn't see Yoshikazu Hara, nor anyone who appeared to be posting tweets at the moment.

Compared to when he first did these checks, though, he was now able to recognize each person individually by their distinctive features. A slimy-looking man stood alone, holding a Rubik's Cube in front of him and smiling blankly, as if he had finally managed to solve it after much effort. It wasn't at all solved, however, with a rainbow of colors on each side. Another man clutched a convenience-store bag, staring intently into the sky. His eyes, which seemed to be in a realm beyond anger and disappointment, were moist with tears.

Several hoodies that probably belonged to young people were hanging on the fence surrounding the columns supporting a pedestrian bridge. Okuyama told him that recently more teens were living on the streets to escape domestic violence. Maybe they were sheltering under the bridge to avoid the wind and rain.

Most of the homeless people he saw on the streets were men. It was more dangerous for women, so they preferred to hide out and sleep on the roofs of buildings at night.

Mitsuhiro also stopped by a location where a camp had been evicted not long ago, but even there, he saw a homeless-looking elderly man standing alone in a daze. He seemed unable to believe the only place he had to live had just vanished without a trace. It occurred to Mitsuhiro that the place might have burned down in a fire, but he quickly dismissed the thought—he didn't want to trigger that fear again—and walked away.

But something was still pursuing him in his mind. Images of burning houses flashed through his head. His father stood trembling, illuminated by the flames. And they were standing on top of countless victims of fires that had built up over hundreds of years. When would it be their turn?

—This is ridiculous.

He had never experienced a fire. Neither had any of his friends or acquaintances. Mitsuhiro himself was always careful with fire; he'd opted for a condo with all electric appliances and no gas connections at all, because of the fire risk in case of earthquakes or the like. But the strange, unsettling feeling that his own home could end up in ashes followed him all the way to the rail station. Before entering the ticket gate, he took a plastic bottle out of his bag, drank the remaining third of its contents, and threw it away. It calmed him down considerably.

On the packed train ride home, he braced himself for the possibility of another panic attack, but he managed to make it safely back to his condo building. But when he got out of the elevator on the fourth floor and stepped into the corridor, he was startled by an utterly bizarre sight.

The floor of the elevator hall was covered in a massive number of white footprints. They varied in size, as if dozens of adults and children had come up here together, stepped out of the elevator barefoot, and stomped through the hallway, leaving behind traces of chalky white powder.

As he stood there in a daze, the smell gradually wafted toward him. It was a dry sort of smell, reminiscent of a crematorium. Mitsuhiro hugged his bag to his chest, covering his mouth and nose with both hands. He felt like the dry air was burning his throat.

Shaking from the shock, he dragged his feet along, adding his own footprints to the cluster as he staggered out into the hallway. Under the fluorescent lights, they looked like patterns floating on the cream-colored floor. The multitude of footprints overlapped each other, rushing straight toward the entrance of his apartment.

Halfway down the corridor, Mitsuhiro's body began to shake. He froze, covering his lips with both hands, his wide eyes stinging and watering up from the dryness. He was in such a state of confusion that he didn't immediately recognize his own terror for what it was.

—*What is this? What the hell is happening? Is this some kind of malicious prank? Did someone who knows about the investigation do this to harass me?*

He tried desperately to stay calm and consider the situation rationally, but his mind was already on the verge of panic and urging him to scream.

No matter where I sleep, I smell fire. I'm completely cursed now. Please don't let me die in these flames.

Just as he remembered one of the posts, he suddenly heard screams—Miyoko and Sae.

Chapter 3 With My Father

1

Mitsuhiro stiffened, as if lightning was running across his body. He hurriedly opened his bag, took out the key, and rushed to the front door, stepping all over the footprints.

From behind the front door, he heard Miyoko shouting "Sae!" The blood drained from his face as he inserted the key into the door handle and unlocked it.

The moment he pulled out the key and opened the door, the air behind him violently rushed past. He felt like something had entered the room with him, but he was in no state to think about it. Smoke was slowly drifting from the ceiling in the corner of the front foyer.

"Miyoko! Sae! What's going on?"

Mitsuhiro threw down his bag and ran in, still in his shoes.

The smoke was coming from the kitchen. Miyoko was trying to put out a fire inside the open microwave with a wet towel while Sae stood behind her, shoulders hunched.

Mitsuhiro turned around and ran back, grabbing the fire extinguisher from the bottom of the shoe rack. Fortunately, by the time he got there, the fire was already out.

Miyoko coughed and turned the exhaust fan all the way up. As it loudly sucked the smoke away, Mitsuhiro covered his mouth and placed the fire extinguisher on the floor.

"What did you put in the microwave?" he asked Miyoko, who was blinking her apparently irritated eyes.

"It was Sae, but she didn't mean to…"

Miyoko stopped talking, coughed, and backed away from Sae, who was crouching down to escape the smoke. Mitsuhiro frowned and picked up the towel that had been thrown into the microwave. Beneath it was a set of burnt tinfoil containers—probably the au gratin potatoes they had in the freezer. There were three of them stacked on top of each other. They were meant to be heated in an oven, or a toaster oven at least, but instead she'd just put the whole bundle in the microwave.

"You can't *do* that!" he reflexively shouted. "You'll burn the whole place down!"

He was taken aback by the intensity of his anger, while Sae turned pale and stared at him, shaking slightly.

"Don't yell at her. I should have noticed it."

Miyoko hugged Sae around her shoulders. Mitsuhiro's anger quickly subsided, replaced by regret and self-loathing. He realized that his palpitations and thirst were making him prone to losing his temper.

"I'm sorry, Sae. That was too much."

Mitsuhiro bent down. Sae pouted, looked at the floor, and began to cry.

"A fire is really dangerous, okay? I was scared, too, so I accidentally shouted at you. I'm sorry."

"It's all right, Sae. Mommy and Daddy aren't angry at you anymore."

"But I pushed the button," Sae muttered in a small voice, her head bowed.

"If you put tinfoil in the microwave like that—"

"I pushed it! I pushed it!"

Mitsuhiro felt his anger rising again. "All right. One minute, okay? Daddy's thirsty."

He took a mug from the shelf, trying to calm himself down. He filled it up to the top, then drank it all in one go. He was thirstier than he thought, so he had some more.

"I want some, too," Miyoko said, supporting her large belly with her hands, so Mitsuhiro poured some water into the mug he was holding and handed it to her. While Miyoko drank it down, Mitsuhiro stroked his sobbing daughter's shoulder.

"Sae, does your throat hurt at all from the smoke?"

"I pushed the button..." Sae shook her head, repeating herself.

"Yes, but you can't put tinfoil in the microwave."

"Mommy said to push it."

It finally dawned on Mitsuhiro what his daughter meant.

"Does she mean the oven function?" he asked Miyoko. Indeed, the multi-function microwave they purchased for their condo had a conventional-oven mode as well. Mitsuhiro didn't use it all that often, so he had forgotten about it, but that mode wouldn't have set the metal on fire.

"I thought we had it on. I must have not been paying attention."

"Ahh, okay... I'm sorry about that, Sae."

Sae sniffled and hugged her mother.

"Here, Sae, drink some water."

As Miyoko comforted Sae and gave her a cup of water, Mitsuhiro checked that the burnt trays inside the microwave had cooled down enough and threw them away in the trash, along with the partially burned towel.

"I don't think it's broken..."

But as soon as he peered inside the microwave, a pungent odor assaulted his nostrils, and he recoiled. The stench of a crematorium.

No, that's ridiculous. It's just the smell of burnt tinfoil. He quickly dismissed the thought, grabbed some paper towels, dampened them with water, and wiped the inside of the microwave.

White powdery residue was clinging to the turntable and inner walls. Some of the aluminum had burned up and turned into ash. That's what he told himself as he wiped away the powder, but that same powder was faintly covering the buttons and dials on the outside of the microwave. Why was it on the outside, too? Well, the lids were open, right? The ash must've blown out with the fire. There was no other explanation.

"If the smell doesn't go away, maybe I should just buy a new one," he muttered to himself, quickly wiping down the outside of the microwave with the paper towels and throwing them in the trash. Then he suddenly remembered the trail of footprints leading to his door. His heart skipped a beat. An unusual sense of anxiety swarmed over him. He pulled the trash bag out of the bin, roughly tying it up.

"I'm gonna take this out."

"Oh, Daddy! You're still wearing shoes!" Sae, who had finally calmed down, pointed at Mitsuhiro's feet.

"Hey, you left footprints. Make sure to clean the floor, too." Miyoko smiled and stroked Sae's head.

Sae suddenly smiled. "Yeah, Daddy. You gotta clean the footprints."

"Okay, okay."

Mitsuhiro smiled back at them, took off his shoes, and realized that he was desperately trying to suppress the urge to clean them immediately.

He had to wipe those footprints away. If he left them, there'd just be more and more. Driven by this urgent thought, he took his shoes and a trash bag and headed for the front door. No, no, he didn't want to see them. He didn't want to touch those bizarre footprints. A childish voice cried out from somewhere in his head, but he forced it down with all his might.

In his condo, there was now one set of white footprints here and there. They were his. His bag and house keys were still lying on the floor.

Mitsuhiro left his shoes and trash bag at the front door, picked up his keys, put them in his pants pocket, and took his bag to the bathroom. He placed it on the floor, took out his jacket, hung it on the edge of the washing machine, and rolled up the sleeves of his shirt. Suddenly, he noticed his tense face reflected in the mirror above the sink. He looked away. He didn't want to see the glimmer of fear in the depths of his eyes.

Opting against using a rag, he instead grabbed the floor wiper and attached an adhesive sheet to it. This way, he wouldn't have to touch that white substance directly.

Quickly, he wiped the dust from the kitchen to the hallway. Miyoko and Sae were preparing dinner now, as if nothing had happened.

After he was done with that, he put on his shoes and wondered if he should wipe up the common hallway as well. The floor out there had a non-slip surface, which meant the floor wiper might not work on it, but he had no choice but to try. He had been living in apartments like this long enough that he no longer even owned a broom or dustpan.

As soon as he faced the front door, which had closed itself automatically, his heart began to race again. What were all those footprints out there? It was too elaborate to be a prank. His mind desperately sought some kind of rational explanation as dread crept into his heart. Maybe someone from Tamai Construction was responsible. They probably sensed that Mitsuhiro was suspicious of them, so they tried to frighten him and make their story sound more plausible. After all, they were the kind of people who'd do anything to achieve their goals.

For the time being, that reasoning was enough to suppress his fear. Having this happen right at his doorstep was beyond unpleasant, though. If he told Miyoko, she might become so afraid that she'd want to move out, but he'd cross that bridge when he got to it. First, he had to build a logical explanation credible enough to soothe his own mind.

His heart was insisting to him that he didn't want to go out the front door, but another concern now pushed that thought aside. What if people thought his family had tracked footprints all over the hallways? The other residents might complain, and the manager would definitely reprimand them over it. He had to clean it up quickly—or "purify" it, borrowing a phrase from Tamai Construction.

Mitsuhiro gripped the handle of the floor wiper again and opened the door with a new determination. He was afraid someone from Tamai Construction might be there, but the coast was clear. Completely clear. In fact, there was nothing to wipe up at all. As if it had all been neatly blown away by the wind during that fracas in the kitchen, there wasn't a single footprint anywhere in the entire hallway.

Was it all just a mirage? Had he convinced himself he'd seen something that wasn't there, because of the lighting or something? Did his assailants from

Tamai Construction decide they'd given him enough of a fright and cleaned it all up before leaving? Or did the footprints themselves have a will of their own and just walk off somewhere?

Whatever the case, there were still a lot of questions to pursue, but he felt a rush of relief. Nothing more needed to be done. Mitsuhiro placed the wiper on the floor, leaned on it like a cane, hung his head, and took a deep breath.

"What on earth *was* all that?"

He raised his head, leaned the floor wiper against the wall of his front door, picked up the trash bag, and headed for the trash drop-off on this floor.

Or maybe they went into his home?

The thought suddenly crossed his mind. But Mitsuhiro's more rational side decided that he couldn't remain in a state of constant fear all night, so he instantly shut out the thought and ordered himself never to consider it again.

Thanks to that, by the time he returned from the trash room, he felt not only relieved but even a bit joyful. He had tackled a problem, and now it was over.

2

"You know, you didn't have to get so angry earlier. You scared me, too."

They had finished eating and bathing and putting Sae to bed, and Miyoko was still upset with Mitsuhiro about earlier.

"I said I'm sorry," Mitsuhiro said, sipping some sparkling water in the dining room. He was getting fed up with Miyoko's repeated lecturing, but Miyoko seemed to be equally frustrated by not being taken seriously.

He wanted to lay his sheaf of documents out on the table right now, but not while Miyoko was still in a bad mood. Normally, she'd enjoy the kinds of challenges Mitsuhiro was wrangling with right now, as she had the other night…but when she wasn't, she'd start nagging him about "bringing his work home" and so on.

The government had recently approved the so-called Zero Overtime Pay

Bill, something proposed by the business community. To be honest, Mitsuhiro didn't know if it was a good thing or not.

Even before the bill was passed, Shimaoka had been working to eliminate overtime, and thanks to that, Mitsuhiro usually left work at five PM sharp each day. But the fact remained that this was such a radical departure from their previous MO that not even the department heads and division managers really knew how to react. The talking-head experts on TV said that the bill would eliminate not only overtime pay but also potentially any limits to the number of working hours. The big move had caused chaos within the IR team for a while, too. Even Mitsuhiro could see that if this resulted in a big drop in salary, it could affect their ability to cover their mortgage, even with both him and his wife working full-time.

However, the management team, including the chairman and his board, repeatedly assured employees that there would be no pay cuts as a result of this, which helped assuage some of the concerns. The loss of overtime pay, they said, would be compensated in the form of bonuses, benefits, and after-hours training.

But measures like these were something only a huge company like Shimaoka could afford, and it was all bound to shake out differently from department to department, so the confusion was likely to continue for some time.

"Hey, is something bothering you? Is that why you're so tensed up?"

Miyoko's question only served to further irritate Mitsuhiro. He thought he was free of worries now, but at this rate, she'd make him talk about all the weird stuff he'd seen—those countless footprints. Even though they were gone now. As if they'd never been.

"Am I tensed up?"

"Yes, you've been like this all day. You haven't been listening to me. Don't you realize Sae is scared you're going to scream at her again?"

"No… I didn't. Maybe I'm just tired."

"Really? Are you sure you're not worried about anything?"

Miyoko's genuine concern was evident. Mitsuhiro smiled, not wanting her anxiety to rub off on him. He wished she would just go to bed already.

"Did you have a problem with the contractors over that underground ritual hall?"

"No, not that."

Mitsuhiro thought about discussing Tamai Construction's strange behavior and what he had seen in his tour of that site. But he decided against it because he didn't think he could make it sound like something to laugh off. This wasn't funny at all, in fact. He was facing the possibility of being exposed to some kind of...*thing* because of what he did in the East Wing basement.

Miyoko frowned. It was half directed at Mitsuhiro and half at the kitchen.

"Ugh, it *still* smells weird. How many times do I have to wipe it down?"

She was talking about the microwave. Mitsuhiro didn't really notice it anymore, that weird odor that floated in with the dry air. He didn't know if it had faded or if he was starting to become numb to it.

Mitsuhiro stood up and turned on the kitchen exhaust fan again.

"We can buy a new microwave, okay? You should calm down a little, too. I'm just kind of tired. I'm sorry if I'm being irritable..."

Suddenly, Mitsuhiro was startled by a small figure in the dark hallway.

"Ah... Sae?"

Miyoko stood up from the dining room table.

"Oh, is she awake?"

Before Mitsuhiro could answer, Sae came into the kitchen, rubbing her sleepy eyes.

"I want some water," she muttered as she passed Mitsuhiro and headed for the sink. Ignoring Miyoko, who had stood up to fetch a cup, she climbed up on her stool and turned on the faucet with the water purifier attached to it. She was trying to drink directly from it.

Just like in the dream.

Mitsuhiro instinctively reached out and grabbed Sae's shoulder to stop her. In his mind, he imagined himself rushing to get the fire extinguisher.

No matter where I sleep, I smell fire. I'm completely cursed now. Please don't let me die in these flames.

* * *

Something terrible was about to happen, just like in that post.

"What's wrong, Sae?" said Miyoko. "You gotta use a cup."

Sae took the cup from her mother. Mitsuhiro let go of her and stared intently as she held it under the stream. He could feel his heart savagely beating. His mind was ordering him to go get the fire extinguisher at once, but he couldn't take his eyes off his daughter.

Miyoko turned off the tap, looked up, and frowned in surprise when she noticed Mitsuhiro.

"What's wrong? What is it?"

Sae gulped down the water.

Then she suddenly clutched her throat, reared back, and fell off the stool.

She collapsed onto the floor, and the sound followed the loud clatter of a glass dropping into the sink. Miyoko screamed.

"Sae?!"

Miyoko hurriedly tried to lift Sae up, and Mitsuhiro also jumped in to help. But Sae recoiled violently, scratching at her throat with both hands and kicking her legs wildly.

"What's wrong? You can't breathe? Sae!"

Miyoko called out to her, but Sae kept struggling and making thin, wheezing sounds.

"I'll call an ambulance!"

Mitsuhiro jumped over to the dining room and grabbed his phone from the table. He dialed 119, held the phone to his ear, and waited for a response, his heart pounding so wildly that he felt like it'd burst out of his chest.

"Tokyo Fire Department. Is this a fire or medical emergency?"

"M-medical! My daughter's..."

"Keep calm and tell me your location."

Mitsuhiro quickly gave the address.

"What's happening?"

"M-my daughter was drinking water and suddenly collapsed. She's scratching at her throat, and she can't breathe."

"Has this ever happened to her before?"

"No, it's the first time."

"Any serious illness in the past?"

"No."

"Does she have a regular doctor?"

"Yes, a GP and a dentist in the neighborhood."

"Have they treated her for anything?"

"Just things like colds and dental work."

"Okay. Can you give me your full name and the full name of your daughter?"

"My name is Mitsuhiro Matsunaga. My daughter is Sae Matsunaga."

"Please give me the number you're calling from."

Mitsuhiro answered the questions, trying to resist the urge to shout at them to get their asses over here. He knew just standing there watching Sae struggle in the kitchen and Miyoko frantically call out to her would accomplish nothing, so he paused to put on a hoodie. With his phone still pressed to his ear, he stuffed his wallet and keys into its pockets.

"An ambulance is on its way now. Please have someone go outside to meet them. When the ambulance arrives, wave to them and guide them into your home. If anything changes with her condition in the meantime, please let them know."

"All right." Mitsuhiro ended the call. "The ambulance is coming. I'll go outside and wait for them."

"I'll go too."

"You should watch Sae. I'll guide the paramedics in."

"She'll be in the ambulance faster if we take her with us."

"I don't know if we should move her around…"

But Miyoko was trying to pick Sae up anyway, so Mitsuhiro hurriedly took her place. Following the emergency evacuation training he had received at work, he held her sideways, ensuring she could breathe more easily. He tilted her head back and bent her legs and upper body into a C shape, holding her tightly so she wouldn't fall, and rushed to the front door with Miyoko.

Twisting his feet into his shoes, he went out through the door that Miyoko opened for him.

While Miyoko locked the front door with her key, Mitsuhiro hurried down the hallway toward the elevator lobby.

"You'll be in an ambulance soon, Sae. Hang in there."

He spoke to her, but all he could hear was the sound of her desperately trying to breathe—*huff, huff, huff, huff.* Nothing could be more terrifying. He could say with absolute certainty that it was the worst experience of his life, hoping that his daughter would just continue to breathe for him.

He had just pressed the elevator button with his elbow when Miyoko caught up with him. The doors opened immediately, and both parents got in, still trying to soothe Sae as they went down to the first floor. Even then, the smell lingered in his nose, but Mitsuhiro was in no state to pay much mind to it.

They left the lobby of the building and waited for the ambulance in the stifling air, shivering as if they were about to freeze in the cold. Once they heard the siren, Mitsuhiro's eyes filled with tears.

"The ambulance is here, Sae! There it is!"

The sound grew louder and louder, and then the ambulance appeared from around the corner with its lights flashing. Miyoko supported her large belly with one hand and waved the other wildly.

The ambulance stopped, and two paramedics got out with a stretcher and rushed over.

"I'm Mitsuhiro Matsunaga. This is my daughter, Sae Matsunaga."

"Okay, we'll take her."

The two paramedics laid Sae on the stretcher and immediately carried her into the ambulance.

"Are you riding along?"

Mitsuhiro and Miyoko nodded without hesitation.

Several residents of the building came out to see what was happening, while passersby stopped and looked in their direction. Mitsuhiro helped Miyoko into the ambulance, then quickly climbed in after her.

3

"She was just dehydrated…?"

Mitsuhiro sat next to Miyoko, staring blankly and repeating the doctor's words.

It took nearly an hour to complete Sae's exam, and during that time, the two of them had no choice but to wait, holding hands on a bench in the largely empty lobby.

"That's right," the doctor said, smiling reassuringly at the two of them. "Once the IV is finished up, you can go home. Just to be on the safe side, I'll prescribe some medication to prevent throat spasms and coughing."

"It's not some kind of disease, then?" Miyoko asked, wanting to be sure.

"Well, the difficulty breathing caused by drinking water is one telltale sign of rabies, which would be *really* dangerous, but that's clearly not the case here."

"Rabies? Isn't that serious?"

"It is, but rabies has been wholly eradicated from Japan since the 1950s. There's no way she could have gotten that unless she was bitten by an unvaccinated animal outside of the country, so please don't worry about that at all. Something probably caused her airway to narrow so that she couldn't breathe for a while, but it fixed itself without any treatment."

Sure enough, within a few minutes of being transported, Sae stopped scratching at her throat, and her breathing returned to normal. It was as if the farther she was from home, the more she recovered. Mitsuhiro thought it was because of the oxygen mask they put on her, but the doctor said she had recovered naturally.

"Why would something like this happen?" Mitsuhiro asked.

The doctor smiled, albeit somewhat awkwardly. "Sometimes, people experience sudden tightness and difficulty breathing due to a cold, sleep apnea, or irritation following an endoscopy. It's a spasm of the pharynx that makes it harder to breathe, but it returns to normal in just a few minutes at most."

"You don't think it's asthma?" Miyoko countered.

The doctor confidently returned her gaze. "Well, asthma-related breathing difficulties are caused by the bronchial tubes becoming inflamed and sensitive, which makes them prone to blockage. We could perform a bronchoscopy at a later date, but..."

"Are there any other tests you can do? Because I'd really like to know if...you know, there's something hidden beneath the surface here, like rabies..."

"There's no way to test for rabies before symptoms present, unfortunately."

"But there's nothing else you could test for?"

The doctor hesitated, judging whether to call it pointless, but then bowed to Miyoko's wishes and ordered a test of Sae's blood and saliva, just to be sure. A bronchoscopy would require fasting for several hours and anesthesia, and other further examinations, such as spinal-fluid or corneal tests, would cause considerable pain to the patient, so the doctor strongly advised against rushing into anything. That seemed to be enough for Miyoko.

"It's been very hot this year, too. Be careful not to let her get dehydrated or heat stroke. Make sure she stays cool and drinks plenty of fluids."

This was the doctor's gentle way of reminding them not to be negligent, Mitsuhiro supposed.

After leaving the examination room, Mitsuhiro went to the night window at the pharmacy outside the hospital and picked up the prescribed medication. When he returned, Miyoko was sitting in a chair next to Sae, who was sleeping with the IV still in her arm. She was leaning against the wall with her hands wrapped around her large belly and her eyes closed.

Mitsuhiro sat down next to her, careful not to wake anyone up, and gazed at Sae as she slept, breathing softly. As he waited for the prescription to be filled, he used his phone to search for the assorted diseases that could cause breathing difficulties. Among them was rabies, also known as hydrophobia, because the stimulus of drinking water caused the throat to close up in patients, eventually leading to a fear of all fluids.

—That's no joke. I could never let Sae get that.

Mitsuhiro felt relieved seeing his daughter sleeping peacefully. In her life so far, Sae had received more than ten different vaccines, including the BCG vaccine for tuberculosis. They had gone overseas for vacations a few times, and he always made sure Sae was current on her vaccinations beforehand.

But that really wasn't the issue. He closed his eyes next to Miyoko, finally starting to admit it to himself. He was tired of straining every fiber of his being in the effort to deny it. He tried to recall how Sae had behaved after dinner. There was no reason for her to be dehydrated today. She'd had a drink of water after her bath, and the air conditioner in her room was humming along as usual.

No, it started when he saw those first footprints outside the elevator. Something was slowly progressing, and it wasn't good. At first, it was just this small thing that had followed him into his home. Now it was like a torrent rushing in.

"Don't worry."

In his half-dreaming state, he remembered someone saying that to him.

"Tamai will give you a charm, so don't you worry."

A woman with dementia had told him that. Megumi Hara, the wife of Yoshikazu Hara.

"The two of them are always bothered by that smell."

That's exactly what she told him.

"'Smells like burning bones,' they said."

Suddenly, he sensed someone approaching. He startled himself awake.

Mitsuhiro watched, stifling a yawn, as the nurse checked that the IV was fully administered. She skillfully removed the needle from Sae's arm.

"All right," she said kindly, "you're free to go home now."

Mitsuhiro was grateful that Sae didn't need to be fully admitted. The thought of going to work after spending the whole night sitting next to his daughter was enough to make him feel dizzy.

Mitsuhiro called for a taxi on his phone, woke up Miyoko, picked up his sleeping daughter, and left the hospital through the night entrance. The taxi arrived in short order. He put Miyoko in first, then followed with Sae in his arms.

On the way home, Mitsuhiro and Miyoko were too tired to talk much. Compared to their irritable exchange in the dining room, though, they were much calmer. Relief was the dominant emotion in their minds.

And perhaps because of that, by the time they were back home:

"Don't worry."

The voice echoed in his mind again when he laid Sae down on the bed. This time, his rational side didn't argue or try to think logically about it.

Miyoko looked at the AC remote control to make sure it was set to the usual temperature. "I'm so tired," she said, resting her forehead on Mitsuhiro's chest. He hugged Miyoko around the shoulders, took her to the bedroom, and put her to bed.

Leaving her asleep without another word, he returned to the dining room, sat down in a chair, and sighed. If he had anything alcoholic at home, he definitely would've poured himself a glass right now. He even thought about running down to the convenience store to buy something.

But he had something to do first. Mitsuhiro finished the sparkling water, now wholly flat after being left alone for so long, and picked up his bag. He took out the amulet he received from Yoshio Tamai from the inside pocket and placed the bag back on the floor.

Untying the string on the charm, he opened the little pouch and found a piece of neatly folded Japanese paper inside, protected by a thicker sheet inside the pouch. The Japanese paper reminded him of a seal, inscribed with "Tamai Appeasement Protective Amulet" in Japanese characters, written cursive-style with red ink. When he unfolded this paper, he saw a tiny wooden tablet inside, inscribed with the character for *appease*, 鎮, in red with an intricate pattern stamped around it in red ink.

Mitsuhiro took the paper with the wooden tag and went to the still-running exhaust fan in the kitchen. He placed both of them atop one of the induction burners and took out a roll of aluminum foil. Tearing a large piece off, he folded it several times into a thick square. After that, he folded the edges up a bit to create a makeshift ashtray and put the paper and wooden tablet inside.

But how to burn it? He searched around the kitchen a bit before finally finding their long-necked lighter. He had bought it last summer for barbecue and firework purposes. There wasn't anything else on hand to light a fire with. He wasn't sure if any lighter fluid was still inside, but when he pushed the button, it clicked and created a small flame. He directed it toward the foil ashtray and brought it close to the paper. It caught fire, fluttering and burning brightly. The fire spread to the wooden tablet, making a tiny crackling sound. The two objects promptly became a single ball of fire, and the rising smoke was sucked into the exhaust fan.

Mitsuhiro placed the lighter next to the stove and waited for the whole thing to burn out. It didn't even take a minute. When he saw that they were both a pile of ash, he took a pair of disposable chopsticks and a small glass teapot from the pantry.

He put some water into the teapot and poured a small amount onto the ashes. Then he stirred the ashes with the chopsticks to dissolve them in the water.

—*What am I even doing?*

He was starting to have doubts, but he dismissed the thought, reasoning that he was just doing what had to be done. He took up the chopsticks and opened the microwave door. Immediately, he sensed that strange odor drifting out.

He then rubbed some of the ash on the tip of the chopsticks against the back wall of the microwave. Yoshio Tamai had told him that any sort of writing would do, but he decided to write the character said to be most effective.

鎮

There was only a little ash there, so it didn't leave much of a mark. He was just tracing the character for *appease* on the wall more than anything else.

But even so, he could tell that something was different. That strange smell was gone. And from that point on, Mitsuhiro gave up trying to understand how this worked.

He took the ashtray and went to the front door, being careful not to spill the leftover ashes. After mixing them on the tip of a chopstick, he wrote the same character on the upper part of the front door. He couldn't make it too big—Miyoko would be weirded out and wipe it off—but he still wrote it anyway. Then he did the same on the corner of one wall of his condo's hallway, Sae's door, and his bedroom door.

Returning to the dining room, he placed the ashtray and chopsticks on the table. He hadn't added much water to start with, so the ashes were almost dry now. Mitsuhiro folded the ashtray in half to prevent the contents from spilling out, then folded it again to shrink it down. He then put the small foil packet into the little pouch that originally contained the amulet.

He was about to throw away the chopsticks, but before he did, he took a small box cutter from the shelf and scraped the ash off each stick. He put the ash-covered wood chips in the amulet pouch, tied up the string, opened his bag on the floor, and put it in a pocket.

Back in the kitchen, he replaced the cutter and lighter and turned down the exhaust fan. Then he went into the hallway and took a deep breath. Satisfied that there was no smell remaining, he let out a deep, relieved exhale.

"Well done, Mitsuhiro. You're such a good kid."

The voice came from behind him. He turned around with wide eyes and saw a man standing there. He smiled with joy.

"Thanks, Dad."

4

Kosuke Matsunaga, his father, looked very healthy there in the hallway. His eyes were strong, his complexion good, and his cheeks weren't thin and gaunt. His hair and beard were neatly trimmed, and he was dressed in freshly laundered work clothes with gleaming white socks, not a single stain anywhere. Mitsuhiro felt his heart warm up when he saw the words "Matsunaga Construction" embroidered on the breast pocket of Kosuke's outfit.

When was the last time he saw his dad so full of energy? He remembered the box of Hi-Lites that Kosuke kept with him like some protective charm, saying that he'd smoke 'em up once he got better after being hospitalized with lung cancer. In the end, they'd gone with him to the crematorium.

"You gotta be careful with fire," a suddenly sterner Kosuke said.

Mitsuhiro stiffened, imagining Kosuke going into one of his rages. In that moment, he felt like he had gone from being thirty-two years old all the way back to thirteen.

That was around when Kosuke changed, too. It wasn't like his business had gone downhill or his clients were treating him like garbage. He'd just be constantly tensed up, quick to fly into rages over the tiniest little thing. At first, Mitsuhiro and his mother tried to tiptoe around it, but this soon evolved into basic fear of the man. By the time Mitsuhiro entered high school, though, he was simply tired of the treatment and no longer feared his father. Instead, he actively washed his hands of any responsibility for the man.

When Mitsuhiro turned twenty, Kosuke had been diagnosed with cancer, and his body grew incredibly small and thin. Mitsuhiro felt sorry for having shunned him all that time, but he never shook the feeling that Kosuke had brought it all upon himself. That was his outlook for years afterward, even after Kosuke went to the crematorium.

Now Mitsuhiro was suddenly struck by the feeling that all of his experiences up until now had been a dream. He was actually still just thirteen years old. The anxiety froze him in place.

"You're being strict with your child. I'm proud of you." Kosuke smiled again.

Mitsuhiro lowered his shoulders, letting the tension unwind. It was pathetic how relaxed that one smile made him feel. His heart was pounding, but the relief was far stronger.

"Yeah. I went a little too far, though."

"No, that was just right. I'm sure your wife thinks she can trust you to do the right thing now, deep down."

"You think?"

Mitsuhiro laughed a bit. He had his doubts, but he was beginning to suspect that Miyoko really did think that way.

"Sure I do. Sometimes, you know, it's best to stand your ground and draw a line in the sand. Hell, from now on, you should *always* do that. Not just with your kid and your parents, either. Speak up to those nagging in-laws of yours. Them and the people at work who keep dumping their problems on you."

"Yeah... You're right. I don't know if I have it in me, but I'll try."

He wasn't at all confident, but saying that out loud made it seem surprisingly doable.

"You can do it. Trust me," Kosuke said, seeming to read all of Mitsuhiro's emotions. "Now go hit the sack, okay? You got important work to do. Have to make the hole happy."

"The hole...?" Mitsuhiro asked out loud, but he immediately realized that his father meant the hole in the East Wing basement.

Ah. It made sense. There was no point fighting the ash that was following him around. He had to go down there and give that hole what it wanted.

"I'll do my best to find Yoshikazu Hara."

"You better," Kosuke said, grabbing his son's shoulders and patting them lightly. "It's the most important job your company has. The biggest of them all. Hang in there for me, okay, Mitsuhiro? Your dad's rooting for you."

Mitsuhiro felt his heart warm up again. He never thought the day would come when his father would acknowledge him like this. Encourage him, even.

"...Thank you."

His voice trembled despite himself. He wiped away the tears welling up in his eyes.

"Go to bed, okay? You got your work cut out for you."

"All right. Good night, Dad."

"Good night."

Kosuke disappeared into the living room. Mitsuhiro sniffled a bit, took a deep breath, and headed for his bedroom. There was no one in the living room, but he didn't bother looking for Kosuke. Just seeing him in such good health and getting to speak to him was enough.

Mitsuhiro quietly got into bed, trying not to wake up Miyoko. With another deep breath, he fell asleep.

In his dreams, he began to wonder what he should do about the other person on his mind right now—Mole Unit-01, the owner of that Twitter account. Mitsuhiro didn't know his face or his name. How was he ever going to find him?

...It's okay. Don't worry. He could feel his father standing right beside him, saying that to him again. ***Don't worry about that guy. He's had the ashes on him for a while now anyway. There's nothing to worry about.***

With relief, Mitsuhiro stopped thinking about it.

He didn't sleep for very long, but he woke up in terrific shape, physically and mentally. At least, that was how he felt. But when he finished brushing his teeth in the bathroom, Miyoko stood up, still half-asleep, and blinked a bit.

"Hey, are you okay? You look really tired."

"I do?"

Mitsuhiro stared intently at himself in the mirror. There were dark circles under his eyes, yes, but he didn't feel tired at all, so it couldn't be anything to worry about.

"I didn't get much sleep, but I feel fine, so..."

Miyoko still looked concerned, so he changed the subject.

"What about Sae? Should we wake her up for school?"

"No, let's keep her here today and see how she feels."

"Yeah, that's probably for the best. Oh, by the way, the smell from the microwave is gone, isn't it?"

Miyoko's eyes widened. She backed out into the hallway, turned toward the kitchen, and sniffed. "You're right. It's all gone."

"Guess we don't have to buy a new one after all."

"I hope not."

Miyoko frowned doubtfully, but she went to the kitchen to prepare breakfast.

After getting dressed, Mitsuhiro was eating his fried eggs and toast when Sae woke up, seeming a little dazed, and sat down at the table. Miyoko poured her some orange juice.

"How 'bout we take the day off school today, Sae?"

"What? But I'm just fine!"

The two of them continued their noisy bickering for a while.

What are you doing? Just lay down the law with her. Mitsuhiro could sense his father standing nearby, offering his advice, but he couldn't bring himself to follow it.

Shut up, you two! The breadwinner of this family is trying to have a peaceful goddamn breakfast for a change, all right? So keep your stupid mouths shut and eat!

He vividly imagined himself bellowing like that, and he couldn't stand it. Not even his own father got *that* bad. No, Kosuke was just constantly preoccupied with his work. He barely took any time out at all to eat with his family, much less attempt meaningful conversation with them.

Still, the urge to raise his voice at his wife and child grew stronger...but he knew it'd just make his relationship with Miyoko worse, so he couldn't bring himself to do it. Now he just felt weak. Like he had disappointed his father somehow. And as he watched Sae reluctantly agree to Miyoko's persuasion from the corner of his eye, he silently trudged out of the condo.

It took buying a bottle of water at the station and riding the train for a while before he regained his composure. ***Why let that discourage you? You'll have plenty of opportunities to discipline your family in the future.*** He felt like his father was sitting next to him, giving him life advice.

When he arrived at the office and put his bag on his desk, his boss, Takenaka, came right over. As soon as he saw Mitsuhiro's face, he frowned and peered at him closely.

"What's wrong? You look tired."

"Uh...well, my daughter had a medical emergency last night, so I didn't get much sleep."

"She did?"

"It was dehydration or something… She's fine now."

"Oh. With this heat, I get it. That must have been tough. How're you feeling?"

"Good, thanks. I'll be in the company car starting today anyway."

"Don't get into any accidents."

"I won't. If I find Yoshikazu Hara, I'll need to bring him into the car to talk, though."

Takenaka frowned again, as if just realizing that for the first time. "You're gonna put a homeless person in the car?" he reflexively replied, then turned his eyes aside, a tad embarrassed. "Well, I guess you'll have to, yeah. Just, uh, try to keep the car clean, if you can."

Mitsuhiro couldn't help imagining himself laying newspaper on the car seat and sitting Yoshikazu Hara down on it. Like spreading a bath towel over the back seat after a trip to the beach so you didn't get it all wet and sandy. He wondered for a moment how the other person might feel, being treated that way, but quickly pushed the thought out of his mind. He could worry about that when the time came. For now, he had something more important to bring up.

"Right. I'll do my best to find him before Tamai Construction does."

"Yeah… I don't know what kinda religious ceremony is involved here, but we need to confirm with Mr. Hara whether he's being forced to do it. If we don't, things could get real complicated real fast. And as for the Twitter poster, Legal advised me it's unclear how long it'll take to get the account's personal info disclosed. They asked Twitter to suspend the account, at least, but no response so far."

Don't worry about that. Mitsuhiro felt his father standing next to him again. He popped an idea into his son's head, and Mitsuhiro decided to float it to his boss.

"What do you think about reaching out to the account owner? We can send direct messages to them via Twitter."

"We can contact them personally? I mean, without it being made public?"

"Sure, as long as neither of us makes the messages public."

"Well, what would you say, though? You can't mention the company name, no matter what."

"They posted that they lost their home. How about contacting them and offering to introduce them to a support organization? If I created a personal account, it'd just look like a kind gesture."

Takenaka frowned, deep in thought. He wasn't familiar with social media, so he probably didn't know what call to make.

"Yeah, we can do that much, at least. All right, give it a shot."

"Thank you, sir. I'll report back when I've made contact."

"Please do. As for the ritual hall in the East Wing, I received a report from Chief Sugawara. He confirmed that a man named Araki from Tamai Construction manages the site, and that Yoshikazu Hara was brought in for the rituals involved. However, only Tamai employees were going in and out of the site, and they don't have any idea how the Twitter poster got in."

"What about the fire?" Mitsuhiro asked softly so the employees around him couldn't hear. Criminal cases like arson were the responsibility of the crisis-management team, and the rules stated that they couldn't discuss those with people from other departments, in order to prevent unnecessary rumors from spreading.

"Chief Sugawara said that the police will be investigating. You might be questioned as well."

"Were the workers at the scene questioned yet?"

"Yes, both of them. Oh, but no one suspects you. Everyone knows why you were there that day, and you had no reason to set the fire. Someone from Tamai Construction also confirmed that Yoshikazu Hara was at the scene with you."

Still, remembering the reactions of those workers at the time made Mitsuhiro uncomfortable. Even when he'd insisted there was another person down there, they still looked at him like he was lying.

Ah, well. It's not your fault. Not many people understand how vital your job is. He felt his father next to him again. ***You have an important role to play. Don't let the responsibility get to you. Have some pride in yourself.***

Mitsuhiro smiled. He was already feeling better.

"What's up?"

Takenaka seemed puzzled by his smile. Mitsuhiro began to feel stranger and stranger.

Even your boss may not necessarily understand your role, you know.

Yeah, you're right, Dad, Mitsuhiro replied silently in his mind, and he kept smiling at Takenaka.

"You know, if Yoshikazu Hara set that fire in order to escape, that'd be a big deal, right? Or if the Twitter poster did it out of spite."

"Why're you smiling about that?" Takenaka grew sterner.

Mitsuhiro bowed his head. "I'm sorry. My father told me I shouldn't take on too much responsibility. I shouldn't have said that."

Takenaka gave him a look. "...Didn't your father pass away?"

"Yes. I...I just feel like he said that to me, I mean."

"...Are you sure you're not too tired for this?" Now Takenaka seemed concerned. "It hasn't been long since the fire. Are you okay to drive?"

"I'm fine, Mr. Takenaka. I'm in great shape."

Mitsuhiro brushed away the idea. In fact, he felt like he could do pretty much anything at the moment.

After that morning meeting, Mitsuhiro immediately registered a free burner email address on his cell phone, opened the Twitter app, and created an account for himself. He wanted to use a name that'd make people feel an affinity for him, so he chose "Mr. Scraping By."

It was a little hard to believe that he could send anonymous messages across the world so easily. He didn't know if that was a good thing, but at the very least, there was this one person on Twitter attacking a major project, and so far, nobody had been able to stop him—a worst-case scenario.

Mitsuhiro thought about what to write, typing a draft into the memo app on his phone.

Sorry to contact you out of nowhere. There's a group called Helping Hands Mutual Aid that does a lot to support people in need. They're a bunch

of really trustworthy guys, so I'd like to introduce them to you if you're interested. Hoping you'll reply before your situation gets any worse.

If he phrased it like this, then even if there was no direct reply, the person who received the tweet might contact Helping Hands, and Mitsuhiro could get in touch through them.

He showed the message to Takenaka at his desk, got the go-ahead, and then, as Takenaka watched, he pulled up Mole Unit-01's account and sent the direct message over.

"Let's hope he takes the bait," Takenaka said.

"Yeah," Mitsuhiro replied.

Taking his bag over to General Affairs, Mitsuhiro filled out the company-car paperwork, accepted the keys, and walked over to the lot. Now that he was approved, he wouldn't have to go through the same procedure every single day; filling out a time record and submitting it to General Affairs would suffice. This car was his alone for the next week, and he couldn't have been more grateful for it.

He found the company car assigned to him and got in, but the direct sunlight made the interior a sauna, so he left the driver-side door open and turned on the AC.

"Right. Once the temperature is comfortable, let's get going."

That was Kosuke. Mitsuhiro hadn't noticed him before, but his father was now in the back seat.

"Feels kind of funny, driving my dad around."

"Yeah, same here. Fasten your seat belt, okay? And watch the road. This is important work, so you gotta do it right."

Mitsuhiro closed the door, fastened his belt as instructed, and started the car. Feeling almost giddy with excitement, he checked the map on his phone and looked at the route he'd worked out in advance. The sight of Kosuke in the back, visible every time he glanced in the rearview mirror, was tremendously reassuring.

He really needed that encouragement, too. The rest of the IR team was busy with the important, exciting task of rehearsing for the upcoming shareholder meeting, and here he was, prowling the streets of Tokyo in search of a couple of homeless people. Of course the task would get him down.

This morning was devoted to casing the main parks, the railway bridges and overpasses, and the vacant lots along the railroad tracks and riverside around Shibuya Station—the places that Okuyama from Helping Hands had informed him of—but all he saw were homeless people from various walks of life, none of whom were Yoshikazu Hara. It was a real slog from start to finish, but despite spending the entire morning searching in vain, Mitsuhiro still felt fulfilled. He even had a sense of mission, like he was doing something only he could do.

At noon, he stopped at a fast-food parking lot, bought a burger combo for himself, and was returning to his car when his phone rang—his personal phone this time. Looking at the screen, he saw that it was his mother-in-law.

"Hello?"

"Oh, Mitsuhiro? I'm at the hospital with Miyoko right now."

"What? The hospital?"

"She said she suddenly fell ill—there was some kind of awful odor, and it made her sick. So I rushed over to her, but she was asking if you could leave work early today, because Sae's all alone at home right now."

5

"I'll be back there as soon as I can," Mitsuhiro replied before ending the call.

He wasn't just worried about his wife. This fulfilling, exciting work had just been rudely interrupted, and he was angry. Who cared if it smelled bad? This was an important assignment he was chasing. Ever since she got pregnant, Miyoko had constantly been complaining about one thing or another. Couldn't she put up with something smelling bad for a little bit?

On the other hand, he was also shocked at himself for thinking that way. She was experiencing a whole wealth of physical changes all at once—how could he just order her *not* to change? Mitsuhiro had assorted ways to escape his stresses, but Miyoko didn't. In fact, she was always the type who went out of her way not to cause trouble for her husband—and Mitsuhiro himself didn't want to just stop caring about his wife and children like his father did. At least, that's what he thought. Used to think.

Mitsuhiro sat there confused, unable to understand why he was so angry with Miyoko, when Kosuke leaned forward from the back seat.

"You can't help it. It's natural to get angry at times like this. Here you are, the breadwinner of the family, out handling a huge job, and now you're having to deal with all these stupid complaints."

"I know, right? It pisses me off."

"Well, you're partly to blame yourself. You've been spoiling your wife and child. Discipline is important, you know? It's what you need if you want to keep a household running smoothly. You have to think of it as part of your job and do it *properly*, or else you'll get interrupted like this when you're doing something really important."

"Yeah. I hear you. I'll try."

Kosuke smiled and patted Mitsuhiro on the shoulder, then leaned back in his rear seat.

Mitsuhiro took a deep breath to calm himself. A pleasant smell emanated from the fast-food bag on his lap. It made him hungry, but *apparently*, he wasn't going to be afforded the luxury of having a decent meal in peace today, so he plopped the bag on the passenger seat and called Takenaka.

"*Wow. Okay. Yeah, no helping that,*" Takenaka said with a sigh. "*Gotta wonder if it was too early for you to have two kids, huh?*"

Mitsuhiro apologized and ended the call. Then he was struck by the urge to ask Takenaka what he meant by that last comment. When *would* be the right time to have two kids? Miyoko was in her thirties now. What did he mean, too early? He trusted his boss a lot, and now he was saying that it was wrong for employees to enjoy having a family? That really stuck in his craw. It was probably just a frustrated slip of the tongue, yes, but that slip was more than enough to shake his trust in Takenaka.

After returning the company car to the parking lot, he went to the office to bring back the time sheet and sign out early, then went home without saying goodbye to anyone. He was still angry as he rode the train, holding the bag with his now-cold burger combo. The only thing that saved him was Kosuke's presence nearby.

"Y'know, back in the day, people mocked men who couldn't discipline their families. You know what your bosses are gonna think if you just spoil your wife and kids, right? But I gotta say, your boss has some problems, too. Relying on you alone for such an important task like this…"

"Maybe I should ask for more staff? I thought I could handle this alone…"

"Really, everybody in your department should be attending to that hole, you know. Everybody in your whole damn company. That's how important it is. And that's why you should take the initiative here and set an example for everyone else, okay? Then the tide will really turn. Everyone will wanna be like you. You'll be the one who moves the whole company."

Kosuke's words had a powerful effect on Mitsuhiro. Now he felt like the board of directors, not his boss, had given him this very special assignment.

"All right. I'll do my best, Dad."

He got off the train and hurried out of the station. He was worried about Sae being alone, but he also wanted to get to the burger in his bag as soon as possible.

Really, why didn't they just take Sae to the hospital with them in the first place? Did his mother-in-law want to say she had a granddaughter without actually putting in any of the work required to raise her? He stewed over it as he entered the condo building. He noticed that same parched, desiccated smell as he passed through the automatic doors—it was pretty intense, in fact—but he didn't pay much attention to it. Instead of fear, he felt anger and hunger—and thirst.

Part of him knew he wasn't in a very stable mental state, but he believed he'd calm down after talking to Sae and eating at home.

As soon as he opened the door to his condo, he was struck by the same strange burning smell as the night before and saw smoke drifting from the ceiling of the hallway. He threw down everything he was holding and ran over in his shoes, almost bumping into Sae as she came out of the living room crying.

"Sae! What's wrong?" he asked, holding her. But Sae flinched and stiffened in his arms. She stared up at him, and her expression was full of fear.

She wasn't afraid of what was happening in the apartment but of the man in front of her. Mitsuhiro had just yelled loudly at her yesterday, and she was afraid of being yelled at again. So she froze, unable to explain what was happening.

He understood well how she felt. He had been the same when he was a child.

Discipline. He felt like Kosuke was standing right behind him, telling him to do it. ***Discipline her now. It's your fault she started that fire.***

He had to put it out. His rational mind attempted to push aside his anxious feelings. There was a fire somewhere in the house. If he didn't put it out before the alarm or the sprinklers went off, it'd become a huge scene.

"Sae, go outside and wait for me."

Mitsuhiro let go of Sae's hand. Then, just like yesterday, he took the fire extinguisher out from the shoe rack, covered his mouth with his jacket sleeve, and rushed into the living room. He had learned in a company-evacuation drill that toxic gas rises up from the floor, so he quickly looked around the room, keeping his head as low as possible. He immediately found the source of the crackling sound and smoke.

It was the electric fan. He had no idea one of those could ever catch fire.

Mitsuhiro stopped pressing his jacket sleeve against his face, pulled the pin out of the fire extinguisher, aimed the nozzle at the fan, and squeezed the lever. He sprayed it out from a distance at first, closing in as the fire died down.

Once it was out, he set down the extinguisher and unplugged the fan itself. Clenching his lips tightly to hold his breath, he opened all the windows, along with the sliding door leading to the balcony, and went to the kitchen to turn the exhaust fan up to maximum.

Breathing heavily under the roaring fan, he grimaced at the unpleasant smell. The air was filled with it—burning metal, plastic, and carpet, along with that now-familiar distinct, intensely dry smell. Returning to the living room, he confirmed once more that the fan was no longer burning. However, just like the microwave last night, that unmistakable, crematorium-like smell was clearly emanating from the fan.

Hot, fresh air blew in through the window. Still grimacing, he thought again about how weird it was that the fan had caught fire. Come to think of it, he remembered hearing on the news that fans could catch fire after being left unmaintained for years and years...but he didn't think the fan in this place was that old. They'd better contact the manufacturer. Maybe it was defective and a recall was in order.

With that in mind, Mitsuhiro cranked the AC to the lowest temperature possible and set the AC's fan speed to maximum. Miyoko had always insisted that they use the electric fan in conjunction with the AC to help it cool more efficiently. Sae had probably left the fan on all day, since she thought that was the normal thing to do.

"Daddy, are you okay?" Sae timidly called out from the hallway. She was standing with half her body hidden behind the door, looking scared that she was about to get scolded.

You told her to stay outside! Kosuke grimly pointed out right next to him. ***She can't do what she's told. That's why the fan caught fire. You have to be careful with fire. Get it through her head already.***

Mitsuhiro almost did just that. He fought to keep himself from glaring at Sae and shouting *Get out of here! This is all your fault!* Even if it meant disappointing Kosuke, he just couldn't bring himself to do it. Sae had come back here out of concern for her father, braving her fear, and he couldn't punish her for that.

"I'm fine, Sae. Are you okay? Did you get burned at all?" he asked as gently as he could, but Sae bit her lip and lowered her head. He had managed to stop himself from shouting, but she'd still seen the hard look in his eyes.

"Daddy, I'm thirsty."

He was aware that the hot wind, the hunger, and the thirst were making him angry. Mitsuhiro took off his jacket, draped it over his shoulders, and—just like last night—went to the kitchen, filled a glass with water, and knocked it back to calm himself.

"Would you like some, Sae?"

Sae, who was still staring at the floor, slowly trudged over and shook her head.

Tell her to get over here right now!

He felt as if Kosuke was shouting orders in his ear.

She needs to come over immediately when her father calls for her.

I can't, Dad, Mitsuhiro weakly replied in his mind. *Please don't make me.* He drank another glass of water, straining to ensure he didn't follow Kosuke's orders, and put it in the sink.

"Sae, you didn't get burned, did you?"

Mitsuhiro examined his silent daughter's face and arms. Nothing was red or blistered. That was a relief.

"I'll take care of the fan, so stay in your room, okay? It's gonna be hot in here with the window open."

With that, he gently coaxed Sae toward her room. Sae shuffled her feet, and he became anxious that Kosuke might say something, but he didn't—which brought its own form of anxiety. He knew Kosuke would scold him eventually.

After sending Sae off, he returned to the living room, threw his jacket on the sofa, and looked down at the fan, which had been warped by the heat. Then he looked at the throw rug, with all the burn marks and fire-extinguisher foam bits on it, and sighed. He thought about sealing up the fan (which still had that strange smell to it) in a garbage bag, but before doing so, he took his phone out of his jacket and shot some pictures. He captured the manufacturer's name, model number, and the area where the fire seemed to have started with his phone's camera. Then he went to the kitchen, grabbed a large garbage bag, put the fan inside, and took it out to the balcony. He thought he should have the manufacturer retrieve it instead of spending the money to throw it out as oversize garbage. After all, there was no guarantee that a similar accident wouldn't happen in some other household. He should really have them investigate the cause of the fire.

He wiped off the extinguisher foam with a rag, left the rug as it was, and put the fire extinguisher back on the shoe shelf. He thought about how he'd have to inform the management company and get a new extinguisher as he picked up the keys, bag, and fast food he had left in the hallway.

"Sae, did you eat?" he asked from the doorway.

"Mm-hmm," replied Sae, who was sitting blankly on the bed.

Mitsuhiro nodded silently and took the things he was holding to the dining room.

When he opened the bag on the table, he found that the drink had spilled out and the burger and fries were all wet, but he didn't care. He laid them out on the table and devoured them, as odd as it all tasted. By the time he finished, the air in the room had ventilated out, and the smell of the fire faded considerably.

Mitsuhiro put all the wrappers in the fast-food bag, crushed it, threw it in the trash, and closed the windows in the room. Then he sat down in a chair, grabbed his bag on the table, and stared into space. He waited for Kosuke to say something, but there was no sign of him.

He felt calmer now, but perhaps that was why he could clearly smell the odor now. Even though he had taken the burnt fan outside and left the exhaust fan on, the smell of dry ash wafted in from some unknown place. It came from everywhere in the room, really.

No, it was definitely the throw rug, Mitsuhiro told himself, hugging his briefcase to his chest. He'd roll up the rug, take it outside, and that'd be that. But somewhere in his heart, he knew that wouldn't solve the problem.

So what should he do? As he sat there, Sae suddenly came over.

"Are you doing work?"

Mitsuhiro raised an eyebrow. He wondered why Sae would ask that, but then he realized it was because he was hugging his bag. He knew what he had to do—and why he was holding it so close.

"No, not work."

Mitsuhiro opened his bag and took out the amulet from the pocket. He put the bag on the floor and placed the charm on the table.

Sae sat down in her chair, curiously looking at the amulet.

Her father untied the string and took out the aluminum foil and wood shavings from inside. When he opened up the foil, he saw some dried ashes stuck to the inside. He thought about dissolving them in water, but something told him that this wouldn't be enough. He didn't know if that was because of the amount or quality of the ashes, or how they had been burned, but something was missing, and now that smell was back.

Was it because he hadn't written those characters in enough places around the condo the first time? As he thought it over, Mitsuhiro looked at the pouch that had contained the wooden tablet. Maybe he could use that, too. That'd give him more ashes, and then he'd write as many characters as possible.

Mitsuhiro took the wood pieces and the amulet pouch and placed them on the open aluminum foil. He went to the kitchen, while Sae followed him with a puzzled look on her face.

"Dad, what are you doing?"

"Um, it's a kind of magic spell."

That just intrigued her more. When Mitsuhiro placed the foil and the amulet on the cooktop, Sae moved her stool closer and stood next to him.

"Don't touch it," Mitsuhiro said gently as he took the lighter out of the drawer.

He applied it to the foil. The wood bits and pouch smoldered, the smoke rising up and getting sucked into the exhaust fan. Mitsuhiro lit it several times, burning the wood chips, the string, and the pouch, until everything was ashes.

Then he took a small teapot from the shelf, filled it with water, and poured it little by little over the ashes. Taking up a pair of disposable chopsticks, he stirred it carefully, then took it all over to the front door.

Sae followed him as he stared at the character he had written on the top of the front door last night.

鎮

"What did you write?"

"That's kind of a difficult character. It means 'to appease,' which means, uh. . .you know, to quiet something down."

"Okay."

Mitsuhiro wrote the same character on the walls of the hallway and above the doors of each room. He also wrote it on the edge of the kitchen exhaust fan, the microwave, and the walls of the living room and dining room.

"Can I try?" Sae asked.

He handed her the other chopstick. "Can you put some little dots around here?"

Yoshio Tamai had told him that simple lines or dots worked just fine too. Sae did as she was told, tapping the tip of her chopstick on the wall. Most of the ash had dissolved into the water, so it only left a few water marks, but Sae looked up at Mitsuhiro with a satisfied smile. In a rather unexpected fashion, they had buried the hatchet, and now he smiled back at her. Sae wanted to keep going, so he let her do the same thing on the walls by the bath and toilet.

The ashes in the foil were almost gone, the water all dried up. Mitsuhiro folded it up and placed it on the top shelf of the shoe rack, along with the chopsticks he had used for the ritual. He stood in the hallway and took a deep breath. Sae did the same, and her face lit up.

"The smell's all gone!"

She smiled. Mitsuhiro stroked Sae's head and felt like he could hear his father saying, ***I wonder how long it will last***. He didn't know. But he didn't think the effect would fizzle out.

As he returned to the living room with Sae, the thing on Mitsuhiro's mind was who he should tell about burning the amulet. He had several business cards from Tamai Construction. Which one should he call?

6

But he didn't have time to contact Tamai Construction right away. After he was done writing the messages in ash, he received a call from his mother-in-law, Michiyo Umehara. She said the exam was over and he could see Miyoko over at the hospital.

"Just to be on the safe side, she's going to be admitted for now and undergo another exam tomorrow. She asked for a change of clothes and things, but would you mind bringing those over for me?"

She probably didn't want to make a round trip. Mitsuhiro's mother-in-law acted like everything she did was out of the goodness of her heart, but the truth was that she tried to make people do things for her instead of doing anything herself, which often angered her daughter.

Mitsuhiro wanted to tell her that he was busy taking care of Sae, but he just said "All right" in response. If he asked his mother-in-law to do something, she'd berate him later about all the trouble he was putting her through. Besides, Mitsuhiro wanted to give Sae a chance to see that her mom was fine so she wouldn't worry. Of course he wouldn't say no to that.

"Let's go to the hospital and see Mommy."

Sae was overjoyed to hear the news. Mitsuhiro got a change of clothes for his wife and put them in a bag. He didn't change his own, just threw his jacket over his shoulders as he left home with Sae.

They took the bus to the hospital, where the front desk told them that she was in a four-bed room in the OB-GYN ward. When they went in, all the beds were surrounded by curtains. Mitsuhiro checked the name tags to make sure he had the right room, then walked over to one of the beds.

"Miyoko, are you there?"

"Oh, is that Daddy? I'm right here."

Miyoko's voice came through the curtain, and Sae pulled it back and rushed inside.

"Mommy!"

When Mitsuhiro entered, he saw Miyoko sitting up, leaning against the back of the bed, with Sae clinging to her.

"Where's your mother?"

"She had an appointment with someone from the neighborhood association."

Mitsuhiro shrugged and barely kept himself from rolling his eyes and making a snarky comment.

"I'm sorry I made you leave work early. My dad's out, too. I know your mother would've come, but I'd hate to make her come all the way over from Hachioji in her condition."

"Sae was off school today, too," he added, hoping to convey that he thought this was just supremely bad timing for everyone. He was frustrated that his in-laws wouldn't even watch their own grandchild at a time like this, but for now, all that had to be shunted aside. "What did the tests say?"

"Nothing so far. They said it's probably just severe morning sickness."

"There was a smell that made you feel sick?"

Miyoko's face darkened. "I think we should throw away that microwave after all."

Sae's head snapped up. "Mommy, the house doesn't smell bad anymore! Dad did a magic trick!"

"A magic trick?" Miyoko repeated suspiciously.

"Yeah, just a little one."

"He lit a charm on fire and wrote a spell with it!"

"What did he set on fire?"

Miyoko frowned at Sae's proud explanation.

"It was a fire-prevention amulet. I did it to make Sae feel safer. Kind of like you and your 'power spots,' right?"

"No, not really. You've never done anything like that before."

"I learned it at work. It was all done safely."

"What if Sae tries to copy you?"

"You won't do that, will you, Sae? Not unless Mommy or Daddy's around, okay?"

"Okay! But, Daddy, why did the fan catch fire?"

"Wait, what?"

Miyoko was visibly startled. Mitsuhiro hurriedly explained what had happened after he got home. He had come here to help reassure her, but instead he had made Miyoko more fearful than ever.

"There was almost a fire? When Sae was home alone?"

"No, it wasn't big enough for the fire alarm to go off yet. I think someone from the manager's office would have come running if it was."

"It could have been too late then!" she said, her face white with fear.

It ultimately took Mitsuhiro about an hour to calm her down, and after that, the three of them went to the hospital cafeteria for an early dinner.

"I'm so glad you're all right."

Miyoko kept hugging Sae, until Sae herself realized that she had been in serious danger after all, which made her anxious. Mitsuhiro had to keep talking about complaining to the fan manufacturer to distract them from their feelings.

He discussed tomorrow's plans with Miyoko, and by the time he took Sae home, it was past sunset. He put Sae in the bath and then to bed, then took a bath himself, feeling wholly drained. After getting out, he poured himself some sparkling water in the living room and picked up his phone, intending to message Miyoko that he was going to bed.

He found several notifications waiting for him, from Twitter and from his call log. Holding his breath, Mitsuhiro opened the Twitter app. There was a reply to his direct message.

I have nowhere to go, so I'm looking for a place in Jingu-dori Park to sleep tonight. They'll kick me out of there during the day, so I'm doing day-labor work until it gets dark. Mom said I should. Tell me where else I can sleep, please.

* * *

The sender was, of course, Mole Unit-01. He had reached out after all. The trains were still running. If Mitsuhiro picked up the company car from Shimaoka, he'd be there in a flash.

Okay, I can be at Jingu-dori Park in about an hour. Let's meet there.

Mitsuhiro hurriedly sent his reply, then realized just what he had done. He'd be leaving Sae behind. He tried to delete the message, but it was too late.

Thanks. I'll be waiting.

Mitsuhiro groaned when he saw the immediate reply. Should he send a message saying that he'd have to do it tomorrow night after all? But if he hesitated, Mole Unit-01 might think he was just screwing with him and stop replying.

As he stared at the screen, hesitating, someone else suddenly spoke to him.

"Go ahead. Your dad's watching."

Mitsuhiro spun around. Kosuke was standing next to him.

"Your dad'll watch over Sae. You've got important work to do. Get to it."

"All right. Thanks a lot, Dad. That really helps."

"Don't forget the voicemail," Kosuke reminded him. "There might be a message there, too."

"Right," Mitsuhiro said, figuring he could check it on his way to the station.

In a hurry, he got changed, grabbed his bag, and quietly left the condo, locking the door behind him. On his way to the station, he checked his phone and saw that he had a call from an unknown number. Just as Kosuke told him, he had some voicemail to play back.

"I apologize for calling so late. My name is Sota Araki from Tamai Construction. I had something to discuss with you regarding Yoshikazu Hara, and I'd appreciate if you could call me back when you hear this."

7

Mitsuhiro had received messages from both the Twitter user and Tamai Construction at the same time. Was that a coincidence? Or was there some connection here? He wondered if he should call Araki back right away, but he decided to put it off until later.

So he got off the train at Shibuya Station, finding it choked with the crowds. People in business attire going home and people going out to enjoy the city were rushing around the platforms, trying to avoid each other. Mitsuhiro hurried out of the station, careful not to bump into anyone, and headed straight for the parking lot with his company car. He got into the car, glad he hadn't returned the keys, and wondered if he'd be written up for going out at night with it. Considering the situation, though, he was sure they'd understand. If he missed this chance, it'd be back to aimlessly patrolling the streets tomorrow.

Mitsuhiro drove out of the station, navigated the narrow, twisty side streets of Shibuya, and came out onto the main road. He turned left in front of the station onto Meiji-dori Avenue and stopped at the side of the road near Jingu-dori Park, turning on his hazard lights.

He got out of the car, locked it, and checked the time on his phone. It had been a bit over thirty minutes since he last exchanged messages with Mole Unit-01. No new messages had come in.

I'm here at Jingu-dori Park. Where are you?

He sent the message as he followed the railroad tracks toward the park.

The tracks between here and Shibuya Station were lined with parks and bicycle lots on one side; on the other side, there were lines of tiny eateries that could only hold a few customers at a time. The whole area, including the overpasses in the vicinity, was known as a gathering place for homeless people, with several blue-tarp tent houses lined up in the darker alleys.

The park where Mitsuhiro was headed was similarly lined with cardboard signs and plywood boards, painted with slogans like "NO EVICTION" and "HOMELESS RIGHTS" and "STOP REDEVELOPMENT!" on them and attached with wire to the park fencing. From where he stood, he could vaguely make out people standing in the shadows here and there.

The people in the park would have been able to see Mitsuhiro clearly as he entered. He stood at the entrance, but no one approached him. He didn't approach any of them, either; he didn't want any unnecessary conflict.

Was it the next park over, maybe? The long, narrow park was divided in half by a building in between. There was a public restroom in this half, so that made it a more likely place to stay, but he wasn't sure. He checked the messages again.

I'm sitting on a bench.

Mitsuhiro glanced at the benches, but there was no one who seemed to be looking at a phone. He left the park and headed for the one next door. As he walked along the side of this long, thin park area, he saw a faint light coming from a bench at the far end, near the railroad tracks.

Mitsuhiro entered the park and approached the person looking down at his phone.

"I'm the one who messaged you."

When the person slowly looked up, Mitsuhiro was so surprised that he blankly stared in amazement. Yoshikazu Hara was sitting on the bench.

"Are *you* the one who tweeted about the East Wing?"

The man on the bench looked puzzled. "Ah, yes… Have we met before?"

"In that hole…"

Mitsuhiro stopped himself, remembering that Yoshikazu Hara had dementia. Instead of explaining everything over again, he opted to get to the point.

"Yes, we *have* met. In fact, I've been trying to find you. Um, my car is over there. If you could come with me…"

"You have somewhere I could sleep? Everywhere here is taken. If I go anywhere else, the locals get angry and kick me out. My mom keeps nagging me, but I'm just so tired..."

"I'll find somewhere. We'll ask Helping Hands. Come on, let's get in the car first."

Mitsuhiro wanted to pull him up by the hand, but Okuyama from Helping Hands had expressly warned him against that sort of thing, so he had to rely on words. Fortunately for him, the man stood up immediately and followed quietly. It was summer, and the body odor was overwhelming, but Mitsuhiro pretended not to mind.

When they returned to the car, he unlocked the door and opened the passenger side.

"You can take the passenger seat."

The man sat as instructed. He seemed genuinely exhausted, collapsing into the seat with a thud.

"I'll close the door for you."

Once he did, Mitsuhiro got into the driver's seat. He tried to start a conversation, but the smell made it hard to breathe, so he reflexively opened the window. "Pretty hot night out," he said, trying to make an excuse for it, but the other man just stared blankly at the windshield, not caring much either way.

"Let me ask you a few questions. Is it okay if I get this on video? I want to record our conversation."

"Eh? Oh, sure. Whatever you want. I don't care. I just wanna sleep."

Mitsuhiro turned his phone camera on and started filming.

"Now, um, I want to confirm something. Was everything in the East Wing your own decision?"

"Huh?"

"Did you go to the East Wing on your own?"

"Ahh, yeah. They gave me the job."

"You weren't forced to by Tamai Construction?"

"Forced? Huh? Oh, you mean the electrical work in that hole?"

"What?"

"I was doing electrical work. The lights weren't workin' anymore. Too old."

"Okay, so you were doing electrical work. You went to that hole on your own—"

"Ahhh…"

Suddenly, the man let out a painful-sounding groan, bowed his head, and looked downward.

"It's all 'cause of that hole. Fire keeps comin' out of it. Everyone's been sayin' that this whole time. They tried exorcism after exorcism, but it keeps happening. They've all gone crazy, and there are so many construction mistakes that the electricity doesn't even work properly anymore. Taking apart the piles, lowering them down… Hell, getting them set up takes over a month by itself. I just don't wanna do this anymore. Just let me go!"

"Were you forced to perform work you didn't want to do?"

"I asked to do it. Of course I did. It was good pay. But I never thought I'd end up like this…"

With that, the man began to sob quietly.

Mitsuhiro felt sorry for him, but he was relieved to hear there were no discrepancies with Tamai Construction's claims. Yoshikazu Hara had gone down into that hole of his own volition. He had probably helped install the lighting and bring in the pile driver and so on. The "construction mistakes" he kept bringing up only concerned the ritual hall with that hole in it.

Mitsuhiro certainly didn't expect to kill two birds—Yoshikazu Hara and the Twitter poster—with one stone. He stopped filming, feeling very proud of himself.

"All right," he told the sobbing man. "I'm going to make a phone call so I can find you a place to sleep."

He got out of the car. The smell inside was so strong that he relished the fresh air. But as he was about to call Helping Hands to fulfill his promise to the man, he received a call from an unknown number. It might be Sota

Araki from Tamai Construction; he'd left a voice message earlier. He was… the general manager, right?

Mitsuhiro was done interviewing Yoshikazu Hara for the moment, so he casually answered the call.

"Hello, Matsunaga speaking."

"I'm sorry to bother you. This is Araki from Tamai Construction. I left a message in your voicemail earlier."

"Ah, yes, sorry I didn't call you back sooner. I was busy with something else. So, how can I help you?"

"Well…I got a call from Yoshikazu Hara."

"Huh? A call?"

"Yes. He's definitely somewhere in Shibuya, but I think his illness has left him a little befuddled. We're looking for him at the moment, but I thought you might have heard from him."

"Oh, um, right. As a matter of fact, I'm with Yoshikazu Hara right now."

"You are?"

"Yeah. I was about to call Helping Hands and ask them to help find a place for him to sleep."

"Okay. We can definitely provide that for him. We haven't even paid him half of the mi-keshi *fee yet. If the ritual's left unfinished, it might curse all of us. Would you mind bringing Mr. Hara to the ritual hall in the East Wing? I'll contact the on-site staff and let them know. I'll head right over there, too."*

Mitsuhiro hesitated for a moment. But if Yoshikazu Hara wanted this job, maybe it'd be best to hand him over to Tamai Construction and settle this matter for good.

"All right. I'm in the neighborhood, so I'll be right there."

"Thank you very much. Goodbye for now."

Mitsuhiro hung up the phone, feeling refreshed, and returned to the driver's seat.

"Okay, Tamai Construction will provide a place for you to sleep. They said they'll pay you as well."

"Huh? What? Why?"

"Because they only paid you half of it so far. There's still work left to do, too."

"Ehh? I thought it was done. Ugh, that's all I need..."

"Well, I think it's better to finish it all up, okay? You'll get paid for it."

"Ahh, are you kidding me...?"

"And the guy from Tamai Construction said they'll make sure that nobody gets cursed, too."

"They'll do something about all of this?"

"Yes. Probably. I think so."

The man let out a painful sigh. "Well...all right. My mom says I should do it, too, but... *Oooh,* but I really don't want to..."

Mitsuhiro had obtained consent, so he put the car into gear, made a U-turn, and headed for the station. He stopped at the nighttime parking lot between the construction site and a bus depot just before the intersection in front of Shibuya Station's east exit. He thanked his lucky stars he'd brought his employee ID with him as he got out, walked around to the passenger side, and opened the door. The man, seemingly resigned to his fate, left the car and followed him, head bowed.

Mitsuhiro entered the code for the soundproof barrier around the site and went inside. It was the middle of the night, but the site was illuminated by bright lights. He showed his employee ID to the busy work crew on the site and went to the East Wing staff room, leaving the man waiting outside where Mitsuhiro could see him. He couldn't afford to have him disappear again.

He borrowed two sets of helmets, gloves, and flashlights from the office. Outside, they both equipped themselves and headed for the East Wing basement.

There was no construction work going on below, so they relied on their flashlights as they descended the stairs. The noise from above gradually faded away, and soon the men could hear nothing but their own footsteps.

When they reached the lowest level, Mitsuhiro traced his memory to find the place they needed to go. It didn't take long.

鎮

The now-familiar character was written large on the wall, and the stairs leading down to the ritual hall were fully illuminated by their flashlights.

"Let's go," said Mitsuhiro. "This way."

As he began to descend the stairs, the other man followed with a sigh of despair. They went down the long stairway in silence and emerged into a narrow passageway.

"I can smell it again," said the man from behind. Mitsuhiro smelled it, too, but he felt optimistic now. Finally, this was almost over, and his mission would be accomplished.

He'd expected the door ahead to be closed and to have to wait there for Araki from Tamai Construction. But when he reached it, he noticed it was wide open. It looked like a dark hole leading to nowhere.

Mitsuhiro paused, reluctant to go inside. Then he heard his phone ringing in his jacket pocket. Surprised that he could get a signal all the way down here, he took it out.

The call was coming from the phone he had given Sae to use. She must have woken up and called him when she found him missing.

He hurriedly answered.

"Sae?"

"It's me, Mitsuhiro. Your daughter's doing fine. I'm keeping an eye on her."

"Dad? What's up?"

"Listen, Mitsuhiro. Don't stop where you are. You have to put him in that hole. If you don't make the hole happy, weird things are gonna keep happening all over your home."

"Really?"

"Yeah. You sure got a lot to learn if you don't even know that."

"I know… I'm sorry."

"Nah, nah, you'll learn it all, okay? Your dad here will teach you. Now, first thing, take the man with you into the hole as soon as you can. Don't let him escape like last time."

"All right. I'm on it."

The phone went silent after Mitsuhiro's reply, so he put his phone back in his pocket.

"All right, let's go. Please come inside with me."

"Ohh, I don't want to…"

The man hesitated, but he timidly followed. Mitsuhiro was determined to do what he had to. All that fear from last time was nowhere to be found. He wasn't aimlessly wandering around in the pitch darkness any longer, and his mind didn't nag at him about the white dust he kicked up with each step he took.

He proceeded mindfully, taking care not to fall into the hole, and when he found the shrine, he went over to it and flipped the light switch. The orange light illuminated the room from all four corners, and he could see that his partner, who had been cowering a moment ago, was much more relaxed. But when Mitsuhiro placed the flashlight on the table and picked up the stepladder on the floor, the man's expression changed.

"Huhh? What are you doing?"

It was so obvious that Mitsuhiro didn't bother answering the question as he slowly lowered the stepladder from the edge of the hole to the bottom. When he felt the rubber feet dig into the bottom of the hole, Mitsuhiro let go.

"All right. Climb down, please."

"What? Me? Why?"

"That's what your job is. I think your illness might have caused you to forget."

"I'm not sick!"

"Um… If you're anxious, I can come down with you, and we can wait together."

"If I go into that hole, I'll be even more cursed than I am now!"

Mitsuhiro was getting angry with the stubborn Yoshikazu Hara.

"That's not going to happen."

He grabbed the man's wrist, pulling him. Okuyama had warned him never to do that, but come on—it's not like he'd have to deal with homeless folks again after this anyway. If the guy would just listen, everything would work out fine—but to his surprise, the man resisted, trying to break free.

"Whoa. Don't fight me, all right? It's your job."

"Ahh! No, I don't want to! No, Mom! Stop it, Mom! Ahh!"

Mitsuhiro grimaced at the shrill sound of the man's voice echoing around him.

"Be quiet, please!"

He suddenly felt thirsty, which only made him angrier. The air was hotter now; the sweat on his forehead and the smell of dust in his nose made everything seem uncomfortable.

Desperate to get this over with, Mitsuhiro grabbed both of the man's hands and dragged him to the edge of the hole where the stepladder was. But the man violently twisted himself around, shaking off Mitsuhiro. He turned his back, trying to run away. Mitsuhiro hurriedly chased after him, grabbed him by his clothes, and pulled him back.

"Ahh! Let me go, Mom! Ahh! Please, I'm sorry!"

The man hit Mitsuhiro with the flashlight, and Mitsuhiro grabbed it from him, tired of all this. Hara grimaced back at him, taking off his helmet. Before Mitsuhiro could react, he was hit on the side of the head with it.

Mitsuhiro reared back from the impact, letting go of the flashlight. But he was determined not to let the man escape and grabbed his clothing with one hand. The man swung his helmet over and over, hitting Mitsuhiro's own helmet and shoulders repeatedly. No longer willing to deal with this, Mitsuhiro gave up trying to hold on and finally pushed the man away with both hands.

He saw the man fall backward out of the corner of his eye. A moment later, he heard a dull thud, but he couldn't tell what it was from. The shove had sent him sprawling too.

Quickly getting up, he looked around for the man. He was gone. The helmet Hara had been given was lying near the hole. The rest of him had disappeared.

He's escaped, Mitsuhiro thought, and he shivered. He tried to rush back toward the entrance, but screeched to a halt, realizing there were no footsteps coming from the pitch-black corridor up ahead. He looked back at the helmet, then at the hole beyond it. Now he was shuddering for different reasons. For the first time since arriving here, his heart pounded violently as he approached the edge of the hole and peered down into it.

The bottom was pitch-black, far too dark to see anything. Mitsuhiro bent down, reached for the flashlight he had dropped earlier, and shone it into the hole.

Then he realized what the dull thud was. The man had fallen right into the hole, lying on his back with his limbs spread out. But he couldn't have fallen neatly on the ground down there. He must've landed on the concrete block. Nothing else could have made that particular *thud*.

Dazed, Mitsuhiro stared down at the motionless man, but then he came to his senses and moved along the edge of the hole to use the stepladder. Being careful not to fall himself, he climbed down, flashlight in one hand.

When he reached the bottom of the hole, he took a deep breath and shone the light on the figure. The fallen man's face was turned toward him. He was staring at Mitsuhiro in a stupor, not even blinking, as if inviting him to come lie down there with him.

Mitsuhiro recoiled from the sight, and his back bumped against the stepladder. The problem wasn't that the man didn't close his eyes, even with the flashlight shining right on them. Nor was it the dark liquid oozing out from under his head. No, the issue was the face itself.

—Who is this?

It wasn't the face of the Yoshikazu Hara that he remembered. This man was much younger. His features were completely different.

—How could this happen? Why did I give him a ride, then? Why did I believe it was Yoshikazu Hara when I questioned him in the car?

He screamed the questions inside his head, but there were no answers. He had no idea what to do. He pressed his back against the ladder, staring at the unfamiliar man and his vacant eyes, frozen in place.

Chapter 4 Belongings

1

"What? Why?!"

Mitsuhiro grabbed his head with both hands and let out a pitiful groan. There was no way this should be happening. Nothing this strange should ever be happening.

—*Think!*

He desperately ordered himself, pressing his back against the wall at the bottom of that dark hole, hoping against hope that something would come to mind from somewhere in his confused head. But nothing did. There was no answer to be found. The realization that nothing could explain what was happening filled him with an overwhelming sense of anxiety, and he began to writhe in agony.

The man who had been Yoshikazu Hara just a moment ago—the man who *had* to be Yoshikazu Hara—was now lying on his back in the light of the flashlight, head hanging upside down. He was bathed in intensely bright light, but he didn't blink, and nothing came out of his half-open mouth. The wrinkles in his clothes, stiffened as he bent backward, did not move at all. There was no sign that he was breathing.

"Why did this happen…?"

Mitsuhiro stamped his feet like a child. Why was this man no longer Yoshikazu Hara? He was overcome with a feeling of helplessness he had never experienced before, unable to believe his own eyes, his own mind.

Tears began to spill down his cheeks. He felt like he had been transported back to his childhood and locked in a dark room with no way out. It brought him to the verge of madness.

But after a period of sobbing, Mitsuhiro finally came up with a theory from some corner of his mind that sort of made sense.

—This guy was already here.

That's right. He was at the bottom of the hole from the beginning. He was there before Mitsuhiro came with Yoshikazu Hara.

He must have just been mistaken when he concluded that Yoshikazu Hara had fallen into the hole. When he lost his footing in the darkness where the flashlight couldn't reach, Mitsuhiro had only assumed he had fallen into the hole.

While Mitsuhiro hurriedly climbed down, Yoshikazu Hara got frightened and ran away. He'd abandoned his duty here—no, he *forgot* his duty, because of his dementia. And then he just ran off, no clue what was going on. Mitsuhiro didn't even register in his mind any longer.

And while Yoshikazu Hara was disappearing into the darkness where Mitsuhiro couldn't see him, Mitsuhiro's gaze had landed on *this* man. Thanks to that, it looked like Hara and this stranger had switched places, as if by magic.

That was the only reasonable explanation. At least, he couldn't think of anything else at the moment. What else could it be? Was he going crazy? Did he bring some random person here, thinking he was Yoshikazu Hara, and then push him into this hole and make him completely limp like this? That was ridiculous. There was no way that could be true. There's no way that could have happened. This guy was here before they ever showed up. Mitsuhiro wanted to shout it out. But there was no need.

Way to figure it out, Mitsuhiro. His father was right next to him. ***This guy's been covered in ashes for a long time now. Look. They're piling up on his body.***

Mitsuhiro wiped away his tears, moved away from the wall, and looked closely at the figure. At some point, his hair and face had been covered with a thin layer of white powder. That familiar powder, Mitsuhiro realized, was now covering the wide-open eyes that had frightened him so much. His motionless chest, stomach, arms, and legs, as well as the ground around him, were covered with ash that had fallen from seemingly nowhere. He looked like a large, silent statue.

Relief welled up from the bottom of his heart at the sight. Tears formed in his eyes again.

This isn't anything you need to take the heat for. Mitsuhiro kept nodding in the direction of his father. ***You were just doing your job. An important job. Better hurry, now. Take what he has and clean it up.***

Mitsuhiro wondered for a moment what he was meant to take, but soon he realized. A phone had fallen out of the man's breast pocket and was lying next to his white-ash-covered face. Strangely, there was no ash on the phone, so Mitsuhiro gingerly approached it and picked it up.

The screen lit up. It wasn't protected by a passcode. Smartphones hadn't been around for very long—just a few years—so the idea of putting a passcode on it wasn't as common back then. Mitsuhiro saw it as a must for company equipment due to confidentiality requirements, but he also felt that putting a passcode on your personal phone so no one else could use it was all but admitting you wanted to hide something.

Thanks to that, Mitsuhiro had no problem accessing the man's phone. From the call history, he found out that the man had made previous contact with not only Mitsuhiro himself but also Okuyama from Helping Hands.

He opened the Twitter app, checking its post history. It was logged in, of course, to the Mole Unit-01 account. He tried to delete the tweets attacking the East Wing, along with the private messages he exchanged with him, but he couldn't. He wondered why, but soon realized it was because there was no reception this deep down.

He'd have to go back to the surface to clean this up. Resolving to do just that, he thrust the man's phone into his pants pocket. Suddenly, his eyes were drawn to the man's limp hands. They both had gloves on, and like the phone, there was no ash on them.

Mitsuhiro bent down, took the gloves off his hands, and put them in the other pocket of his pants. Now he'd be able to return with all the equipment from the office. The man had probably borrowed them from the storage room anyway, so there was no harm in returning them on his behalf.

Mitsuhiro didn't look at the man on the floor again as he staggered back to the stepladder, body aching, and carefully climbed up one step at a time. He emerged up top on all fours, heaving a languid sigh. He even thought about lying down and sleeping there, but he was worried about Sae, who was still at home. His father *was* watching over her, but considering her recent health scare, he couldn't stay here all night.

Mitsuhiro stood up and turned around, about to force himself to pull the stepladder back up, when he was suddenly blinded. A bright light froze him in place. Someone was standing on the other side of the hole, shining a large flashlight at him. The glare prevented him from seeing the person's face. He thought for a moment that Yoshikazu Hara had come back, and he almost smiled.

But the next moment, the flashlight was lowered, and a different man appeared.

It was Sota Araki from Tamai Construction. He stared suspiciously at Mitsuhiro on the other side of the hole, then noticed someone at the bottom and shone the light there. His eyes widened.

"Oh, *that's* not Yoshikazu Hara, either," Mitsuhiro said, obvious disappointment in his tone.

"What?" Araki replied in surprise. His voice seemed to echo loudly, maybe because of the hole between them.

"I brought Yoshikazu Hara in here, but then he went crazy on me out of nowhere. He hit me with his helmet and ran away."

Araki shone the flashlight on Mitsuhiro, walking around the hole to get closer to him.

"So who's that in the hole?"

"I don't know," Mitsuhiro said, in the tone of one trying to insist he wasn't lying.

"You don't know…? Didn't you bring him here?"

Araki stopped and shone his flashlight on the man lying at the bottom.

"He was here from the beginning."

"The beginning?"

"After Yoshikazu Hara got away from me, I noticed that person in the hole. He was already there when the two of us went inside."

Araki stretched out one side of his lips in a sneer, then the other, as if thinking about something.

"The bone ash that came out of the seal is returning to the hole."

"What?" Mitsuhiro had no idea what he was talking about.

"This might be someone who was cursed while working here."

"Cursed?"

"Yes. He left the site, but then he got called back to the hole. Just the other day, the previous head of Tamai told me to be careful in case something like this happens."

Araki stroked his hair back and sighed softly, as if expecting to be scolded by this former president later. Mitsuhiro couldn't understand any of this, but the important thing was that whoever was in the hole had been there from the beginning. Araki didn't seem to question that, which was a huge relief.

"Well, I'm the supervisor of this site, so I'll handle matters from here. You can go ahead and return home, Mr. Matsunaga."

Mitsuhiro felt a weight lift off his shoulders. He almost smiled, but he quickly resisted the urge. He needed to be considerate of Araki, who had just been called out on short notice on something that'd take him all night to work out. Mitsuhiro shouldn't show *too* much happiness around him.

"All right. Sorry for the trouble. What about Yoshikazu Hara?"

"On the phone, he told me he was going to his wife's facility…but he didn't seem to know where he even was at the time. You were lucky to run into him."

"I'll find him again and bring him here for you."

"Right. And I'll keep asking around to see if I can find him. Would you mind if I kept in touch with you, Mr. Matsunaga?"

"Yes, please do."

Mitsuhiro bowed his head, and Araki did the same, like they were business partners. In this deep underground space, illuminated only by their flashlights, it was an unusual, even comical situation. Considering the man lying motionless at the bottom of the hole, their calmness seemed downright eerie. But Mitsuhiro didn't want to think about that. He believed with all his heart that he should just leave everything to Araki.

"I'll head out, then."

Mitsuhiro tried to pass by Araki, then stopped suddenly. "Oh, one second. I had a question about the amulet."

"The amulet?"

"Yes. The president of Tamai Construction gave me one the other day. Would it be possible to get another one of those from you?"

"Well, they don't come cheap, but… What did you do with the one the president gave you?"

"I used it, actually."

"Used it? How?"

"Like he instructed me, I burned the contents, dissolved them in water…"

"So for appeasement?"

"Yes… Well, actually, I ran out of ashes, so I ended up burning the outer pouch as well."

"The pouch, too? Not to pry, but could you tell me why you did that?"

"Well…there was a little fire in my apartment. A family member left this old fan on too long, and it burned out. It made me kind of anxious, so…you know."

"Are you being cursed?"

"Huh?"

"Do you sense that your home, or your family, or you yourself are being cursed?"

"No, not at all. I just felt uneasy because…you know, I've had a couple small fires in a row now, so…"

"Have you smelled anything strange, like burning bones? Or has your family been feeling unwell because of it? Or maybe you didn't notice some bone ash stuck to you, and it reappeared somewhere in your home?"

"Nothing like that, no," Mitsuhiro said without hesitation.

That was the truth. He couldn't take such silly stories about curses or whatever seriously at all. All he wanted was to get that amulet. That would solve everything. He didn't need to go telling some guy he barely even knew about what had happened to Sae and Miyoko.

"Well, as I think the president mentioned to you, Tamai's amulets are quite expensive, even for a single body."

"A single body?"

"That's how we count them—one body, two bodies, three bodies. They're divine bodies, having been bestowed with their power by the gods."

"All right... So how much does one cost?"

"Even the cheapest one is two hundred thousand yen."

Mitsuhiro's eyes boggled. Two hundred thousand for a little good-luck thing? Did he hear that right? Even two thousand was too much, in his opinion; a hundred times that amount was completely insane. It even angered him a bit.

"What? Two hundred thousand? Isn't that a little too much?"

Araki snorted. *If you don't want it, don't buy it*—that was the attitude he presented.

"Our amulets are the real thing, you understand. They're not like the cheap ones, the ones made by college students doing seasonal work for a shrine when they're on break. It takes a lot of time and manpower. We also properly reward our *mi-keshi* so that we can receive the blessings of the gods."

Mitsuhiro felt an urge to argue the point, but his lips were too tightly sealed to open. He had no idea how to refute the strange, almost occult reasoning of this man.

"But if you're not being cursed, then you don't need it. I'd suggest you leave quickly, or something might leave with you that you don't want."

"No, um...I mean, yes... Excuse me, then."

Mitsuhiro turned away from Araki. He immediately changed his mind. He turned back toward him.

"Actually, I'd still like one, please."

"An amulet?"

"Yes. How long will it take to get?"

"Not long at all. I'd just have to go get one from where we keep them."

"How about tomorrow?"

"Certainly. It'd be in exchange for your harvest offering, though."

"My what?"

"Money offered to the gods, that is. In olden times, it would have been the first ears of rice harvested at the start of the season."

Araki scratched his neck as he spoke. He seemed to be getting annoyed with talking to someone so ignorant on this subject.

"And that's the two hundred thousand yen?"

"Yes. There are more expensive ones, too."

"All right. I'll have the money. Is it okay if I contact you tomorrow?"

"That's fine, Mr. Matsunaga, but..."

"...But what?" Mitsuhiro urged, a little irritated. He was getting tired of talking so much in this dry cavern. He wanted to get back to the surface and drink all the water he could.

"Are you being cursed?"

Araki asked the same question again, leaving Mitsuhiro even more frustrated than before.

"What? No. Of course not."

Araki was not satisfied. "If you see anyone in your life who shouldn't be there, please let me know."

"Shouldn't be there how?"

"In most cases, it'd be someone deceased. If someone who died long ago starts appearing around you, that's a sure sign you're under a curse. The bone ash in places like this can often transform into the deceased, so it can break through the barrier. By 'barrier,' I mean the one protecting a certain plot of land, or house, or even a person's body or mind. When bone ash makes its way through a barrier, the evil spirits that cause mischief on earth will gather around it and join forces to curse you together, often creating accidents involving water or fire. If you don't realize you're talking to the dead and start seeing or hearing things that aren't real, then in the worst case, it could endanger your life and the lives of those around you."

Mitsuhiro couldn't help but chuckle. He wanted to ask Araki if he really believed all that nonsense, but Araki's tone was serious. The guy was just living in a totally different world from the modern one Mitsuhiro called home. He and his kind had turned the propagation of stupid old superstitions into a kind of business.

"I'll be careful about that," Mitsuhiro said. He wanted to end this conversation on a polite note, as irritating as it was, mainly because he didn't want Araki to get angry and refuse to sell the amulet to him.

"If you *do* happen to see the deceased, please wear or take possession of one of their belongings. That alone will do much to prevent the bone ash from transforming."

"Okay. Thanks for telling me. I'll keep that in mind."

Mitsuhiro bowed, making it clear he wanted to end this chat. Araki remained silent, nodding slightly. He, too, found it frustrating to advise someone who seemed to barely even speak his language.

"I'll contact you again tomorrow. Thank you."

Mitsuhiro said goodbye as if he had just wrapped up a client meeting, and this time he turned away from Araki. He walked toward the open door, picking up the helmet and flashlight Yoshikazu Hara had left behind. They both belonged to Hara, not to whoever was in that hole. Mitsuhiro was firm with himself about that.

"Hopefully the bone ash will come back… I'll have to consult with the old president again."

Mitsuhiro could hear Araki griping to himself behind him, but he ignored it and continued on his way. He turned around at the door, but Araki was already climbing down the stepladder into the hole, so with no further goodbyes, he entered the passageway and climbed the stairs.

—Am I being cursed?

As he headed toward the ground floor, a laugh suddenly welled up from his throat again. The stories from Tamai Construction's employees certainly *seemed* convincing when told in such a creepy place—that was the annoying part about all this. A lot of people actually believed all that crap, Mitsuhiro was sure. Maybe not even that many, but just a few staunch believers were all Tamai Construction really needed. Charging hundreds of thousands of yen for a single amulet? No wonder they demanded millions for some barren room underground.

But despite his opinions on Tamai Construction, his desire to get that amulet of theirs ASAP was a wholly different matter. That was that, and this was this. Needing something to get rid of that weird smell was completely separate from being cursed or whatever.

—Isn't that right, Dad?

Mitsuhiro smiled as he looked up at the reassuring sight of his father climbing the stairs ahead of him.

2

Returning his helmet and the other equipment, Mitsuhiro headed for the gate on the soundproof wall, surrounded by the noise of the night crew. No one stopped him along the way, but as soon as he stepped outside, he noticed that his clothes were covered in grayish dirt. He sighed. This dirt was normal within these walls, but it looked out of place at the station's ticket gates, with so many people coming and going.

But he didn't have time to go to a restroom and clean himself up. It was almost time for the last train of the night.

Mitsuhiro hurriedly got into the company car he had parked there… and then groaned to himself. The smell of Yoshikazu Hara still lingered in the car.

Mitsuhiro started the engine and opened all the windows. When he looked in the rearview mirror to check behind him, he was shocked by the sight of his own face. Not only were gray dirt and white ash caked on his hair and cheeks, but he also had cuts and bruises from being hit repeatedly with Yoshikazu Hara's helmet.

He had never seen himself in such a sorry state before, but there was nothing to be done about it. He wiped his cheeks with his sleeve, but that only rubbed the ash deeper into his skin. Quickly giving up on the idea, he drove off in the company car.

On the way back to the lot, he kept wrinkling his nose because of that lingering smell—the smell of Yoshikazu Hara. Tomorrow, he'd need to put some deodorizer and wet wipes in his briefcase before going to work. For now, though, the most important thing was to get home.

After returning the car to the company lot, he hurried into the station. He walked onto a platform with a large crowd of people rushing to catch the last trains, arriving just as one pulled in.

It was actually the train before the very last one of the night. He sat down in a seat, relieved that he didn't have to hail a taxi home. If he was going to buy a two-hundred-thousand-yen amulet, he'd have to avoid unnecessary expenses for a bit.

Wait. Two hundred thousand yen for *one*? Well, that was the kind of money you needed to bring a small god into your life. A necessary expense to get rid of that smell.

With these thoughts in mind, he took a phone out of his pants pocket, the one that belonged to the man on the ground in the basement. He turned it on, opened Twitter, and deleted all the tweets about the East Wing. He also made sure to delete the messages the man had exchanged with him directly. As soon as the deed was done, he threw the phone into his bag with a deep sigh of relief.

The sense of ease and fulfillment at finally completing the task gave a pleasant patina to his fatigue. Looking back now, it was clearly his job to retrieve Mole Unit-01's phone and delete any and all posts that could've impacted the project and his company's stock price.

You need to thank Yoshikazu Hara for leading you to this solution, don't you? He could feel his father there again, talking to him. ***That man talked too much about the hole. He told his pals that the hole was too big—that we should fill it in. He even put dirt in the hole to keep it from getting bigger. That's how he wound up covered in ash. Listen, Mitsuhiro. You must never do anything to anger that hole.***

"Right. I hear you, Dad," muttered Mitsuhiro, just as the train stopped and a handful of people got on. Two of them—a woman in a suit and an elderly man—made a move to sit next to Mitsuhiro but then passed on by, as if they had reconsidered, and sat down elsewhere.

Mitsuhiro thought at first that this was because his father was sitting next to him, but that wasn't the case. The seats around him were empty. No, they'd avoided him because he was dirty, and his face was covered in cuts and bruises. Realizing this, Mitsuhiro frowned, feeling a tad uncomfortable. Maybe Yoshikazu Hara's body odor had rubbed off on him. The company car still stank to high heaven. The smell might even make people think he was homeless or something.

Something about being blatantly avoided, like a mud puddle on the road, was humiliating. Anger, frustration, and sadness stole into his mind.

How was this his fault? Didn't they ever think about how he wound up like this? Didn't they realize how hard he'd been working, no thought given to his own needs? Why couldn't they show a little sympathy?

As he muttered to himself, he was overcome by the urge to stand up, march over to the people avoiding him, and sit his ass down right next to them, but he managed to reel it back. He'd avoid someone in this state, too. He lowered his head, fighting back all the unpleasant feelings, and got off the train as soon as it arrived at his stop, almost fleeing the people inside.

Caught between the repulsive idea of people seeing him in this state and the desire to retain his pride, he took the stairs instead of the escalator to avoid strangers' eyes. He hurried into his condo building and inserted his key into the door of his home, ready to finally relax. No one would see him now, and he could finally take his time in the shower.

But something odd caught his attention. The door was already unlocked.

—Did I forget to lock it?

Frowning, he opened the door and saw a pair of men's shoes that shouldn't have been there. They were old-fashioned dark-brown leather shoes, the kind Mitsuhiro would never wear.

As he closed the door, wondering who they belonged to, the person in question tromped into the hallway. It was his father-in-law.

"Where the hell have you been?"

The stern, reproachful expression on his face was replaced by a blank stare as soon as he saw Mitsuhiro.

"Whoa, what happened to you?"

"I had to go to the office for an emergency," Mitsuhiro said, his tone just as threatening, throwing his house keys into his bag.

"An emergency? What would you need to do at this hour?"

"Plenty. I had to cover all the bases."

He deliberately kept his answer vague to keep Choji Umehara, his father-in-law, at bay. It did nothing to improve Choji's bad mood.

"Well, why didn't you answer your phone? Sae called Miyoko crying because you weren't home. She said she called you, but you didn't answer."

"I was underground the whole time," he replied, mentally chastising himself for not checking his phone when he came back up. He didn't expect Sae to be awake and calling people; still, he should have at least asked his father about her. But how? He didn't have any time to think about that anyway.

"So Miyoko asked you to come and watch her?"

His tone was meant to imply that he didn't think that was necessary. He could see that it took Choji by surprise.

Calm down, he told himself. *You're losing control.* He was tired and parched, and he couldn't stand the way his father-in-law was staring at him with pity. Choji had made his fortune with an industrial-leasing start-up he founded, and he had a bad habit of constantly imposing his authority on others. He had close ties with Shimaoka, and he was also the kind of man to grumble about the "cheap" hotel restaurant Mitsuhiro had booked so he could discuss marrying Miyoko with them all.

"It's only natural to worry about Sae being alone, isn't it? I know you didn't think you'd be running around at this time of night, but still…"

Instead of refuting Mitsuhiro, Choji spoke in a conciliatory tone, which was unusual for him.

I must look really miserable right now, Mitsuhiro thought, and that just made him angrier. His father-in-law must think of him as this horrid, miserable, dirty man whose words didn't matter at all.

And Mitsuhiro wasn't alone in thinking so. Behind Choji, his father was nodding vigorously.

"This guy doesn't understand anything. I was watching over Sae. If anything happened, I would have told you right away."

Mitsuhiro nodded.

Choji frowned, glanced behind him, then quickly turned back to his son-in-law. "What? Is there something behind me?"

"My father was watching over Sae," Mitsuhiro said, ignoring him. "I'll call Miyoko tomorrow—"

"Wait. Wait a minute. What do you mean? Your father? Not your mother?"

Mitsuhiro frowned, not understanding why Choji was so surprised.

"Your father died years ago, didn't he?"

"Yeah. So what?"

He was finding it difficult to control his irritation. He wanted to take off his shoes, drink a glass or two of water, and get his body under a hot shower. Why did he have to stand here by the doorway, like he was nailed to it? He could feel his innards boiling.

Miyoko's father was always like this. It made him sick. Mitsuhiro tilted his head slightly toward his father standing behind Choji. His father smiled.

"Oh, I get it, trust me. I went through something similar."

He and his father had Choji on the ropes now. That made Mitsuhiro feel much more confident.

Choji looked behind him again. When he saw nothing there, he held both hands out toward Mitsuhiro, slowly raising them up and down. He was acting like he had encountered some kind of attacker in this narrow passageway, with nowhere to escape. His only choice was to try to calm his opponent.

His father-in-law was acting more submissive toward him now than ever before—Mitsuhiro could even see the fear on his face. Meanwhile, his own anger was slowly subsiding.

He'd thought this whole thing would leave a bad taste in his mouth, but it wasn't so. All he felt was reassured. He even wanted to scare Choji some more now.

"Well, here, Mitsuhiro, you've had a long day. Why don't you get some rest for now? I'll be leaving soon, so… Oh, that's right. Miyoko's worried about you, so can you give her a call?"

I want to, but you're too busy getting in my damn way, aren't you?

He thought about yelling at him, but he no longer wanted to expend the effort. All he wanted was to shower and relax as soon as possible—and, really, he was glad his father-in-law had rushed over, which meant he didn't have to face Sae all crying and lonely.

"Right. I'll be sure to do that," he said confidently. "Sorry for all the trouble."

Choji hurriedly came to the front door, as if he could hear Mitsuhiro's inner voice telling him to get the hell out. He pressed himself against the wall to make room for Mitsuhiro as he took off his shoes and stepped out of the entryway and into the condo. Once Mitsuhiro was done, Choji swiftly reached for the door handle.

"Take care of yourself. And Miyoko, too."

He left without waiting for Mitsuhiro's reply and closed the door behind him.

"Ran away with his tail between his legs," his father said, smiling in the hallway. Mitsuhiro chuckled a bit as he locked the door.

"That's the first time I've ever seen him like that. I owe you one, Dad."

"You got me on your side, okay, son? Now go get cleaned up."

"Thanks, Dad."

Mitsuhiro went to the kitchen, put his bag on the floor, and drank some water. He was so thirsty that he really did want to drink directly from the faucet. After rehydrating, he took a deep breath, went to the bathroom, looked in the mirror, and sighed again. His face was covered in ash, and some blood was seeping out of his nose. He didn't even notice the bleeding until now. Dried blood was stuck around his mouth, too.

He looked terrible. No wonder he scared people off on the train and shocked his father-in-law.

He took his phone out of his jacket pocket and placed it on the sink. Once he turned it on, he'd undoubtedly see an avalanche of missed calls from Sae, Miyoko, and Choji. But he didn't feel like contacting Miyoko quite yet. He wanted to at least clean himself up first, or he might wind up yelling at her out of frustration. His father would probably say that he ought to do just that, to teach her discipline or whatnot, but he wanted to avoid antagonizing his wife when he had so much hard work to do.

Mitsuhiro took off his clothes, being careful not to scatter the ashes and dirt around, and nearly put them in the laundry basket before he thought better of it. Everything was so dirty and smelly that he put all of it, including his underwear, straight into the washing machine, added detergent, and turned it on. He didn't want Miyoko to nag him about the smell later.

As he showered, he felt a sense of joy, as if the difficult day had all been worth it. It was frustrating how little Miyoko and Choji understood him despite all the work he had. When he thought about it, he felt less angry and more resigned to his fate. And why not? People like them couldn't possibly understand what it was like so far beneath the ground.

Exactly. You can't understand what that hole is like unless you've been inside it. Mitsuhiro thought he heard his father's voice outside the bathroom. ***You wouldn't understand that the hole gets bigger as more ash comes out, and then it starts wanting even more. No one understands how important your work is. But that doesn't mean you should fold, all right? Keep going.***

Yeah. Thanks, Dad.

After washing himself thoroughly under the warm, clean, inviting water,

Mitsuhiro left the shower. As he was drying himself, his phone rang on the sink. The screen showed it was from Miyoko. He picked it up.

"Hello? Miyoko?"

"What are you doing? Why didn't you answer?"

Miyoko's voice was quiet, but her tone was harsh. She must have been calling from her hospital room.

"I couldn't help it. I was at work until just now. I just finished showering and changing. I'll call you back in five minutes."

"Can you explain what you were doing?"

"I will. Just give me a minute."

Mitsuhiro hung up the phone, put on a shirt, underwear, and pants, and used the hair dryer for a minute or two. He was concerned that the white powder might sprinkle off him like dandruff, but his hair was perfectly clean.

He put his phone in his pants pocket, left the bathroom, and went to check on Sae. Quietly opening the door to her room, he listened carefully. Once he heard her peaceful breathing, he left her alone.

He then went to the kitchen and picked up his bag from the floor. Sure enough, there was gray dirt on it. He used some paper towels to wipe it clean so that Miyoko wouldn't complain later. Then he took a plastic bottle of sparkling water from the refrigerator, sat down on a chair in the dining room, and placed the bag on the floor.

He opened the bottle, took a sip straight from it, and took a deep breath. Now that he was more relaxed—in the right mindset, he was sure—he picked up his phone and called Miyoko back.

"Hello?"

"It's me."

"Why'd you leave Sae out of nowhere?"

"I got a call from someone I was looking for. I had to go see him right away."

"You were looking for someone?"

"Yeah. Someone involved with that ritual stuff Tamai Construction is doing in the East Wing basement. I needed to confirm the man wasn't engaged in forced labor down there, but he didn't have a fixed address, so..."

"Oh, he's homeless?"

"He sold his house to put his wife in a memory-care facility. He developed dementia, too, not long after, and his wife didn't even know where he was."

"I see..."

"Yeah. So, I managed to find him. I asked him some questions, took him to the site, and then I tried to hand him over to a Tamai Construction employee, but he started fighting me out of nowhere, and then he ran off."

"What? Fighting you? Why?"

"I don't know. Maybe his illness was making him imagine something. He clocked me good with his helmet."

"Oh no. Are you okay?"

Miyoko's tone was now completely sympathetic toward Mitsuhiro.

He smiled at this, satisfied. He wanted everyone who'd avoided him on the train to hear this conversation. He was doing a job that deserved people's sympathy and appreciation, and he couldn't have been prouder of it.

"Yeah, it's no big deal. But I'm sorry for what I did to you and Sae. And to your father, too."

"That's okay. Dad just sits around watching TV every night anyway. But...he called me earlier. He said you were acting strange."

"I'm sorry. You know, I was just exhausted. I was trying to help someone, and he beat me up."

"You said something about your dead father watching over Sae?"

"It was just a figure of speech. I didn't know what else to do. I didn't think I'd be away from home for so long."

"You should have called me! I could have asked Mom or Dad to look after her."

"You were in the hospital. I thought you were already asleep. Sorry, it was all so sudden, and I was tired, so I wasn't thinking straight. I just wanted to finish my work."

"I understand, but...Sae was crying really hard, you know. I don't want her to get so worried that she has trouble sleeping. When she wakes up, give her some attention, all right?"

"Yeah, I should have left a note for her in case she woke up."

"And pick up your phone, too!"

"I couldn't get reception down below. I'm sorry."

Miyoko sighed. "*Well,*" she said, her tone lighter, "*I'm not exactly able to help, myself, so I know it's no use blaming you. But these are the times when Sae gets bad dreams and wakes up.*"

"She had a bad dream? Did she say that?"

"If she still remembers it tomorrow, try to comfort her, okay? Because it was scary even for me."

"What'd she dream about?"

"Ohhh..."

Miyoko let out a groaning sort of sound, implying she didn't want to talk about it.

"She said someone took her away and threw her into a hole—this square hole—and she couldn't get out. She was crying about it."

The scene vividly played itself in Mitsuhiro's mind—Sae being abducted and thrown into that hole. Sae chained up, crying at the bottom of the hole. White ash falling on Sae's face and body.

—Quit being stupid. How could something like that happen?

But his arms were covered with goose bumps. A rush ran up his spine, and he was overcome by the vague feeling that the hole really was capable of that. But he quickly pushed the thought away.

"That sure is a scary dream."

"Yeah. So take the time to listen to her, all right?"

"Sure. Are you going to be discharged?"

"Yeah. They said there's nothing wrong with me, so I should be able to come home tomorrow afternoon."

"I'm sorry I didn't answer your phone call."

"No, it's fine. The doctor's about to make his rounds, so I should hang up."

"Okay. Good night."

"Good night."

Mitsuhiro put his phone on the table and looked at his arms, still covered in goose bumps. He tried to drink some sparkling water, but his hands were shaking so much, he almost dropped the bottle.

Falling into a large, dark square hole, unable to get out.

—*Calm down. You won't let Sae go through that. You won't let that happen.*

Mitsuhiro took a few heavy breaths. When his hands stopped shaking, he grabbed the bottle with both hands and gulped the water down.

—*It'll be fine. I'll get the amulet.*

That thought came to him with the sensation of the carbonation.

—*Then I'll have a god or two on my side. I'll have an amulet worth two hundred thousand yen protecting my family.*

But as he took the bottle away from his mouth and stared at the fizzing bubbles inside, he wondered if that would be enough. Would having some tiny little god on hand really guarantee an escape from that hole? What if he needed more? Would he have to ask Araki or Tamai Construction to get something else for him?

—*The same people who charge ten million yen for a tiny shrine?*

Could it be *him* in a metaphorical hole right now? Was he being dragged down, step by step, into something he could never escape from?

Because he had freed Yoshikazu Hara?

The man had volunteered to be a human sacrifice, but then his dementia made him forget all about it and he fled. So now Mitsuhiro was being called to that hole instead? It was an absurd thought, but he couldn't dismiss it as such. In fact, it seemed supremely logical to him.

Mitsuhiro stared at the bubbles popping in the bottle and finally admitted it to himself. He was in a serious predicament, one he had no real explanation for. He shivered.

3

The edges of the square hole were slowly undulating.

Watching it, Mitsuhiro pictured a giant jellyfish dancing in the sea. A creature that expanded and contracted as it floated along, following some ancient rhythm. Sucking in the seawater, filtering out the organisms that provided its food, and expelling whatever it didn't need. But this was more than repeating its primitive life process—occasionally, it followed its survival instincts, using its own intelligence and the toxins it possessed to repel enemies or capture prey.

The hole was the same. And it was more cunning, more ferocious, and more ravenous than any jellyfish. The thing was alive. Not in any metaphorical sense. The hole itself, cut out of the ground, was breathing, expanding as its desires did, calling for the nourishment it needed.

Convinced of this, Mitsuhiro squirmed at the thought of the ground he relied on suddenly disappearing beneath him, his spine being rendered useless. It was similar to the feeling of the moment a roller coaster hurtled downward. The feeling of being pushed off some high place with no hope for survival.

The reality he once believed to be solid under him crumbled away, and his mind was sucked into an unknown darkness. Overcome by this feeling of despair, Mitsuhiro screamed out loud, just like the riders on those roller coasters.

Well done. Look. The hole is happy. His father was next to him.

What is it? What is it, Dad? Why is it alive? Mitsuhiro was crying out, regressing to his childhood.

It's a throne. What remains after the water god was appeased in a previous ritual. The ashes that the god kept in place came out, and a hole was left in its place. It wasn't dug up by anyone. It just opened up on its own. Isn't that amazing?

I'm scared, Dad. I'm really scared. Get it away from me.

Ignoring Mitsuhiro's cries and pleas, his father continued to explain, smiling the whole while.

Once the hole opened up, various things came to it and became one with it. The ashes kept on coming out, and eventually they started inviting **mi-keshi** ***into it. It was born in the remains of a ritual hall, so it knows what to do to appease itself.***

"Appease"? What's that mean? Will it disappear then?

Ha-ha-ha! His father laughed. ***No, Mitsuhiro. Appeasing means keeping it in place. There are appeasing rituals to keep gods like that from leaving.* **Mi-keshi,** *too. And look. This hole is happy. It's glad that it could invite you to be the*** **mi-keshi**.

I'm not a mi-keshi, *Dad. Please. Let somebody else do it.*

You are the **mi-keshi** ***of the hole. You are the one who will obey the hole and the ashes that come out of it. Isn't that amazing?***

No, I don't want to. I don't want to.

If you're disobedient, you know, you'll be punished for it. Do you want to make your father punish you?

Mitsuhiro was suddenly speechless. He began to cry softly. His father gently stroked his head. ***Listen. You released the water god's*** **mi-keshi.** ***Yoshikazu Hara. And the*** **mi-keshi** ***of fire and smoke took the*** **mi-keshi** ***of water and hid him away. He's gone now.***

Fire and smoke? Mitsuhiro had to ask, despite his fear of punishment. *Is that me, too?*

What, so obeying the hole and the ashes isn't enough for you? You want to obey the fire and smoke, too?

Mitsuhiro's tears grew. He couldn't bear to experience anything more frightening than this. If something like that happened, he would lose his mind.

Don't worry. His father smiled. ***The fire and smoke*** **mi-keshi** ***is already here.***

It's not me?

No. He works near the hole. He keeps starting fires at the construction site to delay the water-god ritual.

The water god? If the water god comes again, will that make the hole disappear?

It'll be filled in, his father muttered. ***It's doomed to be filled in eventually. But if we can appease it properly, then even when it's filled with earth again, what was once the hole will still remain. It will become an*** **aragami,**

a powerful guardian spirit, together with the water god, and remain there forever.

Dad, I'm scared.

Don't worry, Mitsuhiro. They're all scared at first. But once you understand how important a job this is, you won't be scared anymore. If you keep refusing, I'll have to punish you, and everything above the hole might collapse.

Collapse?

That big building you're trying to build. The company you work for. The condo you're paying off. The daughter and wife who live with you—it'll all collapse. And then it'll be gone. If that happens, we'll both have to live the rest of our lives being constantly mocked by your spiteful in-laws.

No. I don't want that.

Then you have to understand the importance of this work. Stand proud, Mitsuhiro. If you become an **aragami** ***yourself, you'll feel so brave, so happy. Even your daughter and wife would gladly sacrifice themselves for the hole, maybe. You might even feel like becoming a*** **mi-keshi** ***yourself.***

No. Please no.

I'm just trying to help you. I'll support you, whatever you decide to do. Your old dad is here with you, okay? So don't sit here crying forever. Just relax and do your best at your work. Do you understand, Mitsuhiro?

"Yeah," Mitsuhiro sadly replied as he woke up. He sat up in a panic, thinking there might be a large, living, breathing square hole somewhere in the dimly lit bedroom.

But there was no hole. The voice of reason told him there couldn't be. He yawned, relieved.

He got out of bed, careful not to wake Miyoko, but when he looked back, no one was there. Then he remembered that Miyoko was in the hospital. Barring unforeseen complications, she'd be back home today. Talking to her over the phone yesterday, it didn't sound like anything serious.

Besides, he'd be able to get the amulet today. There was nothing to worry about.

So he went to wash his face in the bathroom. He saw his reflection in the mirror, and it looked like something hard had collided with his face. The cuts and bruises from Yoshikazu Hara's helmet were still there. He sighed, wondering if it would scare Sae, as he washed his face and brushed his teeth. He was in his clothes and cooking up a breakfast of fried eggs, toast, and vegetable juice when Sae woke up, seeming a little dazed.

"Daddy, did you fall?"

Sure enough, Sae's first words were tinged with worried surprise.

"Yeah," he replied, as cheerfully as he could. "I fell down the stairs while I was at work. But I'll be okay."

"Work?"

"I had some work to do last night, when you were asleep. Sorry I left you alone like that. I got back as soon as I could."

"Oh… Um, I called you." Sae seemed to have just remembered.

"Yes, Mom told me on the phone. Were you lonely? I'm sorry."

"Um, when you came home, was Grandpa here?" She looked up, trying to remember.

"Yes, he was."

"Mommy's daddy?"

"Huh?"

"I think there was a man here. I didn't know him."

"Right, Mom's dad. We talked for a bit, and he left right after that."

"Oh, okay. I was scared when I called Mommy, and he told me he came so I wouldn't be scared. But it was weird, and I got even more scared."

Sae suddenly tilted her head. This sequence of events must have stopped adding up for her. She had made a phone call, and then her grandfather showed up…but there was someone else here before that. It didn't make sense to her, but it seemed natural enough to Mitsuhiro. He had asked his father to watch Sae, after all.

So he decided to ask.

"Was your other grandpa there with you?"

"No, I only heard his voice. Wait...but he rang the doorbell, and then I opened the door? Hmm... Maybe I had a dream?"

Sae stewed over this a bit, anxiety flashing across her eyes. Even a first grader could see that this was odd.

"Well, I'm sure your other grandpa was worried about you. He was watching over you."

Sae's eyes widened with even greater anxiety. She had never met her grandfather, so this encounter probably seemed unwelcome to her.

"In your dream, I mean."

When he added that, Sae slumped, looking uncomfortable. "Really?"

"I think so. He was trying to cheer you up because you had a scary dream."

"Hmm. *Did* I have a scary dream?"

"That's what Mommy told me."

"Oh. I guess I forgot it. I don't remember."

Sae looked at Mitsuhiro with frightened eyes, as if she didn't want to try to remember.

"That's fine. It's okay to forget about scary dreams. They don't mean anything anyway." Mitsuhiro compassionately stroked his daughter's head. "Ready for some breakfast real soon?"

"I wanna wash my face. Come on, Daddy."

Sae grabbed Mitsuhiro's wrist, and her grip was surprisingly strong. As if she was clinging to him in fear.

"Okay. I'll make sure you get all clean."

Mitsuhiro took Sae to the bathroom, holding her by the shoulders. She said she was afraid to change her clothes by herself, so he helped her with that, and then they finally set the table for breakfast.

"Hey, can we call Mommy?" Sae asked at the table.

Mitsuhiro pulled out his phone and dialed. There were ten or so calls made to him last night alone, so he reminded himself to delete them from the log later.

"Hello?"

Sae's face lit up when she heard Miyoko's voice. "Hi, Mommy! It's Sae!"

"Good morning, Sae. Is Daddy there?"

"Yeah! We just finished breakfast. Daddy fell and hurt himself!"

"He fell… Yes, I heard. Daddy is so clumsy, isn't he?"

Sae giggled loudly. "Are you coming home today, Mommy?"

"I should be able to, yes. So go ahead and go to school, okay, Sae?"

"Okay!"

Sae wanted to talk to Miyoko, so Mitsuhiro left his phone on the table while he put the dishes in the sink. He didn't have time to wash them, so he just put them in the water for now. He got Sae ready for school, said goodbye to Miyoko, ended the call, and put the phone in his bag.

Then he noticed the other phone in there. He frowned, unsure who it belonged to at first, but then he remembered. It was from the man at the bottom of the hole. Yesterday's sense of accomplishment at stopping all those negative rumors on Twitter had long faded; instead, the unpleasant problem of what to do with the phone now arose.

He had taken it from a man collapsed on the ground. If he were accused of theft, he couldn't plausibly deny it. He had even deleted the man's Twitter posts without permission. Why did he do that? Because his father told him to, of course…but he hadn't considered the consequences. Should he tell Araki that he found it near the hole and give it to him? And be honest about the deleted posts, too?

Why don't you just throw it away and pretend you don't know anything? He felt like his father was beside him. ***No one saw you take it, after all.***

Was that really true? The man lying there in the hole had been staring right at him the whole time. Hadn't he? Or was he too covered in ash to see anything at all?

"Daddy, I'm ready!"

Sae called out to him as she put on her schoolbag, so he stopped thinking about it for the moment. He left their condo with Sae, thinking over which tasks to tackle first before meeting with Araki today.

"See you later!"

Mitsuhiro waved goodbye to Sae as she walked toward school, and then he headed for the train station. On the train, he took his phone out of his bag to check his call log. He didn't think he had any, but after all the commotion last night, he didn't want to miss an urgent call from his boss.

Fortunately, there were no work calls—but there *was* one from an unexpected source. His mother, who still lived in the old house in Hachioji, west of Tokyo. Again, the call had come while he was deep underground.

Mitsuhiro pondered what it could be about. His mother, Akiko Matsunaga, was of the opinion that no news was good news. She didn't bother keeping up with family members, and she never sent cards out for New Year's, either. This had caused some friction with Miyoko's parents, the Umeharas, who were both diligent letter writers and believed connections mattered in everything. The total lack of response to the New Year's cards, Christmas cards, and any sort of other seasonal greeting they sent Akiko was, in the Umeharas' eyes, simple rudeness (and yet another thing to complain to Mitsuhiro about).

Miyoko and Mitsuhiro had convinced them that it was just an innocent difference in personality and customs, and that settled the matter—but as a result of that, the two families had maintained little to no contact for a long time. Maybe Mitsuhiro and Miyoko didn't talk with their parents all that much, but at least Akiko would step in to help when the couple needed something, which wasn't so much the case with the Umeharas. There was a point when Miyoko relied on Mitsuhiro's mother more than her own parents—another nit for the Umeharas to pick. Now that Akiko had developed diabetes, however, Miyoko was more reluctant to over-rely on her.

Did she fall ill, maybe? Mitsuhiro thought about calling her during his lunch break, but instead of putting his phone in his bag, he reconsidered and put it in the pocket of his jacket instead. If he kept two cell phones in that bag, he might accidentally take out the wrong one.

While he was at it, he also turned off the Twitter poster's phone entirely. He considered what to do with it but failed to think of a good solution. By the time he arrived at Shibuya Station, he'd given up on the problem entirely, too tired to think. For now, he opted to wait until he was sure nobody knew he had picked it up. Throwing it away now would be like admitting his mistake…but if he gave it to Araki right away, that'd cause more headaches for him, so he decided to just hold on to it.

To be honest, he didn't want to think about Twitter guy's phone at all anymore. He had something much more important to do. Stopping at a convenience store, he withdrew money from the ATM there—the two hundred thousand yen for the amulet. The… What was it? The "harvest offering." It was pretty unusual for Mitsuhiro to withdraw such a large amount at one time. *Very* unusual, in fact. If he ever took this much cash out at once again, it'd be for the assorted stuff they'd need to buy after their second child was born.

As he put the stack of twenty bills in an envelope and put it in his bag, he wondered how he should explain this to Miyoko. No good excuses immediately came to mind. He'd just have to come up with a reason before Miyoko noticed and said something.

Would a two-hundred-thousand-yen amulet really solve everything? He didn't know that either. Their living expenses, the mortgage, and Sae's college fund kept running through his mind. But by the time he reached Shimaoka, he had pushed all those thoughts out of his head.

The moment Mitsuhiro arrived at the office and put his bag on his desk, Takenaka immediately approached him. "Hey, can we talk for a moment?" he began, but when he saw the cuts on Mitsuhiro's face, his mouth fell open.

"What happened? No, wait—let's talk over here."

Mitsuhiro took his bag along, following Takenaka's gestures. It had both a large amount of cash and someone else's phone in it, and he didn't want to let go of either.

In a few seconds, they had sat down at a partitioned-off conference room.

"Did you find anything yet?"

"Yes, a little. I found Yoshikazu Hara, the person I saw at the East Wing's ritual hall earlier. I questioned him, but when I tried to hand him over to an employee from Tamai Construction, he suddenly grew violent."

"Violent? You mean he hit you?"

"Well. . .yes."

Takenaka's face became stern. If an on-site worker assaulted a Shimaoka employee, it'd call the project's site management into question—and if news leaked out, they'd have to take measures to stave off the rumors. Takenaka himself would have to answer some tough questions, too, about giving his staff tasks that exposed them to physical danger.

"No taking it back now, though," Mitsuhiro quickly added, trying to reassure him. "I think I took the wrong approach with him, sadly. I know my face looks bad, but it's really nothing serious."

Not serious enough to make it a criminal case or claim workers' comp, anyway. Making this statement to Takenaka didn't mean Mitsuhiro was waiving all his rights along those lines, but he felt a need to calm his boss down a little. Otherwise, Takenaka might start thinking about taking him off the team as the first step to control the damage. Mitsuhiro wasn't about to stand for that. After all the hard work he'd put in, losing his position within the company would be a disaster.

Takenaka seemed sympathetic to Mitsuhiro's frame of mind and nodded slightly, softening his expression. "Don't be too hard on yourself. This is just about a ritual hall anyway, not actual construction work. Did you record your interview?"

"On my phone, yes. Would you like to hear it? It's a bit long."

"Not right now, thanks. I'll be late for my next meeting. Just submit the transcript with the rest of the data. Oh, also, all the tweets got deleted."

"Yeah, I saw that, too."

"So your feelers did the trick?"

"I suppose? All I did so far was introduce him to a support group." Mitsuhiro chose his words carefully, trying not to say anything unnecessary.

"Well, good work on that. Legal channels didn't seem to be going anywhere anyway."

"Thank you."

"Fortunately, it didn't attract much attention, but this is an area we definitely need to watch in the future. I'll want to see a detailed timeline."

"Understood."

I didn't really do anything, Mitsuhiro resisted the urge to say. *All I did was take a phone from the man at the bottom of that hole and delete his posts with my own two hands. In other words, I stole it.* If that came to light, it'd be over for him. Now the contents of his bag were a major concern.

Don't worry about it. He suddenly felt his father next to him. ***No one will ever find out. Don't forget the most important thing here.***

The most important thing?

Takenaka looked at Mitsuhiro's seat next to him.

"What's wrong? Something on there?"

"Huh? Nothing..."

The fire. His father's voice rang in his ears. ***I told you. If we want to keep that hole from being filled, the fire will be so important.***

Right. You're right, Dad. I'm sorry.

"Matsunaga? You didn't hit your head, did you?"

"Sorry. I'm fine. Come to think of it, I remembered that I haven't investigated the arson case yet."

"The arson? The one that happened while you were there? I'm sure the Chief's taking care of that."

"Well, just in case, I think we should make sure that it wasn't Yoshikazu Hara who did it."

"That's more the police's job. If we interfere with them, it'll look like we're trying to hide something. We'd get investigated for no reason."

"But someone who had access to the site must have started the fire. It could have been Yoshikazu Hara, or maybe the Twitter poster. If they have a grudge against the company, who knows what they might do next? They could set fire to our actual homes."

"Whoa, keep it down!" Takenaka raised his voice to interrupt him. "What are you talking about? Stop saying these ridiculous things without any evidence. Or do you know who the arsonist is?"

"No...but shouldn't we have a plan in case there's another arson later?"

"I told you, that's the director's job. Stick to your own duties. I don't want complaints that Crisis Management is meddling with construction work. People already dislike us for prying into employees' business."

Mitsuhiro bowed his head, intimidated by Takenaka's stern response.

"Right. I'm sorry."

"Now, let's get ready for the meeting. Also, that company car ain't yours forever, remember."

Without waiting for a reply, Takenaka got up and left the meeting space.

Mitsuhiro slowly stood up, bag in hand, and returned to his desk. He hadn't meant to set off Takenaka, and now he felt depressed. If the boss retaliated by revoking his company car rights, it'd become much more difficult to search for Yoshikazu Hara.

But his father next to him had some advice. ***That guy doesn't know the job that really needs to be done here. Don't worry about him. You're doing far more important work than he ever will. Do a good job and show him what you're made of.***

I will.

Mitsuhiro instantly felt better. Takenaka was busying himself with first-half financial reports and investor relations and so on, but Mitsuhiro was conducting important investigations for a construction project that could determine the fate of the entire Shimaoka Group. That thought alone gave him a natural high.

At least keep your head down, though. Don't want your boss getting too jealous of you.

Mitsuhiro couldn't help but smile, finally putting down the bag in his hands. After turning on his laptop, he began to tackle the first task of the day.

4

"The upcoming completion of the Scramble Walk is the biggest piece of good news we've had so far this quarter," said a smiling Chief Sugawara.

The others gathered in the conference room smiled with him. Some even attempted applause.

"We have avoided making overly optimistic predictions until we entered the final stage of the project, but I am pleased to report that the large-scale construction of sidewalks crossing all major roads and railway lines around the station is now well on its way to completion. As a result of this, the foot-traffic capacity is expected to rise sharply, and the projected economic effect is estimated to be comparable to that of building another Tokyo Station at this point."

This time, genuine applause broke out.

"Additionally, turning our attention to pedestrian-walkway construction along the tracks connected to the Scramble Walk, we have simultaneously launched eleven projects that address more recent challenges, such as installing greenery and improving river water quality. Each project will be audited every two weeks, ensuring everything is carefully checked over at every point in the process. Are there any questions?"

With such good news, there were no questions from either Finance Planning or Corporate Planning.

"Now," Sugawara said, "I would like to answer a question from the IR department."

Takenaka let out a small gasp. No one but Mitsuhiro had expected this. The team members looked at each other, trying to figure out who had asked the question.

Seeing this, Sugawara frowned a bit.

"The police and fire department conducted an investigation into a small fire that broke out in the East Wing basement and determined that it was caused by human activity. This resulted in a temporary closure of the site, which had a slight impact on the construction schedule, but we expect to be able to make up for the delay at this point."

Takenaka slowly turned his gaze to Mitsuhiro. His expression was nothing short of ferocious. Everyone else on the team glanced at Mitsuhiro, then averted their eyes.

Mitsuhiro didn't meet his boss's gaze. Instead he looked toward his father, who was standing next to Sugawara with a smile. He was gently nodding in a gesture of silent praise.

Sugawara noticed Mitsuhiro's gaze and glanced to the side, then turned back and took his glasses out of his breast pocket. Everyone, including Mitsuhiro, thought he was going to put them on, but instead he held the glasses in one hand and continued speaking.

"At this time, the person who started the fire has not been identified. As a result, we are increasing security patrols and monitoring for any suspicious people entering or leaving the premises, as well as for any inappropriate behavior by workers. No similar fires have been spotted since then. The damage is extremely minor, and it will cause no significant change to the construction schedule, so I think it is worth considering whether this should be disclosed to shareholders or not. That's all from me."

Sugawara sat down, his report finished. His hands were still clasped around his glasses; instead of putting them on, he seemed to be pressing them against his chest. Mitsuhiro didn't wonder at all why Sugawara was doing this, though. He looked around for his father, only to find he had disappeared from the conference room.

Takenaka stood up quickly. "Regarding the report just now from Chief Sugawara, we believe that this should be treated as a minor accident. Chief, thank you very much for taking the time to report this to us."

With that, Takenaka bowed and immediately sat down again. He didn't look at Mitsuhiro again for the rest of the meeting. Neither did any of his teammates.

Later, when Mitsuhiro was at his desk and about to leave work with his bag, Takenaka shot him a hard glance as he walked up to him.

"Matsunaga…"

He motioned with his eyes for him to enter that partitioned meeting booth. Mitsuhiro obeyed, feeling the rest of the team watching him. Takenaka sat down at the table, Mitsuhiro across from him.

"It was you, wasn't it? You reported it to the Chief."

"Um, yes. It was," he replied, sounding perfectly natural about it.

Takenaka seemed more taken aback than angry. "Don't you understand what you've done by reporting it to the Chief himself? I made you part of this team because I trusted you, and now you're going off on your own. Don't you feel sorry at all?"

Mitsuhiro certainly didn't. But he knew that any further defiance right now would cost him his company car. After all, Takenaka was his boss… even if Mitsuhiro was much more important in terms of the work they were doing.

"I'm sorry. I thought the East Wing was the key to this whole project. I went too far."

"It *is* the key, yes, but… Are you okay? Do you understand what I'm coming from here?"

"Yes. From now on, Mr. Takenaka, I will follow your instructions. My father told me that this was an important job, so I may have gotten carried away."

"Your father again?"

"Eh? Oh… I'm sorry. I thought that's what I was told."

"Maybe you should take a break." Takenaka was studying Mitsuhiro's bruised face.

"I'm fine, sir. I'll find Yoshikazu Hara right away so we can wrap up this case."

"What about the interview report?"

"Oh, yes. Can I ask for some help with the transcription?"

"…Look, assigning these tasks to other people is the way information starts leaking out. I taught you that we complete all our work within the team alone. That's the iron rule here."

Takenaka's tone suddenly grew cold. It felt like he was reevaluating Mitsuhiro in his mind—was he just having a bad day, or was he always this error-prone? It was an unbearably unpleasant experience. Mitsuhiro could sense the mutual respect that had existed between him and Takenaka vanish, like turning off the light.

"I'm sorry. I've already made an appointment to meet with Tamai Construction…"

"You were going to go without even giving me your interview report?"

"No, there was a sudden request last night. I didn't have the time to tell you until now…"

"All right. Fine, then. Finish your report by the end of the day. I'll contact the Chief, so go apologize to him. You don't need to attend the meeting with the PR team."

"Yes, sir."

"And you've got company car access until the end of this week. Is that clear?"

"Yes, sir," Mitsuhiro softly replied. He wasn't all that discouraged, but the anger was making his voice a bit raspy.

Takenaka frowned, but he left without further comment.

Intensely frustrated by all this, Mitsuhiro clutched his bag tightly to his side as he left the HQ building and walked through the scorching sun, uphill toward the company parking lot. When he opened the driver-side door, the smell made him flinch. The sauna inside had only served to intensify Yoshikazu Hara's body odor. The sweat and grime stung his eyes. He had completely forgotten to buy the deodorizing tools he meant to.

Covering his mouth with one hand, he sat in the driver's seat and placed his bag on his lap. Starting the engine with the door open, he turned the air conditioner on full blast.

What an incredible asshole your boss is, said his father in the back seat. ***I'd love to see that prick covered in ashes someday. Then he'd understand how important your work is.***

"Can you do that?" Mitsuhiro asked aloud, looking at him in the rear-view mirror.

If you want me to, I can. His father grinned. ***The ash is kind of like your footprints. Just watch, all right? Keep your nose to the grindstone, and just you wait and see what happens to him.***

"Okay, I will."

This unexpected jolt of encouragement gladdened Mitsuhiro as he closed the door, fastened his seat belt, and drove off.

First, he parked near a row of big-box stores and bought three bottles of deodorizing spray and two boxes of large alcohol disinfectant wipes. Returning to his parking space, he quickly gave the car's interior a touch-up. It did the trick well enough that he could finally close the windows again.

Feeling the cool air flood the interior, he took his phone out of his pocket. He checked his call log, noticing that his mother had called him yet again, but he had other things to do at the moment. He selected Araki's number from his call history.

"Tamai Construction, Araki speaking."

"Hello, this is Matsunaga from Shimaoka. I'm calling about the amulet we discussed."

"All right. Everything's ready with that. Would you like to receive it today?"

"If I could, yes."

"I'm planning to visit the East Wing at one PM. Would you like me to visit your office afterward?"

"No, I'll be out all day today. How about we meet at the East Wing's construction-zone parking at twelve thirty?"

"That works well for me, actually."

"Good. Let's go with that. Also, I'm sorry to ask, but I have one more request..."

"Yes? What is it?"

"I was wondering if it was possible to talk you down on the price a little...?"

He could hear Araki sigh over the phone. It was the sound of someone wondering why he had to put up with these unreasonable people all the time.

"I'm afraid that we cannot lower the harvest offering for Tamai's amulets. There is no deadline for this purchase, however, so I can provide it whenever you are ready with the fee."

"Okay. Sorry to bring that up. I have the money for you."

"Well, I hope you don't put yourself into dire straits over this, please."

"It's all right, thank you. I'll see you at twelve thirty."

As soon as he hung up, he let out a sigh. *"Harvest offering," he calls it. More like extortion.* But—as Mitsuhiro tried to tell himself—he had no choice. Drastic times call for drastic measures. As long as he had the amulet, everything would be fine. With that reassurance in mind, he called the office at the construction site.

The staffer there confirmed that Takenaka had made an appointment with Chief Sugawara for him. He told him he'd be right there, hung up, and as he took the wheel, he suddenly wondered what happened to the man collapsed at the bottom of the hole. The Twitter guy. The owner of the other phone.

That's not your problem, said his father behind him. ***Mr. Araki didn't say anything about him, did he? Just focus on your job.***

"Yeah. All right, Dad."

Mitsuhiro nodded to his father in the rearview mirror and put the car into gear.

5

He felt uneasy about entering the director's office, but Chief Sugawara himself didn't seem to mind at all. In fact, when they sat facing each other on the sofa set in the reception area, Sugawara was quite polite with him despite the considerable age difference.

"To be honest, I'm glad you contacted me, Mr. Matsunaga. It's better to disclose things like this early on. We can't impose a gag order on our crew, either; that'd just lead to more rumors."

"Thank you, Chief. I didn't expect you to welcome me in like this."

"If I could ask, Mr. Matsunaga—during the meeting, was there anyone standing next to me?"

Sugawara looked serious. Mitsuhiro blinked and stared back at him. He understood that Sugawara was referring to his father, but he didn't understand why he was bringing this up. Did his father's presence bother Sugawara? He hadn't interrupted the meeting; he was just standing near the Chief.

Mitsuhiro ventured a timid nod.

"Um… Yes…"

Sugawara let out a deep sigh, took his glasses out of his breast pocket, and held them in one hand. Still no sign he'd ever put them on.

"You always have those glasses with you, sir," Mitsuhiro remarked, not knowing what else to say.

"They're a memento from my younger brother. They're not mine."

Sugawara looked around the room, as if he was expecting someone else. Mitsuhiro was flummoxed, unsure what to say next.

"Mr. Matsunaga, you went into the ritual hall in the East Wing basement, didn't you?"

"Yes, sir. I was investigating, and, um, I didn't know anything about it…"

"I stumbled into one of those once myself, at a different site. Since then, I've been following the advice of the director of Tamai Construction and keep at least one belonging from a late family member on me at all times."

"I see," was all Mitsuhiro could manage.

"Did he tell you to do that, too?"

The question seemed very sudden. But Araki had said exactly that to him.

"Yes, sir. A member of Tamai Construction did say that. I thought it was pretty farfetched at the time, so I forgot about it…"

"It *is* farfetched, these ritual halls sitting deep underneath all sorts of buildings…"

"Yes…"

"But if Tamai Construction advised you to do that, I think you should make sure to follow through. I was very skeptical about it at first, but it led to some delays, you could say."

"Right," Mitsuhiro said.

But Sugawara dropped the topic. "Well, that aside, we'll be conducting a thorough investigation into the cause of the fire. Please tell Mr. Takenaka not to worry about it."

So Mitsuhiro left the office, and Sugawara saw him off with what could be described as a convivial attitude. Once he was back at his car, Mitsuhiro breathed a sigh of relief.

He hopped in and looked in the rearview mirror at his father, smiling in the back seat. ***The Chief's really siding with you, isn't he? Your boss can't act so tough around you anymore. Maybe you'll get to keep this car awhile longer.***

"I sure hope so."

His father's outlook seemed overly optimistic. Takenaka was sure to get jealous over this.

Hey, don't worry. His father leaned over, smiling right behind Mitsuhiro. ***You won't have to worry about that guy at all pretty soon. Let's get some work done before we meet Mr. Araki.***

"All right," Mitsuhiro replied as he drove away.

The work at hand was, of course, to find Yoshikazu Hara.

At this point, he hadn't heard any news either way from Okuyama of Helping Hands. What he dreaded the most was a call saying that Yoshikazu Hara had been found dead. Okuyama had already reported him missing to the police, so if his body was found, the police would let them know…and if he was wandering the streets in this heat, the worst-case scenario could soon be reality.

It was up to Mitsuhiro to find Yoshikazu Hara before that call arrived. To that end, he decided to visit all the places where support organizations were active, following the list Okuyama had given him.

By "active," he meant distributing meals. Some groups served things like pork miso soup or curry at parks and government grounds, while others gave out small portions of bread and soup to those who lived on the streets. The people working for these groups often served as counselors, too, referring people who were escaping domestic violence to shelters and attorneys.

These groups ran the gamut from nonprofits to religious organizations, corporations, corporate-sponsored volunteer groups, and university clubs. Some among them were more of a racket than a charity, aiming to fleece people of their welfare benefits. Public institutions were also engaged with the homeless, of course, but Mitsuhiro's impression was that they had their hands full with providing temporary housing. These institutions were just not large enough, and since every person using these services had their own unique circumstances that had brought them there, it seemed all but impossible to handle and care for everyone. And that was without taking into account altercations among the homeless themselves, or between them and volunteers, and wherever young people with nowhere to go gathered, so did criminal groups ready to prey upon them.

But regardless of the circumstances, no one could survive without food, so these soup kitchens had become part of the unique daily routine of the unhoused. They usually tried to live within walking distance of food sites, and if they were fortunate enough to find a place to sleep, they tried to keep themselves there as much as possible. For them, changing their sleep site meant carrying all their stuff with them and building a new knowledge base from scratch—food-drop locations, dates, and so on. Without a phone, it'd be a total nightmare.

If Yoshikazu Hara was lucky enough to find a place to sleep, he would've stayed there all day except when he had to get up to receive food. With his dementia, though, he might've lost track of his sleeping spot and wandered off somewhere. If so, Okuyama said that Hara would probably remain in the same ward of Tokyo, as walking any farther would be too much for him. Taking a train or bus was also unlikely—he couldn't afford the fare, and the stations would get swept clear, so you saw far fewer homeless riding the rails all day to shelter from the sun, wind, or snow.

A lot of them were instead using places like internet cafés and love hotels—that was the big new trend, and unfortunately, their proprietors weren't as upfront about who they sheltered. It was impossible to keep track of every single one of those. But even if Yoshikazu Hara was living in a twenty-four-hour internet café or something, he'd still need to venture out in search of free food. Thus, the most efficient way to find him was to visit soup kitchens and case the surrounding areas.

Following the route he'd worked out in advance, Mitsuhiro went down the office buildings between Mitake-dori and Aoyama-dori Streets, parked his car in a lot, and walked with his bag under his arm. There were several parks in the area where free meals were available.

When you find Yoshikazu Hara, his father suddenly said behind him as he headed toward one site, ***you better take a gift with you. If you have something he wants, that'll make it a lot easier to get him on your side.***

It was sound advice, so Mitsuhiro stopped at a convenience store on the way. What could he find that wasn't available at soup kitchens, something Yoshikazu Hara couldn't access very often? It seemed like almost everything. Mitsuhiro tucked his bag under his arm, grabbed a shopping basket, and started with some chocolate and potato chips. What else should he get? Socks, underwear, shirts? Sandwiches or rice balls? Juice? Or maybe alcohol or cigarettes?

Booze first, his father said. ***No way anyone's been offering him booze or cigs, I'm sure. Get him just the right level of drunk, and he'll start listening to you, trust me. Add some cigarettes to the mix, and I bet he'll do whatever you want.***

Again, this sounded right on the money, so Mitsuhiro put a few tallboys of beer, a small pack of sake, and a travel-size bottle of whiskey in his basket. He then went to the counter and, without really knowing what he was doing, ordered a pack of cigarettes, a lighter, and a chicken skewer from the fryer. The clerk gave him an odd look, no doubt wondering what kind of party he was shopping for on a weekday morning, but said nothing and stuffed it all into a plastic bag.

Holding his "gifts" in his right hand and his bag in his left, Mitsuhiro headed to the park. There was a soup kitchen going on right now, and a small crowd had gathered around three large steaming pots. Several volunteers were chopping up vegetables on folding tables.

In addition to a sign that read "SOUP KITCHEN—PORK SOUP," cardboard and plywood boards were attached to the fence around the area, displaying protest messages like "STOP FORCED EVICTION!" and "END DEVELOPMENT NOW!!" and "HUMAN RIGHTS **IGNORED**" and so on. This park, too, was slated for redevelopment. For the people who had finally found a place to sleep here, eviction meant losing their home and their daily routine all over again.

Mitsuhiro walked slowly around the perimeter, feeling supremely uncomfortable. He certainly couldn't give out his Shimaoka Group business card to people around here. But as he observed the people gathered in the park from outside the fence, his father spoke up.

There he is. Look. Yoshikazu Hara.

Mitsuhiro's heart swelled with joy and surprise. He stared at the man, who was sitting on the ground in a corner of the park, leaning against the boundary fence and staring blankly into space.

—*It's true!* Mitsuhiro shouted with glee in his heart. *We did it, Dad!*

He never thought in a million years that the man would be this close. It was within easy walking distance of the East Wing site. Hara must've vaguely remembered his original job and couldn't bring himself to stray too far from it.

Mitsuhiro approached the man, marveling at his success after narrowing his search to the soup kitchens. Instead of entering the park, he went around to the other side of the fence the man was leaning against. He didn't want to attract attention, and Okuyama had informed him that alcohol was strictly prohibited around soup kitchens.

"Mr. Hara? Yoshikazu Hara?" He crouched down and whispered from outside the fence. "It's me. Matsunaga."

The man turned around blankly.

"Eh? Who're you?"

"I'm Matsunaga from Shimaoka. I'm sure glad to see you. I feared the worst when you suddenly disappeared like that."

"Have we met before?" The man seemed uncomfortable. He had forgotten meeting Mitsuhiro at all. That, or maybe he felt guilty when he saw Mitsuhiro's bruised face and remembered what he had done.

"You left your worksite. Remember?"

The man frowned silently, his eyes fixed on Mitsuhiro's plastic bag. He could see what was inside. Now he was sure he had the man's attention.

"Look, no need to stick around here. Let's go back to the site and have a couple drinks while we talk things over. I bought some stuff I thought you might like, but I can go back if you want something else."

"What site?"

"The site in the East Wing in front of Shibuya Station. You were working there, remember?"

"What kind of work?"

"...Well, as far as I know, you were just sitting there next to a shrine. It's underground, so it's kind of dark."

"A security guard?"

"Something like that, I suppose. The construction company paid you."

"Are you really from Shimaoka...?"

Mitsuhiro took a business card out of his bag. The fence was too finely meshed to hand it over, so he just showed it through the gaps. The man looked left and right, as if he wanted to consult someone. When Mitsuhiro saw him from the side, he suddenly seemed a tad unfamiliar. He *looked* like Yoshikazu Hara, but not quite. Maybe a not-quite-perfect match? Mitsuhiro stared at him intently.

The man noticed and turned his face back to Mitsuhiro.

"Um, why are you staring at me?"

"Oh, I'm sorry. I thought I might have mistaken you for someone else."

The man blinked nervously, apparently unsure whether he was about to let a golden opportunity slip through his fingers. As long as he could get that plastic bag, it seemed, he'd do what he was told.

"It's not dangerous work, is it? Uhh, sometimes people give me money to stand in line for them and stuff. Is it like that?"

"Yeah. Would you mind coming with me and taking a look at the site? I think it'll jog your memory. If you don't want to do the job again, that's fine, too. I'll bring you to Tamai Construction, and we'll file a complaint together."

"Well, if it's not dangerous, I'll do it."

"Great. Um... I'll wait at the crosswalk by that intersection, okay? If you can head over there for me..."

The man nodded. Mitsuhiro took his two bags and stood up. Meeting at the park entrance seemed unwise. It'd probably attract the attention of the soup-kitchen staff. He didn't want to get into trouble over the alcohol, and he didn't want Yoshikazu Hara to change his mind while he was explaining himself. For all he knew, he might quickly forget the conversation they had just now.

But he didn't have to wait long at the crosswalk. The man half jogged up to him. He was wearing a tattered coat, a fanny pack, and a backpack. Judging from all that luggage, he probably didn't have a regular place to sleep. Mitsuhiro counted his lucky stars that he'd found him where he did; tracking him at night would've been all but impossible.

The light turned green. Mitsuhiro started walking, and the other man obediently followed.

"Would you like one on the way?" he asked, taking a tallboy out of the bag.

"Oh, yes, thank you."

The man bowed his head repeatedly as he took it, flipped the pull tab, and kept right on walking as he drank from the can. His Adam's apple bobbed up and down a few times, and when he pulled the can away from his mouth, he exhaled deeply with a light burp.

"*Ooh*, that hits the spot."

The man smiled and looked up at Mitsuhiro, who nodded back with a smile of his own. At this rate, it would be a cinch to take him to that hole and chain him up down there.

6

This was crazy. What a trickster Yoshikazu Hara turned out to be.

Mitsuhiro opened the door of the company car parked in the lot, put his bag and the convenience-store shopping bag in the back seat, and sighed in frustration. The guy got away again. He just couldn't believe it.

Sitting down in the driver's seat, Mitsuhiro started the engine, letting the cool air from the AC wash over him as he tried to calm himself down. Maybe he had underestimated Yoshikazu Hara after all. He was so unpredictable; he'd be following Mitsuhiro, and then he'd just magically disappear. If he was intentionally trying to confound him, he was really good at it.

But Mitsuhiro could learn from his mistakes. After all, everything had gone well until he entered the East Wing. As soon as he unlocked the door of the soundproof wall around the construction site, the man said, "Whoa, you really *are* from Shimaoka," seemingly trusting him completely. It was lunch break, fortunately, and few workers were still on-site, so nobody called out his bag of alcohol.

This time, Mitsuhiro didn't stop by the office or borrow any equipment. He didn't want to get attacked with a helmet or flashlight again, for one, but this also saved them a whole lot of time. It was against the rules to walk around the site without a helmet, of course, but even if a worker found them, Mitsuhiro could just say he was from Shimaoka HQ with business at the ritual hall, and he was sure no one would stop him then. Takenaka would probably lecture him about it if he found out, but Mitsuhiro didn't care about that.

But maybe he should have brought along his own flashlight, at least. Without any site equipment, all he had to rely on was his phone's flashlight mode. That made for tricky footing, to say nothing of how uneasy it made his companion.

"There's no electricity here," Mitsuhiro reassured him after the man kept stopping in his tracks, "but the basement is fully lit."

Holding the bags in one hand and the cell phone in the other proved to be quite a struggle. He considered handing the plastic bag to the other man, but he couldn't risk him running off with it, so he had to endure the hassle and keep moving.

Then there was the hallway door with the lock. He had completely forgotten about it. Luckily, it was open as usual, but if it hadn't been, he would've have had to wait for Araki to show up. He should have asked him for the unlock code earlier.

Finally, Mitsuhiro made it to the basement. After assuaging the man, who was starting to freak out a little in the darkness, he carefully walked toward the hole, making sure not to fall in.

His problems began after turning on the light in the hall. He stepped over the ladder lying on the floor, placed all his luggage on it, and turned around. The man was still standing bolt-upright near the entrance. At that moment, he was certain that this painful ordeal was finally over.

But then Yoshikazu Hara ruined all his hard work.

"Here's the hole. All you have to do is go in here."

"Which hole?" the man asked, walking straight toward him.

"The big one right in front of you!" Mitsuhiro couldn't believe the man couldn't see it. "Don't fall in!"

"What hole? Huh? Where's the hole?"

Before Mitsuhiro could wonder if this was a joke or a dementia flare-up, the man walked straight ahead without hesitation…and disappeared. It was like he had been swallowed up by the hole. More like sucked in, really.

There was an unpleasant *thud*, followed by the sound of something heavy being thrown onto the ground.

"Hey! Are you okay?!"

Mitsuhiro frantically picked up the stepladder by the table and lowered it into the hole. He put his cell phone in his pocket, climbed all the way down, and then took out his phone again and turned on the flashlight.

He walked around the bottom of the wide hole, looking for an undoubtedly limp Yoshikazu Hara, but he was nowhere to be found. The only person there was a man lying face down, shuddering and breathing heavily. To Mitsuhiro, it sounded like snoring.

The can of beer Yoshikazu Hara'd had on him was lying next to the man, but Yoshikazu Hara himself was nowhere to be seen. What *was* clear was that the man lying here wasn't Yoshikazu Hara at all. His hair was black, not gray, and he was much shorter.

The Twitter guy!

Mitsuhiro was shocked. Was he still there after Mitsuhiro took his phone the other day? No—maybe he talked to Araki and became his *mikeshi* or whatever.

Right now, though, Yoshikazu Hara's total disappearance was much more of a concern. Mitsuhiro wandered around the bottom of the hole for a while. Then he suddenly looked back at the stepladder.

He got me.

Only then did he realize that the man had escaped. He must've climbed back up the ladder while Mitsuhiro was bumbling around searching for him.

He hurriedly climbed back up, phone still in hand.

"Mr. Hara! Yoshikazu Hara!"

The voice echoed. Yoshikazu Hara wasn't there. He hurriedly pulled the stepladder back up out of the hole, grabbed his bags, and ran to the entrance.

He walked down the passageway, stopped at the bottom of the stairs, and listened carefully. He thought he heard footsteps going upward, but it might've been normal construction work, too. He couldn't be sure.

So Mitsuhiro climbed the stairs, lighting his way with his phone. He couldn't run—not with all the stuff he was carrying. He was impressed that Yoshikazu Hara could navigate those steps in total darkness.

By the time he returned to the underground construction site, he had completely given up. He couldn't look around the premises or ask witnesses for help, either—not with alcohol in his possession.

He looked around carefully as he passed through the site, but it was useless. Yoshikazu Hara had disappeared for the second time.

Mitsuhiro leaned against the steering wheel, unable to shake off his sense of futility, when his father spoke up.

Don't be discouraged. This is another learning experience for you. Yoshikazu Hara was never gonna be an easy opponent. You gotta brace yourself. He might get away more times than this, too.

Are you serious? Give me a break.

Oh, don't be that way. You'll beat him in the end. You just have to learn his tricks. Eventually, the time will come when you'll outsmart Yoshikazu Hara. And not just him. You'll outsmart your boss, and the site manager,

too. C'mon. You can do it. You've only just started working today. Go get something to eat and cheer yourself up before you meet Mr. Araki.

"Okay. I'll do my best, Dad."

Mitsuhiro replied to him out loud as he drove out of the lot. Navigating a series of one-way streets, he returned to the rail station and stopped in the East Wing's construction parking lot.

As his father had advised, he had lunch at a ramen place within walking distance, replenishing his motivation and physical strength, then returned to his car and waited for a bit. As he strained his eyes in case Yoshikazu Hara passed by, another car pulled in. Seeing Araki in the driver's seat, Mitsuhiro got out. Araki parked the car and walked toward Mitsuhiro, bowing his head slightly. Mitsuhiro bowed back.

"Thanks for coming all this way. It's hot out here. Do you want to talk in the car?"

"Yes, let's do that."

Mitsuhiro returned to the car, and Araki settled into the passenger seat. Araki didn't mention any strange smell, so it appeared he had finally eradicated Yoshikazu Hara from the company car. Instead, Araki frowned at what was in the back seat.

"Is that alcohol?"

"I had it ready it in case I found Yoshikazu Hara. I haven't had any."

Araki shrugged. He trusted Mitsuhiro on that, but still, it was probably better to place it somewhere less visible.

"Yes, the previous president also said that Mr. Hara enjoys drinking. But please don't let him into the ritual hall intoxicated. As you know, falling would be very dangerous."

"Ah, yes. I apologize. I'll be mindful of that."

"Drinking in the ritual hall itself isn't a bad thing. Sometimes cups are exchanged during the ceremony, and sometimes the *mi-keshi* brings their own sake. However, you have to be sure to offer some to the gods. If only the *mi-keshi* gets drunk, the gods won't come near them."

"All right. Thanks for telling me. So, about the amulet..."

"I have it right here."

Araki took a white envelope from his jacket pocket, shook it lightly, and dropped its contents into his palm. Sure enough, it was an amulet with "Tamai" embroidered on it.

"Your harvest offering," Araki said, as Mitsuhiro started reach out to it.

"Oh, right."

He felt a bit rebuked as he took his bag from the back seat, removing the envelope of bills from it. Handing it over was almost physically painful. It was an outrageous amount of money. But even so, when he exchanged it for the amulet, he suddenly felt a great sense of relief.

He put the amulet in his bag. It was expensive, yes, but now he believed his problems were behind him.

Araki put the envelope in his pocket with practiced ease, like he dealt in this kind of cash all the time.

"Now, about the ritual hall in the basement—do you think you could tell me the code for the door in the hallway? That way, if I find Yoshikazu Hara, I can take him there without any delays."

He tried to present it as a favor to Araki, not a request for his own sake.

"Hmm… All right. But I'll change the number once Mr. Hara is found, so please don't try to go in after that."

"Sure. Thank you very much."

Araki told him the number, and Mitsuhiro made a note of it on his phone.

"Are you all right, Mr. Matsunaga?" Araki asked as he put the phone away. He was looking not so much at Mitsuhiro's face as the cuts and bruises on it.

"It's nothing serious."

"No, I'm talking about curses. I know that it's your job, but to be honest, I wouldn't recommend continuing to be involved with the ritual hall. Even if you don't get cursed, if you become too connected to the site, the previous president said that you could become its *mi-keshi*."

Mitsuhiro was stunned by Araki's matter-of-fact warning.

"Me? You mean instead of Yoshikazu Hara?"

"Yes. When I told the last president about you, he said you may wind up taking his place as *mi-keshi*."

"You mean I'd have to stay in that hole for days on end?"

"You'd be lucky if that was all it was. Sometimes a human sacrifice is required."

"A human sacrifice… You don't, like, bury people in there, do you?"

Mitsuhiro gave Araki a joking smile. He couldn't imagine such a thing happening in modern society. Araki was sounding like some yakuza thug from a bygone era.

But distressingly, Araki said nothing in response. After an uncomfortable silence, he changed the subject.

"As I mentioned earlier, if you ever see the deceased around you, please start keeping one of their belongings in your possession immediately. And if they continue to appear, please consult with me about it. I would…not recommend contacting our president or our company directly. As the manager, I will do my best to resolve any matters peacefully."

Mitsuhiro wasn't sure if Araki was making sense to him or not. But he seemed sincere, at least. So it was worth asking.

"What if…it's not in reality? Just in a dream or something?"

"That would be more serious, actually. The heart is the center of a person's spiritual barrier, so appearing in your dreams means they have penetrated that barrier. Have you experienced that?"

"No, I was just curious. I think the amulet you gave me will be enough."

Araki pointed at Mitsuhiro's bag. "Well, if it doesn't work, I'm afraid you may need some more money soon, because the next step would be a full exorcism."

"Right," Mitsuhiro replied. He didn't want to ask how much that would be. He knew he wouldn't like the answer, and it might leave him completely hopeless. "Um, what about sprinkling salt or placing lucky charms around?"

Araki sighed at Mitsuhiro's alternative proposals, a troubled look on his face. "If you make a mistake in setting up a barrier or performing the purification ritual, it could trap whatever's inside, or even make them a permanent fixture. If so, you'd be far better off having done nothing at all. Either way, I hope you'll consult with me first."

"All right."

"Well, I'd best be going now. Take care of yourself."

Mitsuhiro felt like he was being treated like a terminal patient, but he simply replied, "Yes, thank you." He watched Araki get out of his car and enter the construction site, the envelope of cash still in his pocket, and let out a sigh of neither relief nor regret. What Araki had said seemed logical enough, but at the same time it made no sense at all. It just felt like blackmail. That two-hundred-thousand-yen amulet was definitely in his case, though, so that was a relief, at least.

Regardless, he had to find Yoshikazu Hara. He couldn't ever let himself become a replacement in that hole. The guy still had to be nearby, he told himself encouragingly, and as he reached for the parking brake, his phone rang from his pocket. Thinking Miyoko might be letting him know she'd been discharged, he took his hand off the brake and took out his phone.

It was his mother from over in Hachioji. It wasn't like her to call on a weekday afternoon when she knew Mitsuhiro was at work. "No news is good news"—that was her motto in life.

"Hello?"

"Oh, Mitsuhiro? I'm sorry; you're at work, aren't you?"

"Yes, I am. What's wrong? Did something happen?"

"Well, that's what I want to ask you, you know. Your in-laws called me up and said you were acting strange."

"I've just been really busy. Miyoko isn't feeling well, and I have some urgent work to handle."

Mitsuhiro's face stiffened with displeasure. Those sneaky bastards, getting his mother involved! He could barely resist calling his in-laws right away and telling those arrogant, unhelpful, selfish pricks that it was all *their* fault.

"Well, all right, but I had something strange happen here, too. I wasn't sure whether to tell you about it or not..."

"What do you mean, something strange?"

"The grave was broken."

"Huh?" Mitsuhiro exclaimed. That was the last thing he'd expected to hear. "What do you mean, the grave? Whose grave? Dad's?"

"That's right. Your father's. The staff at the cemetery said that one corner of the gravestone suddenly made this loud cracking sound, and now a whole piece of it's fallen off. They said they couldn't just throw the piece out, so they sent it over here, and, um, it's pretty big. They suggested we should hold another memorial service or purify the gravesite or something like that before we repair it, but really, I don't know where to begin with that sort of thing."

"What about the priest who came for the funeral?"

"I asked, and he said they don't deal in grave maintenance. He said it'd be strange to hold a second memorial service after all this time. He suggested hiring a professional to repair it, but, I mean, is this our responsibility? It's not an old gravestone, you know, and now it's in two pieces. So I thought maybe your company might know someone who specializes in that kind of thing. When you guys finish a big building, you do purification rituals on the site, don't you? Do you know any companies dealing in that?"

7

Listening to his mother's voice on the phone, Mitsuhiro recalled the elegant home in Tokyo's Setagaya Ward, where he'd lived through high school.

The house, a testament to his father's success as a contractor, was apparently not good enough for Dad to spend his final years in. One day, out of the blue, the Matsunaga family had moved to a house along the Tama River in Hachioji, well west of central Tokyo. Mitsuhiro later learned his dad made the move because he wanted to live near water. That same river already flowed through Setagaya, but for whatever reason, he insisted on living more upstream.

After his father died from cancer, his mother had made some jokes about how he must have had salmon blood in him and so on, but she also said the move did a lot to calm his temper. Mitsuhiro's own memories of the time were fragmented at best. He'd begun living alone soon after getting into college, so the house in Hachioji always felt more like his parents' home than his own.

Maybe it was that yearning to return to his childhood hometown that had driven him to settle down back in Setagaya with his wife and daughter after kicking off his career. He knew he had at least some attachment to the area, something beyond it just being convenient for commuting and building a family, and his wife Miyoko seemed to sense that as well. Maybe that's why she kept using vague terms like "power spot" whenever he suggested moving to a place with a cheaper mortgage.

"Hey, are you listening?"

"Ah...yeah."

Mitsuhiro's wandering thoughts were brought back to the present. Why was he thinking about his old family home? It had long since become someone else's property. He went past it once, after it had been remodeled into a completely different shape. He didn't really feel anything, though, and he hadn't been back since.

"You want to find a company who'll perform a purification ritual on our gravesite because Dad's gravestone got damaged?"

The face of Araki from Tamai Construction flashed before his eyes. He quickly pushed it out of his mind. If they charged two hundred thousand yen for an amulet, who knows how much they'd try to bilk his mother for?

"Oh, right! The stone itself is insured, so the stonemason will work out a new one for us."

Mitsuhiro blinked. He'd never even thought about that sort of thing. "You took out insurance on the grave?"

"Well, the company I worked for had a good policy, so I went for it. They can get damaged by earthquakes and erosion, you know."

Mitsuhiro was impressed. His mother, who worked for an insurance company, was what you'd call a hard-nosed saleswoman. Thanks to her, even after his father decided to close the business and retire, they were wealthy enough to never worry much about money. Mitsuhiro was extremely grateful to her for that. Meanwhile, Miyoko's mother had never once held a job since she was born. That, really, was the core reason why they never got along.

"So, I think we can take care of the repairs for the stone ourselves, but could you arrange to have the broken part properly purified, or whatever you're supposed to do with it? Because I have absolutely no idea about all that."

Mitsuhiro sure didn't either, and he was far too busy to start researching it. But his mother rarely asked him for favors like this, and he didn't want to just brush her off.

"All right. In that case, can you send me the broken part of the grave marker? That, and maybe some things that used to belong to him?"

Wait. Why did he ask for that second thing? Mitsuhiro was confused.

"His belongings? Why? Oh, for the memorial service?"

His mother seemed to find this logical enough somehow.

"Yeah, just in case," agreed Mitsuhiro. He had to keep a possession of his father's with him. Just like Chief Sugawara. A part of Mitsuhiro's mind was screaming at him to do it right now.

Now, is that really necessary? He felt like a black shadow had slinked into the back seat. It leaned toward Mitsuhiro up front and whispered in his father's voice. ***There's really no point in doing that, Mitsuhiro. Your father's right here with you. You're happier that way, too, aren't you? Wouldn't life be a lot harder right now if I went away?***

It would be, yes. But this is about Dad's grave. Mitsuhiro had no idea what to make of this conversation.

"His belongings, huh? I'll see if there's anything left, but we got rid of most of it. All the albums and stuff got burned, too."

The sudden sound of his mother's voice snapped him back to reality, further vexing him. "Burned?"

He could smell the dry scent of fire and ash. The smell of a crematorium, mixed with something even more intense. A house burning. The smell of everything in life reduced to ashes. A strange thought flashed through his mind as well—himself sitting on the side of the road, staring.

"Don't you…? Oh, well, it was hard for you, wasn't it? I'm sure you suffered a lot."

"What do you mean?"

"The house in Setagaya burning down when you were in high school, I mean. Your father was devastated, but after we moved, he got a lot calmer, you know. I've told you about it lots of times since you moved out, but you keep on forgetting after a while, don't you?"

Mitsuhiro was stunned. His house in Setagaya burned down. He knew that memory was somewhere in his head, but it haunted him, how unreal it felt. He did vaguely remember sitting on the side of the road, surrounded by several fire trucks. There must have been all kinds of noise, but his memory was soundless. He didn't know where his mother and father were. Whenever he tried to recall that moment, the scene would always shift over to a crematorium. His father, dressed in a suit, laid out in a coffin. The dry smell of fire and ash drifting through the air.

Mitsuhiro tried to organize the sequence of events, but his head felt too twisted up. ***You don't need to remember***, his father said behind him. ***We are the* mi-keshi *of the ashes. That's just the way it's always been.***

"Did you get covered in ashes, too, Dad?"

"What? What do you mean?"

"Ah, nothing," he said. What was he even saying? He was getting more and more confused…and then, suddenly, he felt someone bumping something against the back of his seat.

You don't need any of those belongings. You have to tell her not to send them.

His father was sternly admonishing him. Someone kept kicking his seat from behind. *Stop it, Dad,* Mitsuhiro weakly called out in his mind. *Please, stop it.*

"*Hey, are you okay?*" his mother asked. *"Is work tiring you out?"*

"Yeah… No, I'm fine. Don't worry. But I'm in the middle of work, so if you don't mind…"

"All right, all right. Anyway, see what you can do, okay?"

"Um, Mom…"

"And I'll look for anything your father had and send a package over. Take care of yourself, okay? Bye."

Before he could tell her to wait, she hung up. The saleswoman in her had never retired at all. She retained that same old tendency to set the pace at all times—another reason why she and Miyoko's mother didn't see eye to eye on much of anything.

Mitsuhiro stared at his phone, shrinking in fear of what his father behind him might say.

"She always was a difficult woman."

This time, he could hear the muttering as clear as day. The voice, surprisingly light, was full of sympathy for Mitsuhiro.

"I'm sure you've had enough of this, huh? All this extra work at home and on the job."

Mitsuhiro timidly raised his face. He saw his father smiling ruefully in the rearview mirror.

"No, that… That's just you."

The belongings were being sent. He tried to think about it but couldn't. His father was right behind him, but those belongings still existed. He tried to reconcile those two facts, but his head just spun in confusion. He closed his eyes tightly. An unpleasant ringing sound filled his ears. He feared it might become the only thing he could hear.

The stress is back.

Mitsuhiro didn't think that so much as remember it for the first time in a while. Back when he was living with his ill-tempered father in his parents' house in Setagaya, he'd often experience ringing in his ears. He didn't know exactly when it was, except that it was sometime in his teens.

He felt someone tapping on the seat behind him. It wasn't the same scolding kick as before. It was more like a soothing shake.

"Calm down, Mitsuhiro. Take a deep breath and get those needless thoughts out of your head. You have important work to do. That's all you need to think about right now. Nothing else matters, okay?"

He could clearly hear his father's voice. He took several deep breaths. The ringing subsided. Mitsuhiro opened his eyes and looked around the construction-site parking lot he was in. The reality of this large-scale project right next to him, and the thought of the incredibly important thing underneath it, brought Mitsuhiro back from his state of confusion.

"That's the spirit. Now, let's get back to work. You can still use that same basic method to track down Yoshikazu Hara, you know."

"Okay, Dad."

Mitsuhiro rubbed his brow and blinked a little. He felt much better. He could hear clearly again. The panicked confusion that had just overwhelmed him was gone.

Yoshikazu Hara had to be nearby. He had no other means of transportation. He probably went right back to that park with the soup kitchen.

With that in mind, he got in his car and drove past the park along the railroad tracks.

Sure enough, Yoshikazu Hara was right there, standing in the food line. It was like nothing had happened at all. No, this was just dementia making him forget everything the moment it happened.

But Mitsuhiro didn't panic and pull over. If he did it here, right in front of the construction-choked rail station, he'd instantly get a parking ticket, and then he could kiss the company car goodbye. He steeled his nerves, calmly pulling into a nearby lot and reaching into the back seat. The convenience-store bag still had all the booze and snacks inside.

Okay. Third time's the charm. It's a big job, and I'll get it done this time. Mitsuhiro gave himself that pep talk as he got out of the car and headed for the park where Yoshikazu Hara was.

8

Ice cream. Not the first request he expected, but it made a lot of sense.

When Mitsuhiro found Yoshikazu Hara for the third time, he said he couldn't drink and asked for some ice cream instead. If you had to pick something to have on the city streets in the middle of summer, ice cream would be high on the list. So Mitsuhiro went into a convenience store with Yoshikazu Hara and bought several kinds of ice cream, according to his preferences.

Yoshikazu Hara smiled as he accepted an ice cream pop, the kind that children tend to ask their parents for, and got into the passenger seat of the car, eagerly licking and taking bites. He finished it on the way to the construction site, washed it down with a couple of frozen push-up tube pops, and followed Mitsuhiro to the hole at the construction site. He must have really been obsessed with his ice cream, because he didn't mind the unlit stairs and showed no signs of resisting or trying to escape the whole way.

However, despite this, the third time was not the charm.

Once again, Yoshikazu Hara just didn't see the hole at all. Mitsuhiro didn't know if it was the dementia taking its toll or if it was because the hole was too traumatic for him to recognize.

"Hole? What hole?"

"Be careful! It's right in front of you!"

Ignoring Mitsuhiro's loud warning, Yoshikazu Hara stepped over the edge with the tube still in his mouth. His gait was so natural, Mitsuhiro thought he might just walk across air and reach the other side. But of course, Yoshikazu Hara wasn't a magician. He fell like a rock and disappeared into the hole with a thud.

Mysteriously, at that moment, Yoshikazu Hara had disappeared again. There was no need to lower the stepladder to check. When he shone his phone's light into the bottom of the hole, there was no one there. Just a thick layer of white ash. Well, no—he thought he saw something person-shaped lying near the concrete block, but he didn't think it was Yoshikazu Hara. Someone who fell into the hole just now couldn't have been covered with ash *that* quickly.

All it looked like to him was that Yoshikazu Hara had disappeared. Taking advantage of Mitsuhiro's panic and confusion, he had quickly hidden in the darkness and fled yet again.

With a convenience-store bag in his right hand and his phone flashlight in his left, Mitsuhiro climbed the stairs, scowling at the futility of it all, and returned to his car parked near the construction site.

He started it up, cranked the AC, and ate a cup of ice cream Yoshikazu Hara had left behind. It'd just melt otherwise. He thought about driving around the construction site on another search, but there was no real need. He knew where to go. He'd found him twice in one day, after all. And unlike when he was searching around in vain, he now knew exactly where Yoshikazu Hara lived.

By now, the guy had probably forgotten all about his escape from the hole and was back in line at the soup kitchen. It was very, very likely.

By the time he finished eating that cold, sweet ice cream, the futile irritation was gone. He was determined to take Yoshikazu Hara back to the bottom of that hole. With the right plan and a little ingenuity, he was confident he could do it—again and again, if needed. No matter how many Yoshikazu Haras there were.

"Good job. You're getting better at finding Yoshikazu Hara. Keep up the good work."

Encouraged by his father's words, Mitsuhiro felt another rush of motivation as he tossed the empty ice cream cup into the plastic bag and drove off.

But as determined as he was, the fourth go-around was unexpectedly difficult. He couldn't find him along the railroad tracks, so he checked his cell phone and found out about another soup kitchen going on over in the Yoyogi neighborhood. These kitchens and food distributions took place over a hundred times a month across Tokyo, with some homeless people doing the circle between Shibuya, Shinjuku, and Yoyogi several times a day.

So he drove to Yoyogi Park, parked his car, and looked around, convenience-store bag in hand. Sure enough, Yoshikazu Hara was sitting there on a bench, rolling something around in his hands. The thrill of discovering him had lost its edge by now, though. The cycle was starting to become almost routine.

There was a metal armrest in the middle of the bench, designed to prevent people from lying down on it—just one of many ways to make the homeless move along instead of camping out there.

When Mitsuhiro approached him, he saw that Yoshikazu Hara was holding a faded Rubik's Cube in his hands. He kept playing around with it, observing it from various angles and smiling happily the whole time. His face was full of joy, as if he had finally solved the puzzle, but the colors on each side were all mixed up.

Mitsuhiro recalled seeing someone playing with a Rubik's Cube somewhere else before. Maybe that had been Yoshikazu Hara? No, it probably *was* him. Yoshikazu Hara popped up everywhere, it seemed. It was quite surprising.

"You like that thing?" Mitsuhiro asked as he sat down.

Yoshikazu Hara, clearly wary of this interloper, clutched the cube in both hands and pressed it against his stomach. Mitsuhiro could tell that he was afraid of having it taken away, so he took his eyes off the cube and placed the convenience-store bag in front of him.

"Would you like any of this?" he said with a smile. But Yoshikazu Hara grew even warier, glancing up at him from the corner of his eye. In the end, however, he still relaxed enough to get in the car with Mitsuhiro and go to the construction site together.

Back to the routine.

As soon as they arrived at the ritual hall, Yoshikazu Hara quickly strode into the darkness. He wasn't even slightly afraid of the pitch-black place—in fact, he seemed rather accustomed to it. And he probably was, too; he'd been there many times before.

"Give me one second to turn on the lights," Mitsuhiro said, hurrying over to the shrine. He turned them on. Yoshikazu Hara was gone.

Mitsuhiro was stunned. He felt powerless. Yoshikazu Hara was some kind of denizen of the shadows. He seemed to melt right into the darkness every time he disappeared—and he'd keep doing it, until he remembered his duty and the desire to stay down here. Until then, there was no choice but to bring him here again and again. To remind Yoshikazu Hara of his duty. And that was fine, because Mitsuhiro was sure Yoshikazu Hara *was* remembering, little by little. This time, he had gotten into the hole on his own—what further proof did he need?

Mitsuhiro looked at the square edge of the hole. He thought it seemed wider than when he first saw it. He compared the length of the stepladder placed next to the shrine with the distance to the edge of the hole. The hole *did* seem to be getting closer to the shrine, actually. Like it was trying to swallow it up.

Every time the ashes came out of the ground, the hole got wider. The connection occurred to Mitsuhiro all at once. And, hang on, it wasn't just getting wider—it was also getting deeper. Eventually, it'd become too deep for the stepladder to reach.

The ash emerging from the ground would accumulate at the bottom of the hole, swallowing anyone who entered. Turning them into the same dry ash. Just like a crematorium.

The ash was burning people alive. Countless people had died in this way, and now they were all this ash coming up from below.

Mitsuhiro was startled by what sounded like a low groan. He came back to his senses. He wasn't sure what was going on in his mind.

He looked around for the source, but no one was there. He looked into the hole. Was there someone at the bottom? Come to think of it, someone other than Yoshikazu Hara had been in there before, hadn't he? What happened to him?

But wait a second. Did Yoshikazu Hara really disappear right after Mitsuhiro had brought him down here? Or did he remember his duty on the fourth attempt and climb down into the hole himself?

Mitsuhiro stood at the edge, his hopes high, and searched for Yoshikazu Hara with the light from his phone. But here was nothing but the concrete block and a pile of white ash. It looked kind of like there were people piled up under the ash, but Mitsuhiro didn't really care what the ash looked like from *his* perspective. All he was hoping to see was Yoshikazu Hara sitting there, chained up.

Mitsuhiro flipped the light switch again. Relying on the light from his phone, he made his way out of the space, being careful not to fall in, and went to look for Yoshikazu Hara again.

9

As dusk approached, Mitsuhiro gave up the search for the time being. He returned the company car to the lot and began cleaning the interior, intending to get rid of Yoshikazu Hara's body odor. The odor of many Yoshikazu Haras.

He sent a text message to his boss, reporting that he was ending the search for the day. There was no reply. When he returned to the office, neither Takenaka nor the other team members were there, but he saw on the office whiteboard that they were in an IR meeting—without Mitsuhiro.

Takenaka had told him nothing about that. He hadn't been told to attend the meeting. Nor had he been told not to.

Takenaka really *was* trying to remove him from the team. That was how it seemed, but it didn't discourage Mitsuhiro. It just angered him. He knew his father would tell him not to worry, that he had much more important work to do than listen to that idiot Takenaka.

On his computer, he filled out the return sheet for the company car, along with a request for permission to keep using it, and emailed both to General Affairs. Normally, he would've asked Takenaka to do this for him, but he was unavailable at the moment, and there was no point waiting for him. He needed that car to pick up Yoshikazu Hara.

When he placed the printouts of these forms on Takenaka's desk, he noticed something strange. There were footprints under his desk, made of some kind of white powder.

When Mitsuhiro bent down to take a closer look, he saw several footprints around Takenaka's chair. He looked back at the office door. More footprints led straight to Takenaka's desk, just like the prints leading into his apartment.

But then, as if suddenly blown away by the wind or absorbed into the floor, the footprints disappeared. Mitsuhiro stood there in a daze.

His father laughed.

"The ash has its eyes on your boss now, huh? It's gonna take care of him so he doesn't get in your way."

"What do you mean?"

"It's supporting you now, you see? That's proof you've been recognized as a qualified *mi-keshi*. I'm proud of you, son."

Mitsuhiro smiled. He didn't care if he was shunned by the rest of the team. It didn't even matter if he lost his desk on this floor. He could proudly say that that was how important his current job was.

So he left the office and went straight home. He was still walking on air when he entered his condo.

"Daddy's back!"

Sae ran down the hallway and hugged Mitsuhiro. Miyoko followed, her belly appearing from around the corner ahead of the rest of her.

"Welcome back."

"Hey. How are you feeling?"

"Much better. That smell is still bothering me, though."

The only smell Mitsuhiro could detect was the aroma of a warm dinner.

"I have my amulet here, so we'll be fine."

"Huh?" she said, frowning.

But this was exciting news for Sae. "Oh, are you gonna do the spell again? I wanna do it too!"

"Sure, if it's bad enough."

Mitsuhiro took Sae's hand and went to the dining room with the puzzled Miyoko. The table was already set for dinner, but Miyoko had other things on her mind.

"What kind of amulet is this? The one Sae was talking about?"

"Yes. I got one."

Mitsuhiro took the envelope out of his bag and showed her the amulet with "Tamai" embroidered on it.

"It's the same one!" Sae squealed, taking the charm from Mitsuhiro's hand. "You're going to burn it? Is that okay? It won't undo the charm or anything?"

"That's what I was told to do. If necessary. For now, let's just put it up somewhere."

"On the fridge!"

Sae rushed to the kitchen and hung the charm on a magnetic clip attached to the refrigerator. Miyoko craned her neck to look at it, opened her eyes wide, and shrugged her shoulders.

"Maybe it does have some kind of psychological effect. It's like…that smell bothering me just disappeared."

"Looks like we got a new power spot for our house," Mitsuhiro jokingly announced. Miyoko had to chuckle back.

"You don't even know what that term means, do you?"

"Power spot!!" shouted Sae, making her parents laugh even harder.

After dinner, the family took their respective turns in the bath. Sae and Miyoko went to bed, and Mitsuhiro was enjoying some sparkling water in the dining room, his father sitting across from him.

"Wish I could enjoy a job-well-done drink with you," said his father.

"Yeah. I've always wanted to drink with you like this."

"We can, once you finish up your work. But not yet. I don't want you getting a DUI or anything."

"Of course not."

"So let's get going, okay? Your wife's back. I'll join you."

"Thanks."

"Let's give this our best shot, Mitsuhiro."

He never thought he'd ever go out to work with his father. He picked up his bag and headed for the front door, trying not to make a sound, his eyes stinging with tears. He was able to spend quality time with his dad because of his current job. It was hard work, something his boss just refused to understand, but it was well worth it. Nothing else seemed to give him quite that level of fulfillment and joy.

So Mitsuhiro left the home.

10

His phone rang.

Mitsuhiro threw off the jacket he had draped over his body. The bright light hit him like a blow to the eyes. He covered his face with both hands and groaned.

Something felt strange under his rear end. He wasn't in bed at home, apparently. He blinked his watery eyes and looked around. He was in a car. With a shock, he suddenly realized that he had been sleeping curled up in the back seat of that company car.

He thought someone had shone a flashlight or something in from the outside, but that wasn't the case. It was the morning sun. The surrounding buildings were reflecting the sunlight into the car.

The car was parked in the company lot. He had a vague memory of driving it around last night. After he got home, he went out again with his father to look for Yoshikazu Hara. He remembered that much. But when did he fall asleep in the car? He couldn't believe he'd ever do such a thing.

His eyes cleared up as he searched for his ringing phone. He found it in his jacket pocket and yanked it out. As he feared, it was Miyoko.

"Uh, good morning."

His heart was pounding with shock. He was so unnerved that he almost wanted to ask her where he was, but he still managed to keep it together.

"Hey, when did you leave?"

"I'm not sure what time. I had something I needed to do first thing."

He wiped the sweat from under his chin, reached out to start the engine, and switched on the air conditioner.

"First thing? It's five thirty."

"Well, it is what it is, you know? I wanted to sleep, too."

The AC began to blow out cool air. Spending the night in a car with the engine off in the dead of summer… He could have died of heat stroke. The thought made him shiver.

"Hey, did you really come to bed? I didn't notice you coming in or leaving..."

"I did. I didn't want to wake you up, so I was quiet."

"Hmm..." She sounded less than fully convinced. *"I hear a car."*

"It's a company car. I'm using it for an investigation."

"Is it okay to use it before work starts?"

"I can't just rent a car. I'll explain everything to the company."

"Are you going to work now?"

"Yeah. Sorry to make you worry."

"Well, I hope that investigation ends soon. Also, I'm supposed to have another checkup today. If it takes a while, can you leave work early?"

"I'll...ask my boss. How're you feeling?"

"Not all that great, to be honest. I'm getting that unpleasant smell again. Doesn't the condo feel weird to you?"

"Weird?"

"Like, the smell won't go away. Just being here makes me feel sick. You must think something's off, too, right? You got that amulet and everything."

"I'm fine. Stop worrying. I'll look into the smell and clean it up when I get home."

"I hope cleaning will fix it..."

What do you want us to do? Move out? We're only a few years into our mortgage! He almost blurted it out, but he managed to hold it back. He had just woken up, and he needed to both pee and get something to drink. Both needs were becoming rapidly urgent.

"I'll figure it out, okay? I should get going."

"Make sure you come back home, all right?"

"Of course."

Mitsuhiro ended the call, threw the phone into his bag, and got into his car.

He rushed to a convenience store in the neighborhood and bought breakfast and a drink, along with underwear and a T-shirt. He then went to a capsule hotel about a ten-minute walk away, washed himself up, and finally started to feel human again.

But then he noticed something strange. There were scratches all over his arms, along with the backs of his hands, and bruises were starting to appear. As if he'd gotten into a violent fight with someone. When did that happen? It was because he resisted. He recalled all the many times Yoshikazu Hara had tried to push him away, refusing to go down into the hole. Too many times to remember.

So that was it. It was Yoshikazu Hara's fault. Realizing this, Mitsuhiro put both arms into the capsule-hotel bathtub. The scratches stung a bit, but he didn't care. Even after dark, he'd managed to bring Yoshikazu Hara into that hole. That was something to be proud of.

He got out of the bath, changed into a clean shirt and underwear, and put his dirty clothes in the convenience-store bag.

After throwing it in the trunk of his company car, he went to work. No one was there, however; it still wasn't even seven AM yet. Mitsuhiro finished the report Takenaka had asked him to submit and emailed it over. Then he wrote up a report on his use of the company car. He did this to avoid questions about why he was driving it around in the middle of the night... but that'd require Takenaka's approval. Given Mitsuhiro was now on his boss's bad side, that approval wouldn't come easy—but then again, it was Takenaka who ordered the investigation. As long as he kept hammering that fact, Mitsuhiro would probably avoid taking the full blame.

But that, of course, would probably mean no more company car. If that happened, he'd have no choice but to rent one, which presented some thorny issues. He had already paid a lot of money for that amulet; any further unanticipated expenses would squeeze them hard. He would have to keep car usage to a minimum and get Yoshikazu Hara to the site on foot as much as possible, but that raised the chances of being noticed by someone.

It'll be fine. His father suddenly spoke to him from behind. ***Don't worry about your boss. Besides, look how early you are. Might as well use the car while you got it.***

Following his father's advice, he left the office without greeting anyone or even checking to see if he had any meetings and returned to his company car. Yoshikazu Hara's body odor was pretty strong in there, so he cleaned the interior with wet wipes and deodorizer. Well, he had to be frank—it felt like *he* had contributed to the odor a bit, too. A distressing thought crossed his mind, that he could end up like Yoshikazu Hara himself sooner or later, but he pushed it out of his mind and drove away.

Today, he found the first Yoshikazu Hara within minutes. He quickly took him to the basement and waited until he was out of sight before returning to the surface.

When he got back to his car, he remembered that Miyoko had asked if he could get out of work early. It was already past nine. He called Takenaka. No answer. With no other choice, he sent a message saying that he needed to leave early because his pregnant wife wasn't feeling well.

He wondered where he'd find Yoshikazu Hara next, but less than five minutes later, Takenaka called.

"Matsunaga speaking."

"What the hell is this? Are you crazy?"

"What?" he asked back. He could sense Takenaka's disappointment on the other end of the line.

"I'm asking if you're serious about this," Takenaka said, changing his tone slightly.

"You mean about leaving early, sir?" he asked, frowning.

Then Takenaka suddenly started shouting at him. *"What's wrong with you? You're not the one giving birth, are you? Leave that job to the woman already!"*

Mitsuhiro felt the blood drain from his face. Wasn't it Takenaka himself who said harassment like this was nonconstructive, harmful, and had no place at work? Did something change in Takenaka over the past few days? Or were these just his true colors showing? Whatever the case, any remnants of his trust in his boss were completely shattered.

"So I can't leave early?"

"I don't see how this is your problem, all right? And stop requesting the company car without running it through me, either. Today's your last day in that thing, okay? You're working in the reference room until the shareholder meeting is over."

"The reference room?"

"And lemme warn you—you better not file any stupid complaints over me keeping you here the full day. You should be grateful that no one's forcing overtime on you."

And then Takenaka hung up.

Mitsuhiro clutched his phone. His body was shaking with rage. What was he going to have to do in the reference room? Organize old company newsletters and stuff? He couldn't help but think that Takenaka's personality had done a one-eighty. He hadn't expected such blatant bullying, so the attack had hit while his defenses were down.

He felt a thud on the back of his seat. ***Don't worry about it***, his father said. ***You won't need to worry about a moron like him. Just concentrate on what you have to do.***

Calming himself down, Mitsuhiro called Miyoko. She didn't answer. Must be at the hospital for testing. With no other option, he sent a message saying that his request to leave early was refused.

He then drove to where he thought Yoshikazu Hara was, parked in a lot, and checked his phone. The was a text from Miyoko reading *I can't believe it*, followed by the news that she might have to be hospitalized for observation again and they'd have to ask his mother-in-law to take care of Sae.

Mitsuhiro sighed and sent a message of apology and agreement. If only Yoshikazu Hara would just stay in that hole. He felt sorry for the guy, but right now Mitsuhiro deserved a whole lot more sympathy than that bum, in his own opinion.

No more whining, he told himself. He'd just do as his father said and concentrate on the task at hand. After all, he'd been entrusted with an extremely important job.

Mitsuhiro bought a few things Yoshikazu Hara might like at a convenience store and looked around for places where he might be. He didn't think the blazing sun would be enough to slow him down, but he was overcome by a lingering fatigue. Spending last night in the car must have taken its toll. He was afraid he'd collapse from the heat, but his sense of mission spurred him on…and after a bit more searching, he managed to take Yoshikazu Hara back to the hole again.

For another day, he worked up to quitting time without seeing his boss or anyone else on his team. After returning his car to the company lot, he filed an application to continue using it, even though he knew Takenaka would reject it. If today was the last day, tonight probably still counted. He was exhausted, but he'd have to work overtime again tonight. Takenaka was wrong in that respect. In fact, he was swamped with overtime work right now.

He removed the bag of dirty clothes from the trunk and took the train home.

There were women's shoes at the front door, but they weren't Miyoko's. He knew right away that they belonged to his mother-in-law.

"Helloooo…"

"Daddy!"

Sae ran up and hugged Mitsuhiro. His mother-in-law, Michiyo Umehara, appeared with her handbag.

"Oh, hard day at work?" she said in her patronizing tone, heading straight for her shoes. Mitsuhiro was home, and that meant her job was done.

"Thanks for coming in," he said with a formal bow. Michiyo gave him an exaggerated shake of the head.

"I had to feed Sae, you know. *And* I had to accept a delivery for you. Something your mother sent. I can't *believe* how heavy it was. Okay, see you later, Sae."

"Bye!"

"Whew, I'm all worn out," she said, putting on her shoes. She left without even looking at Mitsuhiro.

He went to the dining room with Sae. He wondered what kind of meal his mother-in-law had prepared, but it was just instant curry poured over microwaved white rice.

"Grandma said we should get a new microwave. She said this one smells funny."

Mitsuhiro sighed. "Still?"

"Uh-huh, a little. Even with the amulet."

"Well, maybe it takes some time to work."

Mitsuhiro stared at the amulet hanging off the refrigerator. Would he have to burn it already? How long would it last? Would he have to pay another two hundred thousand yen to buy a new one? The thought made his heart feel heavy, and fear squeezed against his spine. If he blew all his savings on this stuff and couldn't even pay the mortgage…

"Daddy, did you want some of Grandma's curry?"

Sae's cheerful voice drove away his fear for a moment. Accepting the offer, he heated the curry and rice in the microwave and ate it with Sae. Then he called Miyoko so that Sae could talk to her.

"I'm sorry. I'll get better soon."

Miyoko's voice sounded much stronger than it had early this morning. Did leaving this home make her feel better? He wondered about that briefly but didn't say anything about it.

More importantly, he had to get Sae to bed. He had to find Yoshikazu Hara right this minute. His father had to watch Sae, so he had no choice but to go alone.

"Daddy, are you going out again?" Sae asked anxiously in her bed.

"It's okay, Sae," he replied, dodging the question. "You don't have to worry about me, okay? I'll call your mom when I wake up in the morning."

He decided to relax in the dining room for a while until Sae was fully asleep. Then, for the first time, his eyes fell upon a cardboard box in the living room. He remembered that his mother-in-law said she took a delivery. Something sent by his mother.

Belongings.

The word suddenly popped into his head. He had completely forgotten about it until then. Curious about the contents, he fetched a box cutter from the kitchen, cut the tape securing the lid, and removed the contents from the wadded newspaper it was packed in.

He was startled. For a moment, he thought his mother had sent him a large dark-gray blade of some sort. It was actually a stone, about two and a half feet long, and it was shaped like a kitchen knife, except the handle was attached at a right angle to the blade.

—Can stone really break off into this shape?

If his mother was to be believed about the broken gravestone, that's exactly what this was. It looked like a blade of stone, or a sharp stake carved from stone, but either way, it almost seemed to be crafted for some kind of specific purpose.

What's more, the words "Kosuke Matsunaga" were engraved on the handle of this knife. This was the engraving originally on the back of the gravestone, which was why he thought this might have been intentionally carved off. Plus, there was a white handkerchief near the handle. The initials "KM" were embroidered on it, for Kosuke Matsunaga. It was like he was telling Mitsuhiro to wrap it around the handle and use it. But use it on what?

—The deceased.

Mitsuhiro felt the words pop into his head again. The words of Araki from Tamai Construction, and Chief Sugawara as well.

Just as Mitsuhiro was about to touch the stone, still uncertain, a loud shout reached his ears.

"Don't you dare!"

It was his father. Suddenly, he was standing right in front of Mitsuhiro, his eyes full of anger.

"What's wrong, Dad?"

Mitsuhiro shrank back as his father furiously shouted at him. "You can't bring something like that into the house! What are you thinking? Throw it out!"

"But it's yours..."

"I'm right here! Don't touch that! Do you understand? Don't touch it! Throw it away right now! Do it *now*!"

His father's fierce tone was so frightening to Mitsuhiro that he began to cry. Just like when he was a child, he couldn't even think of disobeying his father.

He wrapped the stone and handkerchief back in the packing newspaper. He took it all into the kitchen, still crying, and put it into the plastic garbage bag lining the bin.

"No! You gotta throw it away! You can't keep this in your home!"

His father continued to yell at him, so Mitsuhiro, trembling with fear and grief, took the trash bag out and tied it shut. He brought it to the front door, put on his shoes, and went to his floor's trash-disposal room. He placed the bag on top of the other trash bags, sobbing.

"But it's yours," Mitsuhiro wept.

A much calmer voice came from behind him.

"It's your mother's fault for sending all this pointless junk. I'm sorry I yelled at you, son, but I was doing it for your own good. C'mon, cheer up. You have work to do. I'll take good care of my granddaughter in the meantime, okay? You should get out there before Yoshikazu Hara falls asleep somewhere."

Mitsuhiro wiped his tears, returned to his room, changed his clothes, and got ready for work. Before he knew it, the thoughts of his father's grave and his belongings faded away, fully replaced with thoughts of the man he had to find.

"Sae's all yours, Dad."

With those words, Mitsuhiro left the house and hurried to the station before he could miss the last train.

Chapter 5 *Mi-keshi*

1

Somewhere far away, he heard the sound of a running toilet. Then there was a loud scream, and Mitsuhiro jumped up, kicking off his blanket.

He was in his bedroom at home. Morning light was streaming in through the curtains. He wasn't in his company car—what a relief it was to find himself in a familiar bed.

Then Sae burst into the bedroom and clung to Mitsuhiro's chest, crying as though something was chasing her.

"What's wrong, Sae? Did you have a nightmare?"

"There's something scary!" she cried loudly. "It's scary!"

"Scary? Where is it?"

"I was in the bathroom! I went in, and I didn't know it was there!"

Mitsuhiro got out of bed, holding Sae in his arms, and headed for the hallway. Suddenly, Sae screamed again and pulled on Mitsuhiro's shirt, trying to keep him in the bedroom.

"Daddy, no! It's scary!"

Tears were now streaming down Sae's face. Her terror was almost overwhelming. "It's okay," he said. "I'll just take a quick look. Stay here, Sae."

He stroked Sae's back to calm her down. It took some doing, but he managed to get her to let go of his hand.

"Careful, Daddy," she said, hugging Mitsuhiro's blanket instead.

"Don't worry," he gently replied and went out into the hallway, blinking his sleepy eyes.

Of course, he didn't really think there was anything there. She was probably just being oversensitive because her mother was gone. Probably startled by her own shadow or something.

He saw that the bathroom door was open and blocking the hallway. It hadn't been thrown open with enough force to bang against the wall—he didn't remember hearing a sound like that. Sae must've used the door as a barricade to protect herself from whatever "scary" thing was there.

The poor girl. It was a childish, unfounded fear, but this was her whole world right now. With that in mind, Mitsuhiro grabbed the doorknob and pulled it toward him.

—See? Nothing there. There's nothing to be afraid of, Sae.

He was going to say that, but when it appeared from behind the door, Mitsuhiro almost leaped backward, stifling a scream.

—Run! Run! Get away!

The words echoed in his head, but his feet were frozen to the floor.

—A horde of the dead, coming this way!

He was terrified. But nothing was physically approaching him…

…because it was just some stains. Mitsuhiro exhaled sharply. Dark-gray stains had appeared across the walls of the hallway, leaving the wallpaper warped and wrinkled in places. All together, the marks joined together to create the forms of dozens of men and women, young and old, who had either been burned to death or were currently burning, writhing in agony. It looked like a large black-and-white photograph of the gruesome scene had been pasted onto the wall.

The stains spread around the corners and onto the ceiling. Mitsuhiro could smell the dry, pungent odor of a crematorium filling the hallway.

Was it a water leak? Mitsuhiro tried hard to come up with a logical explanation. But whatever the cause, the stains were there, and the image they formed was beyond macabre.

—It only looks that way by accident, Mitsuhiro told himself. He had to

tell Sae that, too. But no matter how he tried to change his perspective, no matter how much he moved around in the hope that it'd look different from another angle, that image of people losing their lives, their dignity, in fire did not disappear.

—Let's cover it up for now.

Figuring out what this was could wait. He had to keep Sae from being scared all day. As he thought this, he sensed something moving behind him and whirled around. It was his daughter. She was holding a rolled-up blanket, crouching low as she ran across the hallway to the kitchen. Then she quickly ran back and handed Mitsuhiro something.

"Daddy, do you want the amulet?"

It was the one he had bought from Tamai Construction.

"Ah… Right, yeah."

Mitsuhiro looked at the wall. He really didn't want to perform the little ritual Yoshio Tamai taught him. If burning the amulet solved the problem, then great, but what if it didn't? He'd be out another two hundred thousand yen. The money would just vanish, like ash.

"Let's pin this amulet to the wall with a thumbtack or something."

"Aren't you going to do the trick?" Sae asked anxiously, unsure why he wasn't rushing to take care of it.

"This is probably just water leaking from the floor above. It'll be fine. If we leave the charm there until we replace the wallpaper, it won't get any worse."

"Really?"

"Yeah."

Mitsuhiro nodded, internally hoping it was actually true.

"I'll go get mine."

Sae timidly shrugged and entered her room, trying not to look at the stain on the wall.

He saw her take her corkboard off the wall of her room, her blanket in the other hand. It was for pinning up her favorite postcards and pictures. She handed him the board, and Mitsuhiro took a tack out of it.

"Thank you, Sae."

Mitsuhiro approached the wall with the charm and thumbtack, and Sae retreated back into her room, peeking out from the doorway like the wall was about to explode.

Or maybe this really is *an explosion*, thought Mitsuhiro. From the shades of the staining, he could tell that it had spread from the center of the wall outward in all directions.

Mitsuhiro instinctively searched for the spot where he had written the character for *appease* in ash. Not searching, exactly. He soon realized that he intended to put the amulet there. It didn't take long to find, because of course there were no stains on that part of the wall. That ritual was still working. In fact, he could even faintly see that character still written up there.

鎮

Suddenly, Mitsuhiro realized why the stains had appeared here.

—This is what they're after. The purpose of the stains is to erase the ritual characters. They want to swallow each one we put up in here one by one.

In that case, it made sense to place the amulet here, where the stains first appeared, to maintain its effectiveness. He had long since given up figuring out if this was rational or not. Right now, he just wanted to deal with it and show Sae he was at least trying to do something.

So Mitsuhiro pinned the charm to that one stainless spot with a thumbtack. He could hear Sae breathe a sigh of relief, as if she'd half expected the wall to gobble up her father.

"I think we're safe for now," he said, smiling at her. But Sae's eyes were still open wide. She was beginning to panic a bit.

"That scary thing hasn't gone away, Dad. It's still here. It's still here."

Her tone was urgent, as if she suspected her father couldn't see it.

"I know, Sae. We'll have to replace the wallpaper, so let's just cover it up with something for now."

"With what?"

"Maybe newspaper?"

Mitsuhiro couldn't think of anything else, so he went to the living room with Sae and took out a stack of *Nihon Keizai Shimbun* newspapers that had been stuffed into the magazine rack. It was the largest financial paper in Japan, and he purchased them whenever his boss told him to, usually when they printed relevant articles about the Shibuya area or the construction industry. Even in this allegedly digital age, people in Japan still primarily thought of newspapers as just that—news printed on paper. Maybe that showed how behind the times Japan's media had become, but either way, it meant Mitsuhiro had enough newspaper to cover the stain on the wall.

With Sae's help, they were able to completely cover the hallway using thumbtacks and tape. The newspaper-covered wall wasn't much of an aesthetic improvement—it made the condo look almost dilapidated—but it beat seeing that hellish inferno every time they walked down the hallway.

"I hope it goes away," Sae quietly muttered. He could tell from her tone that she didn't expect it to.

"Daddy will take care of it, okay? Let's get you ready for school."

As he went to the bathroom with Sae and brushed his teeth, he idly wondered how much it would cost to fix the wallpaper. If they could just replace part of it, then that would be great, but what if the whole hallway needed renovations? The potential cost wasn't just depressing; it made him feel sick. If they kept bleeding money like this, their finances would be in bad shape soon. As much as he had been working with the homeless lately, he knew that once you hit rock bottom, climbing out was extremely difficult. Like falling into that hole. If someone didn't lower a ladder in for you, there was no way out.

His mind rewarded this train of thought with an image of his family huddled together at the bottom of the hole, trembling with fear, and he swiftly pushed it away. For now, he had to force himself to forget about the wallpaper and the repair costs, as well as the money he'd spent on that amulet. There was work to be done and breakfast to cook.

He sat Sae down at the table and put his phone on speaker mode so she could talk to Miyoko. This, too, had become the routine, and Sae visibly brightened as she enjoyed her fried egg and juice.

"Something scary came out in here," she complained to her mother. "I went out of the bathroom, and there it was."

"A stain on the wall? Well, that's no good. It's not just a leak?"

There was a slight hint of anxiety in Miyoko's voice.

"Probably. We should tell the condo manager. Are you feeling better?"

"I'll be fine soon. You see? I feel better when I'm not around that horrible smell all the time."

"Oh," Mitsuhiro replied. He wanted to be honest and tell her that *he* sure didn't smell anything, but getting in a phone argument with his pregnant wife when she was under the weather would benefit neither party. His father would probably see it differently, though—but given the important work Mitsuhiro had to do, even Dad would understand that family strife had to be kept to a minimum.

"I'll do something about the smell. You think you'll be back today?"

"I should be. The tests all came back fine. I just hope I don't get sick again."

"Are you sick, Mommy?" Sae asked with concern.

"No, not sick," came the cheerful reply. *"I'm doing great. I'll be home real soon, okay?"*

"Okay!"

In another few minutes, Mitsuhiro left the condo with Sae. He waved goodbye to her on the sidewalk, turned around, and returned to the lobby, where he pressed the intercom button for the manager's office. The door opened, and an elderly man appeared. Before Mitsuhiro could ask him about the water leak, the man's eyes widened.

"Ah, Mr. Matsunaga, just who I wanted to see. I have something I need to talk to you about."

"What's that?"

"The trash. You can't go throwing away something like this. Just one second."

The man went back inside, then returned with something wrapped in newspaper.

Mitsuhiro knew immediately what it was: the gravestone. A piece of his father's gravestone. He was stunned. He had thrown it away last night. Yes, if he'd just tossed it on the pile, someone would have complained, but he had wrapped it in newspaper and everything. It should have looked like normal garbage, really.

"The garbage collector told me this had torn through the bag," the man said, pressing the newspaper-wrapped object into his hands.

"Torn through…?"

"Yeah, he said it almost cut him! And those of us in the office are the ones who take the heat for these things. It's in the rules—if it's over two feet long, you gotta break it into smaller pieces and put it out as non-combustible garbage. Okay? And write something like 'Danger—sharp' on the outside, like you would with a knife. Really, if this is some kinda stonework, you should really have someone in that field pick it up for you."

Mitsuhiro wanted to ask how they knew it was his trash to begin with. Presumably, it was because he'd thrown it away with the envelope the amulet came in, which included his name and address. He was embarrassed to think that someone had gone through his trash, violating his privacy—even though he knew it was all his fault. Being lectured at length in the lobby while other residents were passing by on their way out made him even more uncomfortable.

So Mitsuhiro apologized profusely, changed the topic, received a promise that they'd check for a water leak in the floor above, and returned to his condo. He didn't even think about putting that stone wrapped in newspaper in his bag and going to work. It'd be a heavy load, and he didn't want his father to scream at him.

He put his bag on the floor at the entrance, opened the storage closet in the hallway, took a hammer out from the toolbox, went to the kitchen, and placed the newspaper-wrapped stone on the cutting board. The manager had told him to break it into small pieces, and he was ready to follow orders.

Steadying it with his left hand, he swung the hammer down. There was a loud *bang*, but he didn't feel the stone break inside the newspaper. He struck it several more times, but the stone inside didn't budge. He assumed smashing it with a hammer would break it into three or four more pieces, easy. It already broke once—why wasn't it willing to break further for him?

Mitsuhiro judged that it wasn't breaking because he had laid it flat, so he placed a knife-sharpening stone on the cutting board, set the piece of gravestone upright on it, and pressed down firmly with his left hand. This way, he could focus the hammer impact on one spot. Impatient and afraid he was going to be late for work, he swung the hammer down with all his might.

A sharp pain shot through his left hand, and Mitsuhiro grunted and stepped back. The stone did not break. In fact, the impact had caused it to bounce up, piercing through the layers of newspaper and making a gash across his left palm.

He scowled, threw the hammer on the cutting board, and put his left hand in the sink to prevent the blood from splattering all over the floor. As it dripped down to the bottom of the sink, he reached out with his right hand, tore off a piece of paper towel, and pressed it against his left hand to stop the bleeding. Fortunately, the wound didn't seem too deep, but the pain further provoked his anger. He glared at the tip of the stone protruding from the newspaper, ready to rant and rave and complain about why he had to deal with all of this.

"What am I gonna do with you, Mitsuhiro?"

His father suddenly spoke from beside him. He wanted to acknowledge the effort, but he couldn't hide his amusement at his son's clumsiness.

"But…it won't break. It's too hard to do anything to it."

"Then ask someone who *can* do something with it."

"Like who?"

The first face that came to mind was Sota Araki. There was no one else he could turn to. But he really didn't want to count on him, if he could help it.

"I don't know how much they'll charge me."

"Don't you think the wall might've gotten stained because of that thing? Maybe the ashes were trying to punish you a little because they hate that stone. Hey, stop looking so pathetic! You're a grown man. Go get your hand patched up. And be careful not to touch that stone when you take it with you."

"Can't I just leave it somewhere?"

"No. You can't leave it in this house. That's out of the question."

Mitsuhiro didn't want his father yelling at him, so he reluctantly did what he was told. The bleeding had stopped now, so he took some alcohol and gauze out from the first aid kit. The pain wasn't that bad anymore. In the end, it wasn't much worse than a paper cut.

He had used quite a bit of newspaper to cover the wall, but there was still some left. He folded up a new piece and covered the part where the stone was sticking out, securing it with tape. After stuffing it into his bag, he looked at the clock on the wall. It was past eight thirty.

Great. He was beyond late, and he hadn't thought about the morning meeting yet. He hadn't even received a notification about whether there was a meeting or not. He was all but removed from the team now, he supposed, but he had a reason to show up on time. He wanted to use the company car, even if he had to get retroactive approval for it later. But Takenaka had probably put an end to that by now. He was sure he'd never be allowed to touch that car again.

He had no choice but to rent one. The thought of the expense made him feel sick, but he just had to accept it. That was what Mitsuhiro told himself as he left home again.

2

Surprisingly, his company car access hadn't been suspended. When he arrived at work, he saw a bunch of crisis-management team members rushing around.

"We received a call from Mr. Takenaka saying that he couldn't come to work," one of the members told him. "We're urgently coordinating who'll replace him at his meetings with the other departments."

In order to minimize the risk of data leaks, Crisis Management restricts information sharing and outsourcing as much as possible. As a result, when the man at the top was absent, it quickly became unclear who was in charge of what information. Takenaka's policy was backfiring on them now, which was a relief to Mitsuhiro. He didn't even wonder why Takenaka couldn't come to work.

"Anything I can do to help?" he asked out of politeness, but as expected, no one took him up on the offer. He was still in Takenaka's sights as a target, so no one wanted to touch him with a ten-foot pole at the moment.

But that didn't matter. This was a lucky break. He could use that car all he wanted to while Takenaka was gone, and he was free from the meaningless busywork he was promised earlier. Mitsuhiro quickly turned his back on the office floor and made a beeline for the parking lot. He had a whole lot of Yoshikazu Haras he needed to find today.

As he climbed the hill up to the lot under the summer sun, his phone rang. The caller was Okuyama from Helping Hands. He had promised to share information about Yoshikazu Hara; maybe he had some new clues. Mitsuhiro didn't hesitate to pick up.

"Matsunaga speaking."

"Hi, this is Okuyama, head of Helping Hands Mutual Aid."

"Yes. Thank you very much for your help earlier. Is this about Yoshikazu Hara?"

"It is, yes. The other day, someone who knows Yoshikazu Hara saw him at a soup kitchen in Yoyogi."

Okuyama was referring to the one held regularly at the south gate of Yoyogi Park. This was unexpected. Mitsuhiro had taken him to the East Wing many times, so he'd expected to find him wandering around the Shibuya Station area again.

"Is he sleeping somewhere in Yoyogi?"

If so, that provided easy access to both Shinjuku and Shibuya. He might even be traveling between the two wards of Tokyo. Mitsuhiro cursed his bad luck as he entered the company lot. His search radius had just been expanded a great deal.

"I don't know. He said he had work to do and went off somewhere, I'm told. I imagine he'll show up at the Yoyogi soup kitchen again."

Mitsuhiro held his phone between his shoulder and his ear, took the keys out of his bag, and opened the door. It was still sauna-like in there. He put his bag on the passenger seat, held the phone in his left hand, and got into the driver's seat. His hand hardly hurt anymore. It was just a little itchy.

"Thank you very much. I'll expand the search area to Yoyogi as well, then."

He started the engine and turned on the AC, but the heat inside the car was so oppressive that he got out again. Just sitting there until the temperature dropped might be enough to give him heat stroke.

"By the way, I had another unrelated question."

"Yes?"

"Mr. Matsunaga, have you been talking to the people who visit soup kitchens?"

"Yes, as part of the search for Yoshikazu Hara."

"Are you taking them anywhere?"

He suddenly felt uneasy. Okuyama, it seemed, was wary of something. Mitsuhiro had to proceed with caution.

"I have brought them into my car for questioning at times," he quickly replied. If he talked how about he kept taking them to this underground hole before losing him in the darkness, it might give the impression that he was forcing Yoshikazu Hara into becoming a human sacrifice or something. Considering Yoshikazu Hara's illness, Okuyama might very well see it as coercion.

"You're not bringing them to a support facility or anything like that, are you?"

"I wish I could do that for them, but…why do you ask?"

"Well, we're seeing a significant number of people who left their possessions behind and haven't returned to fetch them."

"Oh?"

"It's often the case that when people move into shelters, they sometimes leave their belongings behind in case they have to return to the streets later. If we've lost track of them, though, we usually report it to the police, in case they were involved in a crime of some sort..."

The way Okuyama's voice trailed off seemed to indicate that he was gauging Mitsuhiro's reaction. Maybe his reaction to the word *police*, specifically.

"Right," he replied, allowing Okuyama to continue.

"Do you have any idea what might be going on with that, Mr. Matsunaga?"

"Me? No... All I'm looking for is Yoshikazu Hara. Someone tried to post photos of our site on the internet, but that's been resolved."

"Resolved."

Okuyama repeated the word, and his tone was heavy with implication. He was starting to rub Mitsuhiro the wrong way.

The car was finally cool, so he hopped in and shut the door.

"Yes, that's right," Mitsuhiro said, halfway ready to just ask what this had to do with him.

"You're not approaching people living on the streets and transporting them so they don't get in the way of construction, are you?"

"Huh? Transporting?"

"I've heard that someone matching your description has been showing up multiple times a day at food distribution points, carrying a convenience-store bag."

So what?! Mitsuhiro wanted to shout back, but he held it in.

"Certainly, when I'm discussing matters with them, I sometimes buy them something in exchange for their time. Ice cream and so on."

"Ice cream?"

"Yes."

"Any alcohol?"

"Well, I try my best to avoid that, but if they're really insistent on it, then—"

Suddenly, he felt a sharp pain in his left hand. It almost made him drop his phone, so he switched to his right. He thought the sudden, stinging pain would irritate him even further, but surprisingly, that wasn't the case. Instead, he wondered why he was feeling irritated at all. That, and a sudden chill in the pit of his stomach. It was confusing.

—What is this? Anxiety? Am I getting anxious out of nowhere? Why?

Hang in there.

Suddenly, he thought he heard his father's voice. What was he supposed to "hang in there" about? Was he being reminded not to tell Okuyama about the hole by accident? Or his important work?

"*So you've purchased alcohol for them at times?*" Okuyama asked from the phone. Mitsuhiro's heart was racing for no apparent reason.

"Ah… Yes, at times."

"Do you know exactly who you purchased it for?"

"No, I didn't ask for their name."

"Because some people saw you talking to someone at the soup kitchen, but we haven't found anyone who said they spoke with you themselves as of yet. Everyone seen leaving with you doesn't seem to have come back."

His stomach sank again. Why? Was Okuyama implying that he was responsible for these homeless people disappearing?

The cut on his left hand throbbed. Mitsuhiro stared at his gauze-covered palm with disgust. *This is all Okuyama's fault. He's making it start to hurt again.* He knew that was silly, but he couldn't shake the feeling that it was true.

Hang in there.

His father's voice rang out again. But Mitsuhiro didn't want to "hang in there" about anything at the moment. He wanted to end this conversation quickly and focus on what he was supposed to be doing.

"Um… From what you've told me, I don't think I can be much help… I mean, first of all, who can say that was really me?"

But Okuyama wasn't done talking.

"I'm saying that if someone's been forced to sleep on the streets, it's not very common for them to suddenly disappear unless they've checked into a support group. And this isn't one or two people—we're talking over ten people disappearing in a row. The only conclusion we can make is that they've been forcibly

relocated, the way big corporations used to do decades ago, or that they were involved in some kind of incident."

"That sounds right to me, but… I'm sorry, I have to take another work call…"

"Ah, yes, I apologize for taking your time. Are you at the office now?"

"No, I'm out on a call."

Mitsuhiro frowned. Why did Okuyama want to know where he was? Was he trying to prolong the conversation?

"Well," he quickly said before another question could come up, "thank you very much for informing me about Yoshikazu Hara. I'll look around for any rumors about the people who haven't returned, too."

"Thank you very much. I appreciate it."

Okuyama's stiff tone conveyed that he didn't particularly appreciate this at all, but Mitsuhiro didn't care. "Goodbye," he said before hanging up.

He tried to make another call, but he was in such a state of turmoil that he couldn't do it right away. He felt an indescribable anger, an inexplicable anxiety, an implacable impatience, and an irresistible urge to start crying. He didn't know what was causing all these feelings, and if he didn't get them out of his system, he wouldn't be able to do anything but just sit there in a fog.

Mitsuhiro turned the AC vent toward his face and let the cool air blow on him. He thought that might calm him down a little, but it didn't seem to work. His left hand continued to throb with pain, dragging his mind down further. At this rate, he'd have to drive around with one hand.

Hang in there.

Dad's voice again. He wanted to cry out and ask what his father wanted him to do. With his injured hand, he couldn't drive or even hold a convenience-store bag, let alone catch or restrain Yoshikazu Hara if push came to shove. His task was vital; how could this piece of his father's grave be hindering him *this* much? It was absurd.

There was a heavy thud on the back of his seat.

"Calm down, Mitsuhiro. Stop obsessing over your hand. It doesn't hurt at all, does it? And forget about that stupid phone call. Besides, didn't you have someone you needed to call right now?"

His father, as usual, was right about everything. Mitsuhiro put his injured hand out of his mind. The pain disappeared instantly—see? It was never that serious to begin with. The turbulence in his heart calmed. He remembered now that he was doing the right thing, and he needed to stay strong.

Yes. This was the right thing to do. There was no way his work in the East Wing—the very foundation of Shimaoka's massive project—could be wrong in any way. Maybe Okuyama was giving him shit about it, but he didn't matter.

His composure completely regained, Mitsuhiro turned the AC vent toward the roof of the car and selected the number for Sota Araki of Tamai Construction from his call log.

"This is Araki."

"Hello, this is Matsunaga from Shimaoka Headquarters. Sorry to keep calling you."

"Not at all. How is it going?"

"Well, I actually have two things I'd like to discuss with you. First, I'd like to ask you about amulets... If you have something more effective, I guess? Something stronger?"

"Yes, we do have something, but the harvest offering will be substantial. The one we can prepare right away is for appeasing spirits, and it costs five hundred thousand yen."

Mitsuhiro's head spun. Between that and fixing the wallpaper, this was now the size of a small renovation project. But if he couldn't stop that stain from reappearing, he might have to renovate the entire unit in the end.

"All right. I'll figure out how to come up with that. Also, there's something else I'd like to have disposed of."

"Disposed of? An older shrine or something?"

"No, it's...part of the stone from my father's grave."

"A gravestone?"

Araki repeated it back to him, his voice betraying his disbelief. Mitsuhiro explained that part of his father's stone had cracked, and his mother had asked him to dispose of it in the ritualistically proper way.

"Yes, stone-purification rituals do happen sometimes. Earthquakes can cause gravestones to topple and crack, or the heads of the shrine guardian dogs can come off."

"All right, but…will it cost me?"

"Well, being related to mourning, this is known as tamagushi-ryo *or* onsakaki-ryo*—that's the name for offering a branch from a sacred tree to the gods. I'll need to discuss it with the previous president, but based on what you've told me, it shouldn't be too expensive if it's only part of the grave. I think it'll likely be about the same amount as the amulet I mentioned."*

Now the dizziness was accompanied by nausea and chills. He was asking for one million yen in total, and he called it "not too expensive." He was taking advantage of Mitsuhiro's predicament to extort as much as he could, wasn't he?

"But that being said, please don't push yourself too hard over this," Araki said, seemingly reading Mitsuhiro's thoughts. *"I don't know why you need such an amulet, but perhaps that piece of grave is causing the problem. Why not have it purified first, and then we can decide whether the amulet is necessary?"*

It was unsettling in a way. First, that stone was delivered, and then that stain showed up. But the prospect of a half-price deal gave him a glimmer of hope, even if the total was still twice his initial purchase.

"All right, let's go with that, please. I have the stone with me, and I'd like to hand it over as soon as possible."

"Certainly. I'll go over the purification ritual with my predecessor. How about we meet at the same place in half an hour?"

"Perfect. Thank you."

After the call ended, a groan escaped his lips. He couldn't tell if he was relieved or terrified of what was to come. Five hundred thousand yen. He prayed with all his heart that this would solve the problem as he turned off the engine and stepped outside. He walked to the nearest bank ATM, withdrew half a million yen, and put it in an envelope. It felt like sawing part of his body off, and he felt dizzy. The thought that he might have to withdraw the same amount all over again later on made it hard to move away from the machine.

It's to protect my home, Mitsuhiro told himself. He had to protect his home in order to keep his very, very important job. Miyoko would eventually find out about this, but he knew she'd understand.

He put the envelope in his jacket pocket. His left hand began to throb again, as if it was telling him to deposit the money back. Was his own left hand accusing him of making a mistake? It wasn't even a serious injury. Mitsuhiro squeezed it in anger, willing the pain away.

After returning to the parking lot, he sped off and reached the construction site in less than five minutes. While waiting for Araki, he checked the map app on his phone to find Yoyogi Park and the surrounding areas where Yoshikazu Hara had been seen. He thought the man stuck around Shibuya Station; Yoyogi was unexpected. Maybe he was wandering around more. Maybe the dementia kept him from remembering where his sleeping spot was.

Once this gravestone thing was cleared up, Mitsuhiro would have to expand his soup-kitchen search. Did he really need to go all the way to Shinjuku? Okuyama knew too many people around Yoyogi and Shibuya. Maybe hitting up other support groups, and the soup kitchens they ran, was his best bet in hunting down Yoshikazu Hara.

"Expanding the search area is fine and all," his father said from behind, "but you should also think about better ways to deal with this whole situation."

He didn't understand what "deal with" meant at first.

"What do you mean? What do you want me to do?"

"If this Okuyama guy's gonna get in our way, we have to deal with him properly. It's easy. Just show him where Yoshikazu Hara needs to be taken."

And then we'll throw him in the hole, and Okuyama will finally shut up. Now Mitsuhiro understood what his father meant. He had no resistance to that idea either. There was no other choice. The only way to convince Okuyama was to do as his father said.

Just as he was vividly imagining Okuyama falling from the edge of the hole, there was a sudden knock on the window. When he looked up, Araki was there, standing on the passenger side.

"Ah, come in."

Mitsuhiro reached out and opened the door, moving the bag that was sitting there onto his lap. Araki bowed his head, got into the seat, and closed the door.

"Thank you. Regarding what we discussed on the phone, I confirmed with the previous president how to purify the piece, and he said it'd be best to offer it to a deity that has already been appeased."

"Offer it…?"

"Yes. Would you be able to drive us to Shinjuku in this car?"

"Oh, no problem."

"There's a good spot at the Shinjuku Imperial Garden. The purification itself won't take long."

"Okay. We can head out right now—"

"Well, before I look at the item to be purified, I'll need to ask for my *tamagushi-ryo*. Is that all right?"

"Um, yes… How much was it?"

"I checked with the previous president, and he said five hundred thousand yen would be fine."

Araki spoke like this was actually a big discount. Mitsuhiro nodded, clenching his jaw to keep from grimacing in front of Araki.

"I have it ready here." He took the envelope from his pocket but didn't hand it over right away. "And this will fully purify it, correct?"

"We will take full responsibility for calming the spirits. I speak in terms of decades, not days. Once we are entrusted with a duty like this, it is passed down across generations. Think of it as building another grave."

From that perspective, maybe the fee wasn't so expensive after all.

Just as he was about to agree, the wound on his left hand began to sting again. He scowled at it. Araki took the envelope, put it in his pocket, and looked back at Mitsuhiro, puzzled.

"I'm sorry… I cut myself on that stone. It still hurts a little."

Araki's gaze fell on the gauze covering Mitsuhiro's left hand. "That might be causing an issue. Can I see the stone?"

Mitsuhiro took it out of his bag, wrapped in newspaper—but the stone slipped out of it. It was the part that had torn through the newspaper last time, when Mitsuhiro was going at it with a hammer.

"Ah!" As he cried out, the stone jabbed into Araki's right thigh.

Mitsuhiro shuddered. It must have just jabbed him. But thanks to the newspaper he had wrapped around the tip, it didn't break the skin at all.

"I… I'm sorry! I should've been more careful!"

He apologized frantically, but Araki calmly picked up the stone by the bit covered in newspaper.

"Yes… It's looking very troublesome."

Araki took a towel from the pocket of his work clothes, wrapped the stone in it, removed the newspaper covering the tip, and handed it back to Mitsuhiro.

"I'm really sorry about this."

Completely flustered, Mitsuhiro took the remaining newspaper and wadded it back into his bag. His heart was still pounding. He had almost injured someone he was relying on for everything right now. If it had turned out any worse, who knows how much compensation would have demanded for that, too? He dreaded the thought.

"Don't worry about it. These things happen. Are you okay to drive?"

"Yes, I'm fine."

Mitsuhiro caught his breath, balling his left hand into a fist to try to chase away the pain. It didn't completely disappear—it was still throbbing, in fact—but it wasn't bad enough to affect his driving.

So he turned onto Meiji-dori Avenue and headed toward Shinjuku, calmly driving through the congested streets. Neither of them spoke. When Mitsuhiro glanced to the side, he saw that the stone, now wrapped in that towel, was on Araki's lap and being held down with both hands.

They turned right at Koshu-kaido Highway and parked in the Shinjuku Imperial Garden lot. Mitsuhiro left his bag in the back seat, got out of the car, and went to the entrance with Araki, paying the admission fee. Fortunately, he didn't have to pay for them both.

Once they were inside the Imperial Garden, he meekly followed Araki as they walked to the pond on the easternmost side.

"This is the pond where a water god lives. It's the source of the Shibuya River that flows underneath the East Wing. Originally, the river flowed from here all the way into Tokyo Bay. The ritual hall in the East Wing was placed there in order to summon the power of the water god here, appease him, and keep him in place right here."

"Okay," Mitsuhiro replied. He had read about the source of the Shibuya River many times in the construction documents, and he didn't find the water-god story strange at all. Unlike his first visit to Tamai Construction, Mitsuhiro was now fully convinced. This was just how things were.

"Considering your duties and connections, the previous president said it'd be best to seal your father's gravestone here. Is that acceptable with you? If so, we can drop this stone into the pond right now."

"Really? Won't someone get angry if we just drop it here?"

"This pond and ritual site are jointly managed by Tamai Construction and several other organizations. Either myself or our previous leader will inform them beforehand."

"So there's one of those ritual sites here in the Imperial Garden?"

"Where we stand right now was originally the site of a mansion belonging to a prominent samurai clan. There used to be a rather large ritual site on this spot. Are you ready? I will now drop the stone into the pond. The waters are regularly purified, so as long as this imperial garden exists, the grave will continue to be properly honored."

"...All right."

Mitsuhiro looked at the stone that Araki was now holding up in offering. He'd wanted to drop it into the pond himself, if that was allowed, but Araki didn't give him the choice. He had almost injured him with it a moment ago.

This wasn't just a chunk of stone any longer. In the hands of an amateur, it might be downright dangerous.

Araki faced the stone and the pond and began to chant something.

"Kakemakumo kashikoki Izanagi no ookami, tsukushi no himuka no tachibana no odonoahagihara ni misogi haraetamaishitoki ni narimaseru haraedo no ookamitachi, moromoro no magagoto, tsumi, kegare, aramuoba haraetamai kiyometamaeto maosukoto o kikoshimese to kashikomi kashikomi mo maosu."

It sounded like a shrine prayer, but Mitsuhiro had no idea what it meant.

Then Araki tilted the stone, removing the hand towel covering it. The stone slipped out of his hands, much like how it had shed the newspaper in the car, and fell into the pond tip first. It didn't make as loud a sound as he expected, and none of the few other visitors in the garden seemed to notice.

"This completes the purification ceremony," said Araki.

"All right," Mitsuhiro replied weakly. He stared at the ripples in the pond as they gradually faded away. He should have felt relieved that it was finally over, perhaps, but instead he felt like he had lost something he didn't need to.

Just like that, the piece of his father's gravestone was gone, out of his reach.

3

"Be careful with the hole."

Araki said it suddenly on the way back from the Imperial Garden to Shibuya Station. Mitsuhiro stopped the car at a red light and looked at Araki in the passenger seat.

"What do you mean…?"

Deep down, he was nervous that even little conversations like this would lead to more fees, but Araki didn't mention anything about money, thankfully.

"The hole where the bone ash is stored. I understand you've been making a number of trips to the East Wing ritual hall."

After that little ritual at the pond, Araki had been somewhat friendlier for some reason. Once the light turned green, Mitsuhiro sped away, wondering if Araki saw him as a walking ATM or something. If so, it wasn't welcome news.

"Whatever you do, don't touch the edges of the hole or go inside. Normally, no one but the *mi-keshi* is allowed to enter the hall. It's in an unstable phase at the moment."

This was only fueling Mitsuhiro's anxiety.

"An unstable phase?"

"We are trying to invite the water god to that ritual hall, but the bone ash accumulated in there doesn't like it. It's trying to prevent it by causing a fire in the area."

"What do you mean…?"

"To put it simply, it's like it's trying to create a smoke screen of fire and pestilence to prevent the water god from coming."

"Um, why would it dislike the god?"

"Those who bring curses into the world refuse to be worshipped. They try to change the rituals into something of their own. All ritual halls require quite a bit of supplication before the gods will actually descend, but the *mi-keshi* of the water god has left, so there is no begging to be done. That's why we can't seal the ritual hall shut."

Araki sounded like he was implying that it was Mitsuhiro's fault for freeing Yoshikazu Hara. How was he supposed to know? The accusation rankled, but he just bowed his head a bit behind the wheel, not wanting to upset his passenger.

"I'm sorry. I went too far with what I did. I'm doing everything I can every day, searching for Yoshikazu Hara…"

"No, Mr. Matsunaga, I'm not saying it's your fault. You were confused by the bone ash, I'm sure. I attempted to calm it down as well, but sadly, I lost sight of Mr. Hara."

"Calm it down?"

"Calm down the fire. It's a ritual involving an amulet."

The term *amulet* did nothing to restore Mitsuhiro's confidence. Instead he felt a sense of dread that his savings were about to be completely wiped out. But that wasn't the concern Araki had.

"What I worry about is that Mr. Hara might be summoned by the water god. Instead of having the water god come to the ritual hall, it'll be the *mi-keshi* going to the water god, and then he'll disappear for good."

"Like a human sacrifice?" Mitsuhiro blurted out without thinking. He wanted to think that was an exaggeration, but Araki's nod made his blood freeze. A moment later, he imagined Yoshikazu Hara sinking to the bottom of that pond in the Imperial Garden. He tried to shake the image from his mind, but it was no use. It was like trying to wipe dirt off the windshield with your wipers, only to smear it around even more.

"Blessings and curses from the gods are like a two-sided coin. The further the water god's *mi-keshi* moves away from the ritual hall, the wider the hole becomes. That's because the bone ash is coming out of the ground. Should the edge of that hole reach the shrine in that room, the water god will lose its place of power there, and if that happens, compensation will be necessary."

So he wasn't imagining it. The hole *was* getting bigger. Mitsuhiro was afraid to ask what *compensation* meant here, so he kept his mouth shut. What if Araki said *he* had to be the next human sacrifice? It made his heart race.

"It is also necessary to appease the ashes that have left the scene. If the ashes continue to wander around, it could lead to unexpected fires elsewhere. Bone ash, you see, is the essence of the regret held by those we must have pity for."

"Have pity for?"

"Yes. My father taught me that we must not only fear them and keep them at bay but also take pity on them and appease them."

"Um, your father worked at Tamai Construction, too?"

"Ah, I'm sorry. I'm referring to the previous president, Yutaro Tamai. I was actually adopted into the Araki family—my uncle is from that family—and changed my surname afterward. Yoshio Tamai, the current president, is my cousin, who was similarly adopted into the Tamai family."

Mitsuhiro couldn't help but ponder this. It sounded like a pair of brothers swapping children or something—not eerie so much as extremely old-fashioned and bizarre to modern sensibilities.

"Um, why did they do that?"

"It's a custom to avoid disaster."

He didn't explain any further, and Mitsuhiro didn't want to pry into family matters. After passing through a busy intersection, they stopped at the entrance to the even busier construction-site parking lot. As they waited for a line of buses to enter the temporary roundabout, Araki looked at Mitsuhiro.

"Mr. Matsunaga, have you ever been involved in a fire or other disaster?"

"What?"

"You've purchased amulets. If you expect to experience a fire, I can burn a fire of my own to appease the spirits."

"Why would you do that?"

"It's a kind of ritual, done to subdue the spirits and make offerings. You may fight fire with fire, or subdue them with pure force, or appease them by giving the bone ash something to keep them happy. There are many approaches."

How much would Araki ask for? How much did he plan to squeeze him for? Mitsuhiro didn't feel angry about it. Instead, he just felt a helplessness that drained all the strength from his body.

"Can I do it myself?" he asked as a last-ditch form of resistance. "Like, burn the talisman inside the amulet…?"

"I wouldn't recommend it. In fact, just the other day, I lit such a fire to calm the spirits, but it almost spread to me and others."

"You got burned?"

"It wasn't serious."

Araki stroked his arm through the sleeve of his work clothes. It must have been at least a minor burn. And he was an expert at this—if someone like Mitsuhiro tried it, Araki was implying, he'd wind up in flames.

"But either way, under no circumstance should you try to handle this yourself. It will only bring disaster to you."

"All right… So how much does it cost to request that?"

"If we treat this as an extension of the ritual-hall appeasement… Well, in order to calm the disaster and pray for the safety of your family, I think around three million yen would cover it."

It felt like a direct blow on the head. As Mitsuhiro parked the company car in the lot, his hands shook, his head spun, and his stomach turned cold. He feared he might run into something, but he managed to work the car into its space.

"Um…" He searched for way out of this. "Does it have to be you, Mr. Araki…?"

"Your other choices would be the previous president or the current one… but if this involves mobilizing our whole firm, it could cost as much as an entire ritual hall."

Three million yen. The shock to his head was followed by a nail driven into his heart. He couldn't breathe. A delayed wave of nausea, like motion sickness, washed over him. Stretching his budget wouldn't nearly cover such an amount. He'd have to take out another loan, leaving him deep in debt. It'd be ridiculous to lose all his money and place in life—all very real-world things—just to be rescued from some strange, invisible threat. But the fear that he had no choice in the matter lurked in the pit of his stomach.

"I can't possibly come up with that kind of money…"

His voice trembled.

Araki nodded back reassuringly with what seemed like genuine sympathy.

"Well, if you ever find yourself in a similar situation, please don't hesitate to consult with us."

With those parting words, Araki got out of the company car, opened the soundproof door with his number code, and entered the construction site.

Five hundred thousand yen for the exorcism. What if that didn't work? What if the strange stain didn't disappear? What if it spread out even more when he came back home? Would he have to buy another amulet for the same amount? What if that one did nothing, too?

There was just no choice. He gritted his teeth. He had to protect his home, even if it meant depleting his savings. Look at all the homeless people he saw. They had nowhere to live, which meant they couldn't obtain proper residence identification, which meant they couldn't get a home *or* a job. If he wanted to avoid that, he just needed to tough it out.

A sudden, excruciating pain shot through his left hand, resting on the steering wheel. It made him scream and curl up in pain.

Hang in there.

His father's voice. What did he mean, "hang in there"? The pain was unbearable.

"What a whiner."

His father's voice was clearer now. It was coming from behind him again.

"Go buy some painkillers. Or maybe you could ask Mr. Araki to fix it for you. He'll do damn near anything for you, won't he?"

"But I don't have any money left."

"You have your daughter's college fund, don't you? You can cancel all your insurance policies. You could all share one cell phone. Lots of ways to make it work. You could even take out another loan."

"I don't want to..."

Mitsuhiro hugged his knees on the seat with both his good hand and his aching one. Tears streamed down his cheeks.

"It's tough, isn't it?" his sympathetic father said. Mitsuhiro sobbed like a child as he looked at his father in the rearview mirror.

"Was it this hard for you, too, Dad?"

"Yeah, maybe."

"Is that why you were so strict with me and Mom?"

"Could be, yeah."

"I'm sorry, Dad. I didn't know about that at all."

"It's all right."

His father patted him lightly on the left shoulder. Instantly, the pain in his hand subsided.

Mitsuhiro wiped away his tears, put his feet back on the floor, and looked around the car. One time, when he lured Yoshikazu Hara in here with beer and snacks, the man had taken one look and said, "Whoa, you live in here or somethin'?" He had seen the convenience-store bag full of dirty clothes he was still carting around. Mitsuhiro had replied that he didn't, but he remembered how he tried to laugh off the question and completely failed to. He saw them every day, but his subconscious regarded the homeless people around him as creatures from another planet. Now that he knew that they most certainly weren't, he didn't know what to say to that question any longer.

Why did he think it could never happen to him? He didn't know anymore, even though he was slowly drifting toward that reality. It felt like a hole of his own, one he couldn't crawl out of by himself, and it made his head spin.

"You are the *mi-keshi* of the hole," his father said. "And that's fine, isn't it? In fact, it's an honor. If the hole wants you to, you should go in there with your whole family."

Mitsuhiro tried to say he didn't want to, but his phone was ringing too loudly to reply. He was still wearing his seat belt, so he twisted his body around to pull his phone out of his pants pocket. The name on the screen made his eyes widen.

It was Takenaka. Wasn't he supposed to be absent from work? Mitsuhiro considered ignoring the call—Takenaka couldn't have been calling about anything except the company car he was about to confiscate—but he didn't want Takenaka looking all around Tokyo for him, so he picked it up.

"Matsunaga speaking."

"This is Takenaka. Where are you right now?"

The voice was cold.

"I'm near the East Wing site, sir. I heard you were out of the office..."

"Come back here right now. I have something to ask you."

"What is it?"

"I can't talk about it on the phone. How long will it take you?"

"About fifteen minutes?"

"You can make it sooner than that. Get over to the team meeting room. I'll be waiting for you."

Then he hung up. It was a most unwelcome call, but it had dragged Mitsuhiro out of his state of desperate melancholy. He gave the phone an irritated snort and parked the car in the company lot on top of the hill. His anger quickened his pace as he walked back to the company building.

He got into the elevator, wiped the sweat from his brow, and entered one of the conference rooms.

Takenaka was there, and the state of him made Mitsuhiro blink. He was wearing his usual short-sleeved shirt and slacks, but the left side of his face was bandaged up, and his left arm was covered in dressings and suspended from his neck with a sling. The second surprise came when three unfamiliar men in suits turned around to face him at the same time.

Mitsuhiro closed the door behind him with his right hand, which was holding his bag. His first guess was that Takenaka had gotten in an accident and was being questioned about it.

"What's going on?"

Takenaka didn't answer, his face still stern, but one of the men in suits spoke for him.

"We're here looking into the arson at Mr. Takenaka's house last night."

Mitsuhiro's mouth fell open. He stared back at Takenaka's angry eyes.

"Detective Kitagawa, Shibuya Police Department."

The man took out his ID, drawing Mitsuhiro's attention. "Kazuya Kitagawa, Criminal Investigation Division" was printed on it.

"So," Kitagawa began as he put his ID back in his pocket, "I hear you spoke to Mr. Takenaka about a problem at a construction site. A possible arson?"

"Um… When was this?"

"About the ritual hall. The one you're so preoccupied with," Takenaka interjected.

"I'm sorry, could you step outside for a moment, please?"

One of the other men stepped in to stop Takenaka before he could be any more intimidating. Takenaka nodded, glaring at Mitsuhiro, and then limped out of the conference in obvious pain.

"Please, have a seat," said Kitagawa, pulling out a chair for himself. It was a conference room at his own company, but Mitsuhiro now felt like he was on a sales call to some outside firm, so he sat down and placed his bag on the floor. The other two sat a distance away, silently observing the conversation.

"Mr. Matsunaga. We heard about an incident involving you and an arson at the construction site. The site manager mentioned you during his interview. I understand that you and your boss, Mr. Takenaka, had a disagreement about whether or not to make this arson public."

"Yes, but I apologized to Chief Sugawara for it…"

"Right, but witnesses told us it was only with great reluctance. Mr. Matsunaga, do you think you have something against your boss, Mr. Takenaka, because you were forced to apologize against your will?"

"No, not at all," he quickly replied. Apparently, he was now an arson suspect. He remembered the looks he had received from the staff after he brought Yoshikazu Hara out of the hole, and he stiffened with discomfort. "I certainly regret making such a fuss over a small fire, yes, but I have no idea about any of this."

"If I could ask what you were doing last night…"

"I was at home with my daughter. My wife is pregnant and feeling unwell, so she was in the hospital for observation. My mother-in-law came over for us, but I still tried to get back home as soon as possible."

"I see."

Kitagawa nodded, but his indifferent eyes made it clear he wasn't ready to end the conversation.

"Do you know Tomohito Okuyama from Helping Hands Mutual Aid Society?"

"Huh? Oh. Yes, I do."

"Mr. Okuyama told us that you are looking for a certain person."

"Yes, a man named Yoshikazu Hara… He was working at the site, and I didn't know he had Alzheimer's, but I wound up letting him leave his post."

"What kind of work does someone with Alzheimer's do?"

Mitsuhiro reluctantly explained, even though he hadn't been the one to hire him.

"He was working at a ritual hall underground… I found out later that he was hired by a specialist contractor."

"A ritual hall? Like what Mr. Tamai the shaman deals in?"

"Shaman…?"

"Ah, sorry."

He didn't know what Kitagawa was apologizing for. He couldn't really picture what he meant by *shaman,* but he frowned at the word anyway. Kitagawa quickly changed the subject.

"So he was hired by Tamai Construction?"

"Yes. Do you know them?"

"Well, they come to our station pretty often."

The Shibuya Police Department was a stone's throw away from the East Wing site. Kitagawa acted like this should be common knowledge since they were all neighbors, but to be honest, Mitsuhiro had no idea where this was going.

"So, Mr. Matsunaga, it seems like quite a few other people besides this Yoshikazu Hara have disappeared."

"I heard that from Mr. Okuyama, too. I don't know anything about it, though."

"Witnesses informed us that people went away with you after you struck up conversations with them and never came back."

"Oh… You know, I'd buy him some ice cream or something so I could investigate Yoshikazu Hara."

"Did you give them alcohol?"

"Well, sometimes but not always…"

"I heard you were using a company car."

"Um…? So…?"

"Do you think the dashcam would show anyone with you in the car?"

"Yes, I think so."

Kitagawa was trying to pressure him, it seemed. Mitsuhiro felt like a deer in the headlights. Then the detective, attempting to elicit more of a response from him, slowed his pace a little.

"We have some evidence here regarding a certain homeless person. This includes both eyewitness accounts and surveillance camera footage showing this person talking with you as you traveled toward Shibuya Station."

"Uh-huh."

"Where were you going?"

"I was trying to take Yoshikazu Hara back to the construction site where he used to work."

"Did you find him?"

"What?"

"Yoshikazu Hara. Did you find him?"

"Yes, but as soon as I find him, he disappears. I think it's because of his illness. We're still looking for him."

"So where did you take the homeless man who *wasn't* Yoshikazu Hara?"

"Ah, no, nowhere… I'm only looking for Yoshikazu Hara."

"You didn't take anyone anywhere?"

"No."

Kitagawa tilted his head and took a breath. Then he spoke up, attempting to guide Mitsuhiro a little more.

"Have you ever thought that homeless people should be put out of the picture because they get in the way of construction work?"

Mitsuhiro's eyes opened wide. "Of course not."

"I heard that sort of thing wasn't so uncommon once upon a time. People getting kidnapped over land-sale disputes and so on."

"That's all in the past. I've never even thought of such a thing."

Kitagawa nodded, as if he hoped that was the case. Honestly, Mitsuhiro hadn't expected the police to stand up for the homeless and their problems so much. Maybe Okuyama's persistence had paid off. Either way, though, he couldn't afford to be a suspect here.

"I mean," he said, "what's the point of chasing away one or two people? There's so many more out there than that."

"No, it's definitely not one or two, Mr. Matsunaga."

Mitsuhiro was taken aback by the matter-of-fact response. Okuyama had used the same turn of phrase with him, but he'd assumed he was padding the numbers.

"Um, are that many people missing?"

"According to Mr. Okuyama, at least fourteen people are unaccounted for."

"Fourteen…?"

Mitsuhiro couldn't hide his surprise. He expected three or four at the most. Indeed, if that many people disappeared at once, you'd want to know what's going on, wouldn't you?

Kitagawa peered at Mitsuhiro, observing his expression closely. "You don't know anything about that, do you?"

"I'm sorry… If I find out anything, I'll let you know…"

"Yes, please do. Here's my contact information."

Kitagawa handed Mitsuhiro his business card. Mitsuhiro took his own card out of his bag and gave it to Kitagawa.

"Sorry to take up your time. Thank you for your cooperation."

"No, not at all—"

As he stood up with Kitagawa and his men, the cut on his left hand began to ache again. He let out another groan. It was impossible for the detectives not to notice. Quickly, they stopped what they were doing to look at Mitsuhiro.

"Where did you get that injury?"

"Huh?"

"Did you get hurt during your search?"

"No, it was at home. In the kitchen."

"A burn or something?"

"No, I accidentally cut myself throwing out the trash."

"All right. Hope it heals up soon, then."

Kitagawa nodded to the two men, and all three left the conference room. Mitsuhiro remained behind, feeling intolerably uncomfortable, like he'd just been subjected to a strip search. He felt even more uncomfortable when he pictured them coming to his apartment and combing his trash for clues.

Just then, Takenaka swung the door open.

"It wasn't *you*, was it?" he barked.

Mitsuhiro, stunned, stared back at Takenaka's pallid face.

"I'm asking if you're the one who burned down our house."

"No... Do you really think that?"

His mind was in a daze, but Takenaka's glare only sharpened; he seemed to believe the facts were obvious.

"Are you still looking for the homeless guy?"

"Yes, sir. I'm pretty close to finding him."

"Don't you think you're causing a hell of a lot more problems in the process?"

"What do you mean?"

"Why do homeless people keep on disappearing? Why did my house have to burn down?"

"Um, is it completely gone, sir?"

Suddenly, he saw his old house burning down in front of his eyes. His mother's words—*"You keep on forgetting about it after a while, don't you?"*—echoed in his mind. He faintly remembered sitting on the side of the road, watching the flames shooting out of the windows and roof of his house.

"Almost," Takenaka said, his eyes bloodshot. "The kids' room was almost completely gone."

"Stop it. It wasn't me."

"But you're the one who pulled the trigger. Why the hell'd you poke the hornet's nest and make everything worse? You were supposed to resolve this incident, and instead you've turned it into this huge deal. And now I've been kicked out of the shareholder conference this quarter because I didn't kick *you* out of here sooner."

"Kicked out? Why?"

"Well, I can't be part of it if *I'm* involved in this huge damn scandal!" Takenaka howled in obvious fury.

Mitsuhiro flinched back, speechless before the rage and hatred in Takenaka's eyes. His boss must have been afraid that everything he had built up in Shimaoka was about to crumble.

Maybe Takenaka should go in the hole ahead of Okuyama. The thought crossed Mitsuhiro's mind for a moment, and he knew his father would've said the same thing. Not that he really meant it—

"And return the keys right now. You're banned from car access."

He threw the order at Mitsuhiro as he stormed out of the conference room. Now even Mitsuhiro had to admit that he would love to see Takenaka weeping at the bottom of that hole.

Disgusted, he picked up his bag from the floor. He did so with his left hand, which rewarded him with a pang of intense pain that made him stumble and drop the bag again. It felt like there were sharpened thorns all over the handle. He wanted to grab it and slam it against the wall in sheer frustration, but instead he sat down in a chair, clutched his head with his uninjured right hand, and sighed deeply.

"It's not my fault, either…"

4

Walking around Shibuya in the scorching sun, holding his aching hand, Mitsuhiro thought about renting a car over and over. But whenever he actually stopped in front of a rental-car center, he succumbed to his fear at the thought of skipping mortgage payments to afford it.

He also opted to quit making his little pre-prep shopping trips at convenience stores. With only his right hand available, he didn't want to have too much luggage on him, and this blast-furnace weather was melting the ice cream and heating up the drinks too fast anyway.

The shopping, he resolved, would wait until he found Yoshikazu Hara. But now the sun was about to set, and he hadn't found him once. He no longer had a car, which was one reason, but a lot of it had to do with his aching left hand. Every park he went to, every tent city he walked around, every time he felt he was *this* close to finding Yoshikazu Hara, the pain in his hand would drown it out.

Like his father suggested, he bought some painkillers at the pharmacy, but they didn't help much. And yet as soon as he started heading back to the station, thinking he should give up for today, the pain faded away. It was like the pain only existed to hinder him from his extremely important job.

Exhausted, he got on the train and returned to his condo, resigning himself to the fact that finding Yoshikazu Hara might have to wait until his hand healed up.

As soon as he opened the front door, he felt a strange emptiness. The lights were off, and Miyoko's and Sae's shoes weren't there. Wasn't she discharged by now? Did she get worse?

He turned on the lights as he pondered the question…and was startled to see that the wall was peeling.

No, that wasn't it; the newspaper had fallen off the wall. He took off his shoes, approached the wall, put his bag on the floor, and picked up two fallen thumbtacks. Fearing the pain in his left hand, he pressed down the newspaper with his elbow and pinned it back with another thumbtack.

The stain wasn't fully covered. It was seeping out from underneath the newspaper, spreading not only on the walls but also on the ceiling and floor. Some of the newspaper was stained now, and the printed text was dissolving into the face of a tormented ghoul. He shivered.

Looking at the amulet pinned near the ceiling, he saw that the white fabric of the pouch had turned a pitiful, dirty gray. That thing had cost him two hundred thousand yen. Mitsuhiro fell to his knees in exhaustion. Would burning it and performing a purification ritual still be effective? It seemed unlikely, but he thought he might do it anyway. If it didn't give him *something* to hope for, why did he spend all that money? Because clearly, purifying that piece of gravestone wasn't enough. He may as well have thrown half a million yen in cash into that pond.

Mitsuhiro stood up on unsteady legs and looked around Sae's room, along with the darkened dining room and bedroom. No one was there. He was in his own home, but now he was overcome with the feeling that he had nowhere to go. He felt like a homeless person, wandering around some building, looking for a place to rest quietly.

If things continued like this, he'd soon think it'd be easier to just throw himself into that hole. The thought had already occurred to him.

Hang in there.

He thought he heard his father's voice from somewhere. *Yeah. He's right.* That was just the kind of encouragement Mitsuhiro needed. If he *didn't* hang in there, he'd lose his home. He had to find Yoshikazu Hara soon. He couldn't give in to the pain of his wounds. Then the hole would be satiated. Surely it would release him.

Suddenly, his phone rang in his jacket pocket. Mitsuhiro took it out and saw the call was from Miyoko. As soon as he tapped the call button and put it to his ear, an onrush of emotion exploded out.

"Why aren't you at home?!"

"What? What do you mean by that?!"

"I mean why the hell aren't you at home?!"

"Because you *weren't! It smells awful! And look at that wall! Why are you still there? You know it's crazy, right?"*

"Then where do you want me to be?"

"I don't know! That's why I'm worried! Please calm down a little!"

Mitsuhiro leaned against a (non-stained) wall and took a deep breath. She was right. What had happened to him?

"Where are you right now?" he asked, his voice suddenly weaker.

"At my parents' house," Miyoko replied, also growing a bit calmer. *"It's the only place I can go. Sae's with me."*

"Why'd you take her with you?"

"Because you can't even feed her properly! You can't even come visit me at the hospital! You were out somewhere in the middle of the night again, weren't you, on whatever work you're doing?"

"Well, if I go to your house, your family's just gonna yell at me and kick me out."

"They told me I could stay here as long as we need to work our issues out. You were the one who yelled at Mom first. She and Dad are holding their ground here."

The moment he imagined his in-laws' faces, his violent side once again surged.

"What issues? I've been working hard all this time!"

"What are you talking about? Calm down."

"I *am* calm!"

"Seriously, what's going on?"

"What do you mean?"

"We have a lot less money in our account now. Did you buy something?"

Mitsuhiro was at a loss. He knew he had to explain that at some point, but now was really not the time. He even resented Miyoko for choosing this moment.

"It's for our home. We need it."

"You didn't spend hundreds of thousands of yen on that good-luck charm, did you?"

He was about to say *The hell's wrong with that?* before stopping himself. This was tiptoeing close to major fight territory. But Miyoko's strong tone didn't relent for a moment.

"Does it have anything to do with the police showing up?"

"The police?"

"They called me. I said I was at my parents', and they came all the way over here. They asked me a bunch of questions about your work, but I mean… Is it true that you're going around talking to homeless people? Are you really taking them somewhere in a company car in the middle of the night?"

He didn't know how to answer that. He couldn't understand why even

Miyoko was suspicious of him now. The throbbing in his left hand made it hard to think straight.

"Why aren't you answering me? Also, did you go to the school today?"

That only confused him more. "Stop talking nonsense. Why would I go to the school?"

"Sae said she saw you standing outside the gate."

"What?"

"Weren't you supposed to be at work? Why were you loitering like some weirdo? Were you trying to take Sae back to the condo?"

The thought that someone was trying to take his daughter suddenly popped into his head, and he shuddered with fear. Why would they do that?

For "compensation." He couldn't find Yoshikazu Hara. His family would have to be put in the hole.

"No! Miyoko, it wasn't me! That's not me! Tell Sae not to believe anything she hears!"

"Huh? Not believe— Tell me what's going on!"

"I don't know either! I'm just doing my goddamn job!"

His emotions exploded again. He just couldn't bear to hear Miyoko's voice anymore.

"Look, can you just come over here for a little bit? Get out of our condo."

"You want me to live with your parents? You know they won't—"

"Just get out of there! You'll feel a lot better once you're out! There's something wrong with that place!"

Mitsuhiro stamped his feet in frustration. He couldn't bear to imagine this home completely empty.

"It'll be over soon, all right? Then our place will be all normal again!"

"Again, what are you talking about? What's gonna be over soon? I'm telling you, I feel so much better when I'm not there."

"How much of the mortgage do you think we have left?! Are you telling me to sell this place? We'll lose so much money! I'm finally home, okay?! Can't you think about protecting this place a little?!"

"That's not the point! What do you mean, you're 'finally home'? Are you talking about when your parents' house burned down?"

The house was on fire. He sat on the side of the road, unable to do anything, watching it burn. He hated it. Why was she making him remember that?

"Just shut up! Stop griping about my work! I have things to do! Important work! Why are you getting in my way?!"

He was almost out of breath now. He braced himself, expecting Miyoko to sass back at him, but all he heard was the sound of sobbing and Sae's voice asking, "Mommy, why are you crying?"

"It's nothing." Miyoko sniffled. *"I'll call you back."* Then nothing.

Mitsuhiro felt his limbs trembling with agitation and guilt as he picked up his bag and entered the dark dining room. He put it and his phone on the table.

Hang in there.

His father's voice didn't make the trembling stop.

As he sat in that dark room, head bowed, he noticed that his father had sat down in the chair across from him. He was smiling.

"Now you can focus on your work, right? And once you're done, the whole family will be together forever."

He imagined the three of them huddled together at the bottom of the hole. No, four. The baby in his wife's womb would be there, too. It was a horrifying thought, but now he realized that it was a relief, too. He couldn't take any more of this. More and more now, he felt like he didn't care what happened as long as this job was over soon.

Mitsuhiro helplessly looked at his father. "You weren't there for me," he said resentfully.

"Where'd that come from all of a sudden?"

"I was lonely for so long. I felt like you didn't even see me anymore. I didn't want Sae and Miyoko to feel the same way."

Hang in there.

His father's voice. It didn't sound quite like the voice of the man in front of him, but he couldn't tell for sure.

"No? Well, I'm sorry I made you feel lonely. But in the end, we'll all be together as a family. Like how the fire turns everyone into ashes and makes them one."

His father looked back at the window behind him. Suddenly, a dazzling light shone through it, revealing his father's silhouette.

Mitsuhiro stood up in a daze and looked over his father's head.

Everything was on fire. Every building around them was engulfed in flames and collapsing. Something fell from the sky with a loud screeching sound, exploding on the street and sending columns of flame into the air. People were burning everywhere, running around in panic, then falling to the ground.

There was an inferno out the window. An earthquake. An air raid. The aggregated memories of countless fires over the years were now dancing around with the blizzard of embers flying past the window.

His father turned his face back to Mitsuhiro. With that turn of the head came a strange smell. The smell of something being burned until even its bones were ashes.

Before Mitsuhiro's eyes, his father's face and body were burned to a crisp. His skin was charred black; his bones cracked with a crunching sound. Blood and pus oozed from his body, which was now swarming with flies and maggots.

There was a small sound from the hallway.

A thumbtack had fallen, leaving newspaper hanging off the wall. The stain on the wall was spreading. Soon it would burn like his father, spilling boiling blood, cracking from the heat, crawling with maggots.

"You see now, don't you? This is how we all become one."

His father smiled. He was no longer burning. Outside the window was the usual quiet night view.

Mitsuhiro slowly sat back down on the chair and nodded to his father. The way fire destroyed people was no longer on his mind. He understood now why his father wanted to live near water. He wondered if Dad had always been this afraid of the scene he just witnessed.

"Were you cursed, too, Dad? That's why you got so angry when I left the kerosene heater on in my room back in middle school."

"Ahh, maybe. But let's get ready for work, okay? We're almost done now. All that effort will go to waste if we just sit around here all night."

"Yeah..."

Mitsuhiro had said yes, but both his body and mind were utterly exhausted. The pain had subsided for now, but he knew it'd flare up again soon. Nothing could have drained his motivation more. But if he slacked off now, his father—and the hole—would be furious with him. He didn't want to think about that hole taking Sae and Miyoko away. He had no choice but to get up. He grabbed his phone from the table, put it in his jacket pocket, and tried to stand up, holding his bag with his right arm.

The wound on his left hand began to throb.

Hang in there.

He heard his father's voice. But it didn't sound like his father smiling in front of him.

Hang in there.

Mitsuhiro looked at the bag he was holding. He finally realized that the voice he had heard so many times before was coming from inside of it.

"What are you doing? You have to get to work, don't you?"

Mitsuhiro didn't leave. The pain in his left hand was still there, but strangely, it didn't bother him.

He placed the bag on the table, opened it, and peered inside. It was too dark to see clearly with only the ambient light, so he reached inside with his right hand and took out everything he could touch, laying it all out on the table.

There was a tablet he had left in the bag, forgetting to charge it. His wallet. His business card case. A plastic bottle with about a third of its contents remaining. A spare key to his home.

A worn Rubik's Cube came out. He couldn't remember when he had put it in there. He stared at it intently.

There was a phone with the power turned off. It belonged to Mole Unit-01, who was there when he first took Yoshikazu Hara to the basement. He couldn't remember why he had left it in his bag or why he had taken it in the first place.

"What are you wasting time in here for? The hole will be angry. So will your dad."

But Mitsuhiro didn't care. He was more concerned about the wad of newspaper at the bottom of his bag. He took it out and placed it on the table. The bag should have been empty now.

But when he looked inside, it wasn't. He saw something small and shiny, half-wrapped in white cloth.

Mitsuhiro reached for it.

His father's face contorted, and his voice was more terrifying than it had ever been as he shouted, "Don't touch that!"

But Mitsuhiro could hardly hear him. The shout reached his ears just as his fingers touched the item in the bag. It was a white handkerchief, a memento from his father, with the initials "KM" embroidered on it. Mitsuhiro could feel not only the softness of the cloth but also the hardness of what was wrapped inside. It was something sharp, reminiscent of a small fruit knife. He felt around with his thumb over the handkerchief and detected a complex pattern carved into it.

No, it wasn't a pattern. It was part of an engraved name. A piece of his father's name.

"Mitsuhiro!"

He realized that his father was yelling furiously in front of him.

Mitsuhiro looked at him, this person he thought was his father. No, the person he'd been made to believe was his father. His whole body was charred beyond recognition. He was covered in boiling blood and the smell of burning flesh. Mitsuhiro, overcome with shock, thrust what he was holding toward the eerie shadow.

There was nothing there.

There was only a chair with its back pressed tightly against the edge of the table. This was the one chair the three-person family usually never sat on. They usually put their things on it.

Mitsuhiro took a deep breath and placed what he was holding in his right hand on top of his left.

The cut on his left hand hardly hurt anymore. When he unfolded the handkerchief, the name "Kosuke Matsunaga" in stone crossed it diagonally, forming a handle. The thinly cracked part extended out like the blade of a fruit knife, just like he had assumed it was at first. But it was a piece of the gravestone, an even smaller piece of it. All those hammer blows must've put a crack or two into it after all.

He had forgotten about the handkerchief in his agitation when the stone hit Araki's leg. That cloth, plus the small stone, had been wrapped in newspaper this whole time...or maybe they resisted being thrown away by Mitsuhiro.

"...Dad?" he said, stroking the stone with the fingertips of his right hand.

Air rushed into his lungs. Suddenly, his body relaxed, his chest muscles loosened up, and he felt his lungs expand. His legs had grown numb from sitting in the same position for so long.

Mitsuhiro, unable to make sense of this, took several deep breaths, waiting for the blood to return to his legs. All the while, he continued to smell that terrible odor. The smell of dry ash filled the whole place.

When his legs were useful again, Mitsuhiro stood up and turned on the lights. He still held the piece of stone in his left hand, along with the handkerchief. Now that it was bright, he noticed a lot more than just the smell. There was a thin layer of white powder on the floor and table.

Even from the dining room, he could hear a crunching sound as the stains on the hallway walls gradually spread. He thought it sounded like a person's skin cracking under high heat, and then he wondered how his mind came up with that analogy in the first place.

Miyoko was right. Something strange *was* going on. Not just in this condo but with himself as well.

Mitsuhiro looked at the things on the table and picked up the dead phone with his right hand. He connected it to the charger and waited patiently for it to turn on.

Before long, it came back to life. It wasn't locked, so Mitsuhiro launched Twitter from the list of apps on the screen. The page for Mole Unit-01 appeared. He searched for the messages he had exchanged with the guy, but for some reason, they had been deleted. No, wait, he had deleted them himself for some reason.

He closed Twitter and opened the settings. The real name and payment details of the owner, sadly, were password-protected and couldn't be viewed.

Next, he opened the call history. There were several months' worth of records, but not that many voice calls had been made. Most were just numbers with no description, with only three entries labeled "Construction," "City Hall," and "Job Center." The "Construction" entry had the most calls. Checking the numbers, "Construction" was a mobile phone number, while "City Hall" and "Job Center" had landline area codes.

Mitsuhiro put the stone and handkerchief he was holding in his left hand into his shirt pocket and switched the phone over to that hand. Then he pulled out his own phone with his right and searched the "City Hall" and "Job Center" numbers. The former was the welfare consultation desk at Shibuya City Hall, and the latter was the job placement office near Shibuya Station.

Neither contained any personally identifiable information, so he opened the phone's text messages instead. This was all spam, with no signs of communication with friends or family. There were several messages from the "Construction" number, some with attached images, but he assumed they were mass texts informing crews of times and locations to report to, so he didn't open them.

Looking for something else to check, he opened the photo album. It was full of images from the East Wing construction site, some of which he recognized from Twitter. There were some other images, too, and Mitsuhiro's eyes were drawn to one of them.

In front of a small shrine, Araki, wearing a helmet, was pointing at a patch of the ground marked with ropes, surrounded by Yoshikazu Hara and five other workers. The body language seemed to indicate that Araki was instructing them to dig the ground in front of the shrine. Based on the shrine's location, Mitsuhiro realized that they were standing right where the hole currently was.

This confirmed that the owner of this phone was one of the workers hired to dig that hole. Mitsuhiro might be able to identify the guy from his company's work records. He closed the image, but then something occurred to him. Mitsuhiro returned to his call history, brought up the "Construction" number, and opened his own phone to check Araki's number.

They matched. The owner of this phone had been in communication with Araki.

Mitsuhiro closed the call log, returned to the phone's text messages, and opened one sent from the "Construction" number. There was no text, just images. Some pictures of the East Wing construction site—and shockingly enough, Mitsuhiro recognized all of them. They were the seven images that Mole Unit-01 had posted on Twitter, the ones that had led Mitsuhiro down to that site in the first place.

—Did Araki send these images to the Twitter poster?

He couldn't come up with a logical reason why. Were they confirming some detail of the construction project? If so, there should have been *some* text accompanying them. There was no reason for Araki to send this guy images from areas outside the ritual hall.

Had Araki sent them to Mole Unit-01 and instructed him to post them on Twitter? That was plausible, but again, there was no reason for that.

—But what if there was?

The only thing Mitsuhiro could think of was that Araki wanted to lure someone into the ritual hall. If Shimaoka noticed the posts and took issue with them, someone would go into the site to check it out. If that was Araki's aim, he would've had Mole Unit-01, a workman at the site, post it on his behalf.

—But what for?

A curse.

Human sacrifice.

Compensation.

The words flashed through his mind, but they didn't form a clear explanation.

Mitsuhiro placed the two phones on the table and thought over what he knew for sure. Mole Unit-01 was definitely not Yoshikazu Hara, not unless Hara gave his phone to someone at the ritual hall and asked them to take a picture of him. Also, the images posted on Twitter by Mole Unit-01 were originally sent by Araki.

—Is all of that reasonable so far?

He realized that he was talking to the "invisible guest," as Sae put it. Now he wasn't so sure. He needed someone to discuss this with. Someone who'd understand the situation. Someone who wouldn't ask for money in return. It was financially impossible to consult with Araki, and his connection to Mole Unit-01 made him very suspicious.

That left only one person. Mitsuhiro picked up his phone, knowing it was a long shot, and made the call.

"This is Sugawara."

The person answered immediately. Mitsuhiro leaned forward on the table.

"I apologize for calling so late, Chief. This is Matsunaga from the IR department at Shimaoka. I'm calling because I'd like to consult with you."

"I heard the police showed up. Has there been another incident?"

Ah, right. He still hadn't ironed that out. But that could wait. He wanted to at least completely regain his sanity first.

"I don't know if this is related to that, but… Um, sorry to bring this up, but you mentioned that you saw your deceased brother at one point…"

"Yes, I did."

"Well, to tell the truth, I saw my deceased father as well. I realized just now that I didn't find it unusual at all, right up to this very moment…"

"And you realize now that it's strange?"

"Yes. The moment I touched one of my father's belongings, I immediately came to my senses. I also suddenly noticed that, um, my home smells bad, and there's definitely something wrong with it."

"Have you consulted anyone about this? Anyone from Tamai Construction Company?"

"Um, yes, I purchased an amulet from an employee named Sota Araki..."

"Purchased? You bought it?"

"It was quite expensive, but yes. Also, my father's gravestone was damaged, and after discussing it with the previous president, he helped provide purification rites for the damaged piece."

"The previous president?"

"Yes."

"Are you referring to Yutaro Tamai, the previous president of Tamai Construction Company?"

"Yes, I believe it was him."

There was a moment of silence on the other end of the line.

"And he said he discussed this with the previous president recently?"

"Yes, just yesterday. Is that a problem...?"

"Yutaro Tamai is dead."

5

"Dead...?"

Mitsuhiro repeated the words, feeling the blood drain from his body.

"Yes. I consulted with Yutaro Tamai himself long ago, back when he was president. He passed away many years ago, and I suppose it was one of his relatives who took over the company instead of his own son. Or is Mr. Araki the son of the previous president?"

"He said he was."

His heart raced. It felt like the pieces of this once-incomprehensible puzzle were all falling into place, and it only made him more terrified. Chief Sugawara, on the other hand, seemed completely unfazed.

"*Perhaps,*" he calmly continued, "*Araki is also seeing the dead.*"

"He did mention his 'predecessor' a lot to me…"

So Araki was cursed as well. But since when? Was it because of Mitsuhiro? Or was he like that long before he dove into the ritual hall?

"The fact that you paid for an amulet from him is also concerning to me. I, too, received an amulet from the previous president and had a purification ritual of my own performed…but as long as it was related to our own ritual hall, I never personally paid money to Tamai Construction."

"What? You didn't?"

"The previous president said they only accept money from companies and government agencies involved with the ritual halls. There were no personal transactions—that was the rule they stuck to. That's why they charged so much for management fees, he said. It didn't seem that expensive to me, since it's a minimum ten-year contract anyway."

Mitsuhiro's astonishment faded and was replaced by anger. He had been potentially swindled out of a large sum of money, which was unpleasant enough, but now he wondered if that amulet Araki gave him, and the whole ritual with throwing the stone into the pond, was actually meaningless. It was a bitter pill to swallow, but worst of all, money didn't seem to be the only motive here. What if he was doing all this in order to curse someone? What if Mitsuhiro had fallen right into that trap?

No. If he hadn't been hoodwinked and lost sight of Yoshikazu Hara, he wouldn't be in this predicament right now. He could've just questioned him down there, confirmed his position at Tamai Construction, and then there wouldn't have been any problems.

Who started the fire?

Appeasement by fire.

He didn't think he could be surprised anymore, and yet he was.

"If you remember that small fire in the East Wing…I think Sota Araki might have started it."

It sounded ridiculous even to him, but Chief Sugawara remained calm.

"Why do you think that?"

"I found out that he was in contact with someone who had been slandering the East Wing on Twitter. Based on the images of the ritual hall he sent this person, it's possible he was trying to get the poster to hurt the reputation of the construction site on social media."

"What would he do that for?"

"Could he have been trying to lure someone from Shimaoka into the site so he could free the person performing the ritual? Because without that arson, that person would still be at the site. That, and maybe he wanted to put me in a state where, um, I could see the dead."

"So not only did this person want to interrupt the ritual—they wanted to specifically curse you, Mr. Matsunaga?"

"No, I think anyone would have sufficed."

Sugawara let out a thoughtful "*hmm*" at this.

"I know this probably all sounds strange to you, sir."

"Well, I'd find it completely bizarre if I hadn't experienced it myself. But maybe we shouldn't assume that there was a clear purpose for this. If you're being enticed by someone you care about who should be dead, well, you'd do almost anything for them. You wouldn't even know what you're doing."

Sugawara's words were convincing. Mitsuhiro didn't know when he might lose his sanity again, and if he did, he didn't think he'd be able to explain his actions in any logical manner.

The phrase "do almost anything" suddenly made him wonder if it was Araki who set fire to Takenaka's house. An "appeasing" fire. Araki himself might have fully believed that he was doing the right thing, too. It seemed very possible.

"We need to see what state Mr. Araki is in. Should we consult with Tamai Construction?"

"Before that, why don't we confront him directly? If we talk to Tamai Construction, they might cut off our means of reaching Araki."

"Certainly, if this is a site matter, we need to start by talking to those involved in the incident. All right. I'd like to accompany you, if possible."

"What? You?"

"This lies under my jurisdiction, including the ritual hall. Whether Mr. Araki is guilty or not, I want to reach a definitive conclusion about the arson. Also, I still have the amulet given to me from their previous leader. That should count well enough as the 'belongings of the deceased' for Mr. Araki's purposes."

Mitsuhiro unconsciously put his left hand in his breast pocket to make sure the stone and handkerchief were still there. He didn't know how effective it would be, but if Araki wasn't of sound mind and they had something that could ward off these visions of the dead, it might be useful. Hopefully, if this was an authentic Tamai Construction amulet, it'd be especially effective.

"Thank you very much. I'd really appreciate that. I'm sorry to put you through all this trouble..."

"Well, we need to consider the safety of the site as well. When will you be meeting Mr. Araki? I can call the office and have him come over if you like."

"I'll call him. If I tell him I want to buy an amulet, he'll come over for me. We usually meet at the East Wing construction parking lot, so I'll arrange to meet him tomorrow..."

Mitsuhiro craned his neck and looked at the small calendar on the TV stand in the living room. Tomorrow was Saturday. Between the odd hours he'd been keeping lately and the way he'd stopped being invited to meetings, he had completely lost track of the days of the week.

"...Ah, but the office will be closed anyway," he said, correcting himself. "I'll try to schedule it for the beginning of next week."

"*Saturday's fine, actually,*" Chief Sugawara said. *"It's actually more convenient. Better to get this done sooner than later. Let me know when you work out a time, and I can drive over, and we can talk in my car."*

"All right. Thanks for all of your help."

He ended the call, stood up, opened the window, and let out a deep breath. He had taken this call in what was now a hot, stuffy apartment with the AC turned off. The memory of sleeping in the company car came back to him, and he was suddenly afraid of being dehydrated and not even knowing it. Leaving the window open, he grabbed the remote, turned on the AC, and wondered just how coherent he was at that moment.

Was this deep sluggishness because he had neglected to eat and sleep properly? If he didn't hold on to his marbles now, he'd never resolve any of this. He'd just collapse, and then he couldn't do anything.

With that in mind, Mitsuhiro went to the air vent, stood under the cool breeze, and called Araki.

"This is Araki."

"Hello, this is Matsunaga from Shimaoka. I'm sorry to call so late."

"Not at all. What's the matter?"

"Well, actually, I need another amulet."

"Already?"

"I wanted to get a set for the whole family. Would that be tough on short notice?"

"I'll ask the previous president about it, but it should be fine. If you need anything else purified, we could meet over at the Imperial Gardens again."

"Thanks, but I'll just need the amulets this time. I know tomorrow's Saturday, but would you mind meeting at the usual parking lot at the East Wing?"

"Not a problem. I was planning to stop by the ritual hall anyway. How does eleven in the morning sound to you?"

"That'd be great. Thank you very much."

So Mitsuhiro now had his appointment. Deep down, he wanted to ask Araki about the East Wing fire and Mole Unit-01 right now, but he couldn't risk doing anything that'd break off contact with him. Besides, he couldn't judge for himself whether his mind was wholly sound right now. He wanted to call Miyoko but didn't. If he lost himself in the middle of the call and flew into another rage, it'd do nothing to calm her or Sae.

For that matter, Mitsuhiro couldn't even really remember in detail what he had been doing since going down to the basement of the construction site anyway. Was that really true? Fourteen homeless people were missing? Even if he did take them all to the ritual hall, he had no clue what had happened to them afterward. Then again, wasn't Araki managing that hall? It was odd that *he* hadn't commented at all, either.

Mitsuhiro put his hand on his breast pocket to check for the stone and looked around the room for a way to keep himself sane. He felt helpless, wandering in complete darkness with only a flashlight to guide him. He could no longer dismiss the idea of "curses" as mere superstition, and thanks to that, he couldn't even tell where the boundary between normal and abnormal lay any longer.

A loud noise echoed through the room. A torrential downpour had begun out of nowhere, pounding against the windows and screens. The kind of sudden, intense rain that had been making headlines in the news lately. Mitsuhiro stood by the window, feeling the wind and rain blowing through the screen. It was surprisingly rejuvenating, almost like it was purifying him. The violent storm seemed to blow away the strange smell and dry air that had taken up residence here.

He wanted to open all the windows in the house, but he didn't. Instead, he closed it and went to the kitchen. He took a wet wipe and wiped down the table, then put everything back into his bag. After finishing off the contents of the plastic bottle, he threw it into the recycling bin. He washed the rag in the sink, wrung it out, and tossed it in the trash as well. Then he used a floor wiper to go over the floors in the dining room, kitchen, and hallway, briskly wiping away the dust-like material that had accumulated while he was unaware.

He discarded the wiper sheet and peeled off all the stained newspaper from the hallway walls. The thumbtacks were blackened and smelly, so he threw them away with the newspaper. He wondered what to do with the amulet up there, but in the end, he took it off and threw it away along with the tacks. It felt like throwing away a bundle of ten-thousand-yen bills, but he didn't let his emotions get the better of him.

He then brought in another rag from the kitchen and used some household cleaner to wipe the walls. The once-gruesome stains were reduced to just some dirty faded marks. He threw away the rag, took the garbage bag from the bin, tied it shut, and took it out to the trash-disposal room.

Upon returning, he filled the bathtub with water and had a late dinner in the kitchen—microwavable white rice, instant miso soup, and whatever else was left in the refrigerator. He still felt pretty lethargic, eating alone to the sound of the rain, but he could tell that his blood was moving around again. It helped him relax, and his back and abdomen were grateful.

After finishing his meal and washing the dishes, he went to the bathroom and threw his jacket into a cleaning bag. Before taking off his shirt, he took the handkerchief and stone out from the breast pocket. He wondered if something resembling his father might appear as soon as he let go of them. How did Chief Sugawara do this? Did he carry his brother's glasses with him into the bath? He couldn't have. If so, he would've advised Mitsuhiro that he really *did* have to go that far.

As a test, he cautiously placed the handkerchief and stone on the sink. Nothing happened. He took a step back and looked around. He waited for a burnt-out corpse to suddenly pop out and grab him, but nothing appeared.

Keeping the handkerchief and stone close at hand, he took another step back and left the bathroom. He felt fine. He wasn't going crazy, at least. He wasn't struck by an urge to lunge for them right away. Perhaps just recognizing that his father's belongings were there had an effect.

Mitsuhiro returned to the sink, still on his guard, and began to unwrap the gauze on his left hand. He braced himself for intense pain, but it just stung a little. As the blood-soaked gauze came off, it revealed a cut running diagonally from the base of his index finger to the heel right above his wrist. It was scabbed up, covered in dried blood, and almost completely closed. He didn't know which line this corresponded to in palm reading, but either way, he didn't think the wound would last long.

He wondered why such a shallow cut hurt so much. Should he take it as a message from his real father? He would've preferred a warning that didn't involve debilitating pain, but it had successfully brought him back to his senses, so he had no right to complain.

So Mitsuhiro stopped worrying about the pain in his hand and looked up as he unbuttoned his shirt. Then he saw it in the mirror—or *them*, that is.

Charred corpses were writhing and screaming behind Mitsuhiro. He couldn't tell how many there were. Faces and hands were everywhere around him, spewing boiling blood from skin torn away by the heat. He couldn't actually hear anything, and yet he felt like he was being swallowed up by a whirlpool of ear-splitting screams.

It had started and ended in an instant. Stunned, he grabbed the handkerchief and the stone—but before he even made the move, the horde of corpses had vanished. It wasn't really a matter of "appearing" or "vanishing"—it felt more like he had briefly shifted into the same wavelength or something with them, giving him a glimpse of the other side.

His heart was pounding violently in his chest, and sweat was breaking out on his forehead. But there was no sense of fear-driven helplessness. It was there to some extent, but he pushed it aside, ardently hoping to endure this inexplicably abnormal experience.

Perhaps it was thanks to his father's belongings that he could think clearly about all this.

The horde was still there. He had driven them out of his mind, but they were still persistently clinging to him. Not just one or two of them but a collective force—something impossible to count, much like a flow of water or a puff of smoke. Unless he drove them out of this home and back to the hole they came from, they'd continue to haunt him forever.

Mitsuhiro pressed his left hand against the mirror and pushed hard. The gesture didn't have much thought behind it, but he needed his own "ritual" to fight this fear. To express his determination.

He felt a sharp pain in his hand, but he ignored it and rubbed it against the mirror. The blood from the wound seeped out, leaving a thin film. He continued moving slowly, writing a large character across the entire surface of the mirror.

鎮

He didn't know if this would work, but he wanted to make this display to whatever was following him around. He needed to show whatever was clinging to him that he wouldn't go down without a fight.

—*This is where my family lives. It doesn't belong to you. You have no right to be here. You're not even alive. I won't let you take this away from me.*

Mitsuhiro held his sharp stone in the air, wrapped in a handkerchief, and shouted:

"Get out! Get out of my family's house!"

6

The heavy rain showed no signs of letting up. The city had only just begun preparing for the sudden, intense storms in the forecast, and now it was about to be hit by disasters everywhere.

The worst was avoided thanks to centuries of diligent flood control and water-diversion efforts. The construction of railway lines in sparsely populated valleys and tunnels made flood prevention an essential matter, leading to measures like underground reservoirs and rivers being turned into channels.

Even in the Shinjuku Imperial Garden, where the water god was said to reside, the ponds that collected rain and groundwater not only absorbed a significant amount of rain but also allowed excess water to flow immediately over a small dam into the nearby underground channel. The fierce flow of water would push at the round, eroded stones submerged in the pond, along with the creatures swimming around in there, but as long as the dam remained, none of those objects would enter the underground channel.

But one stone submerged in the bottom of the pond—shaped like a long, thin blade—may have been more suited to catching the flow of water. Even in the early stages, when rainwater began to drain from the pond, it was already moving around. What set it apart from the pond's other residents was that, despite being pushed against the small dam, its flat shape allowed it to be carried upward by the water flow, slip over the dam, and flow into the Shibuya River, one tributary of the underground channel system.

In the force of the water flow, it moved with an unusual lightness for being made of stone. It moved through the channel like a slightly heavy piece of wood, going from the Sendagaya neighborhood toward Jingumae. It flowed across narrow culverts between densely packed houses, streamed through underground channels where sunlight never reached, collided with concrete riverbanks as it crossed between Harajuku and Omotesando, and finally merged into the Onden River, another old body of water that had been channeled underground.

At the riverbed here, there were low dams constructed to prevent debris from pooling together. The stone got caught on these dams several times, but the force of the current was strong enough that it managed to keep moving forward.

After traveling approximately three miles through the underground waterways, the stone finally came to a vast reservoir beneath the intersection in front of Shibuya Station. There, it seemed to fall out of the current, sinking straight to the bottom and coming to rest.

Rainwater filled the reservoir, the overflow going out into the Shibuya River aboveground. But no matter how swiftly the water flowed, the stone remained motionless, firmly adhering to the bottom of the reservoir, seeming to find its home right above the ritual hall located even deeper below.

7

—*Water.*

The thought came to a half-asleep Mitsuhiro as he watched the pale morning light gather under the curtains. He remembered how his father had wanted to live near water, back when he was alive, and how they had moved to the house his mother still called home. He felt he should give this some closer thought, but he didn't know why.

He sat up and looked at the clock. It was seven in the morning. The sluggishness had mostly disappeared. That was probably thanks to the long bath he took last night—the first in a long time—along with a good night's sleep, free of anxiety or apprehension. Or perhaps it was thanks to the handkerchief and stone he had placed on the side table. Mitsuhiro picked them up in his right hand and went to the bathroom.

He frowned when he saw that the character written in blood on the mirror was gone. Had the things haunting him erased it? He thought they might have, but upon closer inspection, the character 鎮 remained faintly visible on the mirror's surface, only if you were looking for it.

Maybe the blood had just seeped into the mirror itself. Or maybe he was just imagining that the character was there. The blood he thought he had smeared on the mirror last night might've been nothing more than a hallucination. Mitsuhiro looked at his left hand again. He couldn't see any wound that could've created enough blood to write such a complex character.

Unable to figure it out, he pushed the writing on the mirror out of his mind, placed the handkerchief and stone nearby, and washed his face. While brushing his teeth, he thought about looking for the rest of the stone he had dropped into the pond in the Imperial Garden, but he had a vague yet firm belief that he'd probably never find it.

—It's already been offered to the water god. Only the water god knows where it is. Just like Yoshikazu Hara.

Convinced of this, he finished brushing and wiped his mouth with a towel. When he met his own gaze in the mirror, he was surprised at the sight of his own determination. He felt a new, firm conviction that this was the answer after all.

Yoshikazu Hara was the water god's *mi-keshi.* Araki had said so himself. He worried that instead of inviting the water god to the ritual hall, the *mi-keshi* had been invited to the water god instead.

A map popped into his head. There were several places within walking distance of the Imperial Garden where homeless people tended to sleep. Yoyogi Park, where Yoshikazu Hara had been, was also in range.

And there you had it. Yoshikazu Hara wasn't in Shibuya at all. Mitsuhiro had been wandering around the wrong place all this time.

There were still several hours until the eleven o'clock appointment with Chief Sugawara and Araki. Enough time to go to Shinjuku, then make a quick return to Shibuya. Mitsuhiro got ready, dressed as he would for work, ate a quick breakfast, and checked the map on his phone to figure out which route to take.

He put the stone and handkerchief in his breast pocket, grabbed his briefcase, and left the house. The heavy rain encouraged him to return for an umbrella before heading to the station.

This rain was just like when he first went to investigate the East Wing, he mused as he bought a bottle of spring water at the convenience store and boarded the train. After transferring to the subway at Shibuya and getting off at Shinjuku, he headed off through the downpour toward the first site he'd hit.

This was within the boundaries of the Tokyo Metropolitan Government Building, the complex of buildings that served as Tokyo's city hall. Support groups and volunteers provided meals here; over the New Year's holiday, they also set up centers where those in need could meet a counselor and get whatever help they needed to improve their lives.

According to research data, the overwhelming majority of Tokyo's homeless slept in parks, followed by the covered areas underneath overpasses. There were plenty of both around city hall, which led to large numbers of tents and cardboard homes in the area at one point. Most of those were gone now, taken away as part of the Tokyo government's campaign against homelessness, and the number of sleepers in Shinjuku Central Park had gone drastically down.

But they hadn't completely disappeared. When Mitsuhiro detoured over to a large underpass, there were still people squatting in the vicinity. Along the walkway between the assorted city hall buildings, there were around twenty tents of various kinds.

"Yoshikazu Hara? Is Yoshikazu Hara around here?"

Mitsuhiro carried his folded umbrella and bag and called out to everyone he saw. If he didn't find him here, he planned to look around Shinjuku Central Park, then head south toward Minami-Shinjuku, cross the railroad tracks, and visit as many scattered locations as possible around the Imperial

Garden. If he'd still had the company car, he could also have checked out Toyama Park near Takadanobaba and Yoyogi Park as well, but that was impossible on foot. He had already ruled out Kabukicho and Okubo Park; the former was mostly filled with young drifters, not the elderly, and the latter had a counseling center for homeless women, making it less popular with men.

Saturdays like this one were when volunteers distributed lunches and provided legal and medical consultation services to the homeless in front of city hall. If Yoshikazu Hara was in the neighborhood, there was a good chance he'd be there for the food.

When Mitsuhiro arrived in front of the building, there were about fifty men and women who appeared to be homeless or on welfare. He approached them, hoping against hope.

"Is Yoshikazu Hara here?"

Suddenly, someone tapped him on the shoulder. He turned around with anticipation and saw a man in his sixties holding a boxed lunch.

"If you're looking for Hara, I think he's over there."

Mitsuhiro didn't know if this man was one of Yoshikazu Hara's homeless friends or if they had worked together, but he squinted in the direction the man was pointing.

"Thank you very much. I appreciate it."

Mitsuhiro's heart swelled with expectation. He quickly headed in the direction he had been told.

"Yoshikazu Hara? Is Yoshikazu Hara here?"

A man sitting on a piece of cardboard on the street looked up in surprise. "Uh? What is it? You looking for me?"

Hearing a familiar voice, Mitsuhiro stopped in his tracks and stared intently at the man standing a few feet away. He held his umbrella and bag in his right hand and placed his left hand on his shirt pocket to check for the stone inside.

It was Yoshikazu Hara. The water god's *mi-keshi* was looking up at him with a half-eaten lunch in his hands.

"I've been looking for you... Yoshikazu Hara... I'm Matsunaga from Shimaoka."

He approached the befuddled-looking man and bent down to speak to him.

"I've been looking for you ever since you left the East Wing site."

Now Yoshikazu Hara's eyes widened, welling with tears. "I—I don't know where anything is around here. I try to come back every single day, but for some reason, I always end up here. My wife, you know... I have to put my wife in a nursing home."

"Megumi Hara? Yes, yes, she's doing very well." Mitsuhiro's voice trembled. He wiped away some tears of his own as he sat down next to the man, not even caring how he smelled.

"She is? My wife's well? Oh... That's great. I was so worried." Yoshikazu Hara wiped his eyes.

"Listen, you were performing your duties at the ritual hall in the East Wing, and I interrupted you by accident."

"Ahh, yeah, you. You're from that time..."

"I didn't know what I was doing. I was way out of line. I'm really sorry about this."

"It's fine, it's fine. Just bring me back; that's all I ask. You'll do that, right?"

"Yes, of course, I'll be with you the whole way back."

"Oh, right, right. Here. I've been holding on to this."

Yoshikazu Hara rummaged in his pants pocket and handed Mitsuhiro a folded plastic bag. Wondering what it was, Mitsuhiro took it and found a piece of cloth inside—the handkerchief that Miyoko and Sae had given him on Father's Day. He had given this to Yoshikazu Hara on the day he freed him from the hole, and now it was back with him. This was *the* Yoshikazu Hara. He had finally picked the right person.

"Thank you very much." Mitsuhiro clutched the handkerchief, pressing it to his forehead in gratitude.

"I'm sorry it took so long to give it back. We leavin' now, or?"

"No, no, you can finish your lunch first."

"Okay. I'll be quick."

While Yoshikazu Hara ate his meal, Mitsuhiro took out his phone and made a call.

"This is Sugawara."

"Hi, it's Matsunaga again. Sorry to call so early. I'm in front of Tokyo City Hall right now, and I finally found Yoshikazu Hara, the man from the ritual hall."

"Ah, I see... Very interesting timing. Right after you obtained your own father's belongings?"

"Yeah. So it's a bit early, but I'm gonna use a train or taxi to take him over to the site."

"Let me come pick you up."

"What? You're coming yourself?"

"I was planning to leave early anyway, just to see if the rain was causing any construction issues. I can be there in about twenty minutes. Would that work?"

"Yes, of course. Thank you very much."

He explained that he was in front of Tokyo Metropolitan Government Building No. 1 as Yoshikazu Hara silently looked on.

"The site leader's coming to pick you up," Mitsuhiro said once he was off the phone.

"Oooh, the Chief? He'll hate it if I get in his car in this state."

"Then let's go to a convenience store and get you some new clothes."

"Oh, no, you don't have to go this far for me..."

After lunch (and some more persuasion), he went with Yoshikazu Hara to a convenience store in the city hall building. There, he brought him some razors, a toothbrush, a pair of underwear, a shirt, and a raincoat. They didn't have any jackets or pants; instead, Yoshikazu Hara asked for a raincoat so he wouldn't get the car dirty.

While waiting for Yoshikazu Hara to change in the restroom, Mitsuhiro's phone rang. He thought it might be Chief Sugawara arriving early, but it was Miyoko. He wondered if he should talk to her now, but he didn't want her to think he was ignoring her, so he picked up.

"Miyoko? I'm sorry about yesterday..."

"Hey, did you go to the school?"

Her tone was brisk. She was clearly questioning him.

"What? School?"

"The weather forecast said the rain's gonna get even worse, so they sent everyone home early. Did you go pick her up or not?"

"What are you talking about? It's Saturday— Oh! They have class on the first Saturday of the month, don't they?"

"So it wasn't you who took her?!"

Miyoko's angry tone suddenly changed, and she began to cry. Realizing what Miyoko was trying to say, Mitsuhiro froze.

"Did someone pretend to be me and take her?"

"When I went to pick her up, her teacher said that her dad had driven over to pick her up. She said Sae called the man 'Dad'..."

"That wasn't me! He's just pretending to be me!"

"What?! Don't yell at me! Where's Sae?!"

Miyoko was in tears. Mitsuhiro took a deep breath. He had to stay calm. Think calmly about what happened.

Hang in there.

He heard his father's voice from deep in his chest. His knees, weak with bewilderment and anxiety, suddenly regained their strength. If Sae believed this person was her real father, then it wasn't just some criminal. He wouldn't even be human, strictly speaking. He was something that could make himself look like a completely different person.

Mitsuhiro knew that because he himself had been made to believe that many different people were Yoshikazu Hara. Fourteen homeless people had disappeared. Now he fully understood the gravity of what he'd done. It was terrifying to picture what was in store for him, but now wasn't the time to think about that.

That hole was sensing his resistance.

It knew he was trying to find Yoshikazu Hara and take him back. Did it want to spread around as much ash as possible before that happened? To widen itself? To destroy the seat of the water god? And to do that, it needed something to compensate for the lost ashes. That's why it took her.

A theory began to form in his head. It was nonsensical, but it had to be true. Someone dominated by the hole had kidnapped Sae to "compensate" for Mitsuhiro's resistance.

"It's the East Wing. They took Sae there."

"What?"

"I told you about entering the ritual hall at the construction site. I'm telling you, you lose your mind when you go in there. I lost my own for a while, too. Today, I was due to question someone else the hall had taken over…but they acted before I could."

"Wait… What? What are you talking about?"

"I'm going to the East Wing right now to get Sae back. Chief Sugawara will be there, too. I think we'll be fine."

"Why would the Chief be there?"

"I'll explain later. By the way, you said the police came to your parents' house. Did you get their business card?"

"Yes, from a Detective Kitagawa…"

"Contact him for me. Tell him that a man named Sota Araki from Tamai Construction might have kidnapped Sae."

Miyoko fell silent. Mitsuhiro thought she'd tell him to stop talking nonsense again, but instead, he heard some fumbling around, as if she was searching for something.

"Sota Araki…from Tamai Construction. Right?"

She was writing this down. Mitsuhiro vigorously nodded, even though he couldn't see her. "Right. Tell the detective to check on Araki's whereabouts. We'll work with the police to trap him so he can't escape."

"Is Sae all right?"

Mitsuhiro clenched his fist. ***Hang in there.*** He nodded at his father's voice. "She'll be okay. We'll find her soon. Then we'll restore our home to how it used to be so we can all live there together."

Miyoko sobbed softly on the other end of the line. *"Be careful."*

"Yeah."

"I'll be waiting by the phone."

"Okay. I have to go now."

When he hung up and turned around, Yoshikazu Hara was there, a stern expression on his face. In his hand was a plastic convenience-store bag with the clothes he had taken off.

"Sota Araki's the son of the former Tamai president?"

"Um… Yes."

"Ahh. I thought I was the only one bein' cursed, but it's him, too, huh?"

Mitsuhiro nodded again. "Yeah. It happened to me, too, but I've come back to my senses. I think Araki's looking to offer my daughter to the hole instead."

"Whoa, that ain't good. You better do somethin', quick. Is the director here yet?"

"I'll check."

He returned to the street with Yoshikazu Hara, right underneath the walkway that connected two of the city hall towers. He called Araki, but as expected, he didn't answer. Instead, Chief Sugawara called.

"This is Matsunaga."

"I'm in front of Building Number Two. It's a white minivan."

Mitsuhiro glanced around until he saw a Honda luxury van with the hazard lights on and the driver-side door open. Chief Sugawara was inside, waving. He ended the call, jogged over, and got into the back seat with Yoshikazu Hara.

"My name's Yoshikazu Hara," he said after Mitsuhiro was done thanking the director. "I saw you once, Chief, during a morning assembly when I was workin' in the East Wing. Sorry to get in your fancy car when I'm like this."

"Don't worry about it. Should we go straight there, or should we ask some questions first—"

"Let's go now, please. My daughter's missing, and I think Araki took her."

"Your daughter? Why?"

"It may be 'compensation' for my resistance to the curse."

Chief Sugawara's expression instantly soured. He started the car. "I'll try to hurry."

Mitsuhiro tried Araki's cell again, to no avail.

"Can you not get in touch with Araki?"

"I'm calling him, but he's not answering."

"Here, Mr. Matsunaga, take this."

The director reached behind and handed him something. It was a slightly faded amulet with "Tamai" embroidered on it. Mitsuhiro reached out and took it.

"This was given to me by the previous president Tamai. I'll let you keep it for now, Mr. Matsunaga."

"Thank you very much."

Mitsuhiro put the amulet in the breast pocket of his jacket, alongside his father's belongings. He was afraid he might panic now that his daughter was missing, but strangely, that didn't happen. Mitsuhiro was desperately doing everything he could to remain calm, yes, but Sugawara and Yoshikazu Hara were there to keep him company, and he felt that the items in his breast pocket were mentally supporting him. Even the cut on his left hand was helping.

Chief Sugawara drove carefully and steadily, hurrying but not rushing through the heavy rain, and drove straight for Shibuya Station.

"That smell!" Yoshikazu Hara suddenly cried out. Mitsuhiro detected it a moment later. The dry air was filled with the stench of burning flesh.

Mitsuhiro opened the window halfway to let it escape, sniffed his jacket, then turned his nose toward Yoshikazu Hara. One of them might've been the source.

"I definitely smell it," Sugawara said. But when he stopped at a red light at the Miyashita Park intersection, he leaned forward and looked at the AC vents by the front seat.

"I think it's getting stronger."

Chief Sugawara opened the driver-side window slightly and switched the air conditioner over to straight fan mode.

Instantly, a fierce odor filled the car, and all three of them covered their mouths and coughed. Then the engine suddenly roared with a deafening noise.

Mitsuhiro instinctively removed his hands from his mouth and covered both ears from the blast. Yoshikazu Hara, meanwhile, wrapped his arms around his head, trying to cover all his orifices at once.

Amid the assault of bizarre sensations, Mitsuhiro saw Sugawara quickly put the car in park, apply the parking brake, and try to turn off the engine. But the car didn't fall silent. The engine noise just grew louder, more deafening and intense.

"Get out of the car, both of you!"

Just as Sugawara shouted to them, unbuckling his seat belt and twisting his body out, the hood of the car suddenly flew open, spewing steam, fire, and smoke into the air.

Mitsuhiro and Yoshikazu Hara also frantically unbuckled and tried to open the doors. Just as they did, all the AC vents in the car spewed out blinding flames and intense heat. It was like being surrounded by dozens of gas burners. All three men cried out in shock, desperately trying to open the doors as the sudden heat burned their hair and clothes.

But the doors refused to open, and the automatic window switches had stopped working. The fire spread from their clothes and hair to the car seats. Mitsuhiro screamed for his life, pressing his face against the half-open window. It was pouring rain outside, but the heat inside was so intense that his whole body was in agony. The three shuddered in despair, believing they would be cremated alive inside this car...

No! Mitsuhiro's mind showed him an image of Araki taking Sae down the stairs leading to the ritual hall. *I don't want to die like this! Not in a fire!*

Then someone in front of him started shouting.

"Get back! I'm going to break the window! Get back!"

Through his heat-blurred vision, Mitsuhiro saw a crowd of people gathering, and one of them was holding something up. He didn't know what it was, but Mitsuhiro forced himself to retreat into the burning hell and cover his head with both arms. The pain was sharp, as if countless needles were being twisted into his back and head.

His jacket and shirt ignited, and he could clearly imagine his skin burning, radiating steam. Just then, the window shattered.

Several people immediately grabbed Mitsuhiro by the arms and sides and dragged him out of the window. He felt the water on the street and the pouring rain extinguishing the flames on his body as he was brought to the sidewalk.

Now all the windows of Chief Sugawara's car had been smashed open. A few people in the crowd had brought along emergency-escape hammers, the kind used to break car windows if your car was sinking in water. The motorists waiting at the traffic light with them must have had a few handy. If this hadn't occurred at such a busy city intersection, their chances of survival would have been much lower.

Immediately after Mitsuhiro was pulled to safety onto the sidewalk, Yoshikazu Hara was also dragged out. The clothes on both of them were burned and torn all over, but the men themselves were both on their feet and miraculously free of serious injury.

Chief Sugawara, who had been carried out last, wasn't so lucky. He had been sitting in the driver's seat, with more AC vents pointing at him than in the rear. Both sleeves of his suit were charred black, and his legs from the knees down looked like they had been roasting in an oven. His burnt shoes, feet still inside, were steaming now that the rain was falling on them.

"Chief!" Mitsuhiro yelled. "I'm calling an ambulance!"

Sugawara shook his head, his face contorted in pain. "Everyone in the crowd is doing that already. Get going. I'll handle things here."

"But..."

"This has to be stopped immediately. We can't let it spread any further."

Mitsuhiro saw that Sugawara was clutching the glasses he always kept in his breast pocket, and he nodded, jaw clenched.

"Yes. Thank you. Let's go, Mr. Hara."

"Ahh, Chief, I'm so sorry..."

"It's okay. Please, go."

Mitsuhiro and Yoshikazu Hara bowed to Chief Sugawara. They didn't bother to grab their belongings from the smoldering car as they hurried toward Shibuya Station in the pouring rain, still groaning from the pain.

8

Burned and soaked to the skin, Mitsuhiro pushed his way through the crowd at Shibuya Station and reached the soundproof wall surrounding the construction site. He opened the number lock and invited Yoshikazu Hara inside.

Amid the water pouring down into the semi-demolished old East Wing, he chose the shortest route to the ritual hall without even stopping by the office. At the bottom of that temporary stairway, he came to the wall with that now-familiar character on it.

鎮

Shining his phone light on this glyph written in ash, Mitsuhiro had a strange, complex feeling of déjà vu. He had first lost sight of Yoshikazu Hara in this area, and now it felt like he was retracing the events that had first led him here—right up to being rescued by a third party while surrounded by fire and smoke. On the other hand, fragments of memories of doing the same thing over and over again also flashed through his mind. How many times had he come here? And how many times had he descended the stairs that started at this wall, with someone he believed to be Yoshikazu Hara?

Mitsuhiro illuminated the man behind him with his phone, clutching the stone and amulet in his pocket. He feared the man might suddenly transform into a stranger, but Yoshikazu Hara remained Yoshikazu Hara. However, he was dazed, staring at the floor in confusion.

"Ohh? Wait, was this the place? I was told we were going to dig a hole in the ground."

Mitsuhiro didn't know much about Yoshikazu Hara's illness, but he was starting to not make sense again. Mitsuhiro feared that he might even disappear for the second time. Without the more reliable Chief Sugawara around, if Yoshikazu Hara started to get disoriented, Mitsuhiro would have no choice but to go it alone. But how would he know if he was still sane? Would he lose his mind again? His concern for Sae's safety, which he had managed to hold in check until now, suddenly ballooned to the verge of panic.

He wanted help. He wanted someone, anyone, who could help him out.

Hang in there.

The voice echoed loudly in his head. Mitsuhiro clutched the contents of his pocket tightly. No one was coming. He didn't have time to explain the situation to anyone. He couldn't waste any time getting to the basement. Mitsuhiro took a deep breath, summoned his resolve, took his hand out of his pocket, and grabbed Yoshikazu Hara's wrist.

"I'll take you there. Follow me. If you get lost, call for Matsunaga."

"Ahh, is he the foreman here?"

"Yes. Matsunaga. Let's go."

Mitsuhiro tugged the man's wrist, a little forcefully, and started down the long stairs leading to the ritual hall.

The staircase, illuminated by the light of his cell phone, gave him an even stronger sense of déjà vu. The accumulation of white, powdery ash dancing around his lower legs was something he had seen countless times before. The echoing footsteps, and the strange odor that hung in the dry air, could even be called familiar by now.

Mitsuhiro prayed breathing the air here wouldn't cloud his mind again. With his phone in his right hand and Yoshikazu Hara's hand in his left, he had nothing to cover his mouth with. A silent voice in his head, preying upon this anxiety, told him to go back to the office and borrow a helmet and dust mask.

Hang in there.

But he didn't think he should. Maybe it'd happen going back to the stairs, maybe when he was filling out items, names, and dates on the equipment loan record at the office—he had a feeling the somewhere along the line, he'd lose sight of Yoshikazu Hara again. Or maybe the fire would come back, and he'd be engulfed in smoke.

That won't happen. Go back now. It'll be safer to turn back.

No, don't. Get Yoshikazu Hara to where he belongs as quickly as possible. And make sure Sae is there. Make sure this really was all Araki's doing.

It's a waste of time. You don't even know if Sae's there. Miyoko has to be worried. Go back to the surface and call her.

Hang in there.

No, don't go back. Don't stop. Keep going down.

Don't go down there. Go back. Don't bring that man there.

I gotta take him there right now. The real mi-keshi *of the water god.*

Suddenly, the stairs ended. At the bottom, he shone his light down the passage, confirming that the door at the end was open. The ground was dimly lit by a faint orange light. Light from the ritual hall. Someone was there.

He'd been afraid the passcode on the door might've been changed, but he realized now that maybe Araki couldn't close the door in the first place. If he was trying to release the ashes, he had to keep it open. That was how the ash broke the seal.

"It's right there, Mr. Hara. That's the site."

"Yeah, it sure looks familiar."

"You'll remember more once you go in, I'm sure."

Still holding Yoshikazu Hara's wrist tightly, Mitsuhiro entered the ritual hall.

In the corner to the right of the square hole, a small figure lay trembling.

It was Sae. Even in the dim light, even from a distance, even amid the dry, acrid smell, he recognized her instantly.

"Sae!"

Without letting go of Yoshikazu Hara's wrist, Mitsuhiro put his phone in his jacket pocket and hurried toward his daughter.

"Whoa, what's the rush?"

He could feel Yoshikazu Hara stagger a bit, but he managed to keep his balance.

Araki was nowhere to be seen, and Mitsuhiro proceeded with caution. He glanced into the hole, but Araki wasn't there. He wondered if Araki had followed them down the stairs, gleefully waiting to close the door behind them once they were in the hall, but there was no sign of anyone else.

As he got closer to his daughter, he could see the state she was in more clearly. She was convulsing and arching her back, exactly the same as when she had become "dehydrated" that night. Mitsuhiro was overcome with a dread that made the blood in his veins run cold, but he desperately resisted the urge to let go of Yoshikazu Hara and run up to her. His senses were warning him that Sae would fall into the hole if he didn't do something, but he never let go of Yoshikazu Hara.

When he finally managed to get to her side, Mitsuhiro bent his knees, reached out with his right hand, and grabbed her left arm to pull her away from the hole.

"You don't have to hold me anymore," Yoshikazu Hara said. "I'm back at the worksite now, thanks to you."

Mitsuhiro looked at him, astonished. His usual semi-dazed expression had disappeared, and he was now staring at the hole with determination in his eyes.

He let go.

"Is the girl sick? Poor thing."

"I'm sure she'll be fine once she gets out of here."

"Well, hurry up and do that, eh? I got work to do down here, sadly."

With that, Yoshikazu Hara walked over to the wall where the shrine was located. Mitsuhiro watched him, wondering what he was going do next. Then he saw him reach for the stepladder lying in front of the shrine. Apparently, he intended to climb down into the hole himself.

If he had it handled, Mitsuhiro could focus on getting Sae back up top. If necessary, he could change the passcode on the lock and close the door so Yoshikazu Hara wouldn't disappear again.

Mitsuhiro picked up his trembling daughter with both arms. He wanted to give her something to put in her mouth so she wouldn't bite her tongue during the convulsions. But as he reached into his breast pocket for the handkerchief, he heard footsteps behind him.

Looking over his shoulder, he saw Araki appear, as if he had slipped right through the wall. He was wearing a helmet and carrying a shovel on his shoulder.

Mitsuhiro was stunned. Was he hiding behind the pile driver, crouching in the driver's seat, or maybe hiding among the piles of stakes? Whatever the case, Araki quickly approached the helpless Mitsuhiro and swung what he was holding. All Mitsuhiro could do was brace himself as much as possible and hold Sae to his chest to shield her.

A sound like a metal plate being struck echoed through the basement. The flat back of the shovel had struck Mitsuhiro diagonally behind his head. The impact made sparks fly in his vision. He couldn't stand back up, so he dropped down on one knee to at least avoid falling into the hole.

"Hyaaaah!"

Yoshikazu Hara let out a high-pitched scream. Mitsuhiro's blurry vision caught sight of Araki rushing toward him, but he couldn't do anything.

Yoshikazu Hara had been using the stepladder as a shield, but Araki knocked it out of his hands with the shovel. He pushed the old man away with one hand, and as Yoshikazu Hara staggered, Araki swung his shovel down without hesitation.

There was a dull thud, and then Yoshikazu Hara was motionless on the ground. It sounded like the joint of the shovel had connected with his head.

Mitsuhiro hugged Sae even tighter. He made several attempts to run toward the door, but each time, his head started pounding, his legs tangled up on him, and he fell to his knees again. He had to get Sae back to the surface somehow. He couldn't break his promise to Miyoko. He gritted his teeth and tried to run, but he couldn't.

He slapped his daughter's small cheek, hoping she would regain consciousness and run by herself, but it was no use.

"I'm sorry to be so rough," said Araki's voice from nearby. "I consulted with the last president, and he said this is the only way."

Terrified, Mitsuhiro turned toward the voice, trying to shield Sae, and he felt another heavy impact on his back. The moment he realized he had been kicked, the ground disappeared. He knew that he, and Sae in his arms, had been kicked over the edge and into the hole.

In the short time it took to fall, Mitsuhiro could only think of shielding Sae with his body, trying to wrap himself around her as much as possible. Then something hit his right shoulder with tremendous force, and he was once again struck by a blow so powerful that it temporarily blinded him.

He had hit his shoulder on the concrete block, then rolled onto the far softer ground.

Mitsuhiro's consciousness drifted away as he desperately prayed for Sae's safety.

Hang in there.

But the pungent smell wafting up from the strangely soft ground made his eyes tear up. It irritated his throat enough and made him cough, pulling his fading consciousness from the brink.

"Are you all right, Mr. Matsunaga?" Araki flatly asked from the edge of the hole.

Mitsuhiro lacked the energy to respond. Araki didn't seem to be expecting an answer anyway.

"I see you found Yoshikazu Hara for me. But we can't put him back in the hole yet. I went through all the trouble of digging it the way the old president told me to. If we don't provide compensation for the hole, whatever went in will just come right back out. If the water god comes now, it'll just become a normal hole again. It won't become a seat for the *aragami*, the guardian spirit.

Of course, you did a lot to fill it in for us, so the old president told me it's okay if you two are the last. I'll bring your wife in soon, so don't worry."

Mitsuhiro said nothing in response to Araki's bizarre one-sided argument. He pressed his cheek against the strangely soft ground, all covered with white powder, and panted. His body was numb from the painful blows, but he ordered it to take action; he managed to move Sae's convulsing body to the ground and pull out his left arm.

Hang in there.

He felt a voice encouraging him. His right arm hung limply behind his body, not moving at all. In fact, other than the pain in his shoulder, he couldn't even feel his fingertips.

In place of his useless right arm, he searched his breast pocket with his left hand. The first thing he touched was the handkerchief, and then the stone. He clenched them in his fist, then picked up another item with his index finger and thumb.

"Now, wait there with your daughter, please."

Araki withdrew from the edge of the hole and disappeared from view. *Don't let him go. Make him come down here. I have to get Sae out of here.*

Mitsuhiro dug his left elbow into the soft ground and endured the agony of raising his upper body. Left hand trembling, he held the amulet above his head and shouted, "This is an amulet from your predecessor, Araki! It belongs to your father!"

As expected, Araki immediately returned and looked down at him. His eyes were wide with surprise and anger.

"What is that? Why do you have it?"

"Chief Sugawara gave it to me! You don't want this lying around here, do you? Because every time you come here, you'll be reminded that the 'previous president' is dead!"

Araki opened his mouth wide and let out a terrifyingly shrill scream.

"You can't have that here!"

He sounded like a child speaking through the mouth of his adult self.

"Throw it out of the hole! Now! Before I get angry!"

"If you want it, come on down! I'll give it to you then! Otherwise, I'm gonna bury it in here! I'll use one of your father's belongings to 'compensate' the hole!"

Araki glared even more fiercely and clenched his fists, his body violently shaking. He turned on his heels and disappeared for a moment. Then Mitsuhiro could hear the clattering of the ladder being lifted.

Mitsuhiro hooked the charm around his index finger and clenched the sharp stone in his hand, wrapped in the handkerchief. He pressed the blade against his wrist so that it couldn't be seen from the back of his hand. Then, with all his strength, he pushed himself up with his knees. Swaying, he managed to get to his feet and lean against the concrete block behind him.

Something clinked under his feet: a chain. The restraint that Yoshikazu Hara had requested for himself.

The chain lock around the ankle shackle was still there, just as Mitsuhiro had left it, with the key still in the keyhole. A chill ran through him at the idea of being restrained with this for all time. But he could also use this to bind Araki, so he bent down unsteadily and cautiously removed the key, taking care not to drop what he was holding.

He put it in his pants pocket, took a deep breath, and leaned back against the concrete block again. Every little move he made caused his battered head to throb, and his right shoulder ached enough to make him feel dizzy. But at least now, even if Araki got him with the chain, there'd still be a chance to escape.

He'd expected Araki to come down immediately, but instead, he kept on clattering around with the ladder, mumbling, "Don't touch it, you must never touch it under any circumstances." Araki must have been thinking about how he'd safely retrieve the amulet once he was down there.

Mitsuhiro also thought furiously during this brief respite. If he tried to resist in these circumstances, Araki would easily subdue him. His only option was to reason with Araki, offering to destroy the amulet in exchange for bringing Sae back to the surface—not that Araki was open to negotiation at the moment.

Just then, he felt something strange on the concrete behind him. The part of his back leaning against it seemed to slip on him. He moved away from the block, unsure what was going on, and something thudded to the ground.

It was a piece of concrete. Mitsuhiro stared at it intently. Even in the dimly lit hole, he could clearly see its shape.

He could only assume that it had broken off from the impact of his body, and he was shocked to see that it was exactly the same.

The same as the piece of gravestone that Araki had thrown into the pond.

Hang in there.

Mitsuhiro felt his father's voice more strongly than ever. Maybe it was coming from the stone in front of him...but at the same time, it somehow seemed to be coming from far above his head. Perhaps through the water tank, which was probably filled with rainwater by now.

Suddenly, a stepladder appeared from the edge of the hole, lowering itself down. It wasn't on the wall where the shrine was, across from Mitsuhiro, but on the corner of the wall to his right. Perhaps Araki didn't want to climb down with his back to his enemy.

Mitsuhiro quickly knelt down on one knee, put the amulet, handkerchief, and stone back into his breast pocket, and grabbed the handle of the large knife-shaped stone that had cracked off the concrete block. He grabbed the part where his father's name would have been if this were the gravestone, lifted the back of his jacket with the tip of the blade, and forcefully shoved it into his belt.

He then took out the charm, handkerchief, and stone again and watched Araki descend, holding his breath.

Araki held a shovel in one hand, facing this way. He descended slowly, step by step, ever vigilant. Given the bestial rage on his face, any thought of negotiating vanished. He was so possessed with anger that reasoning with him seemed impossible.

Once both of his feet were on solid ground, Araki held the shovel straight out in front of him and approached Mitsuhiro.

"Put the amulet on the head of this shovel. Be *quiiiet* about it. If you don't do as I say, I'll hit your daughter with it. I'll hit her as hard as I can."

His voice was even shriller and more childlike than before.

Mitsuhiro, still on one knee, lifted the amulet but then placed a hand on the ground, as if the pain prevented him from raising his arms.

Araki scowled and turned his face away from the amulet, but he still kept on edging closer to it. The head of the shovel was now on the ground in front of Mitsuhiro. As soon as the amulet was placed on it, he'd swing the shovel and send it flying out of the hole. Maybe he'd give Mitsuhiro a few blows while he was at it. The state he was in, that wouldn't be surprising, either.

Mitsuhiro focused all his strength into his knees, stood up in a flash, then stamped down hard with his right foot on the joint between the shovel head and the handle. The handle slammed out of Araki's hands and hit the soft, foul-smelling ground.

As Araki scrambled to pick it up, Mitsuhiro threw the amulet at him. Araki recoiled in shock, but as his hand moved away from the shovel, Mitsuhiro thrust out the sharp stone he was clutching and jumped forward with all his might. The stone flew straight into Araki's face. Mitsuhiro could feel it piercing flesh in his hands before hitting something hard. Using the momentum, he threw himself at Araki and pushed him to the ground.

The impact made Mitsuhiro's vision blur. He felt nauseous, as if he had suffered a concussion, and his right shoulder felt as if it had been torn from his body. He screamed.

Araki, on the ground, shoved him back with both hands. Mitsuhiro was lifted back up and then fell on his rear, but he planted his left hand on the ground to keep himself from falling backward. Araki kept a hand to his face as he struggled, raising his upper body and kicking his legs to get away from Mitsuhiro. He got to his feet, back scraping against the wall opposite the stepladder.

Mitsuhiro glared back at Araki with desperation. He could barely take any more pain, but he forced himself to get up on one knee. Then he reached behind his back and fumbled for the thing tucked into his belt.

Araki's shoulders shook, then his whole body. He took his hands away from his face. The handkerchief fell, and Mitsuhiro could see the stone sticking out from the left side of his face. Mitsuhiro realized that he had stabbed through the cheek, but the stone must've been caught by his teeth. It was by no means a minor injury, but it was still insufficient. Instead of being fatal or discouraging him at all, it only enraged him further.

Araki unfastened his helmet's strap, grabbed the stone, and slowly pulled it out before tossing it aside. Blood flowed from his mouth and the wound on his cheek, dark and ink-like.

"That hurt! That really hurt! You make me so mad!"

Araki screamed as he rushed away from the wall to pick up the shovel he had dropped. Mitsuhiro had no strength to stop him. He could only wait with one knee on the ground as Araki grabbed the shovel and stomped across the bottom of the hole.

"I've decided to hit you a hundred times! You won't listen to me! I'm gonna hit you over and over, even if it hurts a lot and you pass out!"

Mitsuhiro stared intently at Araki, who was screaming in a voice that sounded more like a vengeful spirit than a child. He paid no attention to the shovel in his hand. Instead, his eyes were on his opponent's right leg. His right thigh. For some reason, his attention was drawn to that spot. He didn't even look at the other leg.

Now that leg was approaching. It was within reach.

"Okay, number one!" Araki yelled, blood spewing from his mouth and cheek as he raised the shovel.

Mitsuhiro put all the strength he had left in his body into the object in his left hand and stabbed it into Araki's right thigh. The sharp stone easily pierced Araki's work clothes and sank into flesh—and Araki's weight was added to Mitsuhiro's momentum halfway through. The pain caused his right leg to suddenly give way, making his weight shift to that side. The stone blade pierced deeper than Mitsuhiro had expected, running straight through his thigh to the other side.

With a terrible scream, Araki hopped around on his left foot. He used the shovel as a cane to stay upright, but his weight shifted unexpectedly to his left, and he could only manage a few steps toward the concrete block before collapsing with a thud.

Mitsuhiro suddenly realized that he had seen something like this before. It was when that gravestone piece hit Araki's thigh, on the way to the purification ritual. Strangely, the stone had struck him in the exact same place.

But as Mitsuhiro saw Araki still trying to stand up, leaning as best he could on that shovel, he searched for the thing he had thrown away earlier—Tamai's amulet. From where he was standing, it was the only thing within reach. He was afraid it'd be half-buried in that white powdery ash by now, but he found it right away. He crawled forward with his knees and left hand, trying desperately to reach it just a few steps away.

But Araki's helmet hit him in the face, and then the shovel head came down in front of his eyes. Mitsuhiro recoiled and fell backward, shuddering from the pain in his shoulder.

Araki crawled toward him with both hands and his one good knee, raising the handle of the shovel in his right hand.

"Come on, *one*!"

Mitsuhiro desperately backed away. The shovel head came down, vertically embedding itself into the ground.

"I said *one*!"

Araki pulled the shovel out, repositioned his grip, and swung it as if it were a spear. The tip of the shovel came down again.

Mitsuhiro tried to dodge it, but this time, it tore through the fabric of his pants and ripped into his right shin.

"One!"

Gritting his teeth against the new wave of pain, Mitsuhiro waited for Araki to get closer, then tried to kick him in the face with all his might. But he couldn't reach him, and the tip of the shovel cut his right ankle.

"Two!"

Araki shouted angrily, got down on his knees, and grabbed the base of the shovel handle with both hands.

"And *three*!"

At that moment, there was a rattling sound.

Both men froze, thinking the other one and made the noise.

But Mitsuhiro realized first that it wasn't either of them. Yoshikazu Hara had climbed down into the hole and was standing behind Araki, holding up the chain that had once bound him. Araki noticed Mitsuhiro's gaze, sneered, and turned around.

"Why are you butting in? I gotta put my wife in a nursing home!" Yoshikazu Hara shouted loudly as he swung the chain at Araki.

Araki tried to defend himself with the shovel, but he was on his knees with his opponent behind him. There was just no way.

The lock at the end of the chain struck the side of Araki's head.

The shovel fell from his hands. He opened his mouth, but no sound came out. His eyes stared at Mitsuhiro, seeing nothing, and then he fell forward and collapsed. He didn't get up.

9

Mitsuhiro wanted to collapse from exhaustion as well, but he had a duty to bring Sae back to the surface. He couldn't allow himself to pass out.

"Hara...put the chain around that man's legs. And we need to stop the bleeding..."

"What? Ohh, ahh, he's badly hurt!"

Yoshikazu Hara wrapped the shackle tightly around Araki's right leg, locking it in place. It wasn't the politest thing to do, but it both restrained him and provided a kind of lifesaving measure. Without the chain, Araki or someone else could pull the stone out of his thigh, resulting in massive blood loss.

"Can you take that girl upstairs for me?" Mitsuhiro asked, using Araki's shovel to get to his feet.

"Ahh, she sure is sick. I hate that she fell down in here. Okay, okay, I'll carry her up."

Yoshikazu Hara pulled the stepladder over, unfolded it, and placed it so the sides were flush against the wall. Then he easily lifted up the still-convulsing Sae onto his shoulder and quickly climbed the ladder. If it weren't for his dementia, he'd still be perfectly capable of working in construction.

Leaving Sae with Yoshikazu Hara, Mitsuhiro cleaned up the scene and endured the pain as best he could. He put the handkerchief and the smaller stone in his pocket, picked up the amulet, and placed it in Araki's hand. A loud, painful groan escaped from Araki's mouth, but he didn't wake up.

The next task was the most difficult one. He had to climb out of that hole by himself. Clinging to the stepladder, he climbed up step by step, pushing through the pain in his head and right shoulder, not to mention the leg that had taken two clean hits from the shovel. He was nervous that he'd pass out from his concussion halfway up, but he managed to reach the edge of the hole safely.

When he looked up, he saw Sae and Yoshikazu Hara standing in front of the shrine. The table with the paper streamers on it had been knocked over, and Sae was lying on the floor. As he approached the table, he noticed the same clean air as when he first came here.

He didn't know if Yoshikazu Hara had done it on purpose, but now that she was near the shrine, Sae's condition had improved dramatically. Her convulsions had subsided, and her breathing was calm. Another moment later, her eyes snapped open, and once she recognized Mitsuhiro, she got up with a loud cry.

"Daddy?!"

Yoshikazu Hara smiled broadly. "She's feelin' better!"

Mitsuhiro couldn't help but breathe a sigh of relief.

"I'm here to pick you up, Sae. How are you feeling? Can you walk?"

"Um, I think I'm okay. But, Daddy, you're all white. Did you fall? Are you hurt?"

Just as Sae had said, his jacket and pants were covered in ash from rolling around at the bottom of the hole. Mitsuhiro nodded at Sae. His next "curse" would come from Miyoko if he came home looking like this.

"Yeah, a little. Sae, do you remember when you came here?"

"Mmm, I dunno. Oh! I thought you came in a car to pick me up. But it wasn't you."

Mitsuhiro nodded again, took Sae's hand with his good one, and helped her down from the table.

"Let's talk about it when we leave here. Hara, too…"

But Yoshikazu Hara shook his head firmly. "I have to work here. I have to wait for Mr. Tamai to come. Thanks for bringing me here, though."

Mitsuhiro didn't know what to say, so he just bowed his head. Then he suddenly remembered something. He took the key for the chain lock from his pants pocket and handed it to Yoshikazu Hara. Then he took Sae's hand, still suffering from his sore right shoulder and leg, and together they left the ritual hall.

He turned on his phone flashlight, handed it to Sae so she could light the way, and climbed the stairs, counting the steps as he held her hand. He was constantly alert, wondering when the smoke would start to fill the air and where the fire would break out. If that happened, he planned to quickly give Sae the handkerchief in his pocket, tell her to cover her mouth, and hurry her upstairs. He knew he wouldn't be able to run up, so he'd lag far behind her. He might even collapse in the smoke. But he wanted to get Sae to safety.

However, there was no fire. Nothing blocked Mitsuhiro and Sae's way, and they were able to climb all 177 steps, panting for breath.

鎮

When they passed the wall with the character, Mitsuhiro took the phone back, and they climbed the temporary stairway together.

At the top awaited a wall of people. There were construction workers who were waiting impatiently in the office, along with two detectives, one of whom introduced himself as Kitagawa. Yoshio Tamai from Tamai Construction was there, along with the two other employees he had met at their office. Behind them, Miyoko rushed out, crouched down, and hugged Sae as if she would never let her go.

"Sae! Oh, thank heavens! Sae!"

Sae was taken aback by her mother's intense relief and looked up at Mitsuhiro. "Was I lost?"

Mitsuhiro couldn't help but chuckle. "It's okay now," he said, stroking Sae's head.

Kitagawa approached, giving Mitsuhiro a once-over, but said nothing.

"The man who took Sae is in the underground ritual hall."

Kitagawa didn't react to Mitsuhiro's words. "For now," he simply said, "let's get you to the hospital. Your daughter is pretty pale, too."

Grateful for his offer, Mitsuhiro followed their lead. They left the site and got into the back seat of the car Miyoko had been given a ride in, Sae sitting between them.

Miyoko put her arm around Sae's shoulder and touched Mitsuhiro's ash-stained cheek. "Mr. Tamai said he was sorry for the trouble they caused you."

Mitsuhiro groggily nodded.

"The detectives barely listened to me," she whispered, frowning. "They just kept asking Mr. Tamai questions. They asked if he was going down to the basement, and he just said all they could do was wait for someone to come up from there… What was that all about?"

Mitsuhiro squeezed Miyoko's hand with his free one. "There must be some reason for it. I'll ask him what happened."

"And then you'll tell *me* what happened, okay?"

Looking into Miyoko's tearful eyes, Mitsuhiro wondered if he could. But he relented.

"I'll tell you everything. It's all right now."

10

At the orthopedic department of the general hospital, Mitsuhiro was stripped of all his clothes except his underwear and given a hospital gown. An X-ray revealed a fracture of the proximal end of the humerus, something he was told usually happened to athletes or the elderly after falls. He opted not to mention that he had been kicked into a fairly deep hole.

He underwent an MRI scan of his head, got stitches for some of the cuts on his legs, and received treatment for the burns all over his body. Because he had come with the police, the doctor who patched him up assumed that Mitsuhiro and Sae had been involved in a traffic accident, the sort where the car both got torn apart and caught on fire. That wasn't entirely wrong, so he didn't argue the point.

His right upper arm was carefully immobilized, and his forearm was suspended from his neck in a sling. He was given an IV for pain relief and told that he'd need to stay in the hospital for a few days. By the time he learned this, it was already past four in the afternoon, and he hadn't been able to see Miyoko or Sae the entire time.

He was then led to a hospital room—a private room, even though he hadn't requested one. At the door, he was handed a bag with his clothes, and then he was left alone, as if to say, *Do whatever you want in there.*

At that point, he should have sensed the hand of someone else in all this, but all he could think about was lying down in bed—that, or talking to his family. But when he opened the door and entered, there were two men inside—one in a suit, and the other in work clothes.

Detective Kitagawa was holding a can of coffee, and Yoshio Tamai was holding a large paper bag, standing by the window. Mitsuhiro realized that life wasn't going to be that easy for him.

"We're here to see how you're doing. Are you feeling any better?"

The strong painkillers made it hard to stand up for long, so Mitsuhiro put the bag with his clothes on the bed and sat down.

"They said I can be discharged in a few days if I rest enough. My head's still foggy from the medication, so I'm not sure if I can talk too coherently, but..."

"I'm not here to question you," Kitagawa quickly said. "I'm just here to see how you're doing. We heard you hit your head. If you're doing all right, I'll be on my way."

Before Mitsuhiro could ask anything, he shook the coffee can to see if there was any left, took a sip, and left the room.

Yoshio Tamai smiled at Mitsuhiro, who was left in a daze.

"They don't want to get involved, I suppose. Everyone in the Tokyo police force knows about the terrible things that happened to Mr. Sugawara of Shimaoka a long time ago."

"Chief Sugawara…?"

"It was at the construction site when the police department moved to its current location. There was a ritual hall in the basement there, which we were in charge of managing. The police chief must have been *very* afraid of curses, because he strictly ordered all his officers not to go down to the East Wing basement this time, too. Just like before."

"Is he okay now, Chief Sugawara?"

"Well, he suffered serious burns, but his life isn't in danger. I heard that this belonged to you, Mr. Matsunaga, so I brought it over for you."

Yoshio handed him the paper bag, which contained a charred bag. He didn't have any choice but to leave it in Sugawara's car at the time.

Mitsuhiro put the burnt-smelling bag back in the paper bag and wondered what would have happened if the police had confiscated it. What would they have said about the Rubik's Cube of unknown origins? And what about Mole Unit-01's phone?

As Mitsuhiro thought about this, Yoshio Tamai bowed his head.

"We've caused you a lot of trouble. We had changed both our posts and our last names to prevent something like this from happening again, but I suppose the curse was stronger than we expected."

"I heard that Mr. Araki was the son of your predecessor… Oh, right, have a seat."

"Thank you very much."

Yoshio pulled up a chair and sat down across from Mitsuhiro.

"It was a long time ago, but our previous president, Yutaro Tamai, was severely cursed. The owner of a building where a ritual hall was located became involved in a faddish new religion. He wound up tampering with the shrine, and both he and Yutaro, who was in charge of managing it, were cursed."

"Cursed? It wasn't his fault."

"As I suppose you understand now, curses are like that. They spread through people's karma—it's not about good or evil. It's not because someone harmed the gods or because something is right or wrong. It's more like a natural disaster. If a dike breaks, it'll lead to a flood, but you can't say the people caught in that flood did anything wrong to deserve it."

That was the cruelty of disasters, and it was enough to convince Mitsuhiro. Part of him wanted to dismiss the idea as ridiculous, but whether it was the painkillers or the injuries and fatigue, he couldn't bring himself to argue.

"But things often follow the path of karma. If a parent is cursed, it often passes down to their children."

Those words caught uncomfortably in Mitsuhiro's mind. A curse placed on a parent is passed on to their children? For some reason, he felt like Yoshio was talking about his own father. Somewhere in his heart, he feared that he'd mention the fire at his parents' house long ago, but Yoshio seemed indifferent to that.

"To sever the ties of karma, Sota Araki and I swapped homes. Originally, I was Yoshio Araki, and he was Sota Tamai. However, the karma must have returned to its original holders somehow. Perhaps deep down, he was not fully on board with swapping families."

"I see…"

"That, of course, is the situation on our side. Which has nothing to do with you, Mr. Matsunaga. But since we have become connected in this way, I'm afraid I must ask you to participate in the ritual."

The sudden request left him feeling like his heart was being squeezed by a clenched fist.

"But…does that mean I have to go into that hole, too?"

Yoshio waved his hand, dismissing the idea. "No, no, Mr. Matsunaga. you're neither a *mi-keshi* nor a Shinto priest. We just need you to join the circle of the ritual. It will be a ceremony to invite the water god to enter the hall. We cannot return the bone ash that possessed you to its original place and prevent it from ever coming out again, but we'll make sure that it doesn't come out for at least the next few decades."

"I'd…like to talk to my wife and daughter first…"

"I strongly advise you to meet them after the curse has been lifted." Yoshio suddenly looked very serious. The faint smile on his lips only made his expression eerier. His words carried an inexplicable persuasiveness.

"All right. But in the state I'm in…"

"We'll have our staff work something out. Do you have your father's belongings?"

Mitsuhiro searched the pocket of the jacket in the bag and took out the handkerchief and the stone. "Um…yes, right here."

"Then please take them with you. And please take this, too, while I'm here."

Yoshio took a thick envelope out of the pocket of his work clothes and handed it to him. Mitsuhiro frowned as he took it and looked at the contents. Then his eyes widened. It was a thick stack of ten-thousand-yen bills.

"This is your money back, Mr. Matsunaga. We will cover your hospital bill as well, and at a later date, we will transfer the *mi-keshi* fee for the curse that befell you."

"But if I take it…"

"This isn't like what we gave Mr. Hara. You're accepting this in order to be *freed* from the *mi-keshi*. You don't want to remain trapped in the karma of Mr. Hara and Mr. Araki forever, do you?"

"No…"

"All right. Please wait here for a moment."

Yoshio left the room.

Mitsuhiro stared at the paper bag with the stack of bills. Of course, he was relieved that Miyoko had one less thing to blame him for, but this "ritual" he'd have to join in made him extremely anxious.

As he played around with the envelope in his hand, he began to nod off from the medication. That is, until a knock on the door startled him awake again.

"Come in."

Yoshio Tamai entered, handing him another paper bag. When Mitsuhiro took it, he saw that it contained a long-sleeved shirt, a set of underwear, and a pair of pants. Everything was white.

"Shall I help you into it?" he kindly offered.

Mitsuhiro politely declined and asked him for a few minutes of privacy.

Using only his left hand, he took off his patient's gown and, after a struggle, managed to put on the new clothes. They didn't fit perfectly, but it wasn't that bad. He took out his father's belongings and the money envelope from his bag, along with his house keys and wallet, and put them in his pants pocket.

When he stepped out of the room, Yoshio was waiting by the window, leisurely gazing at the evening sky.

"Let's go. I'll take you in my car."

Mitsuhiro followed Yoshio out of the hospital. None of the hospital staff took him to task, even though he hadn't been discharged. What was in the basement of *this* hospital? The question suddenly crossed his mind as they headed for the parking lot. Tamai Construction managed the hospital's ritual hall; maybe that was why no one objected to their comings and goings. Not that he felt like asking Yoshio about it. He'd be in the hospital for the next few days, and he didn't want to think about what was *really* there the whole time.

Guided by Yoshio, he got into the passenger seat of the van. The cargo area was filled with various cleaning tools, multiple helmets, and cardboard boxes labeled with terms like "shrines" and "shrine accessories."

Tamai sat in the driver's seat, started the van, and drove out of the parking lot and onto the main street.

"We will do our best to find out about those invited into the hole," he said, sounding sterner than before. "If they have families, we will distribute *mi-keshi* fees to them. This is entirely our duty, so please don't worry about anything, Mr. Matsunaga. Helping Hands will no longer contact you."

Suddenly, Mitsuhiro felt that sensation again his in left hand. The feeling he had touching the ground at the bottom of the hole while he was desperately fighting Araki.

The ground had been oddly soft and squishy, emitting a pungent odor that stung his eyes.

His impression was that he might have been crawling around where the fourteen people swallowed by the hole had been piled on top of each other... but whether it was the painkillers or the fear and guilt in his mind, all his memories were shrouded in black fog, too thick to form anything coherent.

"Sound money means sound dispelling, you see," Yoshio said in a matter-of-fact tone that made it difficult to tell if he was joking or not. Probably not, though. He had the same no-nonsense attitude as a seasoned construction worker whose livelihood depended on putting in good work.

"We will also have to pay Chief Sugawara and Mr. Takenaka. I'm afraid the ritual-hall-management fee will have to be raised by quite a large amount, but I've already been granted permission from the chairman of Shimaoka."

"Right," Mitsuhiro meekly replied.

Yoshio said nothing more. Once they arrived at Shibuya Station, he maneuvered the van through the crowds of cars and buses and parked it in the construction lot.

"Let's go. You'll want to put a helmet on."

He got out of the driver's seat and took two helmets from the back of the van. Mitsuhiro got out as well, took a helmet with his left hand, and put it on.

When the two of them reached the door of the soundproof wall, Yoshio tapped out the number code like it was muscle memory, unlocked the door, and motioned Mitsuhiro to join him.

Mitsuhiro did so, vaguely thinking about how, for a change, he was actually *supposed* to be here. No one brought it up before, but this really wasn't someplace a guy from the IR department should have had an all-access pass to day and night—something especially true of the ritual hall below.

They wound up not stopping by the site office after all. He descended the temporary staircase he had climbed a few hours earlier with his daughter, soon arriving at the wall with the 鎮 character written on it. It seemed to stick out much more clearly now, as though it had been freshly drawn. Maybe it was paint, or maybe the ashes from burning a bonfire's worth of amulets.

Following Yoshio down the stairs, he immediately noticed that the whole area had been given a thorough cleaning. In Tamai's words, it had been "purified." Thanks to that, the foul odor had completely vanished, and for the first time, Mitsuhiro felt the damp coldness that you'd normally feel belowground like this.

Trying to maintain control of his groggy mind, Mitsuhiro counted the steps on his way down, just like he did with Sae on the way up. He must have been muttering numbers out, because Yoshio glanced back at him at one point, but he didn't offer any comment.

Sure enough, there were 177 steps between the top and the passageway. The door to the ritual hall was open, and the lights were on inside. Yoshio bowed toward it, and Mitsuhiro followed suit, taking care not to strain his right shoulder.

Following him into the ritual hall, Mitsuhiro was surprised to find himself in what seemed like a much different place. The floor was brightly lit by the orange lights, and he could see that everything had been swept clean. Four mounds of dark soil had been piled up over the edges of the hole, all the same size and shaped like geometric cones. To prevent the mounds from collapsing into the hole, there was an arrangement of boards, ropes, and temporary wooden pillars around the edge, decorated with paper streamers and sakaki branches.

Stakes had been driven into the four corners, with more branches lashed to them. Square ropes ran between the stakes, streamers hanging down. The entire hole now looked like a full-on shrine for an earth-appeasement ceremony.

Around each mound of earth were three small pyramids made of pebbles, twelve in all. Mitsuhiro thought they looked like the rock used for making crushed-stone piles. In this method of pile creation, vertical holes were drilled with a pile driver, then filled with crushed natural stone to firm up the foundation and improve earthquake resistance.

—They're going to fill the hole?

As he realized this, Mitsuhiro noticed a small white curtain set up next to the pile driver on his right, with a group of ten men and women standing in front of it. They were of varying ages, some in their twenties and others in their sixties or older. None of them appeared to be construction workers. They were dressed in white kimonos with *hakama* trousers of different colors and white *tabi* socks—a bit like they were preparing for a festival, Mitsuhiro thought. Some had shovels, others had flutes, and one was holding drumsticks next to a large *taiko* drum that had been brought in.

"These are all our employees. Please wait there for a moment."

Yoshio headed toward the group. They shifted aside to make a path for him, and when one of them opened the curtain, Yoshio went inside. The curtain closed, and a few minutes later, Yoshio Tamai emerged again, having completely changed his attire. He was now wearing the traditional *eboshi* black hat of medieval Japan and holding a wooden *shaku* ritual baton in his hand. Out of the crowd, he was the only one wearing all white.

"Please show Mr. Matsunaga the way. Oh! He's still convalescing, so prepare a seat for him."

One of the women went into the curtain and came out with a circular straw mat.

She was a member of the crowd who had been waiting up top as Mitsuhiro took Sae out. He remembered that she had introduced herself as Chiyo Tamai from General Affairs when they first met. She approached Mitsuhiro with a solemn expression, her cheerful office personality gone.

"I will guide you, Mr. Matsunaga," she said with a bow.

"Okay."

Mitsuhiro bowed back and followed Chiyo toward the shrine. It was kept out of view by the mounds before, but now he saw that it was decorated with brand-new sakaki branches and altar fittings. The table was lined with Shinto accessories and offerings, and the upper part of the wall was inscribed with a large *appease* character 鎮 of pure white.

Chiyo placed a mat in front of the corner stake to the left of the shrine. "Please sit here."

"Um, okay."

Mitsuhiro stopped looking at the shrine and sat down on the round mat. Kneeling pained his leg too much, so he sat cross-legged and peered down into the hole.

Araki and Yoshikazu Hara were there.

Mitsuhiro froze in shock, blinking a few times to make sure he wasn't seeing things. But it was no mirage. They were both at the bottom of that strangely soft hole. The smell and the heat were terrifying. When Mitsuhiro put his face beyond the barrier of rope and paper streamers, he realized that the stench and heat were all trapped inside the hole, never leaving the boundary.

Yoshikazu Hara was chained to the concrete block. He had a calm expression on his face as he looked straight up, more peacefully meditating than sleeping.

Araki, meanwhile, was leaning quietly against the wall to the right of the concrete block. His head was bandaged, the right leg of his work jumpsuit was torn, and his right thigh, which had been wounded with that stone, was wrapped in thick bandages. The knifelike stone that had stabbed him was placed right next to Araki, and the blood seemed to have been wiped clean.

He was staring at the amulet in his right hand, but when he felt someone watching him, he suddenly turned his head up and saw Mitsuhiro. Mitsuhiro shuddered, thinking that Araki was going to yell at him for causing this, but Araki seemed indifferent, turning his attention back to the amulet in his hand.

—What on earth are we going to do now?

Despite being in this cold ritual hall, Mitsuhiro felt an anxious sweat beading up on his forehead. If they filled the hole with the soil from those mounds, then what were Araki and Yoshikazu Hara doing down there? What exactly was the plan? The question seemed too morbid to ponder. He was too shocked to ask it out loud, but before he could even try, Yoshio and his employees gathered around the hole.

Holding his ritual baton in front of him, he passed right by Mitsuhiro. He tried to give Yoshio a *what's going on?* look, but Yoshio didn't even glance back.

Just as Yoshio fell out of view behind one of the mounds, there was a creaking sound. Mitsuhiro leaned over, peering under the ropes and paper streamers stretched over his head. He saw the stepladder in the corner and Yoshio climbing down it. When he reached the bottom of the hole, he coughed at the smell, then walked toward Araki.

"Sota."

Araki stopped staring at the amulet. He turned his gaze toward Yoshio.

"Sota, were you cursed along with the previous leader before he passed away?"

"Maybe. I really don't know anymore."

Yoshio nodded gently and pointed at the amulet Araki was holding. "Is that the one our late leader prepared for Chief Sugawara?"

Araki smiled happily. "Yes. The paper inside was written by my father. Should I give it to you?"

"Keep it. I'll give the director something else in its place."

"Sorry."

"It's nothing to be sorry about. Is there anything else you want me to do, Sota?"

"Nothing. Let's get this appeasement done. Be careful with it. Make sure nothing comes out for thirty years."

"Okay. I'll take good care of this place."

"Please do, Yoshio."

Araki and Yoshio bowed to each other. Then Yoshio went over to Yoshikazu Hara.

"Mr. Hara."

Yoshikazu Hara opened his eyes and looked at Yoshio.

"Don't worry about Megumi. We will take responsibility for her and make sure she has everything she needs."

Yoshikazu Hara sat upright and bowed deeply. "Yes, please. Whatever you can do."

"I truly appreciate the long relationship you've had with us."

"The pleasure is all mine. Thank you very much."

Yoshio bowed to Yoshikazu Hara, held his baton forward, and quietly returned to the stepladder, as if the ceremony had already begun. Yoshio was no longer looking at Araki or Yoshikazu Hara, and the two of them quietly closed their eyes.

Once he climbed out of the hole, an employee pulled up the stepladder and placed it under the table in front of the shrine.

—*Wait!*

Mitsuhiro wanted to shout it out loud.

—*Why are you taking the stepladder? Those two are still in the hole!*

But the atmosphere was so quiet, the scene so otherworldly, and most of all, no one else seemed to question the situation. All he could do was sit there in shock.

The ten attendants scattered in all directions, while Yoshio stood at one corner of the hole. Fourteen living people were in here. Mitsuhiro thought about that. The same number as those swallowed by the hole. He didn't know if that meant something.

He was wondering if the number was deliberate when he heard a loud thud. Someone was beating a drum. Along with the constant *boom, boom, boom*, the sound of flutes began to echo underground. Yoshio began to chant something loudly, making the hair rise on Mitsuhiro's arms.

Hifumi yoimunaya kotomochirorane
Shikiru yuwitsuwanu sowotahakumeka
Uoe nisarihete nomasuasewehoreke

Mitsuhiro had no idea what he was saying. Was it for a standard earth-appeasement ceremony, or a special prayer to summon the water god? Or was it to call back whatever had come out of the hole?

But it was all of those things at once—something more than Mitsuhiro could ever understand.

Hifumi yoimunaya kotomochirorane
Shikiru yuwitsuwanu sowotahakumeka
Uoe nisarihete nomasuasewehoreke

As Yoshio repeated the chant, the pile-driver machine suddenly roared into action, shaking the air in the sealed ritual hall.

Before he knew it, four of the ten Tamai employees, two men and two women, began a strange dance in a line, circling the hole clockwise. The four of them chanted the same syllables in unison with Yoshio Tamai, and the pitch gradually seemed to rise.

Mitsuhiro felt like he was in some realm that was not his own. His vision grew distorted, and everything seemed to be spinning around him. He wanted to shout *Stop!*, but for some reason, he found himself whispering the words repeated by Yoshio and his team. If he didn't, he feared, he'd eventually be swallowed up by the hole himself. If they didn't purify everything here and now, he might face this terrifying ordeal all over again—and this time, he may really lose everything.

The sound of the drum and flutes, the rumble of heavy machinery, and the incomprehensible prayer continued. As the four dancers circled the hole multiple times, the boards holding back the earthen mounds were removed one by one.

—Ah, they're filling it in.

They're going to fill in this whole thing.

And irreplaceable human sacrifices will serve as its foundation.

As the thought raced across Mitsuhiro's spinning head, the mound at the edge in front of him collapsed into the hole.

The soil, as dark as store-bought fertilizer, poured down on Araki at the bottom. Then the mound on the right collapsed, followed by the one on the left, instantly engulfing Yoshikazu Hara. Finally, the pile of earth on Mitsuhiro's right fell, and the hole was now completely filled in.

The four dancers picked up their shovels. Still chanting the same words as Yoshio, they scooped up the remaining earth and threw it into the hole to the rhythm of the drum, flutes, and heavy machinery.

No, there was no hole now. There was only a mound of earth.

To the left of Mitsuhiro, Chiyo Tamai removed the rope and paper that had been tied to the stakes. The pile driver moved straight toward the spot, making tracks in the dirt.

If something that heavy went on top of a hole filled with loose soil, wouldn't it sink right in? Whatever rational part of Mitsuhiro's mind remained considered the thought. But while the caterpillar tracks did sink in a bit, they didn't get stuck beyond retrieval. In fact, the machine was moving back and forth, rotating itself over the hole to compact the soil.

It was like a dance, Mitsuhiro thought, watching the pile driver repeat its little sequence of steps. It was running over people in its soil-compacting dance. Like when they drove piles during construction. It was dancing, and compacting the earth, and compacting the people buried below.

Hifumi yoimunaya kotomochirorane
Shikiru yuwitsuwanu sowotahakumeka
Uoe nisarihete nomasuasewehoreke

Eventually, the pile driver stopped moving. The four dancers went to the wall, put down their shovels, and began to install one of the concrete piles that had been laid out.

Mitsuhiro watched in a near daze as these people in traditional Japanese clothing worked with practiced hands, following standard safety practices, as if this were nothing more than a regular ground-improvement job.

The concrete pillars, which looked like giant stakes, were adjusted by the pile driver operator to ensure they were perfectly vertical, and then they easily sank into the soft soil. Right where Araki had been.

Once the first concrete pile was completely hidden in the ground, the pile driver moved slightly, and the next one was installed. This time, a hard pillar was driven into the soil near where Yoshikazu Hara had been.

When that was finished, the concrete-pile work continued at pace, one by one, along the edge of the hole. After that, crushed-stone piles were put in place around the hole, just as Mitsuhiro had anticipated. These two types of pile work were carried out with a strict, practiced procedure, even with Mitsuhiro on his straw mat and Yoshio chanting right nearby. Mitsuhiro was the only one wearing a helmet, though. The others were all dressed in traditional Japanese clothing, which wasn't really safe. Any of it could easily be caught in machinery.

No, this wasn't construction work. It was a ritual.

He still couldn't believe that they had to break out the pile driver. They weren't building a house underground. And yet, at the same time, Mitsuhiro never doubted that this place needed to be built as solidly as possible.

When the last crushed-stone pile was driven into the ground, the drum and flutes stopped. Yoshio and the others stopped chanting, and Mitsuhiro watched silently as the pile driver returned to its original position. He had lost track of how long the ceremony went on. His head was too foggy to keep track of the time. His whole body felt numb, and his ears rang from all the echoes.

When he glanced toward the door, he saw someone standing there. Someone who wasn't among those standing here on the ground, alive. Someone who shouldn't have been there, but his face was blurry and unclear.

He thought it might be Yoshikazu Hara. No, actually, it might be Araki. Or maybe his father, Kosuke Matsunaga, had made this his second grave. Or maybe it was all three of them at once.

"Please stand up, Mr. Matsunaga."

Before he knew it, Yoshio had come up to him. Mitsuhiro unsteadily got to his feet, supported by the other Tamai Construction employees. He felt an immense fatigue, as if he had just finished working a long shift.

"You must not say a word about what happened here outside of this place.

Do not tell anyone, unless you want to be bound by karma once more. This is very important."

Mitsuhiro gave Yoshio several deep nods. He didn't want to tell anyone. He didn't even want to tell his family.

So he left the ritual site with the assistance of the Tamai employees. He needed them because either the ritual or the painkillers had made him impossibly groggy.

He climbed the 177 steps, followed by the temporary stairs, but he almost fainted several times during the climb. By the time he reached the surface, he was being all but dragged along, virtually unconscious.

When Mitsuhiro came to, his helmet had been removed, and he was in a car driven by a Tamai Construction employee. It was night. They arrived at the hospital, and someone was waiting with a wheelchair out front. He was carried to his hospital room and put into bed, still wearing his white clothes and pants stuffed with the assorted things he'd taken with him.

Without even the energy to thank those who had carried him over here, he fell asleep.

His sleep was restless, coming in waves both deep and shallow. He saw someone sitting in the hospital room, but his mind told him it was a dream. Everyone involved in this whole thing was now in that hole, deep underground. Everyone except him. That's why, even when he saw Araki sitting in the hospital room chair, staring at him with those emotionless eyes, he didn't shout out. He just reflected on how he'd probably be having these dreams for a while to come.

The night passed, and he woke up to bright sunlight and the sound of the door opening. When he turned his head, Miyoko and Sae rushed over to him.

"Daddy!"

Sae zoomed straight to Mitsuhiro's left knee and clung to it. Miyoko must have given her precise instructions on where to hug and where not to hug.

"This was hard on you, wasn't it? The president of Tamai Construction gave us a lot of money. He called it compensation."

"Yeah. It's okay to accept it."

"When we got home, you know, the smell was gone. We deep-cleaned all the stains, too. They're almost gone."

"Yeah! I got rid of all the scary stuff!" Sae laughed cheerfully to herself.

"Sae helped, too," Miyoko added with a smile. Neither of them seemed to be forcing their cheeriness too much, which Mitsuhiro was thankful for.

"There's nothing to be afraid of anymore, Sae."

"Yeah!"

"But maybe we should move," he half-unconsciously muttered, eliciting stares from his family. "We don't have to force ourselves into this mortgage or anything. I'm sorry."

Miyoko smiled a bit. "Why are you apologizing?"

"I don't know," he said to himself with a laugh. Miyoko and Sae laughed along with him.

The realization that his family was back to normal was such a relief after they had almost taken away by something truly terrifying. He couldn't have been more grateful.

But even so, part of his mind would never quite return to what it once was. Just like that soil, tamped down and pinned with stakes, it would remain sealed away for decades to come, appearing only in his dreams. He would just continue to pray that he could endure it without screaming.

Final Chapter Completion—2019

"It's *huuuuuge*!"

As soon as they stepped outside the east exit of Shibuya Station, amid the remaining soundproof walls, Sae shouted, as if she had been waiting for this moment, "You built such a huge building, Dad!"

"Calm down, Sae," Miyoko said. "You'll scare Kota."

Mitsuhiro was pushing a stroller with their four-year-old son, Kotaro, sitting in it.

"C'mon, Kota," Sae said, turning around to lecture him. "How long're you going to stay in the stroller?"

"No! No! Sae, no!" Kotaro immediately started kicking and flailing his arms.

"No teasing Kota," Miyoko said, waggling her finger at Sae. "You'll make him cry."

"Okay…"

"Don't stop," Mitsuhiro said. "People are going to run into us. Let's go."

He kept pushing the stroller, paying no attention to Kotaro's struggling. He wanted to get away from this intersection, with people constantly coming and going everywhere. There was a water tank deep below where they were standing, and although he had never seen it with his own eyes, Mitsuhiro was convinced that a piece of his father's gravestone was still there.

It was Miyoko who first suggested that the family go see the newly completed East Wing. She said it was a normal thing to do, since the company she and her husband worked for spent so much time and money to build it. That was certainly true, and not even Mitsuhiro wanted to shun the place for the rest of his life. Yoshio Tamai had taught him well what wasn't much of a concern and what he should avoid at all costs.

They now lived farther away from here since the move, but he had a premonition that he'd be a more frequent visitor in the future. He was told not to offer flowers or anything like that, but there were other things he could do. For example, he could hold his father's belongings in his hands, recite words of appeasement in his mind, and just pray that he would never be cursed again.

Chief Sugawara told him that he made a regular habit of that. The burns he'd suffered from the car had apparently pained him for the following month, and some of the bruise-like lesions he suffered from had stubbornly refused to go away, but he was able to have them removed by Tamai Construction. Mitsuhiro didn't ask what kind of bruises they were. He guessed that it had something to do with Chief Sugawara's younger brother, but both Mitsuhiro and Sugawara avoided the topic. They didn't want to create needless karma between each other.

It took Takenaka several weeks to heal the burns he'd suffered in the arson attack as well. He formally expelled Mitsuhiro from the IR department in the meantime, but Chief Sugawara scooped him up, inviting him to join the Materials Management department. It was a challenging job, as the system improvements this department oversaw had a direct link to the company's stock price, but it was rewarding work, too.

He often thought about the construction company his father had run, and on rare occasions, he also received documents related to the ritual hall. His former colleague in the IR department had told him that the investigation work he did had become a pet project of the chairman, and its purpose had shifted to supporting the unhoused population around Shibuya Station. Maybe Takenaka and the IR team wanted to use this movement for some kind of upcoming business strategy, but Mitsuhiro didn't really care any longer.

After that whole thing, he never heard from Okuyama at Helping Hands again. That stuck in his mind a bit. He wondered if Okuyama still concerned himself about the whereabouts of the fourteen missing people. Would Mitsuhiro ever feel the urge to call up Okuyama and tell him something he should never say to anyone? Those were questions that, for good or bad, he had a duty to bury deep inside himself.

Mitsuhiro's family braved a long line of families and couples, went up the elevator, and ate at the restaurant they were looking for.

"Good thing we made a reservation," said Miyoko, expressing her relief as she surveyed the massive crowd inside.

As they enjoyed their meal, Mitsuhiro caught a glimpse of someone standing at the entrance. He recognized the vague silhouette. Making sure his family didn't notice, he checked the feel of the stone wrapped in the handkerchief in his breast pocket before taking a second look.

Araki was standing there, and Mitsuhiro felt a dull pain in his right shoulder. That always happened when it rained or whenever his heart raced. He was supposed to be completely cured, but sometimes his shoulder would just go numb on him, and he wouldn't be able to lift his arm at all.

Mitsuhiro held his breath, trying to avoid attracting attention, and waited for the pain to go away on its own.

The sight of Araki didn't panic him. This wasn't a ghost escaping from the ritual hall.

Yoshio had described it as something akin to a reflection on a glass window. A reflection of fate. The mere sight of it didn't cause any harm, and it soon disappeared anyway, but he was advised to not stare. Apparently, if you started to look directly at it, it'd gradually drift closer to you. That wasn't a big deal, either, but it certainly wasn't a pleasant experience.

Mitsuhiro looked away from Araki, smiling as Sae fed Kotaro pancakes and Miyoko admonished her for putting so much syrup on them. Then he looked out the window. Just as Shimaoka had hoped, crowds of young shoppers would return to this station soon. Plus, the Tokyo Olympics were next year, and with that would come even more tourists. Regardless of whatever unexpected disasters awaited them in the future, the future of the city was bright. After all, they had done all the necessary compensation to ensure it.

Thanks to those Olympics, though, construction-material costs were rising, and distribution channels were getting constricted. Those problems would inevitably dampen investor sentiment, so there'd probably be another meeting on the subject at the beginning of the week. As he considered these things, he found himself naturally, unintentionally staring back at the people standing on the sidewalk below, looking back up at him from ground level.

There were two of them. His father and Yoshikazu Hara. He should have looked away, but he couldn't. He put his hand on the window, wishing he could call them over.

"What are you looking at?" Miyoko asked, following Mitsuhiro's gaze.

—Did you know that we're all living on top of the dead?

He wanted to say it so badly, but of course he didn't. He couldn't bring himself to. He could imagine Miyoko or Sae someday feeling obligated to carry a belonging of his around—that Father's Day handkerchief, maybe—and he just couldn't say it.

"Oh, just thinking about how there're more people around now."

His father and Yoshikazu Hara stopped looking up and began walking with the passersby, as if they were alive, too. Mitsuhiro didn't bother following them with his eyes. He just quietly turned his face back toward his family.